MATTHEW PEARCE

PASSION

Book Two in the Adam Series

Published in the United Kingdom by:

Red Falcon Publishing, an imprint of
Blue Falcon Publishing Limited
The Mill, Pury Hill Business Park,
Alderton Road, Towcester
Northamptonshire
NN12 7LS
Email: books@redfalconpublishing.co.uk
Web: www.redfalconpublishing.co.uk

A CIP record of this book is available from the British Library.

First printed July 2023
ISBN 9781916321687

For the man who found joy in all things.
Andy Crawley

BOOK 2

PASSION

MATTHEW PEARCE

Prologue

Passion

A fragment of what it is to be alive. Like blood, surging through the body, so does passion flow within. It lingers in our every action, clandestinely fuelling every choice, every thought, every desire. Through passion, our existence is given meaning, our purest of emotions intensified. We find the shrouded meaning of love and the truth behind the hollowness of despair. Interdependent of passion, we are often swallowed by the beast, bringing bliss or sorrow; yet without it, without passion, we would cease to be human.

He awoke with a fire in his heart and a hunger in his belly. The sun had barely breached the horizon and the coolness of the nights chill still lingered. He had decided that today would be the day. The day for achieving his goals, for pursuing dreams. He had seen the red and orange glow whilst he slept; it was the twelfth night in a row that he had dreamt the same dream. It would always begin the same way, with him walking through the grasslands near their home. He could smell the pungent scents of herbs and flowers, the perfume of the grass. He would walk to a fruit tree and grasp one of its ripened young; the sweet juice would flow over his lips as he bit into its flesh. Yet, as he ate, he would see another tree in the distance, the elder tree as he and his brother had come to know it. He would drop the half-eaten fruit and as it hit the ground its rosy skin would shrivel and blacken, and it would instantly feed the earth around it. Walking towards the elder tree, he would see his father standing beside it, talking to it, and it would answer. He had been forbidden to ask the pale oak for anything, yet on this occasion, the wind would rattle the baron branches and he would hear it calling to him. His father would tell him to leave, however, the voice on the breeze would urge him to come closer, and upon touching its bark, a tremendous blaze would be set at its roots, stripping its shell and turning it to ash. He would look down at his hands and just before he woke from the dream, he would see the fiery glow radiate from his palms.

He threw off the skins that had sheltered him from the cold and ran out of the cavern they resided in, out into the morning air. *Amazing.* He stared, looking up at the reds, oranges, the sunglow and the burnt umber shades of the sunrise that spread across the heavens. He ran up the grassy mound and past the crystal-clear waters of the lake; he was heading for the woodland. *I know exactly how to make father proud.* He foraged for the tools that he would require to complete his task. An assortment of sticks, rocks and dried grass; such simple things that would light up his father's face and bring pride to his eyes. He craved it more than anything. He had decided that he would need to practice first, to ensure he would get it right when the time came. He meticulously arranged the rocks in a circle, with the dried grass in the centre. Using sturdy sticks, he managed to create a frame, securing them together with kindling; he decided that they could perhaps hang things from it, such as food. He grabbed two stones, one sharp, and one rounded and dull, and he began striking them together again and again. Bashing the stones against one another close to the dried grass he stared unblinkingly, waiting, praying for a spark. After many attempts, he was yet to see even a flicker. 'Come on!' he pleaded with the earthen tools he held, and gave them one last chance. But there was nothing.

'What are you doing?' a voice asked from out of the bushes behind him. He knew it to be his brother. Younger than he, his brother stood taller than him and carried a muscular physique that had often been used against him. 'What on earth are you attempting this time, little brother?' he asked with a belittling tone; for no one could ever have quite the sibling rivalry as them.

'Go away,' he let slip, hoping to be left in peace to practice.

'I think I'll stay and watch, I could do with a good laugh!' His brother taunted him. Trying to ignore him, he struck the stones once again, only for them to create nothing but a fit of laughter from his heckling audience. 'Try this one!' his brother shouted as he threw a stone that hit him across his shoulder. The stone was too large to use and the strike hurt him somewhat.

'Go away!' Getting to his feet he ran at his younger brother, an anger possessing him. He lashed out, swinging his fists, aiming to strike him across his face; yet he missed, and his brother laughed at him once again. Swinging once more, his eyes closed to prevent them from welling up and he felt his knuckles impact his brother's cheek. He opened his eyes to see the rage filled stare of his taller, broader opponent.

'You'll regret that,' his brother threatened, shoving him hard, causing him to fall backwards. He lost his footing and tumbled into his own creation, scattering the stones and obliterating the frame he had worked to build. 'Ha!' was the only sound his brother made before walking away, disappearing into the woods. He grasped at the dry grass whilst tears began to stream from his eyes.

'Why didn't you just work!' he shouted at the dead plant in his hands. 'I needed you to work.' His heart began to beat faster and he struggled to control his breathing; it was as if someone was sat upon his chest, each intake of air pained him. His head was spinning and the trees themselves appeared to be closing in on him, like giant wooden demons; they smelt his fear. Getting to his feet he began to run towards home, frantically fleeing the world as it seemed to close in around him. 'Mother!' he cried as he ran over the grassy mound. 'It... it's...' he struggled to gain enough breath to speak as his whole body shook uncontrollably. Falling to the ground, his arms and legs stiffened, his eyes hurt, and his fingers and toes felt as if they were being ripped from their sockets.

'My poor boy! Drink, drink!' His mother's voice helped to ease the pain, but it was the cocktail of herbs she was force-feeding him that would put his body to rest. 'My poor fragile boy...'

He had passed out. He knew it by the position of the sun, but thankfully his mother's medicine had worked: the shaking had stopped, and the pain had subsided. Drowsily looking about, he realised that his mother was no longer by his side.

'Mother?' He had hoped she had remained close by, yet he received no answer. He climbed to his feet and looked about; for as far as his eyes could see, he was alone. 'Where... ' but as the first word left his lips, he heard a horrifying scream that he knew to be the sound of a deer in distress. Following repeated bleats and screams he laid eyes upon the young animal just as his mother slit its throat. She sat within a strange circle of barren grassland, each blade wilted and brown. She was holding father's knife, its brownish-white edge dripping with the animal's blood. Scattered about the circle were several other small animals, a hare, a bird, a rat; eleven in total. As he looked at them, he felt a welling inside of him. Was it grief? 'Mother?' he questioned, his tone giving away his fear. She looked at him, and for a moment his heart stopped; he did not see his mother in her eyes at first, as if the woman before him was a stranger.

'My boy. Do not be afraid. Come, see what your

brother has done.' She rose from her seat and ushered him to join her across the grass towards his father's garden. There, amongst a variety of plants and bushes, sat his younger brother. 'Look! How inventive!' his mother exclaimed with glee; he had rarely seen her so happy. He moved closer to inspect what was happening, what his brother had been up to. Infront of his sibling was a circle of stones with a wooden frame above and a rabbit hanging down over a crackling red and orange flicker. 'Your father will be so proud,' she said, and it was as if a switch had been flicked within him. His eyes burned with hatred and his clenched fists grew warm in anger as he stared at his brother, revelling in his stolen accomplishment.

'AHH!' He screamed as he charged towards he who had taken everything from him. 'It was mine!' he shouted as his brother jumped up from his perch and evaded his attack. 'Why?! Why take it from me?!' he lashed out, missing with every swing. His brother goaded him, laughing at his anger.

'Boys! Enough!' his mother called, but he would not hear her words. The rage he had burned beneath his skin, and if he could land a single blow, his brother would feel his wrath.

'Enough!' a commanding voice bellowed, and the fire within him was doused. His father stood with arms folded, scowling at his feeble attempt at claiming retribution.

'Father!' he hoped to state his case, but the look in his father's eyes compelled him to remain silent.

'Father, look at what I have built,' chirped his brother, giving him a quick look; he wore a sickening grin. His mother and father both looked at the flames and smiled, a smile that was meant to be his. He felt a hole develop inside of him as he looked on at his invention being claimed as his younger brothers; a sour taste filled his mouth.

'How could you!' He charged once again at his brother. His heart pounded to a hateful rhythm. He threw himself at his sibling but sadly his attack was easily parried, and he found himself hurtling towards the fire.

He screamed out in agony as the heat struck his skin and bit at his hands, yet the pain only lasted a few moments, and he found that his flesh could somehow withstand the burns. His mother gasped in horror and his brother flew to his side; yet his rage persisted. Grasping a stone from within the flames, he rolled over and sat up next to his brother. In one swift movement he struck his sibling across the head and watched as he slumped to the floor.

'Stop!' his mother screamed frightfully as she rushed to her son's aid. She howled in agony as she failed to wake him. 'Abel!' she cried as she shook him, but she received no response. He looked up at his father to see his saddened expression, a tear ran down his cheek from his emerald green eyes. 'What have you done, Cain?!' his mother shrieked. She looked at him with such disgust before striking him, cutting his face from temple to cheek. Cain's blood continued to boil beneath his skin, and he looked down at the stone in his hand; its surface glowed, still holding the heat of the flames, and so too did his hands, glowing, with a fiery passion.

Enraged by what Cain had done, his father stormed towards him, his eyes glowing with a furious red instead of their natural green.

'What have you done, boy?! What have you done! You've...' His father stopped in his tracks and clutched at his own head. 'What... what is this... you dare take from me?' The hatred in his father's eyes was absolute; whatever was happening to him clearly pained him and he wanted to take vengeance on the cause.

'Adam! No!' his mother shouted in Cain's defence. She moved to defend her child from his father's fury.

'You would protect him?! He is a murderer!' His father screamed, shaking the earth beneath them in his rage. He reached out with one of his hands, pushing the boy's mother out of the way and placing his hand onto Cain's chest. 'If I am not to claim vengeance, then you will forever claim it in my stead... sevenfold!' His father's touch ate at his flesh, burning away his skin and leaving an eternal mark; he had been branded.

'So, where does the name 'Brandt' come from?' Markovic questioned, 'I understand Serena was from ancient Greece. How about you?' He had no intention of answering the pathetic mortal. For almost two months now he had been cooped up with the man, following Evelina's orders, when he'd like nothing more than to rip his head clean off and bathe in his blood. She had commanded that he protect the Serbian until things quietened down and he became useful once again. Evelina, Matthias; they had both spent so much time telling him what to do, he was growing tired of it. 'Humour me... what's your story?' Markovic asked, every word acting like a pin, piercing Brandt's eardrums. He sat in the lavish hotel room, tapping his fingers on the surface of a desk, gritting his teeth and forcing his anger to remain in check. However, a fire burned within him, an all-consuming blaze, that if unnourished, would set the world aflame.

'You really *do not* want to know his story, Vlad...' Nahki appeared to the right of the rooms closed entrance. 'Brandt here... let's just say, he likes to leave his mark,' he grinned. Nahki's presence pleased Brandt. It was a sign that he could have a respite from his guard duty, and for a short time at least, enjoy his freedom. 'Your shift is over, brother, go sulk somewhere else for a while,' Nahki announced, taking a seat on the sofa. 'It is almost time to get some use out of this one.' His words were ominous, yet Brandt cared little to what the plan for the whelp was. He just wanted out, out of the room, the building; he had made little use of his free will, and like an animal that had been caged for millennia, the untameable beast wanted nothing more than to run wild.

'What? No goodbye?' Vladimir asked sarcastically as

Brandt rose from his seat and headed for the exit; he chose to ignore the comment and left the room with haste.

He stepped out into the fresh air; the world was at eventide. The blood in his veins ran warmly and the fibres of his muscles twitched. He was restless. He needed to release the tension he carried but was on strict orders to maintain a low profile. Whilst he stood deliberating on where to go, his cell phone began to ring; it was his dear sister, Serena.

'Tired of working on your tan?' he quipped, answering her call. 'Where are you? While I sit wasting away, listening to the drones of a god forsaken...!'

'Do shut up and listen, brother,' Serena cut his rant short. As always, he did as he was asked. 'Is that traffic I can hear? I assume that means you are out of the room?' Brandt merely grunted in reply. Regardless of where he was, she was no doubt in a better position. 'I need to find Adam, brother, have they told you where he is being kept?' Her question was forward, but not surprising, Serena never was one for patience.

'I have no idea...' Brandt confessed; however, he too had a desire to know; his hatred for Adam persisted. 'Why the fuck do *you* need him?'

'Never you mind.' Brandt could hear a tremor in her words, a mortal quiver that was unbefitting of her. 'We've moved into the house, do visit as soon as you can.' Before Brandt could say anything else, Serena had hung up on him.

I need something... someone to... He clenched his fists and gritted his teeth. He looked out across the road to the adjacent parks and gardens, and then up and down the avenue. The city wasn't home, it wasn't even Manhattan; he was a stranger in this so-called windy city. Heading north until he reached the river, he crossed a bridge; he could hear the unmistakable sounds of laughter, of merriment. *Perfect.* Cracking his neck, he had decided on his heading. Casually dressed, he was wearing a plain V-neck long sleeved top that hugged his burly upper body. His jeans were of a darker shade of black to his top and he had donned his usual stomping boots. Like a beast on the hunt, he stopped in his tracks a couple of blocks short of where he thought the sounds were coming from, he closed his eyes and opened his other senses. A *tavern*, he surmised, cutting out the noise of the traffic and focusing on what he wanted. *Ales, food, perfume...* he continued. He could see it all in his mind's-eye as if he was already there, down to the impatient wife complaining about her husband nursing his pint, or the sleaze-ball, eating the double-stacked burger with bacon and cheese, that kept leering at the waitresses. Yet Brandt was searching for something else...

'I'm tellin' ye, one punch n' he was out,' a voice said by the bar. Brandt smiled, opened his eyes and continued on his way. Walking into the pub, his powerful figure caught the eye of almost everyone he passed. He headed for the bar, walking past the perverted businessman's table as he did. Before the man could blink, Brandt grabbed the back of his seat and pulled it from under him, causing the oaf to hit the floor.

'Wha' the fuck!' he groaned, looking about until he saw who had held of his chair, and then unsurprisingly, he made no further protest.

'Bourbon,' Brandt ordered from the barman, whose jaw had dropped at the size of the man before him. 'Keep 'em comin',' he waved two one hundred-dollar bills in front of him until the barman took the cash. Brandt knew all he had to do now was sit and wait; his target would come to him, like a moth to a flame.

'Well feck me, you're a big cunt 'ent ya?' the voice said from beside him. The voice belonged to a short stocky fella with red-brown hair, cut short, and a beard to match. His nose was mishappen and he had the look in his eyes, one of determination; a fearless passion for the fight. 'Tha names Cillian,' his words carrying a purpose, his accent clearly Irish.

'Get to the point, Cillian...' Brandt glanced at the man, before knocking back another drink. He had no time for chit-chat, the fight was what he was after, man on man, knuckles on flesh, on bone.

'How'd ya fancy making a lot of cash?' Cillian asked with a smile on his alcohol flushed face.

'Keep your fucking cash.' Brandt tapped on the bar to get the barman's attention; his glass was still empty. Cillian looked as if he did not know how to react, Brandt had disrespected him, but was far too large a man to take on. 'I'll fight...' Finding the confused Irishman's expression amusing, Brandt laughed before slamming his fists down onto the beer-soaked surface, fracturing the wood and finally gaining the attention of the seemingly death-wishing barkeep. 'Give me the bottle,' he groaned as the man went to pour his drink. Brandt then smiled with his eyes, causing them to flicker a fiery red. The startled barman gingerly placed the bottle on the bar before swiftly moving on to another customer.

'This address, this time,' Cillian explained as if talking to a simpleton as he handed Brandt a piece of paper. The short stocky man then left Brandt to enjoy his drink and sauntered over to the next broad-shouldered man he saw.

One hour to kill... Brandt looked at the card before grasping the bottle by its neck and heading back out into the city.

Heading south, Brandt crossed the bridge again and continued until he reached the parks. People bustled about, coming and going to and from the show. The Buckingham fountain was alight; an array of colour danced within the jets of crystal-clear water, lighting up the eve along with the hearts of those stood watching. Brandt stopped to take it in, humanity's gracefulness. Taking something so simple, something so achingly quotidian, and turning it into a marvel, a bewitching spectacle for all to look upon in awe.

As he watched the radiant sprays gracefully shoot out across the evening air his gaze was caught by a young family of four. A father, a mother, and two young boys, capturing memories of the fountain's presentation. Clearly tired and irritable, one of the boys flicked the other on the ear, causing an argument to ensue. As Brandt watched the parents attempt to discipline their children, he couldn't help but recall how he was with his own brother; and then the pain set in. Suddenly this wide-open recreational space began to feel like a tiny prison cell. He could hear the chatter, the footsteps, even the heartbeats of a hundred souls nearby; it was deafening. His head pounded aggressively and the blood under his skin flowed rapidly towards the boundaries of his being, searching for cracks in his armour, a means to erupt. People around him hurriedly moved away as he grasped at his head and roared in agony. His eyes burned and the whole world became brighter, as if he were seeing it through a deep red filter. He looked out across the night sky and saw the city's skyscrapers in the distance, as clear to see as if the sun was at its peak. Yet, the pain persisted and he could feel his scar, his mark, the constant reminder of what he did, flare with such intensity. He stomped towards the fountain, continuing to howl with inner turmoil. His hands smouldered and his life's blood boiled. Throwing himself forward, he plunged his paws into the fountain's depths in the hope that its cool, calm waters would ease his pain; however, the jets glowed with a vicious red and the water boiled rapidly to the point of evaporation. Brandt pounded the stone of the fountain until a piece of it, no bigger than a baseball, broke away. He grasped the rock and starred at it. He could see his brothers blood smeared across it. He held it tightly, ferociously squeezing it within his burning hand until his pain, his anger, won out. Reality steadily returned and the pounding within his head subsided; within the ecstasy of his guilt, the molten rock had run between his fingers, scorching the earth.

He walked the city streets, basking in this newfound light, despite the absent sun. Something within him had evolved: day, night, it no longer mattered to him. Everything had a heat, a warmth, and it lit up his world. Shadows could no longer have secrets and the black of night no longer existed, for to him, the world was on fire.

''Bout fuckin' time!' Cillian slurred as Brandt approached the darkened, graffitied exterior of the address he had been given. 'Tomasz, this the big cunt I were tellin' ye about. Fighting for free!' He was talking to the large, bouncer-like man that stood beside him at the entrance.

'Lead the way,' Brandt snarled. He was almost at breaking point, his hands, arms, body, ached in anticipation of a release, and the idea that this stocky Irishman was going to gain something from this amused him. 'Let the fun begin,' Brandt grinned. Tomasz held the heavy metal door open for them as Cillian led Brandt inside. The door then closed and was locked from the outside. Brandt was buzzing, his anger, his frustration, it would finally have a target. They walked a dark, dank corridor: the floor was wet from leaks in the ceiling above, the power to the lights stuttered and the walls were hard and cold. They turned right at the end of the passage and passed through a door that led to a descending staircase. As he walked down, Brandt could hear the roar of the crowd, the excitement, the passion. He could hear the calls for bets, money exchanging hands as one person struck another within the arena. The smell of blood, sweat, drugs, smoke, it all filled his senses as he continued to follow Cillian down another corridor.

'Jus' through 'ere.' Cillian opened a door, letting a wave of cheers flood out into the hallway. 'It's t'ree fights, usually four hundred bucks a win, but... you apparently 'ent in need of the cash!' They entered a large underground area. Tables swimming with glasses lined the outskirts of the room; a hundred or so people, here to watch the brutality of man. Men, women, suits and last chancers, the room contained them all. In the centre of the area stood four thickened steel mesh barriers that combined to form a cage, where blood was spilled and lives were either made or lost.

Not exactly the Colosseum... There were a lot of eyes on him, he was the largest in the room, he would attract the most attention. *Good,* he thought as he looked about the mortals. He grasped the collar of his top and tore it in two to reveal his scarred and tattooed skin.

'What's your name?' an older gent asked. He was wearing a tuxedo, standing out from many of those around him. 'I cannot announce you without a name...' he said condescendingly.

'Big cunt!' an intoxicated Cillian laughed, but soon he cowered away once he realised the look of exasperation on Brandt's face.

'Brandt,' he answered plainly, looking down on the nights host. The little man nodded in reply and shuffled over to the cage to make preparations.

'Ladies and gentlemen!' The voice sounded over the speaker system. 'At a height of six feet and four inches, weighing in at two hundred and thirty-five pounds! I give you... Aniot Wojcik!' As he was announced, a large muscle-bound man entered the cage. He wore shorts and had short, dark-brown hair and a beard. He starred at Brandt, unblinkingly, attempting to intimidate him. 'And his opponent! The first man to step inside this ring for free...' he paused for a moment allowing the crowd to either mutter between themselves or laugh mockingly at the idea; 'at a tremendous height of over eight feet and weighing in at...' he stopped again whilst Cillian ushered Brandt onto a set of scales; 'two hundred and eighty-five pounds! Ladies and gentlemen, I give you... Brandt!' There were some cheers from the less than sober on-lookers, whilst the rest of the audience mainly looked on in awe of his gigantism. He looked down on his opponent and grinned. Once within the reinforced steel cell the entrance was sealed, leaving the two men captive together.

Bide your time, make it last, you're gunna enjoy this... Brandt rolled his shoulders and cracked his neck. He shifted his weight back and forth as he impatiently awaited the fight to begin. The supposed heavyweight before him had already began to sweat, the glistening moisture glossing his skin.

A bell rang and the fight began. His opponent gingerly approached. The crowd were alive, but the noise was mostly chatter. Brandt allowed the fighter to land a swift blow to his jaw, revelling in the feeling as flesh and bone collided. The strike had caught the crowd by surprise and a few cheers rose from beyond the cage. He let the man land another hit, and then another; he even backed off slightly, listening to the roar of those who had bet against him, toying with them. Their acclamations caught the attention of those less interested, perhaps those who had initially thought the match to have a given result. Suddenly there were jeers of disapproval as Brandt's opponent landed a hard kick to his abdomen. *Three fights... I'll give you entertainment.* And with that, he smiled maliciously and swung his huge fist, hitting his opponent between his arm and his sternum, sending him bounding through the air and crashing against the steel wall behind him, shaking the arena's foundations. The noise rose as winners on the betting scene cheered victoriously, and others cried out for their losses. Brandt bellowed and stooped, smashing his fists against the floor, further motivating the crowd. The bell tolled and they quickly removed the unconscious, broken man, and a new fighter entered. This one was of a similar height to the last, but his muscles were toned to perfection. Dark of skin, he was quick on his feet, nimbly dancing around Brandt, landing sharp jabs again and again. Brandt swung for him but missed. Surprised by the man's speed he laughed at his own blunder, and with him, the crowd roared. Brandt snatched the man in mid attack, lifting him up by the throat, listening to the sound of the theatre rise along with him. He looked to the crowd, taking in their desire for more animosity, and he threw the man upwards against the roof of the cage, quaking the whole structure and riling his audience further. As the man fell back down and hit the ground, the bell rang once again, signifying another victory.

His third opponent took him by surprise. Under six foot, he was a dwarf in comparison to Brandt. His skin was dry, and his eyes were red and sore. He wore a hooded jacket, jeans, and was barefoot. If Brandt had to assume, this character looked to have been dragged in off the street. A homeless addict, a pathetic excuse for a man in Brandt's eyes, one that could barely stand.

'BRANDT! BRANDT! BRANDT!' voices from the crowd cried out. He wanted to give them a show, a spectacle to applaud; yet looking at what he was up against, he could probably break him with a harsh stare.

'This? This is the best you could do?!' Brandt roared at the host, hugely disappointed. But then his assumption showed an unexpected consequence. Whilst Brandt looked to the organisers of this event, his weary opponent sprang upon him and hit him with an unnatural force to his chest, propelling Brandt backwards into the wall of the cage, shaking the arena. The crowd were as speechless as Brandt. As for the whelp, it was as if his senses were suddenly awakened and he looked anomalously confident despite his odds of success. An unbidden fire flushed within Brandt's eyes; this opponent had a secret, one that he would happily beat out of him. The crowd would finally have a fight to savour. 'Hmph.. who are you?' Brandt righted himself, but the man merely smiled back at him.

'Someone who...' He shook his head as if in pain, 'someone who's getting paid a lot to kick your ass.' The tired red of his eyes now resembled a fury, an unrelenting passion to fight. One that Brandt knew all too well.

'HA!' Brandt responded, 'then let's begin!' He flashed

towards the man, hitting him hard against the opposite wall of the cage before punching him with force, his fist crashing against the man's temple, a hit that would usually kill a mere mortal. However, as the man fell to the ground, he coughed up blood, his life splattering across the hard floor. Brandt began to smile, though, it was soon wiped from his face as the man stood back up. With a speed stolen from his kin, the man zipped toward Brandt and struck him three times across the face, the third hit drawing blood.

'He said you'd underestimate me...' A droplet of blood seeped from the fighter's left eye. 'He told me to ask you...' He was struggling to speak, whatever was happening within him, it was taking its toll; 'to say...' he coughed up more blood. The on lookers were growing impatient, they had not come to see a conversation, they craved death and destruction, and despite his curiosity, Brandt was more than happy to deliver. He marched towards the man, grasped him by the throat and slammed him into the floor. The man laughed as he spat out more blood.

'Who are you?!' Brandt demanded to know.

'A messenger, son of... Adam.' His words hit Brandt harder than any physical blow could have ever done. He looked at the man, puzzled by his words. 'He told me to say... "therefore... whoever kills Cain shall suffer sevenfold vengeance".' The man smiled again as more red tears ran from his eyes. His words infuriated Brandt.

'Who told you? Whose strength flows in your veins?!' but his words were lost on the rapidly diminishing mortal. 'AHH!!' Brandt screamed as his fury bit down on his heart like a rapid dog; his hands glowed bright red and his head throbbed with despair. He raised his hand and slammed his palm into the chest of his opponent, pushing through flesh, smashing bone and crushing his heart against the stone beneath him. There were screams of terror from the spectators as they witnessed his rage. Brandt's head snapped back and he frantically look around at the panicked crowd;

everything burned with a deep red, his anger possessing the world around him. Fear filled the arena as people rushed for the exit. He could see their fear, feeling the heat it produced as their hearts raced. Standing up, he burst through the metal of the cage, his heat melting the steel mesh. He whistled ebulliently as he began to tear through anybody he could lay his hands on, basking in their blood and taking pleasure in the melodic concinnity of their combined horror.

1
Claire Davenport

Where did you go?

It was the question that had plagued her since the festive period. Every day had been an internal battle. For something she had had for a long time but not been aware of, had suddenly presented itself, and before she had had the chance to understand it, it had been stripped from her. She couldn't explain it, she wasn't even sure if she was right, but the voice that had resided in her mind, Carmen, had saved her life; she had given her a second chance, at the expense of herself and the only person that could possibly help her understand why had been gunned down that night and was now lost within a web of C.I.A. lies and shadows. Mike had warned them that Adam would become untameable, that the longer he lived the more powerful he'd become and so out of fear they had acted that night, taking him down and handing him over to Zane and his agency of spies. But what Claire could not shake, was a deep desire to find Adam, to protect him. Their team was continuing with their investigation into Markovic, Cardoza and their affiliates, but they had been ordered to hand anything regarding the Avunaye over to the C.I.A. Strict orders, that Claire couldn't fully comply with, as her allegiance was conflicted. So, when she wasn't examining evidence, or attempting to solve the interrelation between the ever-increasing number of players in Vladimir Markovic's empire, she was hunting for Adam, hacking into C.I.A. databases, searching for the only person that might provide the answers to fill the void within her.

'Ah! Another dead end!' she exclaimed in frustration. Her pursuit of Adam had been arduous to say the least. Today Claire had decided to wear a pair of black suit pants and a dark blue, long-sleeved blouse, with the sleeves rolled up. She had tied her hair up, except for the blonde strands that hung down over her glasses. The colour was a constant reminder of what she had lost that night, but also a gentle reminder of the strength she had had within her. She hoped that one day that strength might return. Her display of exasperation caught the attention of her co-workers. After the assault on the bureau, she had been piecing together a new team of lab technicians. Malique had returned to work, but their relationship had been altered by the attack. Claire was not certain as to how much he knew, if anything at all, but she had to be careful. Since Christmas, she had not been contacted by the mysterious caller that had threatened to expose her. She often wondered if they knew that there was now nothing to expose. The team felt strong as a group, but individually everyone was still recovering. Mike would be returning to work soon, Krysta was still fragile after learning the truth about Jake, Solomon had been reprimanded for the high casualty count at Times Square, only Lucy and Hale appeared to be their usual selves. Claire understood that wounds took time to heal, her own issues were a constant reminder of that, but she looked forward to the day when everything returned to how it once was.

'Hey, Claire, whatcha up to?' Krysta had entered the room. Claire hastily swapped the information on her screen for data related to Cardoza. 'Jumpy?' Krysta said with a concerned look, 'you okay?' Claire wasn't sure what to say, she didn't want to lie to her friend.

'Fine! Me, yeah... fine, fine, fine...' she answered quirkily, yet, beneath her desk, her feet were tapping together nervously.

'I wanted to speak to you about... you know who...' Krysta had seemingly accepted Claire's ruse. Claire smiled in reply, although as she thought about it, she wasn't quite sure who Krysta was talking about. Krysta took a seat. She was wearing her F.B.I. jacket, opened at the zip, over a grey coloured tank top and blank pants.

'Huh?' Claire screwed up her face with a puzzled look.

'The...' Krysta looked about as if to check that no one else was listening; '...the mole. We haven't heard from them in months.' Her words started a panic within Claire, and she started to shuffle in her seat.

'Well, we don't know who it is, was, do we...' Claire tried to keep herself in check, answering as quickly as possible.

'Well, no, but the timing... I had a thought. Well, I've wondered for a while now...' As Krysta spoke, Claire's eyes darted about impatiently. She needed to know where Krysta was going with her ramblings.

Does she know? How could she? Claire feigned a smile.

'It could have been him, right? Adam?' Krysta's words almost knocked Claire off her seat as the relief hit her.

'Adam?' Claire responded unconvincingly.

'Well, he posed as Jake, maybe he pretended to be god knows how many other people in my life. In our lives.' It was all about Adam. Claire relaxed as Krysta continued to divulge her theory. She felt betrayed by what he did, but there was more to it. Most of Claire's and Krysta's conversations over the past couple of months were concerning Adam; it seemed neither of them could get him off their minds. Yet for Krysta it seemed as if she had been hurt twice, she had fallen for Jake who turned out to be Adam, yet she had had some feelings for Adam as well, who in turn had betrayed her trust twice over? The whole matter was deeply, emotionally confusing.

'I, I don't think it was him, Krysta...' Part of Claire wanted to confess the fact that she knew who their guardian angel is, or was, but she was afraid. Krysta looked disheartened by her words, so Claire quickly added, 'but you never know, I'll keep looking into it.' She smiled at her friend hoping to reassure her. Krysta smiled back. However, there was a lack of hope, and a sadness to her tone as she thanked Claire for her help.

'Anyway, what are you working on?' Changing the subject, Krysta looked back at Claire's screen.

'Oh, erm, Kyle has me doing a report on some new findings we've made regarding Cardoza. Seems he and his men have been up to a lot recently,' Claire replied coyly.

'Kit? Joy... Isn't it weird that he's the normal one in all of this?' Krysta admitted glumly.

'Don't even go there...' Claire said abruptly, 'there's nothing normal, or good for that matter, about that sleaze-ball.' Claire hadn't forgotten seeing Kyle flee the moment Markovic took over the tower on Christmas Eve; and besides, she also didn't know if he'd seen Carmen's display during Brandt's attack on the lab. As far as she was concerned, Kyle was one to be wary of.

'Ha!' Krysta laughed at the idea of "going there" again, 'I know he's a dick, I just meant that, he's a normal human being.'

'Yeah, a two-faced, cowardly, lying, normal human being.' The pair looked at one another and then laughed at his expense.

After repeating her theories regarding Adam, then changing her mind and attempting to defend what he had done, Krysta left Claire to continue with her work feeling mentally exasperated. *Carmen would probably have shut her up about an hour ago,* Claire pondered. She missed the company, strange as it was: despite her intrusion into Claire's mind and body, Carmen's character was one that she had begun to take a liking to.

'Claire?' Malique sounded from the entrance to the lab. 'I'm heading off. I have some errands to run. I've sent the results of those tests to you, so you should have those.' She smiled at Malique in reply, it was the most he had said to her since he'd come back, yet for the life of her, she wasn't sure what to say. 'Okay then, see you tomorrow...' Malique raised his hand in a half-hearted wave, before heading out of the room. Claire merely smiled again, oblivious to what he had said for a moment.

Tomorrow? she questioned, looking at the time in sheer disbelief. *Whoa! Where did that day go?!* She wasn't quite sure what she had achieved all afternoon. Deciding to call it a day, she grabbed her bag from the locker room and headed out.

Driving home, she checked her rear-view mirror again and again. It wasn't that she was nervous, or that she thought she was being followed, she was looking, checking her eyes for something, some sign that she was not alone. It was, however, by chance that the last two or three times she checked she noticed the same silver hatchback ten or fifteen meters behind her. She made a right turn and then a left, the vehicle behind doing the same. Her pulse hastened as she began to wonder who it could be; she was only a minute or two from home, perhaps she could lose them. She instinctively pushed harder on the accelerator, racing towards the finish line. *Drive straight on...* she willed her pursuer to drive past the turning for the street on which she lived and as she drove up to her humble abode, she saw the silver car drive past the opening and vanish from sight. She pulled over, her breathing uncontrollable. Gripping the steering wheel tightly, she sat for a few moments looking into the wing mirror, looking down the street for any sign of movement. *This isn't rational.* She tried to slow down her heartrate and take deep breaths. *It was nothing,* she told herself over and over until she had convinced herself that it was okay to climb out of the car. She was afraid, but the fear she felt was amplified by something; was it her now, more evident vulnerability? Carmen had offered a level of protection, but without her, she was just herself. Mortal. Mortality was suddenly a scary thought now that invulnerability had been stripped from her. Fumbling with her keys she stamped a foot and clenched her fists in frustration; 'God, Claire, get a grip!' she raged at herself. Once safely inside she sighed as she changed into her powder-pink cotton pyjamas. It had been a long day and she was exhausted, tired out by work, by the long hours she had put into looking for Adam, and stressing about her friends. She was emotionally done for the day, for the more she thought about how alone she was inside, the more that loneliness began to resemble a feeling of grief, of loss.

It had taken her so long to drift off to sleep that when she woke only a couple of hours later, she was so annoyed and frustrated with herself. *Seriously!* She looked at the time; what was worse was the fact that she couldn't simply lay her head down and go back to sleep: nature was calling. 'Fucking takes the piss... heh, takes the piss...' she chuckled as she sat relieving herself. 'And now I'm awake.' She left the bathroom and stomped off to the kitchen. She needed a drink, but coffee was not the answer, that wouldn't help her drift back off to sleep. *Hmm...* she held up a bottle of cabernet sauvignon, contemplating using it for medicinal purposes. However, she then recalled how she felt the morning after a night of drinking. *I'm such a lightweight...* She opted to pour herself a glass of water instead. She took a few sips and began to head back to bed, taking the glass with her. Exiting the kitchen into the hallway she found it to be illuminated, as if the sun had risen early. The light gleamed from the glass in her front door, flurries of dusty rays spreading out across the floor, clambering toward the darkness of the other rooms and the staircase. *What is that?* she questioned stepping out into the light, but as she did, the soft subtle glow exploded into white hot beams that dazzled her. *Hey! What the...* She tried to think of what it could be out on the street that was emitting so much light. *Headlights? Aliens?* She was chuckling to herself as she searched for her keys, intending to open the front door and head out to inspect the source of the light. The chill of the night bit through her pyjamas, causing her skin to bobble and her hairs to stand on end. She tried to shield her eyes from the glare as she stepped out from the safety of her home onto the pavement. 'Hey! Do you mind!' she called out into the light, hoping to grab the attention of whomever was at the lights origin. Yet as she got closer and it became more apparent that there was no-one sat in the silver car that was pointed at her house, she started to panic; she recognised the car from the drive home, but where was its driver? Unsure of what was happening, she backed away and hurried back inside, locking the door and taking a deep breath to calm herself. *It's okay, Claire, you're safe here, back to bed.*

She tried to reassure herself as she carried her glass upstairs to her room; her firearm was next to her bed; she was going to be fine. Believing that it was probably nothing, no more than a mere coincidence, she climbed into bed. She closed her eyes and stretched out; 'Ah!' she said aloud as she tried to de-stress. *All is fine.* She opened her eyes again, but instead of her ceiling, she saw what appeared to be the case of one of her pillows. 'Wha...' she attempted to say, but the case came down over her. She kicked out in fear, and as she did, she could feel them climb on top of her to pin her down. She tried to pull the pillow up off of her face, feeling the arms and then the hands of whoever it was trying to smother her. It was of no use, she needed something. She reached out and fumbled with her fingertips until she felt the smooth surface of the glass of water from her bed side. Clutching it, she swung it in the direction of her attacker, hearing it smash against them. They yelled out in distress, lessening the pressure that they were exerting on her, allowing her to wriggle free. Claire ran from the bedroom only to find another person just outside the door. The man grabbed her and forcefully pushed her against the wall.

'Kryln wants the job done properly this time, love. See, he's pissed that you made him miss his big day,' the man said. He smiled, revealing a golden incisor within his set of teeth, before shoving her towards the stairs. She reached out for him, trying to grab hold of him, trying to take him with her as she began to fall. Her fingers touched the space between them, and she felt her heart leap as she flew through the air. She didn't hit anything until she was halfway down the flight of stairs; there, the steps hit her shoulders and then her back hard, her head whipping backwards at the impact. She tumbled, rolling down each step, each blow as hard as the last, until she eventually crashed at the bottom. Laying in the hallway, the light from outside once again blinding her, she could feel the drops of blood trickling down the back of her head onto the floor. She looked up wearily to see two men descending slowly down the steps; the world was turning dark.

Cardoza... was her last thought, as she closed her eyes and slipped away from the world.

'Claire, you okay?' a voice asked from the darkness. Her voice was familiar, but Claire struggled to think of who it was, or where she was; and just like that, the world seemed to switch itself back on like a lightbulb.

'What the fuck!' Claire jumped out of her seat. Her pulse raced and her head felt like it was about to explode. There were so many people around her, each of them looking at her with either curiosity or concern. She didn't understand. Where was she? What was this?

'Claire?' Lucy was sat opposite her, the table between them covered in glasses and plates of food.

'What the hell? Where...?!' Claire's words burst out, tumbling from her lips. She looked down at her hands and at her clothes. She was wearing her favourite black pin-striped work suit, but she didn't understand how. She fell and then, darkness. That was all she remembered.

'Claire, seriously...' Lucy looked about at their nosy neighbouring diners; 'what's up with you, you hit your head again?' Her head, that was it, she had hit her head.

'My head...' Claire ran her fingers through her hair, feeling about her crown, searching for blood.

'You fell down the stairs, like, two days ago... how hard did you hit that noggin of yours?' Lucy's words confused Claire even more.

Two days? Claire lowered herself back into the chair. Her head was spinning, it was either sit down or fall down. *Breathe, Claire, breathe...* she coached herself, calming herself and taking back control.

'Claire?' Lucy had a worried look, her eyes asking an endless number of questions.

'Fine!' Claire responded quickly. 'I'm fine, fine. Sorry.' Claire smiled, attempting to remain in control and pass herself off as normal as humanly possible.

'Okay... Look, I know you're... quirky... it's who you are, hon', but the last couple of days you've seemed a little... over quirky, if that makes sense. I'm just concerned.' Lucy smiled at her. She was in her casual attire, blue denim jeans, white patterned shirt and brown leather jacket. Her hair was curled but held up in a ponytail.

'The last two days –' Claire considered the truth of the matter. She had apparently fallen down the stairs two days ago, but what had happened since?

'I know, they've been nuts. Arguing with the C.I.A. over the bodies, I mean, it was bad enough that they took us off the Avunaye case, but now they're interfering with this too –' Lucy seemed frustrated.

'Bodies?' Claire questioned curiously.

'The two fucked up Cardoza guys, and that poor woman.' Lucy looked at her as if she should know what she was talking about.

'Right...' Claire feigned her agreement to Lucy's statement. Yet the thought of two of Cardoza's men turning up dead troubled her. 'I fell down the stairs...' she said whilst trying to process everything.

'I know, banged your head pretty hard. But you look better now than you did yesterday.' It was a compliment from Lucy that was about as good as she'd ever receive from the hardened army brat. 'Your team are looking into the cause of death, aren't they? I wouldn't be surprised if it was Avunaye related. Probably that red-headed bitch –'

'They are? The team I mean...' Claire interrupted, partly agreeing, but mostly questioning the fact. If the bodies did belong to the men that had attacked her, perhaps *she* was the cause of death. 'They are...' She needed to get to the lab, and quickly. 'Luce, lunch was great. I think I forgot something back at the lab...' She stood up looking to leave. Lucy merely smiled in response with a look of bewilderment in her eyes.

'Hey, there's my quirky friend. No worries, my treat, you go do what you gotta do.' Lucy smiled before taking a bite of the indulgent looking chocolate cake that sat before her. Claire gathered her things in a hurry and left her friend to finish her lunch alone.

'Malique, update me!' Claire ordered as she entered the lab. Malique, stunned by her abrupt entrance, dropped the paperwork he was holding all over the floor and then followed it, collapsing to his knees and panickily attempting to gather it all back together. Claire's head throbbed with pain and she winced, pinching the top of her nose with her thumb and index finger, hoping to appease the pain. 'Malique...' She tried to focus, 'I'm sorry, I'm having a strange day. Well, less strange now, or maybe stranger... I haven't quite decided...' Her honesty took Malique by surprise as he knelt, gawping up at her.

'No, no problem, Claire,' there was a semi-stutter to his words, 'two seconds.' Malique hurriedly tidied up his mess and brought a tablet over to her. He quickly briefed her on the latest update, but Claire stopped him mid flow.

'Malique, sorry, can you start from the beginning?' He looked at her curiously, but then obliged. Three bodies were discovered in a dumpster on the corner of Van Nest and Hunt in the Bronx yesterday morning. Of the three, two were male; both were South American as far as they had been able to determine.

'Both men have tattoo's suggesting some affiliation with Kryln Cardoza.' Malique pointed out an image of part of one of their arms; it had a snake tattoo. They had both been torn apart, and in some areas burnt.

'These burns...' Claire said as she pointed to a separate image; her finger trembled as she touched the surface of the screen. Malique stated that they appeared to be electric burns, that the men had possibly been tortured or tasered. 'What's that?' she squinted, looking at a smaller blurred image to the right. Malique quickly opened the file to enlarge it.

'It's a gold tooth. I'm hoping we'll be able to use it to confirm an I.D.' The sight of the tooth sent a wave of terror through Claire's body, one that made her feel physically sick. Malique then went on to explain that the third body was that of a young woman's; they had surmised that she was a potential witness to the crime as she had died at a similar time as the men, but she had not been burnt or ripped apart in the same fashion. Claire looked at the woman's body on the screen and her eyes welled up. She felt as if she was about to hurl. 'Are you okay, Claire?' Her quiet unresponsiveness was no doubt unusual to him.

'I'm... I'm not feeling well...' Claire admitted as she slowly backed away and turned for the exit of the lab. Stumbling out of the room, she headed for the toilets, her mind racing. She burst into the stall and fell to her knees, throwing up what she presumed to have eaten that day, yet she could not remember. She fell backwards, sitting on her heels, grasping and pulling at her hair as she cried, tears flooding her cheeks. 'AHHH!' She exclaimed and she tried to will herself to recall the time she had lost. She was certain that the men in the pictures were those that had visited her home; what had she done to them? And the poor woman, her eyes were still open in the image. How could she have killed an innocent woman, how could she... *Carmen*? She was scared, the feeling of despair sickened her, the grief; it made her angry. CARMEN?! she screamed inside, demanding an answer. 'I couldn't have done this... It must have been her. She must have...' But looking at her own hands she realised that regardless of who it was, it was her hands that had torn apart those men, and had broken that woman's neck. Her hands and her fingerprints, her D.N.A. was what would turn up in the results. Regardless of whether Carmen was still alive or not, it was her body. She had committed murder.

2
Seamus McCarthy

It was the ticking of the clock that woke him from his slumber; the hands of time flinching in sync with the quivers of his body. It was as if death wore stilettos and she was walking towards him, down the corridor of darkness that had held him captive, confined, within an indefinite void. His senses switched on one by one. Following the short, sharp tick-tock that seemed to strike across his ear drums, the smell of iodoform, that sharp disinfectant odour, penetrated his nostrils. His eyelids ached; small shafts of light chipped away at the crevices along their margins. An escape from the black. He lay, raised slightly by supportive cushions, the occasional bleep of a monitor keeping him company. His first instinct was to move, to sit up, but his body resisted his actions. It was then that he recalled the sharp stabbing pain in his back, he felt the blades phantom touch as if it was sliding in once more.

Moira, Alannah, Declan... He began to panic. Their absence, the lack of cards and gifts, even flowers. *Are they okay?* he worried, *where are they? How long have I been here?* The thoughts accelerated his panic, the beep of the monitor sounding more and more frequently. 'Hello?' His voice croaked; his mouth was incredibly dry and his throat was stiff. He couldn't shout despite his desire to do so. *The button,* he suddenly thought as he tried to think of a solution; he must have a button here somewhere to call for a nurse or a doctor. It was on his bed, resting just below his knee, just out of reach unless he was able to bend or sit up further. His arms were heavy and weak and the labour of lifting himself was too much for him to bare right now. 'Hello?' He called out again, hoping that there was someone waiting just beyond the closed door. 'Help...' he whimpered. He breathed in and then out, preparing himself. In, out, in. He had decided to simply bend forward quickly and grab the button. One quick motion. Taking a deep breath in and then exhaling, he channelled all of his might into the single movement, willing his abdominals to work, to help him bend and lean, but they were so weak, still recovering from the damage of the attack and time unused. They failed him. 'Ahh!' he groaned in defeat, 'Ah, AH, AHH!!' he finally yelled. The door to his room eventually swung open and in walked a young man dressed in coloured scrubs.

'Hey, hey!' the man called as he rushed over to the bedside, 'take it easy man, you'll do yourself some real damage if you're not careful.' His name tag read James Daniels, and his uniform stated, New York Methodist Hospital – Brooklyn.

'Brooklyn?' Seamus was confused as to how or why he had ended up here.

'Yeah, that's where you are. If you're feeling up to talking, there's a couple of people that would love to know who you are. Plus, there's the little matter of insurance...' He grimaced as he spoke, as if the mention of insurance, of requesting payment for care at this point in time, made him feel uncomfortable.

'My name...' Seamus began, his head felt light and confused. 'I'm Officer Seamus McCarthy of the N.Y.P.D,' he finally said clearly, his name giving him some power, a feeling of assuredness. He was alive.

'Well, officer, you're gunna need a couple of days to get used to moving about again. If you ask me, you're one lucky guy.' His words didn't seem to make sense to Seamus, who in response, looked at him, questioning his meaning. 'You were found and brought in by some guy, you were nearly dead, and to top it off, it turned out you two were a match for blood type. He donated there and then, saved your life seeing as there's a shortage on AB neg right now.' The man smiled as he helped Seamus get comfortable. He then turned and went to leave, but Seamus quickly asked of him.

'Hey, who was he?' Seamus needed to know who he owed his life to.

'The guy? Didn't catch his name...' the nurse continued to walk away, 'but he has one sweet ride, he's been popping in on the same day every week, same time, so you'll no doubt meet him soon.' He glanced at his watch briefly before exiting. Seamus couldn't help but wonder who his mysterious saviour was.

Sweet ride... Seamus flopped his head back onto the pillow.

He dreamt. It was pleasant, for all he could recall from his time slumbering, was darkness. His dreams showed him his wife and children, safe and sound, back at their family home; they welcomed him with open arms, like a returning hero. The escape from reality felt so good. However, reality soon caught up with him and with it the fear for his family. He needed to get out of here, to go and find them. He could just call Moira, but he owed her so much more than a phone call. The mere thought of seeing her again warmed his heart, but he had not forgotten that night, the night he left them to go and see Dante; the look in her eyes as she knew that he had made the decision to go. The thought, the memory, it pained him. He pictured seeing her again, and pondered on what he would say. In his mind he stood before her, pusillanimous, unable to speak his feelings, the opposite of in his dreams. It was these thoughts that forced him to make the decision to recover, to get stronger before he saw them; they didn't need to see him like this. He asked the nurses for the daily papers and with them he realised just how long he had been away. He learnt of the supposed terror attack within Times Square on Christmas Eve, the failed attack on his city. The knowledge, the hope, that his message to Lucy had had something to do with the success of preventing what the papers called "A Christmas Nightmare", helped to ease his inner turmoil a little. He also learnt of his friend's death, his colleague Axel. For some reason the knowledge of his demise did not hurt him as he would have expected; instead, he felt a flourishing flame within, an anger and a questionable sense of betrayal. *What is wrong with me?* His attention was then drawn towards the door to his room as it opened.

In stepped a man, smartly dressed in a dark grey suit, white shirt and a midnight blue tie. His silverish-brown hair was perfectly styled, and he bore a smile at the sight of Seamus.

'You're awake!' The man appeared happy, clapping his hands together. He was pleased to see him, yet Seamus was unsure as to why.

'Edgar?' Seamus remembered him from that night, but, if he was his supposed saviour. *How could it be him?*

'Confused?' Edgar walked over to the window and adjusted the blind. 'I dropped you off that night and drove away, however, that was one dodgy neighbourhood you were in, so I thought I'd check to see that you'd got on alright. Only by the time I got there you were bleeding out on the snow-covered pavement.' He exhibited a soft, subtle smile, but his eyes showed concern.

'The nurse said you gave blood?' Seamus felt so weary. Despite his nap, he was still exhausted.

'Yeah. Well, they panicked when they worked out your blood type, something about a shortage. Lucky for you I'm the same.' Edgar smiled again and then sat down beside the bed.

'Most amount of luck I've had in a long time...'

Seamus half-smiled and then put his head back, 'thankyou... ' he said, and then sighed with a sense of relief.

'Anytime, mate.' Edgar then stood up and grabbed Seamus by the hand. 'Edgar Young.' He introduced himself in a formal manner.

'Seamus McCarthy.' Seamus shook his hand.

'Right, now that that awkward moment is out of the way, how are you? You need anything, mate?' Edgar was asking sincerely. Seamus was taken back by the question, it was he who owed Edgar, not the other way around.

'I'm okay,' Seamus' words left his lips unconvincingly.

'Lost two months of your life... yeah, sure, you're okay...' his newfound friend retorted, 'honestly pal, I have nothing better to do right now than help you out. Well, except maybe charming the pants off some hot nurse, but that can wait... I guess...' He looked back at the door and then grinned with raised eyebrows.

'I just need to get out of here...' Seamus fidgeted in his bed. He tried to climb out of it to show that he was ready, but his efforts were bordering on pathetic.

'How about you stay put, at least for one more night, and we'll see about getting you out of here. Maybe steal you a set of wheels.' Edgar smiled with his eyes. 'You got a family to get back to Seamus?'

Seamus nodded in response. 'My wife, Moira, and two kids. At least as far as I know I have them to go back to.' His worry was obvious within his timorous voice.

'Tell you what, how about I go find out how they are, to put your mind at ease. Then tomorrow you can go surprise them with your newfound lease of life.' His offer was kind, and more than generous. He was a stranger, yet something about him told Seamus he could be trusted.

'Thanks, Edgar, just –' he was interrupted mid-sentence.

'Don't mention it, and don't worry, discretion is my middle name, well, that and Hugo, but that's just 'cus my parents hated me.' He smiled again before he up and left to carry out his task.

Whilst Edgar carried out the favour of finding information on Seamus' family, Seamus was visited by a couple of Brooklyn's finest. The officers questioned him, asking for details of the night that he was attacked, what he remembered, trying to piece together a description of the assailant. However, Seamus' recollection of that night was poor to say the least, all he could recall was her voice. He felt the need to leave Dante's name out of his statement, the kid needed a fresh start, and having the police looking for him wouldn't help; besides, Dante had already left when he was stabbed, he couldn't have seen anyone. The officers took note of everything that Seamus divulged, they'd no doubt file their report later that day, or tomorrow, Seamus figured, which meant that he had maybe a day before Chief Pérez, his other colleagues and potentially the F.B.I came looking for him.

I need to get out of here as soon as possible... He forced himself to rest as much as he could, until Edgar returned later that evening.

'So, you're N.Y.P.D.' Edgar closed the door, giving them some privacy. 'You realise that you're "presumed dead", right?' His words didn't come as a surprise, Seamus had presumed that that would be the case, however, it did mean that his desire to get back to his family was even greater.

They need to know I'm alive. A war began inside him. His weariness battling against his desperation.

'Your family is okay, sounds like they're back at home. Whatever mess you were all in, apparently it calmed down after you disappeared.' Edgar looked at him, his expression one of apprehension. His eyes asked many questions. 'I don't expect you to tell me your life's story but, what doesn't make sense to me is, you were involved with the feds, C.I.A and god knows who else, and yet, no one checked out a John Doe that turns up in Brooklyn just after your disappearance?' Edgar's point was concerning. How did he go unnoticed for so long?

'I need your help, I need to get out of here tonight,' Seamus pleaded, asking this stranger for assistance once again. Edgar took some time to reply, contemplating what was being asked of him; Seamus half expected him to turn and run, yet his kindness, however, appeared to know no bounds.

'I'll get you to your family,' Edgar finally responded, stroking his short-boxed beard. 'But you have gotta explain some of this shit. I don't need to know everything, but if I am going to be helping you, I'd like to know what kind of shit I'm going to be wading through.' It was an act of compassion beyond what was due, and his request was reasonable; Seamus was inviting him into something that he still didn't fully understand himself, it was only fair that Edgar should know what it was he was enlisting for.

Helping Seamus to his car, Edgar drove whilst Seamus explained, loosely, what had happened to him during the last nine or so months, most of which even sounded unbelievable to Seamus as he said it out loud. Edgar listened intently, seemingly taking in everything Seamus said.

Well, he's not laughing at me. I guess that's a start. Seamus decided that was at least a consolation as they drove into the city.

As they drew closer to Seamus' home, there were a few minutes of silence within the vehicle, giving Seamus time to appreciate the familiar views and the musical chords deriving from the car's powerful engines root notes. 'Pull up here.' Seamus requested that Edgar stop part way down the street from his house. It was close to midnight and the car was loud enough to wake the dead.

'Nice street.' Edgar glanced up and down the tree lined pavements either side of the road. It was cold, but Seamus didn't feel the chill, his heart was warm with the thought of seeing his darling wife, his Moira. He sat for a moment, breathing deeply, collecting his thoughts and silently piecing together some form of an apology. Yet, nothing that came to mind felt anywhere near good enough.

Maybe I can just wing it, speak from the heart... he contemplated as he failed to string together more than two words. *But she deserves so much more than that...* He hesitated as he pulled on the handle to open the car door.

'Seamus? You alright?' Edgar must have noticed his havering.

'I love my wife, but, right now, I feel as if she is better off without me,' Seamus quickly replied, yet his reply seemed to shock Edgar. He stared at his home, trembling at the idea of not seeing them, of prolonging his return, but there was something inside of him, just beneath the surface of his flesh, weaving itself down into the depths of his being, that whispered to him. An emptiness that felt strange and yet also so familiar. Memories of hitting the child in Dante's flat, of losing control at the station, of blood-soaked hands, leeched his thoughts. 'She would want all of me, every ounce...' he admitted, the words quivering as they left his lips. 'But until all of *this* ends, I can't promise her that.' He let go of the handle and sank back into the seat, defeated.

'You think she'd care?' Edgar's words carried an almost angry tone. 'Do you know how rare it is to find someone you truly love? More than passion, more than lust. Truly, love, and who loves you back.' Seamus looked at him as he ranted. 'I don't think she'd care about whether or not she gets one hundred percent of you back right away. Something, anything is better than nothing. Seriously, stop being a virtuous pussy and go and show your family that their husband, their father, is still with them.' He gave Seamus a friendly yet stern look. His words hit Seamus hard, breaking the bricks that formed the foundation of the wall he had begun to build around his heart. They fuelled a flame, an undying fire that he would forever carry for his love, and so, he grasped the door handle once again, this time with confidence.

'Thank you, Edgar.' Seamus began to exit the vehicle, yet Edgar called to him and handed over a card with his contact details suggesting they remain in touch; the thought made Seamus smile as he closed the door and began to walk along the street-light lit path. Barren basswood and elm trees were evenly spaced up and down the street; the leafless canopy no doubt beginning to bud as winter came to a close. Seamus raised a hand and gave a gentle wave as the roaring engine passed him and sped off up the street. As he slowly walked, he repeated Edgars words of advice over and over in his head until he reached his home.

As he ascended the cold, frost-bitten steps that lead up to his door, he endeavoured to reach their summit, despite the nagging images in his mind of a boys mutilated corpse lying upon them. Each step felt like a tiny victory, giving him hope. He made it to the top and reached out with a weary hand to knock upon the barrier that separated him from those he loved, but as he did, he could hear the sound of the door unlocking, and it opened to reveal a woman. She stood in the doorway, with perfectly curled dark hair and a gentle loving face. The sight of her tore at him, mangling his insides like a rabid dog; guilt, love, remorse, hope, fear and most of all passion bombarded his senses all at once. The chill on the nights air grasped at his throat, taking his breath away. She looked cold as well; her lips shivered as she tried to speak. She stood, misty eyed, trembling at the sight of the ghost of a man before her.

'I just... had a feeling that someone was at the d–.' Tears escaped her eyes and fell gently down her flushed cheeks. Seamus stepped forwards, filling the space between them; yet, the intense feelings that flurried within him must have disrupted communications between his brain and his legs, as his weight-bearers buckled at the request to move and he fell to his knees in front of her. She quickly joined him on the cold hard flooring, wrapping her arms around him and embracing him. As he held her as tightly as he could, enduring the physical pain it caused him, he breathed in her scent and tears flooded from his eyes. He hoped in that moment that she never let him go.

They eventually moved inside, out of the cold, black of night. Curled up on the sofa each of them basked in the fact that they were able to look upon the other once again. They took it in turns to attempt to apologise through their tears of joy and sorrow, instantly exonerating one another of any blame. Yet, despite Moira's admission of forgiveness, Seamus could not quite shake the guilt he felt; as far as he was concerned, his penance would be long lived. He held her close, embracing the exchange of body heat between them and gently stroking her hair until she eventually fell asleep, emotionally exhausted. His homecoming had also taken a toll on himself, as Seamus too drifted off shortly after his wife, opening his subconscious to all his thoughts and worries, dreams and nightmares.

Within his slumber, he relived the deaths of fallen friends and colleagues, feeling Sam's life slip away as he held the dying cadet in his arms. His dreams felt so real, but his body would not allow him to escape. Finally, it appeared that the nightmare had ended as he found himself standing in the middle of a huge green oasis. Rolling hills, hundreds upon thousands of coloured flowers, a clear blue sky above.

Is this heaven? his subconscious questioned. He walked through the luscious, bountiful green plains that were brimming with life, watching small animals at play and feeling the gentle warmth of the sun above caress his skin. He walked across a field and up onto a grassy mound. From here he could see far into the distance in every direction. A huge tree caught his gaze as he scanned the horizon. Something about it called to him, a gut pulling sense inside urging him to investigate. He marched across the grass towards the oaken behemoth. He was so fixated on the tree that, at first, he did not notice that the grass around him had withered and died. He stopped for a moment and looked around at the circle of death that surrounded him. *The tree.* The words rang out within in his head, forcing him to continue onwards. It was a pale oak; it's cracked white bark allowing Seamus to see the flesh beneath. As he held out a hand to touch it, he heard a familiar voice urging him not to. The voice told him that he was to never ask the tree for anything, that its fruit would bring only pain. Seamus slowly closed the fingers of his outstretched hand and searched for where the voice had come from. He recognised it, but from where? It had been so long. Could the voice really be that of his father?

The morning passed so quickly that Seamus struggled to take it all in. Reunited with his wife and children, his family sat down together to eat breakfast, celebrating his return, before vanishing to attend their daily lives. Declan and Alannah begged to spend the day with him instead of attending their classes, however, Seamus thought it best that they did not disrupt their studies. Besides, he would have a busy day ahead of him, reinstating himself into the world. Moira reluctantly headed off to work after receiving several messages that they were short-handed. His homecoming had been brief, yet, it was all that he could handle right now, he needed time to build his strength back up. He also had a number of tasks he wanted to complete today. Like a hangover, the eeriness of his dream clung to his thoughts as he proceeded to have a shave and take a shower, tidying himself up. He stood in front of the mirror with a towel about his waist, turning, examining his body, looking at the strangely, almost unscarred back and abdomen he saw before him. He felt the phantom pain of the blade pass through him, yet the wound had all but vanished. He needed answers. Why was he left unnoticed for months? How did he survive? The more he thought about it, the more he questioned Edgar's version of events. *There must be more to the story.* He got dressed, putting on a pair of blue denim jeans and a red, cotton, front-buttoned shirt. He straightened up his hair, slicking it over to one side, creating a clear parting; ideally it needed cutting, but it would do for now. Throwing on some shoes and a black coat he left the house and went to find some answers to his questions, starting with a visit to someone he knew he could trust.

The F.B.I would have requested a statement sooner or later, so he decided it would be easier to get it out of the way. For two pain-staking hours he talked them through the events of the evening of his attack, repeating what he could recall to agents Johnston and Grey over and over again. Their insistence that he must be able to remember more resulted in a headache as he pushed himself to think harder, but he did well to remain composed. He decided to leave Dante out of it, protecting the boy as much as he could; he didn't need the F.B.I looking for him, what he needed was a fresh start. They also wanted information about his whereabouts for the last two months, to which, evidently, did not amount to much.

'Seamus!' Lucy yelled as he exited the interview room and came face to face with his friend. She was pleased to see him, indicated by her eyes as they began to well up, as if she hadn't quite believed his revival to be true until now. 'I can't believe it...' she said before hugging him. Her embrace was unexpected, yet it surprisingly comforted him. She was wearing black suit pants and a light grey blouse, the colours adding to her already formidable demeanour.

'Sol? Mind if we use your office for a bit?' Lucy asked of her superior. She clearly wanted some privacy, and thankfully she did not want to use the interview room, or more aptly, the interrogation room, again. Solomon gave her a quick nod before looking at Seamus, his eyes scanning him, seemingly unsure as to whether or not he could be trusted. His stare made Seamus feel rather uncomfortable, but thankfully Lucy quickly moved into the large windowed office and he was able to follow suit, closing the door behind him and allowing himself to relax on one of the chairs.

'So, what do you need?' Her blunt question was accompanied by a smile; her forwardness throwing Seamus. 'I know you didn't come all the way down here to just make a statement. What can I help you with?' The look in her eyes let him know that she was sincere in her offer to aid him.

'I just wondered how you were, your team... How's your partner? Mike was it?' Seamus attempted to disguise the reason for his visit. The truth was, he knew that she would be able to see through his rouse.

'You... You wondered how we were?' Blatantly unconvinced, she continued regardless. 'We are okay, good, even. The team is recovering well.' Seamus could tell that she was holding something back as she fidgeted slightly in her seat. 'Mike is okay, he's coming back to work soon. Actually, he is doing better than okay, his wounds are practically gone, it's strange...' Her words were followed by a mild look of concern.

'I think I can relate,' Seamus admitted. 'My wound has all but gone, barely a scar, and I have no idea why or how.' It was but one of the questions he desired an answer for.

'Okay, Seamus, come on, spit it out.' She made it clear that she knew there was more to his visit.

'I need answers to a few questions...' He was gearing up to blurt everything out all at once. *I pray you can help...* 'It's a big ask, Lucy, and I hate to ask it, but I need to know if you're willing to help me... discretely...' He felt guilty suggesting it. He hadn't even told her the information he needed yet, but the thought plagued his conscience.

'Seamus? What is it?' Lucy leaned in towards him, 'I will help, where I can.' He could tell that she was unnerved by his vagueness.

'I need information...' his words were nebulous, but he had her attention. Lucy didn't instantly shoot him down, which was a positive sign. 'I have been lying in a hospital bed for two months. No one found me, hell... I don't even know if anyone bothered looking. How does something like that happen? Are you able to find out why I wasn't found?' It was his first request and probably the least important, but he needed to know how far she would be willing to go.

'I can have a look into it, but...' Seamus couldn't help but feel slightly disheartened as the word "but" reared its ugly head. However, Lucy continued, 'What are you expecting to find? If you were purposely hidden from the F.B.I, the C.I.A... that would take someone incredibly talented... someone who probably won't want to be found...' She was right, but at least it sounded as if she was willing to try.

'There's more...' he said ominously, 'I also need info on my father's death, and any link it might have to the Avunaye.' Lucy sat back in her chair as she contemplated his second request and no doubt the ramifications of aiding him with it.

'Your papá? What does *he* have to do with anything?' She appeared confused, raising an eyebrow and screwing up her face.

'He was N.Y.P.D, killed on the job. It sounds crazy but, I had a dream and I just have a feeling... you know?' He couldn't explain it, he could only hope that she could understand where he was coming from.

'I can't say that I'm not one to follow my gut. I can look into his death for you. With regards to connections to the Avunaye, the C.I.A and the D.O.J are currently shutting us out of the investigation. I might, however, be able to dig up something from back when your papá was killed, if there is a connection...' It was a start, and one that Seamus was most grateful for, however, he felt as if there was another "but" just around the bend. 'But, Seamus, you realise what would happen if anyone was to find out that a federal agent was assisting you? I can't believe I'm considering it.' But she was considering it, and that was all Seamus could ask for.

He was over-joyed inside but managed to remain nonchalant for the sake of any onlookers. He thanked Lucy profusely before promising her that he would be careful and remain in touch. Hopefully with her help he might make some headway into why his world had been turned upside down.

Seamus' next port of call was the station. The last time he was here was a time he would sooner forget, or at least hope that everyone else had. However, judging by the looks of those he passed as he entered the building, he had no such luck. Since the incident at Times Square, the Avunaye had posed no threat to the boys in blue, yet the number of officers lost on Christmas Eve could be read in any of the papers, and the tension within the building was still heavy. His colleagues were still licking their wounds, still struggling with their loss. One such officer was Malik Seif. As Seamus caught his eye, his look was one of pain, anger and hatred. They had parted on bad terms before Christmas and since then their good friend and colleague, Axel, had been slain. Seamus could imagine that Malik felt as if his whole world had been torn apart, and for his part in it, Seamus could not feel more guilty.

Trying to apologise to him now would only cause more issues, it won't bring Axel back.

Captain Wu and the Chief were currently in a meeting, so Seamus had been asked to wait. He decided that it would be a good opportunity to see what ongoing investigations there were, and the best person to speak regarding the daily ongoings of the station was Sergeant McCabe. The well-rounded man appeared as jolly as ever.

'Gotta hand it to you, McCarthy, you make the leap from best to worst attendance look like a doddle!' he chuckled. At least someone was willing to talk to him. Seamus briefly explained what had happened to him and then enquired as to how things had been in his absence. 'Honestly, Seamus, sounds like you've had a rough time of it. Why not forget about work for a bit and concentrate on getting back to full strength?' It was a kind way of saying keep your nose out, but at least he made the effort to be nice to him. Seamus attempted to say hello to several other colleagues, only to be shunned and ignored. 'Punching a fellow officer will not get you any brownie points my friend,' McCabe pointed out the obvious, seeing Seamus' failed attempts to communicate with his peers. 'Look –' but before he could continue, the rosy cheeked sergeant was interrupted.

'Sergeant, you've suddenly got a craving for some pie... you had best go check the cafeteria...' Seamus didn't recognise the voice, or the man himself as he turned to look upon who it was that was making such an absurd suggestion. Yet, confusingly, Sergeant McCabe turned and walked away, heading towards the cafeteria, not saying a word. 'Seamus McCarthy,' the man said, turning to look at him. He had short brown hair and was dressed in a pair of black pants and an off-white, ribbed, long-sleeved top. He smiled as Seamus attempted to take measure of him; his eyes were slightly unnerving.

Who is this weirdo? Seamus wondered.

'Well, I have been called worse.' His words confused Seamus even more, as he hadn't said anything yet.

'I'm sorry, do I know you?' Seamus knew full well that he didn't. The stranger did not answer at first, seeming to discretely look around the room.

'You will, soon enough. Now, I require a favour...'

'Who's your friend?' McCabe questioned with a look of curiosity on his face. He had a plate with a slice of cherry pie in his hand. Seamus was confused.

'Who? What were you going to say?' Seamus wasn't sure if McCabe was purposely trying to mess with him or was simply unintentionally confusing him.

'The guy you were just talking to...' McCabe seemed genuine, but Seamus had no idea what he was talking about, and he made sure his expression showed the fact. 'Never mind... Look McCarthy, just take a seat and I'm sure the Chief will see you soon.' McCabe then began to dig into the pie before him. Feeling downhearted by McCabe's obvious lack of interest in speaking to him, Seamus decided it was probably best to keep to himself, get the statement done and head home. He was determined that he would regain their trust once again, but like all wounds of beast and man, their bonds would take time to heal.

3

Krysta Rose-Anderson

She stood looking up at the triumphal archway, its marble construction standing elegantly, unwavering in the dying light as the sun retreated towards the horizon. *They* had been stood in this exact spot when he had imparted the fact that the arch was made from stone and marble, quarried locally. He had told her of the monuments purpose, the reason for its creation and she had loved him for it, believing the seemingly random facts he carried with him. Yet now, as she looked up and read the inscription that he had translated for her, she could not comprehend how the end justified the deed. She remembered his words, his touch, his smile. She remembered how he had made her feel, yet, it was not real. A creation, a lie, with a purpose that escaped her. For the setting sun cast long shadows, and within them she saw pain, loneliness and sorrow. She thought that she had loved him, but if who she had loved was false, was her love also fabricated? He who had power over emotion, could he have instilled her so? Would he have done so? The two of them had walked these paths on numerous occasions, watching the seasons pass, the colours of the world changing around them. From glorious greens, pinks, whites and yellows to the baroness of what followed the oranges and browns. And with the loss of colour from this celestial garden, so too did the colour wash away from her life, revealing the murky truth beneath.

She slipped her numbing hands into the pockets of her warm black coat and sank her head back into the fur-lined hood. Her avoidance of her apartment, of her home as she had previously called it, had come to an end. Yet, she still frequently found ways to prolong her return to it. Doors could be rebuilt, tables replaced, floors swept and scrubbed clean, but safety, the feeling of homeliness; they took time to return. As Krysta reached the entrance to her apartment building, the sky was on fire. She stood for a moment and basked in the beautiful sunset colours and twilight hues. As the natural spectacle steadily came to a close and the world was merely aglow with streetlights, she breathed a heavy sigh, one not of defeat nor depression, but to eject the dimness of the day, to expel her troubles. As the sun set and darkness fell, the world would sleep, for tomorrow the sun would rise again, and all possibilities would be renewed.

She opened the door and stepped into the foyer, leaving the dark outside. Krysta half-smiled and breathed in the scents of lavender and peach blossom as she headed for the stairs. However, something was out of place, a sound, or sounds, from one of the apartments she knew to be empty. She walked slowly, curiously inspecting every inch she covered, searching for change. She reached the door of the apartment, sounds of movement and muffled voices could be heard from within. She raised a hand to grasp the doors handle, but as her fingers brushed its brass surface, the handle moved, and the door opened. For an instant her heart stopped, expecting *him* to be stood on the other side, but instead a woman stood beyond the threshold, and in her deep reddish-brown eyes a look of curiosity stared back at Krysta.

'Can I help you...?' She stood barefoot, wearing light blue jeans that were turned up at the bottom of each leg, and a white, shoulder-less, free-flowing shirred crop top. Her hair was ebony in colour and fell in plaits over her shoulders and her skin was a golden bronze. Holding a large glass of red wine in one hand, she began to look more and more confused the longer Krysta took to answer.

'I'm, I'm sorry...' Krysta finally answered, breaking the awkward silence between them. 'I live upstairs...' Her brain was not fully computing. The woman smiled.

'Hi, nice to meet you.' Still looking slightly confused, she was obviously attempting to be polite.

'I'm sorry, my head, I... I just didn't know anyone was moving in, you just threw me a little, that's all...'

'No worries, we've only just moved in today. I take it by your confused expression you knew the last tenant?' The woman was clearly attempting to create some form of small talk.

'Yeah, I guess, I didn't know if, I wasn't sure that... he was not coming back.' Krysta tried to smile but she wasn't sure how she felt.

'He... ah, an ex?' Krysta merely shuffled in her boots in response. 'Darlin', don't answer, I understand. Men... am I right?' She seemed friendly; her expression changed to one of understanding. 'I have literally just opened a bottle if you feel like a glass. No offence girl, but you look as if you need one.' Krysta could have easily drowned herself in the bottle, but a nagging feeling, a craving to be alone tugged at her heart strings.

'Thanks, but...' Krysta was trying to piece together an excuse that didn't make her look pathetic.

'Girl don't worry about it. The offer stands, anytime... ' She smiled and touched Krysta on the arm reassuringly. 'Anytime you want to talk or hang out, it's just me and my brother B here, swing by anytime you need. You can tell me all about this asshole who used to live here, or not.' Her invite was kind. Part of her knew that Jake would no longer be living there, but seeing it made it all the more real; too real.

'I will, thanks. I'm Krysta by the way.' She held out a

hand as she introduced herself. The woman pushed her hand aside and leaned in to give her a hug.

'Men shake hands girl, we better than that.' As she pulled away, she smiled and began to close the door; 'call me T,' and then the pair parted ways and Krysta headed for the stairs once again.

As she entered her apartment, she was greeted by the chill of emptiness. She flicked on the heating and grabbed a blanket from off the back of one of the sofas to help warm her until the central heating did its job. She sat and stared solemnly around the place. Timeless echoes of his presence resounded about the room. Light defying shadows of what she knew clung to her world and stood defiantly before her. As real as the seat she sat on, she saw his silhouette stood before the window; it would climb through, out onto the fire escape and take flight into the star filled sky. It would stand in the entrance to her bedroom, unmoving, a shimmer that began to fade as darkness took its hold. Yet, when times were at their worst, those green eyes would glow, bringing light and life back into her world. She curled up into the corner of the chair, clambering to something solid, something that was simple, that made sense. His shadow had touched this seat when he had visited, and when Jake...

Why? she thought frustratedly; *why me?* She sat working through his reasoning. *You made me think you cared, made me feel something, and then you disappear when the lies are revealed!* She threw one of the sofa cushions across the room, trying to hit the shadow that haunted her. As tears began to fall from her eyes, her frustration turned on herself and she felt angry for feeling the way she did. *I trusted you, you were always there when I needed you in one form or another.* 'I don't even know who you are!' She voiced her thoughts at the unmoving memory of Adam. Yet he wasn't here to respond, he wasn't with her, and she needed him to be. 'You saved me, you saved us all, but you lied! Why did you lie?!' She demanded answers from the empty space that resided in front of her. She tried to think rationally and wiped her cheeks dry of her tears. Standing up, she saw the shadow, the memory holding out its hand for her to take. 'You want me to take your hand?' she laughed and cried at the same time; 'am I going mad?' The idea of talking to nothing, amused her, but her memories still filled the space around her. She began to pace back and forth before the outstretched hand that had once reached out for her. 'I'm drowning...' she spurted out with a sob, covering her mouth as she began to weep. She tried to continue pacing back and forth but she weakened as she cried, and soon she fell to her knees before him, where he should be, where he once was. 'I don't hate you...' she struggled to speak. '... No, I couldn't, even if, if I wanted to. But I hate all the pain you've put me through...' The words began to leave her lips a little easier the more she spoke, and as she blurted out her true feelings, in the moment, her present communed with her past.

'You filled me with hope, with passion, opening my eyes to something I wanted, something I needed. But then you ripped it all away!' Part of her was wanting to stop, to realise that she talking to no one, yet the rest of her needed the release. 'Now you stand here, with your hand out. What more do you want from me?! I took your hand. I took it and I felt... I felt, love...' She breathed deeply, sniffling and wiping her eyes again. Maybe it was simply that she needed to relive that moment, that memory. She looked around the apartment and watched as the ghosts of the past disappeared. She had touched his hand that night and she had seen him. It wasn't him making her feel, he had shared what he felt, his emotions. The realisation struck her like a lightning bolt to the chest, because she had taken his hand that day and since then, unbeknown to her, he had held much more than just her touch. It had been so long since everything had felt so right, she now realised how blind she had been. He had made her smile, but the feelings were hers and his.

'Love. That's why you did what you did.' Krysta climbed to her feet and strolled over to the cushion that lay on the floor. She picked it up and held it tightly against her chest and smiled. *I know what I have to do now...* she thought confidently, feeling as if she was back in control of herself, back in control of her life. Walking back towards the sofas, she pictured him standing there, holding out his hand, and she reached for it, intertwining memory with reality. 'I know who you are,' she smiled, 'and I will find you again.'

Her emotional evening had exhausted her, aiding her to drift off effortlessly: forgetting any previous reluctance she had felt towards being alone in her apartment. Even though hatred and betrayal had taken root within her, something else also stirred; like the green, pink and red buds that were newly forming on the trees she had passed earlier, perhaps hope had begun to spring from within.

She awoke the next morning refreshed and rejuvenated as well as sensing a new inner determination. She knew what she wanted now, where she could find all the answers she craved. A newfound passion to explore the impossible, to find Adam. Her new personal mission would not be easy, her team had been strictly ordered to leave the Avunaye investigation alone, any new intel they received or found had to be passed onto Zane Brown. This meant that she would need to disregard and disobey her orders and work alone to achieve her goal; she couldn't risk involving the team, her family, for if she was caught, she could not let them take the fall.

'Hey, Krys, good day off?' asked a smiling Hale as she entered the office from the stairwell. He looked as if he had been working hard; his tired eyes, wrinkled blue shirt, crooked tie and rolled up sleeves gave the impression of having already served a full day's work.

'It was... enlightening,' she smiled back at him. 'Got this song stuck in my head though,' she admitted, hearing it play over and over in her mind.

'Heh, hate it when that happens, especially when you don't really know all the words, so just get the same lines...'

'...going over and over, yeah!' Krysta finished Hale's sentence at the same time as him. The pair laughing at their apparent synchronicity.

'Good to see you smiling again, Krys,' Hale admitted, before speedily moving on to wherever he was headed. Krysta's attention was instantly snatched by the appearance of someone she had not seen in the office for some time. He wearily stepped out of the elevator with an expression on his face that could easily be mistaken for someone who was lost. He had tidied himself up since the last time Krysta had seen him; his hair had been cut and he had trimmed his beard. He was wearing a black suit, black tie, white shirt; she couldn't help but think that he was either trying for a Solomon look-a-like, or he was secretly part of an organisation that fought against alien invasions. The thought made her smile.

'Hey muscles! Looking good!' she bawled across the office, her call making him jump as he looked about the office startled. Yet, he soon smiled as his heart returned to where it should be.

'Krys...' His words carried a half-sigh, probably one of relief more than anything else; 'corse I look good.' He grinned as he parted his suit jacket and placed his hands on his hips.

'So, first day back... nervous?' Krysta teased. She knew that there was a chance that he was, but he would never admit it, and keeping the mood light would hopefully help him slip back into routine a little easier.

'Nerves...' Mike paused, 'like my buns... of steel.' He winked as he successfully disguised any fear or doubt that he might have had. 'Cleared to jump back into the action, so here I am.' He seemed proud of the fact. Krysta was a little surprised by Mike's speedy return to action, his recovery was ahead of schedule.

'Only, unfortunately, you won't exactly be keeping up with the best of us, not toe-to-toe anyway!' Lucy joked as she joined the pair of them, lightly punching Mike on the arm as she quipped.

'Ah! Funny...' Mike retorted, 'picking on the cripple.' He began to pretend to hobble, using the wall for balance.

'Get off!' Lucy laughed, giving him a shove. 'Sorry, Krys, Solomon is waiting for this dickhead, gotta get him up to speed.' The pair of them moved towards Solomon's office. Krysta was glad to see things returning to normal, especially for Mike. It had been a hard time for him sitting on the side lines as he recovered. He had done exceptionally well to be as fit as he was so soon, mentally and physically. Krysta only hoped it wasn't an act, and that he really was coping well.

The hours of the morning raced past as Krysta did her duty and followed up on several leads for a few of Markovic's contacts; yet, between each task she found her mind wandering as she tried to think of places to begin searching for Adam. Finding people who didn't want to be found was not her forte, and finding a hidden C.I.A black site, where they were no doubt holding him, would be near impossible for her to do. However, she did have a colleague, a friend, that was an expert at uncovering the truth, and since she already shared one secret with this friend, she knew she could trust her with another. Krysta headed for Claire's lab, narrowly avoiding Kyle on her way there: since Lucy had hit him on Christmas Eve there had been even more tension between them than usual and Krysta didn't have the time to put up with his drivel. She entered the lab, but it was empty. A hot cup of coffee steamed atop the central interactive screen and a half-eaten burrito sat on an adjacent desk.

Perhaps she's in the other lab... Krysta then moved towards the door that separated the two rooms.

'Krysta?' Malique called as he entered the lab behind her, 'have you seen Claire?' He was frantic, looking about the room as if she was hiding somewhere within it.

'I'm looking for her myself.' She paused her search for a moment as she curiously looked at the desperation in Malique's eyes.

'Damn...' He grimaced and then sighed in angst. 'I've got the results back for the tests we ran on the three dumpster victims, you know the ones?' Krysta nodded in response. 'Well, Claire told me to get working on them yesterday, but I didn't get around to it, and now that I finally have, I need S.A. clearance to view the results. She is literally going to kill me...' His over dramaticism made Krysta smile.

'Malique, let me take it, I'll use my clearance and then forward the results back to you.' She touched his arm in an attempt to calm his nerves.

'I... I don't know, that's sort of a breach of protocol, no?' He began to retreat hesitantly.

'It's either that or you suffer the wrath of Claire...' Krysta replied jokingly, however, the idea seemed to make Malique's decision for him as he nodded in agreement and shuffled off out of the room. Krysta sat down at one of Claire's terminals and logged in. *That was quick,* she thought as an email popped up and she opened the documents that Malique had sent her. *Blood work... Fibres... Hair... Nice and thorough.* She browsed through the results and was reminded of the poor woman that had died along with the pair of Cardoza's thugs. 'Right... Ah, I can just print the results...' Malique would require a hard copy anyway, she had decided. She collected the paperwork from the printer, however, the final page intrigued her. *Blonde hair found on victim didn't match that of the female victim,* she read; the document stated that the D.N.A. from the hair sample had made a match within CODIS. Krysta put the printouts down on a nearby desk and walked back over to the computer. The CODIS data was attached separately, so she accessed it with the intention of printing it; yet, as she read the results, she found herself doing a double take before rubbing her eyes in disbelief. 'What the fuck...' The hair sample contained two separate D.N.A. sequences. The first matched a sample registered within the F.B.I internal database, matching one Special Agent Claire Davenport. Krysta was unsure as to what she was reading, most of the report contained medical jargon that she didn't fully understand but one thing screamed at her: "second sequence contains zero percent non-coded D.N.A. – unknown origin". *Unknown Origin? What the fuck does that mean? And what the hell does this have to do with Claire?* Krysta's mind raced with questions to the point that her head hurt. She sat for a moment contemplating her next action. She needed to speak to Claire, she needed to know what all this meant, but the fear that she didn't know her colleague as well as she had thought crept into her mind. She looked back at the screen to re-read the results for a second time, making sure she had read them correctly, yet, as she did, the files closed, and the screen turned black. Krysta panicked and anxiously tried to get it to work again, but to no avail. She hastily moved to another terminal, only to find that the data, the results, were gone, seemingly deleted from existence.

Claire... She couldn't help her initial thought, despite resisting. *She's the only one capable of destroying the files... but why?* She left the lab and headed out into the offices scouring for Claire, or perhaps she should be look for Solomon. The truth being, she wasn't sure what she should do.

Catching sight of the back of Claire as she walked down a corridor towards the changing rooms, Krysta hurriedly followed in pursuit. Her hand gravitated shakingly towards her sidearm as she walked briskly, unsure as to whether she'd need it After all, Claire was family. Hesitantly, Krysta entered the locker room, only to be grabbed by the throat, lifted off the floor and slammed against a set of lockers. She winced at the impact and then reached for her firearm. She was panicking too much to realise at first who it was that was attacking her.

'Claire needs your help!' Krysta's heart pounded uncontrollably, but after her attacker had spoken, she loosened her grip and slowly began to lower Krysta to the ground.

'Claire?! What the fuck... what are you doing?' Krysta croaked between gasps for air. Staring at her friend with a look of desperate confusion, Krysta struck out, pushing Claire away and pulling out her gun. After instinctively cocking back the slide on her weapon, Krysta didn't even have time to contemplate her next action as Claire moved quicker than her eyes could register. Claire took the firearm from Krysta's hand, unloaded the magazine and discharged the bullet that resided in the chamber.

'What is it *you* do not understand? I told you Claire requires *your* help and so you try to shoot us?' Claire looked at Krysta, yet Krysta could not see her friend within those honey-coloured eyes. It was Claire, and yet, it wasn't.

'Adam?' Krysta was so confused, and Adam had taken the form of others before.

'Adam? No...' Claire appeared insulted, as if it hurt that Krysta had mistaken her for someone else.

'Claire, I –' but before she could finish, she was interrupted.

'Claire is in here, she is sleeping. I am weak, but I must protect her, protect us...' She was afraid, but who was she, what was going on. 'I am Carmen. Claire will fill you in on the details, just promise me that you'll protect her. She did not harm anyone, those men... I had to protect her...' She was tired, broken, but her words were sincere.

'I don't understand...' Krysta admitted, needing more information. 'If you're Carmen, where's Claire?'

'I said...' Carmen flew towards Krysta and grabbed her once again. 'Protect her, find Adam. Don't let *him* hurt her...' She was exhausted to the point of collapse, and as she said the words, she slumped into Krysta's arms, forcing

Krysta to fall to her knees. Krysta, unsure of what was happening, frantically shook her friend, hoping to wake her, praying that it was Claire that awoke. After a minute or so, she succeeded in waking her colleague and Claire looked drowsily up at her.

'Krys? What are we doing on the floor?' Krysta looked at her now gentle, hazel-coloured eyes and this time she could see her friend within them. She smiled and embraced her as if she had been lost. But Krysta soon found herself pushing Claire to arms-length as she questioned everything she thought she knew about her friend.

'Claire, what the fuck is going on? Who the hell is Carmen?' Krysta demanded answers. She had a tentative hold on her friend and colleague, wanting to comfort her, but was she holding onto a murderer?

'Carmen?' Claire recoiled timidly, pushing away from Krysta. 'Where did you hear that name?' Fear flashed across Claire's face.

'I just spoke to you, to Carmen... I don't know...' Krysta grasped at her head, she was confused and babbling; what was it that she had just seen?

'She spoke to you... She's alive?!' Claire exclaimed as she perked up, with a look of relief in her eyes.

'You know about her? Claire, she... you, you've done things...' The long dark shadow that Claire was suddenly casting unsettled Krysta. However, she continued to tell Claire about the lab test results, that Claire's D.N.A. was found on the victims and that now it seems the data had been deleted. 'Tell me... what is going on...?'

'Carmen is one of them, the Avunaye. Only she's been protecting me. Cardoza's men, they came to my home and attacked me... She must have saved me...' Krysta edged away from her colleague, so unsure of who she was anymore. 'Krys? It's still me... heh, it's still Claire...' Claire held a worried expression.

'How long –' Krysta began to ask.

'She appeared during the attack on H.Q. She saved us all. I don't know how long or if she was with me before that...' Claire told Krysta all she knew of the Avunaye that shared her body, she spoke so passionately and kindly of Carmen. It was a lot for Krysta to take in. 'Krysta, Carmen is the mole. The one that had warned us all those times. She acted through me to keep us safe.'

'What? Claire, none of this makes any sense...' Krysta could barely think straight. 'Claire, Carmen told me I needed to protect you, she made it sound like I needed to protect you from Adam. Why did she say that?' Her words seemed to confuse Claire.

'I have no idea...' Claire admitted, Krysta believed her. 'Adam and Carmen are friends, maybe she was confused, she must be weak after what she did on Christmas Eve. She's okay Krysta, I swear, but I don't know what I am going to do... if the bureau found out... if those results come out... please help me.' As Claire began to cry Krysta moved back towards her and pulled her in close. 'I need help...' she repeated as she sobbed despairingly.

'Christmas Eve?' Krysta questioned.

'She saved us all...' Claire managed to say through her sobbing.

Something inside of Krysta told her that her colleague could be trusted, and if she could trust Claire, then maybe she could trust this alter ego of hers. To help protect her, if she was going to protect her, the first thing she was going to have to do was to destroy those printouts. She had left them on the desk in Claire's lab, she needed to get to them before anyone else found them. The pair of them stood up and Claire straightened herself up before they headed back to the lab. Only when they arrived, Solomon, Kyle and Malique were all stood in the room waiting for them. Krysta's heart stopped, and she could sense Claire shared her panic as they entered.

Oh no... Krysta thought worriedly as she looked at

their concerned faces. She glanced over to the desk where she had left the paperwork, trying to act as inconspicuous as possible, but the desk was bare. Solomon had a look in his eyes that Krysta knew to be one of concern. *Does he know?*

'We've been hacked...' Solomon announced in an unsettled tone, with Kyle and Malique nodding in agreement. And with the realisation that it was the intrusion into their system and not the results that their visit regarded, Krysta's heart began to beat once more.

4
Michael Ward

Arms out-stretched, his wrists were bound in coarse leather straps that were rooted deep into the wall. His arms had been pulled to the brink of dislocation, with any movement in his torso paying a heavy price on his shoulders. It was just how *he* liked him; helpless and immobilized. It would take all his concentration to stand still, his bare, sore feet rubbing on the rough stone flooring. The door would open, and *he* would step into the room, ducking to fit under the frame. His choice of torture would not last too long, yet each movement was made to feel like it lasted tenfold and once he was done, she'd be there to heal him physically and break him mentally. *He* cracked the knuckles of his bear-sized hands and swiftly jabbed Mike in the side, splintering ribs and forcing his bodyweight to add further strain to his arms. Mike would cry out in agony at first, but as the sessions went on, he grew to understand that his screams were pointless. The beast would then divert his attention to the opposite side, pushing his fingers into Mike's abdomen underneath his bottom rib, forcing his hot fingertips in deeply until he could obtain a decent grip on the bone. The pain was often more than Mike could bare, causing him to pass out, but the monster would only wait until he woke again, so he soon learnt to fight, to hold on until the end, hoping to reduce the time he spent suffering. Brandt, having gripped the lowest rib, would slowly attempt to bend it outwards until it gave way and snapped.

If the experience had taught Mike one thing, it was that, no matter how horrendous, how traumatic the pain, all physical pain was made equal by the fact that, at some point, it all slips away. Brandt's final punishment would involve him placing his palms on Mike's chest. He would apply little pressure, but his paws would heat up slowly. The warmth would be appreciated at first, a distraction from the eternal cold of the prison. Yet, it would soon become unbearable, singeing the hairs from his skin and burning through. His body would sweat to dowse the fire, and the heat would toy with his nerves, sending signals to his brain, begging him to cry out for mercy. Mike's skin would begin to melt, attaching itself to the hot surface of Brandt's hands and, at that point, Brandt would slowly peel his fingers away, one by one, and lift off his palms, tearing away any flesh that was stuck to them, leaving his body red raw. That would usually be where he would stop and the point that Mike would give up and pass out. *She* would then later mix her blood with his, that was how she healed him. She would want him to wake up quickly, and if he didn't, she would kiss him on the lips, her tongue alight, as if bathed in gasoline.

His own screaming woke him. The nightmares played off his memory of the pain, forcing him to re-live the experience, manipulating his mind into believing he could feel the fire again. He opened his eyes to see a woman's face, and for a moment his dream carried over into reality. He grabbed the red-head by her throat as he panicked, yet she yelled at him with a voice that did not belong to her.

'Mike, stop!'

He recognised the voice as she cried out. He closed his eyes and shook his head. Upon reopening them, reality hurtled to the foreground and he let go of her.

'Mike, baby, it's just me.' Lucy croaked. 'It was another nightmare honey, you're safe now.' But her words could not take away the fear and the pain he currently felt. He looked at her, his eyes starting to sting as tears formed in their corners. He was sorry for grabbing her, for hurting her, but he had such contempt for himself; he did not feel safe.

'Mike?' She looked at him, her deep brown eyes staring into his. They held such worry. She placed her hands on his moistened cheeks and kissed him before embracing him tightly; her scent, her warmth, reassuring him that this was real, and the nightmare was over. However, no matter how powerful her feelings for him were, how happy she made him, he was broken inside; gaping holes resided within from his time of torment. He wanted nothing more than to get better, to be better, to wash the blood from off his skin and to feel whole again; but each time he came close, the nightmares would remind him of how fractured he was. 'You're safe, baby...' she whispered as she hugged him and ran her hand up and down his back to try and soothe him. But alas, he did not feel safe. He had told Lucy much about his time as a hostage, but the times that Serena had visited him, the times she had broken him down to nothing, when she had soothed the flames and forced herself onto him, forced him into her, those memories he did not share, those were the ones he locked away deep inside. Lucy repeated herself again and again, reassuring him that he was play now, but he truly wasn't.

'No!' he exclaimed abrasively, breaking free from her embrace, 'no, I'm...' He could have let it all out there and then, he could have admitted how he felt, but why should she suffer with him. 'I'm fine.' He sighed heavily. His heart was racing from his nightmare and his emotions were teetering on the edge of erupting, but he needed to hold in his pain. He needed to be strong again. Her expression told him that she didn't believe him. She released her hair from a band and ran her hands through it frustratedly.

'I *know* you're not fine, but you can talk to me.' She

looked at him, for a second, just as everyone had looked him ever since his return: a look of sympathy, of pity. He hated that look.

'I do talk, I say I'm fine, yet here you are disputing the idea. I *am* fine.' He gave her a curt look, just for a second before he realised what he was doing, but she saw it.

'Yeah. Okay. You're fine,' Lucy snapped sarcastically, 'screaming out in your sleep, that's fine. I hear that if you listen carefully enough first thing in the morning, you can hear the melodic screams of all the fine people of New York as they wake themselves up. Fuck it, I think I'll fuck my alarm off in future.' She was annoyed, but her anger was poorly timed, as right now he couldn't deal with her emotions as well as his own.

'I'm sorry!' He exploded as he climbed out of the bed, waving his arms frustratedly and gritting his teeth. 'Is that what you wanna hear? Sorry that my anguish disturbed your beauty sleep!' The words spilled out without him even having to think. The look she gave him in reply conveyed a thousand words. She sprung out of the bed and began slipping on the pencil skirt and blouse she had worn the day before. She grabbed her shoes before spouting some incoherent words in Spanish and slamming both the bedroom and front door to his apartment as she left. He shook his head, disappointed with her reaction, but more so with himself. 'ARGH!' he shouted se he threw a punch at the wall, hitting it hard and splitting the skin across two of his knuckles. He looked at the cuts, the crimson colour reminding him of *her*, of Serena, and as he caught himself thinking of her, he hit the brickwork again in anger. He moved through to the bathroom and stared at his own reflection in the mirror as he tried to calm the storm inside him. He could barely recognise the face staring back him. His brow was shining with sweat and his hands shook as he tried to steady himself, clenching his fingers around the edges of the basin. Opening the medicine cabinet, he took out an unlabelled bottle. He tried to remove the cap, but his hands were shaking too much to gain a decent grip. He shoved the cap between his teeth and bit down, pulling hard in an attempt to force it off the bottle, to reach its contents. But upon finally getting it off, he found himself annoyed at the presence of only a single pill. *I need more!* He placed the small red tablet on his tongue and bent to swig some water from the faucet. 'I need more!' he shouted as he slammed the cabinet shut, cracking the mirror. He stared for a moment at the fractured glass and the reflection before him that was now as broken as he felt inside.

He arrived at work dressed in a pair of blue sweatpants and a blue hooded top with a tank top underneath. His hands were already strapped up, ready to fight. The tension he felt in his fingers, his palms, arms and chest was unmanageable, craving release. Thankfully for Mike, Hale was a willing combatant, despite clearly not expecting to be sparring today. He stood in his work pants, a slate grey-shirt with its sleeves rolled up, barefoot with a pair of focus pads on his hands. Hale barely said a word as they warmed up, which suited Mike perfectly; no talking, no questions, just the fight on their minds. Mike's fists clashed with the pads, rapidly landing blows with his right and then his left; he used a number of different combinations, incorporating an array of jabs, hooks and the occasional uppercut. The release of sweat, the pounding of his heart and the concentration he was exerting on his breathing all felt good. Everything helped to keep him focused on what he was punching, and not the reason why he was doing it.

'C'mon then, Mike, you gunna start putting a little bite into these swings or what?' Hale smiled as he goaded him. Mike remained silent as he continued to land jabs and cross blows. The truth was he was growing tired, due to the lack of sleep and, despite his reluctance to admit it, the fact that he was still recovering. He tried to punch harder, but the effort just frustrated him further.

'How 'bout you lose the pads and we'll spice this four-play up a little.' He laughed, half expecting Hale to go all sympathetic on him, but to his surprise, Hale backed away and threw the pads to one side. He then turned around and took off his work shirt to reveal his ink-covered back; two magnificently designed angel wings spread out from his spine, out across his shoulders and down his arms until they met up with the other tattoos on his forearms. Below the wing that covered his right shoulder was a typical tribal tattoo that flowed down to his waistline and, as he turned, around Mike could see it continue around onto his abdominals and up to his shoulder, where it merged with the wing's feathers once more. On the opposite pectoral laid the letters "XII" and the word "duodecim". Hale clenched his fists and took up a fighting stance. Mike, in response, took up the same stance and began to move towards Hale, inching to the side as he moved forward.

'You sure you wanna get your ass kicked, muscles?' A glimmer of mischief flashed in Hale's blue eyes. Yet his words did not discourage Mike at all; his determination to recover, physically and mentally, carried him as the pair began to tussle. However, Hale consistently managed to land blow after blow and dodge each of Mike's sluggish attempts to retaliate, only frustrating Mike more and more. 'Anytime you feel like giving up and telling me what has you all rattled, you feel free,' Hale said between breaths. That was enough to force Mike to snap. He was done with pity.

'Fuck.... You!' he said, feigning a move one way and then hitting Hale across the jaw. 'I'm fine!' He pointed at his opponent to cement his statement before turning away and heading for the locker room.

'Sure you are, mate!' Hale responded as Mike exited, ensuring he said it loud enough for him to hear.

Disappointed with how his attempt to forget the world around him had gone, Mike spent the rest of the working day avoiding the people closest to him as much as possible. He didn't want to deal with Lucy, not yet, which meant that he needed to stay away from Krysta and Claire as well. Hale had let him down as far as he was concerned and Solomon would only ask questions, as was his duty. The only person Mike knew to be completely disinterested in his current wellbeing was Kyle, and so, choosing the lesser of the evils before him, he approached Kyle and asked him if he required assistance. Solomon had Claire working on the recent cyber-hack incident, but Kyle had decided to pursue other angles, and therefore he and Mike spent the day trying to obtain the data that had been deleted from its original source.

'This is starting to look more and more like a cover-up...' Kyle's words held an irritable tone as he and Mike reached another dead end. Kyle's dress sense today was a calmer than his usual tastes, opting to wear a grey suit with a lighter chequered pattern stitched into the fabric, a matching waistcoat and a pair of brown shoes that pointed at the toe. He was right though, not only had the data been destroyed but so to had the original samples, supposedly via an order from the director of the F.B.I.

'Results gone, samples burnt, all data erased... how ever did you come to that conclusion?' Mike responded sarcastically, however, Kyle seemed to rise above the comment and simply responded with a subtle scowl.

'What do you reckon then, Ward? Either the two brutes meant more to Cardoza and co. than we could ever have imagined, or...?' He looked at Mike as if for him to finish the sentence.

Yeah... Like I think like you... As far as Mike was concerned, he and Kyle were un-comparable.

'Our system was hacked, our data and samples destroyed... see where I'm going with this?' he looked at Mike again, this time with an expression that suggested he considered him to be slow.

'Inside job?' Mike said smugly, 'you seriously

suggesting...' but Kyle cut him short.

'C'mon, Mike, mysterious messages that land us in the shit. Missing data. How the team keeps managing to stumble into this Avunaye bullshit. You can't tell me that it hasn't crossed your mind, that maybe they have someone on the inside?' Mike found it hard to believe at first, but Kyle was being serious.

'You're serious? Well, I mean, I hadn't really thought... but hey, you're looking more and more fishy by the minute.' Kyle did not take kindly to the suggestion.

'Ha! Says the guy who somehow escaped unscathed from the super-human jail cells of... where was it they kept you again? Oh right, you forget...' Mike's inner temperature would have exploded thermometers.

'Unscathed?! You'd have lasted no more than five minutes in my position you fucking ignorant son of a bitch!' Punching Kyle right now would land Mike in more trouble than it was worth, but something inside of him was screaming at him to just give in to the temptation. Instead, Mike bit his tongue and took his anger out on the table before him, punching down on its surface as hard as he possibly could, shaking the table top either rattling or knocking over all of its contents. He then gave Kyle the finger and left the lab, heading out of the building and into the city. He needed to get away from everyone that reminded him of how weak he currently was.

Mike drove until the light of day began to fade. His phone was full of notifications. Unread texts, missed calls, but he didn't care. He parked his car, leaving his phone on the passenger seat and took to the streets on foot, searching for nothing, looking for nowhere, a place in which he could be anonymous. As he walked, he felt the eyes of the people he passed, seeing him, judging him. Undoing his tie, he threw it to the roadside, turned up the collar on his jacket and ruffled his hair in an attempt to shed his weakened form and become someone else. He searched for some time, and eventually he felt he had found the place he was looking for as he followed the sound of music down an alley; it was coming from a door, partially lit up with neon blue lights. A nameless club. He looked up and down the dark empty alley as he contemplated going inside. Something inside him warned him to just head home, but then his attention was caught by the sounds of laughter as a group of people entered the alley. Two men walked alongside two women, the men dressed in silken shirts, pleated-pants and shiny shoes, the women dressed up in cocktail dresses, their legs on show, faces dolled up and their hair styled. They opened the door fully and headed into the colour filled corridor beyond it, passing money to a large figure that acted as a gatekeeper to the club beyond. The sounds of raucous laughter and drum and bass music broke the threshold and Mike could no longer resist the chance to unwind; to forget himself. He followed the group inside, passing a twenty-dollar bill to the doorman before heading down the corridor. The path led to a set of stairs that, whilst descending to a mezzanine and further to a dance floor, provided a view of the entire establishment. Tens of intoxicated people simply escaping life, dancing and drinking. Mike proceeded down the steps to the mezzanine that ran around the edge of the building to a bar on the opposite side. Mike decided that was where he was headed. He undid his jacket and stood at the bar, cash in hand, joining the queue of people waiting to be served. The lights were dimmed and strobe flashes lit up the faces of others, appearing and disappearing with the light. The bartender simply nodded at him, requesting his order. She had short wavy hair that was coloured silver with black highlights; her hair caught the light with every flash. She was wearing a purple halter top and black jeans with holes at the knees and she had a small nose ring between her nostrils. The makeup around her eyes was dark, accentuating the brightness of her blue eyes that shimmered like sapphires when the light touched them.

'You here to drink or just stare?' Her words snapped Mike from his daze.

'Sorry!' he called out, misjudging how loud he needed to be to talk over the music, 'beer, please,' he spoke coyly, realising he had drawn the attention of others waiting to be served. She speedily took a bottle from one of the fridges, uncapped it and passed it to him before taking the cash from his hand. He walked out from the bar, drink in hand, onto the balcony that overlooked the floor below, watching the bodies move to the music, unwinding, living. After his second drink he waited at the bar, hoping to grab one of the staff's attention. Catching the eye of the barmaid with the silver hair, she nodded at him, but this time he wanted more than just a beer. He took off his jacket and laid it on the bar. 'Anywhere I can stash this? Pretty warm in here.' She raised her eyebrows at his request. 'And a whiskey?' He smiled and held out his cash. She took the cash, then his jacket, and placed it under the bar before pouring him a whiskey. She smiled as she slid him the glass across the wet surface of the bar, and then moved onto the next waiting customer.

'I've been watching you. Are you not going to dance?' a voice asked from behind him. Mike turned to find a woman stood next to him. She had short blonde hair that she had slicked back and was wearing a one-shoulder, black, ladder cut dress that showed more skin than it covered up; she clearly wasn't shy.

'Just here to relax, thanks, love,' Mike tried to be polite, lifting his glass to further make his point. He wasn't looking for company.

'Buy me a drink and maybe I can help with that...' She smiled and leaned in, placing a hand on his forearm. Mike smiled bewilderingly as he tried to think of a polite way of telling her to move on. He looked away briefly, hoping to find a chance to abscond his current position, then turned back to her to let her down as gently as he could, only to find her collapsing into his arms.

'Whoa, easy, love.' He caught her, but looking at her face he came to realise that she was no longer breathing. *What the fuck?* He quickly gave her a gentle shake, but she was unresponsive.

'She's dead,' a voice said from beside him. He knew the voice, the sound of it seding a deathly chill shooting down his spine; it had haunted him now for too long. 'I wouldn't make a scene if I were you, someone might get hurt.' Mike closed his eyes for a moment, praying to reopen them and find himself at home, in his own bed, safe and sound, only this wasn't a dream. He turned to face his fear, still holding the blonde in his arms. 'For god's sake put her down...' She expressed her impatience before taking the body from him and sitting it down at a nearby table.

'Serena...' Mike sighed glumly as he looked at her. She was wearing a red slip dress that clung to the contours of her flawless body; her fiery hair was curled and hung down over her right shoulder.

'I'll take that as, that I made a better impression than the blonde. A little *forward* wasn't she...?' She walked up to Mike and stood casually before him, as if they were simply old acquaintances. His heart began to beat to a panic infused rhythm as he tried to weigh up his options. He looked about the place. There were so many oblivious people, but how many of them could actually help him? How many would die trying? 'What are you looking for, Michael? An exit? Help? You have nothing to fear from me, my love.' Each time the strobe light passed over her face Mike could see the flicker of fire in her eyes. She took his hand and ran a finger across his split knuckles, before lifting it to her lips and placing a kiss on them that sent a shiver to his bones. Mike's hand trembled as his mind took him back to the prison she had held him in. Flashbacks of blood, pain and fire bombarded the forefront of his mind.

'What do you want?' he asked, shaking his head, clearing his mind. It seemed like the safest question to ask as she released his hand.

'Passion, love. What does every girl want?' She signalled for a bartender.

'You're not exactly the average girl. Woman.' Mike decided to step out onto the proverbial eggshells. She did not reply at first, seemingly frustrated by the lack of service. Mike quickly took out another note and held it aloft, catching the eye of the barmaid that had served him previously. Serena ordered her drink; a scotch, neat, with a single ice cube.

'Michael. I *am* human, and although during our time together you saw a certain side to me, unfortunately, things have changed.' Afraid to move, Mike stood listening intently; he wasn't sure what she meant but he was slightly intrigued; and whilst she was talking, at least she wasn't snapping necks. 'Adam...' she paused and clenched a fist; 'that son of a bitch has cursed me with a host of emotions that, up until this point, I have never had to entertain. You see...' she moved in closer, pushing herself up against him; 'when I was, reborn, I was full of hatred and contempt for your sex. Now, those emotions, those initial feelings during the transformation, they're the ones that stay with you. Think of it like my default setting as it were. We can feel all the usual human emotions, love, fear, joy, but they're alien to us, secondary emotions that linger in the background. But now, thanks to Adam, I am open to them all, and I hate it.' She knocked back her drink and beckoned for another. Mike stood still, trembling within but trying to maintain a stone-like figure. He tried to process what she was saying, but the memories of the pain she had caused him kept forcing their way to the forefront of his mind.

'You're annoyed because you feel?' His question prompting her to continue talking.

'Yes. I detest it. Guilt. Remorse. For fuck sake I feel bad for snapping the bimbo's neck. I feel bad for what I did to you and for some stupid reason I feel as if I need your forgiveness. Since that bastard did this to me, all I have thought about is you. Why? Why you?' Rage swirled within her eyes like a whirlpool of flames.

'You feel bad?' Mike didn't know what to say. Whether to stay quiet, shout at her or mock the idea. So, she felt bad, it was the least she should be feeling; yet the more he thought about it, the more it felt like pity to him. She felt sorry for him. 'I don't need you feeling bad for me,' he blurted out and quickly stepped backwards. 'As for guilt, please... you *should* feel bad for what you do, you fucking kill people, Serena.'

'I chose not to kill you, and Lucy...' She looked at him as if to suggest she deserved some form of commendation for the fact. Her use of Lucy's name angered him.

'You fucking stay away from Lucy,' his words carried a threat that he knew he could never act upon.

'Words that are not accompanied or confirmed by actions are such fragile things, Michael. I could kill Lucy any time I want, yet this pesky feeling that, if I did, it would hurt you, keeps creeping in.'

'I imagine you want gratitude for your restraint?' he replied sarcastically, throwing caution to the wind and stoking the fire. She took a step towards him.

'For thousands of years I have cared about only myself and my family. I don't think you understand what a monumental pain in the ass it is to give a shit about a mere mortal such as yourself.' Her frustration flared; Mike wanted desperately to get away from her. As he ordered another drink for Serena he asked for his jacket. The silver haired barmaid passed it across the bar, but as he went to accept it, Serena grabbed the girl by the wrist. 'Michael!' Serena shouted in disapproval of his actions.

'Enough!' he exclaimed, 'this is what you do,' he pointed at the frightened girl behind the bar; 'you can't help but hurt people!' Much to his surprise, his words had the desired effect as Serena released her grip. Mike looked away from her and then began to head for the exit; he was done with her, he just wanted to get home, to shut himself away where he could feel safe; but as he began to make his way across the mezzanine, she grabbed his wrist and span him around. As he came face to face with her, she moved into him within the blink of an eye, pressing her warm body up against his, running a hand up through the hairs on the back of his head, and forcing her subtle lips onto his. She kissed him with such passion, a passion that was absent each and every time before; her soft lips gracefully connected with his, sending a whirlwind through his head, confusing everything. Before he knew it, he could feel her soft moist tongue caress his own, and then reality hit him hard. He pushed her away with every ounce of strength he had and shook his head in disgust. A look of inadequacy flashed across her face, and for a moment, she looked untethered from the world and he almost felt a sense of pity for her. However, knowing what she was, what she had done, he turned away from her again and continued walking; she was not worth his pity.

He walked the streets aimlessly for a while after leaving the club, trying to undo the damage, the confusion Serena had caused. He was so angry he could barely focus; confused and exasperated, maddened by her actions, by his own frailness, by Lucy. *How the fuck do I get myself into these messes...* The thought repeated in his head. He wandered with and without purpose, fleeing everything, whilst heading toward something, anything. He was so caught up in the maelstrom that life had landed him in that he bumped into a man without even realising; that was until he heard his name being called.

'Hey Mike, where's your head at?' Mike turned to see a familiar face, however, the face just reminded him of how messed up his life was right now. The man had brown hair that was tied up into a top knot and a roughly trimmed beard that was patchy in areas where the hair refused to grow. He was wearing a black puffer jacket and starred at

Mike with his beady brown eyes. 'What? No hello?' He was not someone Mike would have wanted to run into in his current state, but maybe he could help.

'Sorry, D, one of those nights...' Mike stressfully ran his hand through his hair. The man's name was Dennis Straus; he was a businessman of sorts, one that held onto a secret of Mike's that could never get out.

'I have exactly the merch' for such an occasion brother, same as before. Just got hold of a fresh shipment.' Dennis had taken advantage of the absent Markovic, cornering the market for certain types of medications. By all accounts he was a dealer, but instead of dealing heroin, cocaine or meth, he had sourced something new that Mike had found useful in his recovery. 'You look like shit mate.' And Mike felt like it too. In fact, because of how he was feeling, the temptation to purchase another dose from Dennis was too strong.

'Same stuff I had before?' Mike felt his conscience banging on the door to his head and heart.

'Same stuff, mate, same price too, seeing as it's you. Made you feel good, didn't it?' he smiled as if it was a simple transaction, like there were no repercussions for Mike in doing this. Mike took out his wallet and held out the money to complete the deal. 'Y'know, they're calling this shit "Velocity", heh. Take it it does the trick for you?' The truth was Mike had never felt anything like it; it had made him feel so alive, like anything was possible. The side-effect of increased or accelerated healing had also helped him repair some of the damage that the Avunaye had done to him.

'Michael, what the hell do you think you are doing?' Serena had followed him and questioned his actions as she crossed the street behind them.

'You followed me?' Mike was scared as well as annoyed. *What the fuck is she doing?* As Mike retracted his hand full of cash, so too did Dennis step back from the deal.

'Friend of yours?' Dennis looked at Serena.

'Not quite,' Mike responded. Serena stood smiling at them both.

'Drugs?' Serena's query seemed to unnerve Dennis.

'Mike, you know I'm not a fan of surprises.' The dealer frowned before quickly looking around, no doubt checking that their business was still private.

'No, I'm sure in your profession surprises often bring bad news.' Serena had a glimmer of mischief in her eyes that Mike recognised. 'I imagine, for example, selling to an F.B.I agent would be on your list of unwanted surprises.' Serena held an expressionless face, but it wasn't her that Mike was concerned about right now.

'A fed?!' Dennis pulled a gun out from behind him and aimed it at Mike. Mike looked at Serena briefly as he wondered what the hell she was doing, but then his attention was diverted to Dennis.

'Hey man, easy...' Mike turned out his hands and slowly raised them in surrender.

'You're a mother fucking fed?!' Dennis extended his gun wielding arm a little further, aiming at Mike's head.

'That's irrelevant...' Serena's words drew the man's aim away from Mike. 'You really don't want to point that thing at me, darling. All I want is to know where, or should I say who, you are getting your supply of Velocity from?' Dennis and Mike both looked at her; Dennis then laughed.

'You, you want my supplier?' he shifted his aim between Serena and Mike and then back again. 'How 'bout I just shoot you both. You a fed too?'

'No. I'm so much more.' Mike looked at Serena for a second, she was so calm. 'I am going to ask, one last time. You see those pills you are offering, they're not a new craze. I know of their effects, and I want to know *who* it was that supplied the key ingredient. So, who is your supplier?' She smiled at him, but he held his nerve, and stupidly opened his mouth with something other than the answer she wanted.

'You stupid bitch, who the fuck do you think...' His words were cut off by the sound of a gunshot. Mike's heart stopped at the sound. Dennis had nervously discharged his weapon and shot Serena just below the shoulder. She retaliated by speedily disarming him and punching him in the chest. She pierced his coat with her fist and as she removed her hand, she held his heart within her grip. She smiled as blood dripped from her knuckles, and then, as his body began to stumble, the heart in her hand burst into flames.

'Can't say I didn't warn him,' she chuckled. Mike stood in shock, starring at the body.

'You, you didn't...' Mike stated in reply.

'It was implied.' She spoke casually, but then she seemed to wobble a little. She was bleeding heavily from her wound. 'Michael?' Her voice had lost its confidence as she reached out for him, but he moved away, causing her to fall to her knees. He looked down on her. The cause of so many of his problems, he had repeatedly wished her dead. 'Mike?' she pleaded, clutching at her wound; there were tears in her eyes as mortality snuck in.

5

Serena

The tap dripped. Her senses allowed her to live the droplets irksome journey from facet to basin, relentlessly repeating again and again. She could hear the drones of traffic beyond the walls, movement within nearby apartments; a mother eagerly attempting to get her child ready for the day. The taste of her own blood lingered within her mouth, yet, above the din, she could hear him, his heartbeat. He was nervous, his heart beating faster than normal despite his attempt to remain calm and collected. It was one of the things she had found herself admiring about him; despite everything he had endured, he still found time to contain himself, carefully considering his actions with sedulous poise. Serena lay, eyes closed on the sofa, listening and learning from the world around her. She was not bound as she might have expected.

He trusts me enough to not handcuff me, or perhaps he understands it to be futile... Trust, fear, denial, acceptance of the inevitable, emotions were never black and white; humanity and mortality meant living in a world of grey. Serena's understanding of her own emotions was that they neither controlled her, nor could they be controlled. They made her who she was, yet they did not define her. Her passion, supposedly a barely controllable emotion, did not require control, it simply was and always would be a part of her. He entered the room to check on her, the third time he had done so in the short time she had been awake. 'Michael, you can stop pacing.' Her words caused a flutter of anxiety within the rhythm of his heart. She opened her eyes and sat up on the sofa. Crossing her legs, she looked at him sternly until he took heed of her words and stood still. 'Now, Michael, what am I doing here?' She was curious as to why he would have chosen to help her. 'And why are you using Velocity...?'

'You were shot...' He crossed his arms sheepishly.

'You would usually bring someone with a gunshot wound back to your home?' She wanted to know what he had been thinking, what he was feeling. She didn't like it, but it mattered to her. 'You are also avoiding my other question. Do you understand what Velocity is?'

'You were shot, you lost a lot of blood...'

'And hospitals are of no use in those situations?' She smiled as she teased him and then sighed with frustration as he again avoided the subject of the drug.

'You're not exactly... I mean, taking someone like you to a hospital would only...'

'Sweetie, there's only one me. You do realise that I am human, don't you?' Serena was curious as to what he had or did think of her.

'But I wasn't sure if you'd heal. A hospital wouldn't be safe, what if you died and...'

'Then I'd be dead Michael...' She had interrupted him with what appeared to be a statement of truth that he was not aware of. 'We don't all get to come back to life. I'm an immortal Michael, not indestructible.' He sat down on the arm of the sofa, at the opposite end to where she was sitting as he processed the information. 'So, I ask again. What am I doing here?' Confusion flashed across his handsome face, he had clearly thought of her, of the Avunaye as unending. 'I wouldn't have been surprised to have woken up in a jail cell, an F.B.I interrogation room, or even a shallow grave, cemented into the earth. Yet here I am just a matter of feet away from your bed, and without any restraints.' She looked him in the eye and uncrossed her legs. She began to pull at the hem of her red dress, revealing her caramel thighs, but as she did, Mike stood up in protest.

'Serena, come on... What, what are you doing?' his tone quivered, his heart raced. His body temperature rose as his blood rushed beneath his skin; she could feel his heat. As fast as she could, she stood up and rushed at him, grabbing him and pinning him against the wall. He grabbed at her shoulders as she kissed his neck, he was no match for her, she wanted him and, on some level, she knew he had to want her too. She delved into his elasticated waistband and grabbed hold of his penis, caressing it as she continued to push up against him. 'Serena!' He struggled to handle her, his cry only encouraging her. She stopped kissing his neck and went to kiss his lips when suddenly he headbutted her, hurting himself more than he hurt her, but it was enough to force her to pause for a moment. 'Serena! STOP!' Mike commanded. There was such rage in his tone, the heat of his body fuelling his temper. He was angry, but more than that, there was fear in his eyes. Suddenly an unpreventable feeling of contrition possessed her. She pulled away from him sharply, hurtling backwards across the room until she hit the opposite wall. Her withdrawal brought forth a look of surprise to Mike's face, his stare bringing a layer of dirt to her skin. She felt unclean, rejected and wicked; the combination of emotions collided within her like missiles, exploding over and over.

'This... This isn't right...' She was shaking on the outside as well as on the inside. *Run!* her thoughts screamed at her, and so she obeyed, fleeing his apartment faster than he would have been able to register. She reached the outside, feeling the sun on her face and hearing the commotion of the city around her. Yet as she stood on the street, the open road before her, an overwhelming sense of confinement plagued her thoughts and the sky itself seemed to close in on her. Serena ran to the nearest alleyway, crashing against its periphery and falling to the ground in a flood of tears. She cried, for the first time in as long as she could recall; she cried so hard she could barely breathe, and her heart, usually a flame with passion, felt broken and extinguished. Feeling as if she had been stripped of her strength, like an unnatural vulnerability that had crept inside, its parasitic existence leeching her of everything she was, she decided enough was enough. She grabbed hold of the pain she felt and held it like a weapon, turning it towards something else, transforming it into anger, into the rage she knew so well. She knew what she had to do. Family could be a burden, what Adam had done to her, she hated him for it, but they were also her strength and thus she needed to head home.

Since the fire at her previous residence, Serena had searched for somewhere close to the city, but remote enough that she and her siblings could be themselves without drawing too much attention. Some of them had always searched out ways to integrate themselves into society, but a few of her brothers and sisters refused to hide who they were, and so they had always required safe havens to escape to. Port Washington was such a place. The home they shared had become so special to her that Serena would always have her drivers drop her off at least a couple of miles from it and walk the rest of the way; the less people that knew of it, the safer they all would be.

She reached the contemporary styled paving that led to her front door and smiled. The cube-styled building resided on over two and a half acres of land, providing its current residents with plenty of space for each of them to have their privacy whilst remaining close to one another. A combination of bright white outer walls and floor to ceiling windows sat cleanly within its park-like grounds. A huge door opened into an expansive coalescence of foyer and sitting room with stunning walls of glass that lead out onto a terrace overlooking a swimming pool and the emerald green lawns of the landscaped grounds. Serena kicked off her shoes and stepped onto the heated tiled floor of the foyer. *Is anyone else home?* she wondered, before deciding to undress regardless of who else was around. She walked naked through to the kitchen and pulled a bottle of champagne from the chiller, grabbed a glass from the cupboard and headed for the bathroom. One of her favourite aspects of this building, the bathroom was perfect. A vastly expansive room, the floor was tiled using calacatta marble and the walls were gleaming white in colour. There was a central partition with openings that were positioned parallel to a set of windows behind the bathtub, looking out across the gardens. Two large walk-in showers sat either side of the spa-like bath. Serena filled the tub with water too hot for most, poured herself a glass of bubbly and slid into the steaming waters to purify her body and wash away the dirt that she felt clinging to her skin. She was relaxed, to the point of almost falling asleep when she heard the howl from outside and looked out the window to see two of her siblings galloping across the lawns. Nahki's ability to transform himself into the wolf had surprised some, his powers were growing quicker than expected. Tisa, when she could, visited to help him hone his new-found ability. The huge black furred wolf of Nahki and the chocolate, shaggy haired beast of Tisa bounded across the grass towards one another, colliding into one another, lashing out with teeth and claws. The air of peace that had filled the house was now gone.

Serena climbed from the bath and went to her room to get dressed. She hurriedly donned an oxblood coloured, laced, pleated maxi dress from her huge closet and rushed down the stairs, out onto the terrace. Nahki held the means for her to get the answers she wanted; he had Adam locked up somewhere and she was now desperate to know where. She leapt off the terrace, down onto the grass, steadying herself with her hand as she landed. Her crimson hair lashed back as she whipped her head up, her siblings within her flame filled stare. She rushed towards them, her anger driving her, and as the wolves turned and began to charge at one another once more, Serena flew to intercept, landing directly in their paths. Neither of them halted at her appearance, both still charging, canines bared. Nahki's huge brown eyes were fixed on her as he galloped towards her, he cared not who he ended up colliding with. Serena gritted her teeth and created flames within her hands. She looked the black beast in the eye and threw a ball of fire at the ground between them, simultaneously doing the same between her and her sister, who was bounding towards her from the opposite direction. The flames hit the ground and with Serena's will, they rose and formed walls of fire, forcing Tisa to alter her course and for Nahki to lose his footing. He hit the ground muzzle first and tumbled. The chocolate wolf ran away from the flames, and transformed, exchanging her shaggy coat for golden coloured skin and braided black hair.

'Serena!' Tisa called as she marched towards her with intent, 'what the fuck are you doing?!' Serena wasted no time surrounding Tisa with a wall of fire. Her brother, Nahki, had now transformed back into his human form and was rushing towards her with a blade in hand. He went to strike; however, Serena quickly avoided his attack and landed a flame covered uppercut that sent him hurtling through the air. As he landed, he swiftly rose to his feet, only to be met by Serena as she grasped his throat and held him aloft.

'I want Adam! Give him to me!' Her rage was evident in the flames that licked up and down her arms and flashed through her hair, yet she did not get the reaction she desired. Instead, Nahki only laughed.

'Sister, put me down and release Tisa. You'll see Adam soon enough.' His calmness annoyed her, but his words satisfied her demands. Nahki's words did rarely not resemble the truth, his lack of emotion made his decision to speak honestly a simple one; of course, he could lie, when the truth proved to give him a calculated disadvantage, but what harm could her talking to Adam do? So, Serena took him at his word. She squeezed his throat tightly once more to reiterate her threat before releasing her grip and extinguishing all the flames.

'Damn, Serena, whatever pissed you off, tell me, 'cus I don't wanna make the same mistake.' Tisa brushed herself off. She grabbed some clothes from off the grass near the pool and dressed herself in a pair of black leggings and a grey-speckled, long-sleeved sports top that zipped at the front. Since arriving in New York, she and Bomani had taken up residence within Manhattan, but they found time to visit and train their skills.

'You know I hate being made to wait.' Serena began to walk back to the house with her kin in tow. As her anger and impatience subsided, a feeling of shame began to sneak in: her current affliction was one that she felt her siblings could not understand.

The three of them took up seats within one of the dining rooms. Floor to ceiling windows looked out over the garden, and on either side of the room, stood sliding glass doors that led out onto terraces. They sat around a round wooden table on white-covered comfy seats designed to seat two people, allowing them to spread out and relax. Serena wanted answers from her siblings. She had been kept in the dark about many things regarding the ritual, Markovic, the plan to bring the city to its knees; she also wanted Adam, or at least his whereabouts, so he could answer for what he had done to her. Nahki held at least one of the answers she sought, however, she had a feeling he knew more than she had originally thought. 'So, brother. Care to bring me up to speed? I have been away since Christmas... Have I missed much?' She made sure that her words translated her frustration. In reply, Nahki stood up from his seat and looked out of the window.

'Serena, what is it you think we are doing here, in New York?' His words were toneless.

'Matthias ordered...' Serena began to reluctantly say, feeling like a child answering her tutor, yet, Nahki raised his hand and halted her.

'Matthias ordered nothing, your orders came from Evelina...' Nahki's words sparked a blaze within her, she detested being lied to. 'The attack on New York was designed to draw out Adam, to find out what he had been up to, how far his memories had recovered since we had last clashed with him. We had to convince him that we were here to threaten the mortals and after all this time we finally found a weakness that forced him to break the code, the unwritten law we all lived by. The curse of our forsaken freewill.' He turned to face her, his face expressionless, his brown eyes measuring her anger, her contempt, her passion. 'The C.I.A are holding Adam, and as deputy director I have had ample time with him over the last couple months. I have put him down again and again, to the point of eradicating every single memory. However, with each resurrection it seems that, with the known exception of the knowledge of his family, a new memory remains intact.' The idea of Adam managing to retain a new memory unnerved Serena, yet despite her worry, she felt anger more than anything else. For if Adam did not remember why he cursed her with the unpleasant array of emotions, if he did not recall doing it, then how could he provide the answers she desired.

'Why?! Why play me for a fool?!' Her temper flared. 'And if that was the plan, why not bring everyone here now? What's the hold up? We have Adam, if we're doing the bloody ritual, why not get on with it?!'

'Why play dumb Serena?' Nahki stared at her. She felt threatened, her palms heating up, almost igniting. 'You know just as well as I that the ritual will not work...' He looked at her, his stare breaking through her defences to her exposed core. 'Thanks to Adam removing, or destroying some of our memories regarding the ritual, it has taken us some time to piece it all together. The ritual requires all of our participation, all twelve of us. We all know that Carmen is going to be an issue. You also know that there can only be twelve Avunaye at any one time, a fact you have kept to yourself.' The accusation drew a look from Tisa that made Serena feel as if she was being backed into a corner. The fire inside her roared. 'But before you say anything, it is fine,' his words confused her. 'We believe that with the tree, we can overcome that obstacle. The mortals, Vladimir and Kryln, their power, money and influence has proven useful and so for now, we will protect them and continue to promise the idea of becoming one of us. Brandt is currently in Chicago –' Serena chortled.

'Yes, I have heard of his indiscretions. He draws too much attention.' Serena interrupted Nahki.

'Bomani and I are keeping tabs on other assets within the city.' Tisa stretched out and lifted her feet up onto the table.

'Matthias is... exactly where he needs to be,' Nahki continued, 'Evelina and Seymour are looking into the re-emergence of Carmen, trying to work out how she managed to survive all these years. That just leaves the problem children –'

'Now, brother, why not just say how you truly feel...' a voice sounded from the opposite end of the adjoining kitchen. It was a voice Serena recognised, but one that made every fibre of her being quiver with a sense of disquietude. 'Oh, apologies, brother, of course you don't, do you. *Feel*, that is.' He stood assuredly, greeting them all with a strained smile. '"Hateful to me as the gates of Hades is that man who hides one thing in his heart and speaks another..."'

'Tobias...' Tisa stated in a tone of angst. Tobias had a ruggedly handsome face with a sadistically sickening glint in his pale-yellow eyes. He had short brown hair and a fair complexion. Dressed in a black silk shirt, black jeans, black boots and wearing a black overcoat with a dark blue lining, he opened out his arms towards Tisa.

'Is that any way to greet your big brother?' He smiled. Tobias was more than just a "problem child", as Nahki had put it, he was by far the worst of them. Throughout time he had done his best to stand out from his kin, honing his abilities to an unnerving degree. He had regularly put all of them at risk of discovery by following his passion for chaos, bringing despair to mankind, time and time again. He also had one ability that frightened most of his brothers and sisters, one that unsettled Serena at this very moment. Serena fidgeted in her chair. 'Honestly, whatever could be the matter with...' he stopped as his eyes met Serena's. He slowly raised a hand over his mouth. It felt as if she was realising her worst fear as he read her like a book, and the more she tried to conceal, the more she gave away; her new-found emotions aiding him by opening each and every door to her mind.

'Tobias!' she yelled angrily.

'He unlocked you...' He said it so plainly, as if it was nothing, spilling out her secret for all to hear. Tobias had control over the mind, reading thoughts, compulsion, even the ability to destroy memories. As far as Serena was concerned, he received the pick of the litter when it came to the devil's powers, and what was worse, he knew it, and revelled in the fact. Nahki and Tisa looked upon her as if she was tainted, a leper among pinnacles of health.

WHY?! she screamed inside as she scowled at Tobias, yet he merely smiled back at her with his eyes.

Listen sister... She heard his words echoing within her head, yet his lips remained unmoving. *Do not look upon Adam's gift to you as anything but that, a gift. Meet me in the garden later and I shall explain.* He smiled again before turning his attention back to the group. 'So, brother, you were telling a tale of Adam's memories. Do continue. I do enjoy a good *story.*' Tobias slung his jacket over the back of the fourth chair and made himself comfortable. Nahki appeared to be thrown slightly, but soon moved forward with his update.

'The woman, the F.B.I agent... No matter how many times he dies, he remembers her.' Nahki paused for a moment, seemingly expecting Tobias to comment, but just as he began to speak again, it was then that his elder brother decided to interrupt.

'And this is the same woman that he finally killed for, how poetic.' He sat back and threw his feet up onto the wood of the table. 'How ironic, correct me if I'm wrong. You continually kill Adam to prevent him from remembering who he is, what he is capable of, keeping him weakened, and yet now he shows signs of memory retention. So, afraid of what's to come, you seek out the garden and the tree, the source of our knowledge and power. Yet, to get the location of said tree, you need Adam to recall one of the eleven memories that we took from him with our very existence...' He looked around at each of them, yet no one said a word. 'Am I the only one who sees a bloody gaping hole in the logic of your plan?' He was smug, and the silence in the room only fuelled his glee further. 'So glad to be back!' He jumped up out of his seat and grabbed his coat, 'I guess I'll go and unpack,' and off he went with quite the spring in his step.

Serena endured the untoward looks that Tisa was giving her for a while as the three of them deliberated on Tobias' words, but there was only so much glaring she could take. She needed to take the attention off herself.

'Velocity...' She spoke simply, but it drew their attention. 'I came across a dealer last night that sells... apologies, sold, the drug. I'm sure you are aware of this, I just wondered which one of us would be foolish enough to start *that* up again, especially after last time.' By the look she received from Tisa, it was evident that she was not in the loop with this one. Nahki, however, she never could tell what he was thinking.

'You're sure of this?' Nahki questioned her statement. Serena could have taken the bait, snapped his head off, screamed at him for doubting her, but she decided to sit back for a moment and let him accept what she was saying. 'Which one of us would be so stupid... Our blood is not for sale.' He was stern, making his point clear, as if Serena and Tisa needed telling; Serena was just pleased that the subject had moved on from her "unlocking", as Tobias had called it.

She left Nahki and Tisa and headed out into the garden. It was peaceful outside, away from the scheming, but really, she just wanted to know what Tobias had to say. Why did he call this awful jumble of emotions a gift? Ever since Adam had unlocked her, she had never felt worse. If her feelings for Mike were not enough, her conscience was overwhelmed by the thousands of years' worth of guilt that was flooding in.

'I won't divulge your secret, about the mortal...' Tobias said as he approached her. He had swapped his shirt and coat for a grey jumper and black leather jacket. 'They do not need to know.' Serena felt thrown by his kindness, if that's what it was. She wanted to know why he would do that, why protect her, why spare her the humiliation. Tobias indicated that he was listening as she tried to work out his angle. 'No tricks, I promise,' he held up his hands, pleading his honesty.

'Then why?' Serena questioned.

'Let's just say I understand what you are going through, what you are... feeling...' He looked at her sincerely, and something inside her told her to believe his words. Despite his honesty, Serena struggled to believe that he too had been "unlocked". 'It's not the worst thing, trust me. I still can't believe how I didn't want this, before, I mean. It seems so simple, moving forward on a single emotion that you never question what *life* is actually like. I mean, to live, to truly live, *is* to feel.' He spoke so passionately, yet Serena still didn't see a positive side to the whirlwind inside her.

'Why would you want to feel like this?' she asked him, yet really, she wanted to know how he managed to keep it all in; she felt like she was being torn apart, how was it that he stood there so calmly?

'You were born again with such anger and hatred in your heart, such a distaste for men, and a pity for women. You have the ability to create and control fire, manifesting the torment that blazed within you. What would you say if I told you that *now* you were capable of more? More emotion, more power.' The dying sun caught his eyes, giving them an almost honey coloured glow.

That's why you called it a gift? Serena knew that he would be able to hear her inner thoughts.

'A gift it is,' he replied confidently. 'Sister, I require your assistance with something.' His words brought a familiar feeling to Serena's heart. Tobias rarely helped anyone for free, she should have known. 'Hey, wait a minute, hear me out...' There was an air of desperation to his voice as she considered walking away. 'In return for keeping your secret, all I ask is that you assist me, or better yet, you let me assist you in finding out where Nahki is holding Adam. If you recall, I cannot simply enter Nahki's mind. His lack of emotion makes him practically hollow.' His conditions took her by surprise. Yet what did he have to gain from her finding Adam?

'Why do you want Adam?' she asked straightforwardly. She was growing tired of running errands for her siblings without knowing their endgame.

'Do you remember how the Avunaye once operated? In secret, the world unaware of our presence. We prevented humanity from destroying itself so many times. Yet now the world is a mess and we are on the verge of being hunted by the mortals. I want to help Adam return us to our former glory.' Serena began to laugh at him, she couldn't believe the bullshit he was saying; Tobias had never cared for anyone but himself.

'You expect me to believe this bullshit, you of all people want to cover up our existence and go back to saving the world from behind the scenes!' She chortled, yet her mockery of him did not appear to upset him as she would have expected.

'I want us to remain in control of our own destinies!' He shouted in response, yet he wasn't angry, no, Serena had seen him angry enough times in the past to know that; this was something else. 'Who do you think arranged all that you see around you, sister? Who do you believe made it so, that all twelve of the Avunaye were in the same place for the first time in ages...?' She looked at him in disbelief. 'By eradicating his memories, they'll push him away, and when we need him, he'll choose the mortals over us. And when he does, there will be no place on Earth that we can all hide from him.' There was a worry and frustration to his tone that was uncharacteristic of him. 'Serena, Nahki requests that I destroy the memories of these F.B.I agents to hide our existence, but I have always believed in using the tools at our disposal. New York is soon to see some changes...' Tobias touched her shoulder and then grasped her hand. 'We are now different from our other siblings, sister, best we stick together. The fire within you... you could set the world a blaze.' His serious expression held a hidden smile for her.

Serena watched as he walked back to the house, and as he vanished from sight, she repeated his words in her mind, and suddenly she felt the worry that he had shown.

Why would Adam abandon us? Despite the things that they had done over the course of time, Adam had never turned away from his family, not truly. Over the years, members of the Avunaye had been lost, killed by mortals who feared what they were, what they were capable of. Adam had always mourned them. With the exception of when Evelina turned on Carmen, the Avunaye had never in existence been a threat to themselves. Serena began to question whether forcing Adam to lose his memories was the right decision anymore; he had never forgotten his family, but now things were changing.

6
Brandt

As he stood on the sun-scorched sand, he watched and waited for the opportune moment to act. The rash young king had found himself amidst an onslaught of Hittite chariots, his forces either staining the earth or fleeing in panic. Despite being outnumbered, the king stood upon his chariot with confidence. The light of the sun flashed across his metal, scale-covered leather tunic as he fought against the odds to survive. Brandt watched on in admiration as this mere mortal clung to his own existence.

'We should just charge in, take a few hits, and then slaughter them all,' his young sibling stated. Pentaur had only resided with them for the last one hundred summers, and as such his arrogance was still fresh. He was the seventh, and with him their power had grown. Brandt had been ordered to wait for his sister's arrival before acting, but his yearning for destruction was insatiable.

'Come then, brother, let us wreak havoc. They call upon their gods for help, let us show them true power!' Brandt smiled and drew two khopesh blades from their chariot. He grasped them tightly, one in each hand, feeding the metal with the heat of his rage. He wore nothing but a kilt, fashioned from the skin of a lion. The scars on his face and chest glowed as the fire beneath his skin roared with an all-consuming anger. His brother, Pentaur, also wore nothing but a linen kilt and he grasped a composite bow as his weapon of choice. His skin was of a bronze colour and his hair as black as night; his eyes were a sapphire blue and despite his cock-sure confidence, he had a soft expression, a kindness within his smirk. Pentaur had provided them with a new power to utilize, his ability enabled him to ride the wind.

'Let us act now, or Rameses will fall on this day!' Pentaur was eager to move into the fray. Brandt smiled, and as the curved blades in his hands began to glow a deep red, he pushed off and began to bound towards the battle, his brother gliding alongside him.

Brandt threw himself into the sides of the heavy Hittite chariots, shattering wood and sending men flying in all directions. He swung his weapons with force, decapitating horses that ferried their masters against the young Egyptian king. Taking the odd arrow to his torso, he was permitted to act in defence and tear his enemy asunder. Pentaur whipped up the sand, sending waves of it crashing against their adversaries, scratching at their flesh, blinding them. When attacked, he would rise up on the wind and shower his enemy with arrows. Rameses had lost many men; he was surrounded, no officers, no charioteers, no shields or soldiers, yet he continued to fight.

'I like you...' Brandt chuckled to the king as he laid waste to two enemy chariots descending on the Egyptian's position. A brave soldier that had been thrown from his chariot stood up and loosed an arrow that hit Brandt in the upper arm. The arrowhead ripped through his flesh and protruded from the back. Brandt tore away the arrows fletchings in a furious manner and ripped the arrow from his arm. He looked at the archer that had shot him, staring him in the eyes, with his own aglow. Tossing his weapons to his sides, he marched towards the soldier and rid him of his bow before grasping him by the shoulders and lifting him up so that their eyes were level. Brandt roared as he tore the man's arms clean from his torso.

The display of Brandt's ferocity rippled a sense of fear throughout the Hittite army and the tide of the battle turned. With the help of the arrival of his other divisions, Rameses had managed to force his enemy to retreat towards the river, and once surrounded by Egyptian forces, the enemy abandoned their chariots and tried swimming to safety. 'HA!!' Brandt guffawed at the fleeing mortals desperately attempting to escape death, many of them drowning in the Orontes regardless of their will to survive.

'Does the order to wait mean nothing to you two?' Serena spoke in a condescending tone as she came to a halt on her horse. She wore her fiery hair down, straightened. Golden bracelets and armlets shone from her wrists and biceps, and apart from two strips of fine black cloth that ran from her shoulders, flowing down over her breasts and between her thighs, she was naked; her golden painted skin glistened in the daylight. Pentaur joined Brandt as he looked around at the battlefield.

'The child required our assistance,' Pentaur smirked. 'Without Brandt and I, he would have been slain.'

'He was ambushed due to his arrogance. Now, due to your rash intervention, the Egyptians are claiming victory. There is talk of a return to Damascus.' She was unimpressed by their efforts and the glow in her eye suggested she knew more, more that would tarnish their victory further. 'Adam resides in the fortified city of Kadesh. With Rameses riding home, now *we* have to get our hands dirty...' She looked down on Brandt from upon her white steed. He hated that look. A simple glare of disappointment, but one that pierced his armour; one only family could give. As they waited for the arrival of Evelina and Matthias, Brandt walked along the bank of the river. Calming himself, he washed his blood-soaked hands in the waters and then proceeded to forage amongst the trees and shrubs for sustenance. The riverbanks were home to a variety of fruit baring plants as well as wise oaks and poplars; Brandt gorged on citrus and ravaged the white-flowered olive trees of their purple-green fruits.

Joined by Evelina and Matthias, the five members of what the Egyptians had come to call "The Guardians of the Gates", traversed one of the tips of the river and made their way toward Kadesh. Matthias, as theatrical as ever, distorted reality to appear as if he rode a hawk-headed lion, and that he himself had the head of the Setesh animal. Evelina remained quiet as they closed in on Adam's presumed location. Her golden-blonde hair draped over her shoulders and she wore a kalasiris that was beaded with an uncountable number of small emerald stones. She could have been mistaken for a noble woman if it weren't for the straps that crossed her breast, straps that held two golden khopesh swords across her back. Her dress was also torn down one side, enabling her to spread her legs to ride and also aided her movement when on foot. It seemed that Adam had predicted their arrival, or perhaps the Hittites were waiting for an attack from the Egyptians; regardless, the gates of the city were well guarded.

'You take the five hundred on the right...' Brandt chuckled to Pentaur, yet, he was then silenced by a glare from Evelina. Her green eyes conveyed a message of disappointment.

'Hold your tongue and wait here.' Evelina then dismounted her horse. 'I will dispatch these foolish mortals to whichever hell they believe in and then we will deal with Adam.'

One-thousand armed men stood between Evelina and the city walls, yet, she was unfazed. Unlike her children, she could act of her own volition. She walked slowly but confidently, barefoot on the sand and dirt laden floor, only unsheathing her blades at the last moment before she attacked. Cutting through wooden shields, she decapitated, dismembered and cleaved through man after man with ease. Brandt watched on in awe, but with a hint of jealousy in his heart as she killed again and again. Her weapons were like extensions of her arms as she spun and leapt, slaughtering groups of soldiers at a time, all the while avoiding taking any damage herself. Whether out of fear, or as an attempt to overwhelm her, a large contingent of warriors charged at her all at once. Cutting down two enemies closest to her, Evelina leapt into the air and gracefully completed a back flip, landing on the ground with roughly fifty feet between her and the four hundred or so Hittite guards that were charging towards her. The ground trembled as the stampede of men descended upon her, yet she remained still. It was not until they were upon her that she decided to act, stretching out her arms before clashing both of her swords together with such might, such force, that the world itself shook on its axis. Turning to look at Brandt, her eyes were glowing brightly, their green turning white, and as she smiled a sickening grin, the army before her collapsed, as if every heart among them ceased to beat simultaneously. Without a word, Evelina span her blades and sheathed them before mounting her ride once more and leading the way into the city. Brandt and the others followed, stepping over body after body. Brandt had hoped there would be stragglers, but alas, Evelina had extinguished the life from each any every one of them.

The city appeared to be void of life. Anyone who was alive within the walls must have hidden themselves away. 'Matthias, Serena, Pentaur, search for the tree. It must be here somewhere... Brandt, come with me.' She seemed more relaxed. Brandt surmised that slaughtering a thousand men must have helped to ease her frustrations. 'Brandt... Cain.' Her tone changed in an instant, now resembling that of the disappointed mother that he had known for an eternity. 'Regardless of whether the tree is here or not, Adam must die. We have the next initiate prepared, the priest... once revived, Adam *will* complete the ritual. Carmen will also do as we order, whether she wants to or not.' Brandt knew that this fight would not be an easy one. Adam would no doubt resist. It had been a century since their last meeting, a hundred years to grow strong, to remember.

'I will do as you ask, mother...' Part of him wanted her to accept him as her son once again, but the distasteful look she gave him in reply informed him that, despite the ages that had passed, she had still not forgiven him. It was still as if she had lost both of her sons that day.

They rode slowly along paths of sand, dirt and stone until they reached a large open courtyard. The ground here was fertile, covered in grass, plants grew tall, climbing the surrounding buildings. There was life here, colours that were alien to this part of the world. Brandt looked on in awe and was sure that this was the place. 'Where is the tree?' he questioned, unable to see the large pale oak.

'You look upon this marvel, this peaceful oasis bathed in beauty, in wonder, and you question what is missing...' Adam entered the courtyard from the opposite entrance. He walked barefoot across the grass, wearing only a white loin cloth about his waist. As Brandt looked upon him, he couldn't resist acknowledging that Adam's appearance encapsulated perfection.

'If it is not here, my love, then pray tell. Where is it?' Evelina climbed down from her horse and walked towards Adam. Brandt quickly followed behind.

'It would seem that I have misplaced it, my love...' Adam smirked. 'I believe that is your doing...' He stood still and crossed his arms. Looking at Brandt for a moment, his expression read one of disappointment, yet there was also something else.

'Adam...' Brandt acknowledged, testing him.

'Brandt...' Adam's mere reply was confirmation enough for Brandt, for what he thought to be true; it would seem his father did not know him, not for who he truly was. Brandt searched those green eyes for some recognition, but there was none, and a flurry of heat rippled throughout his veins. He was angry. Angry at the fact that Adam did not know him, and angry at the fact that even after all this time, he himself still cared, still craved Adam's acceptance.

'I had hoped that after a century of reflection, you might have at least recalled where you had left it.' Evelina's tone suggested that her patience was waning.

'Your unending search for the tree is beginning to bore me...' Carmen entered the courtyard. She was dressed in a bright white kalasiris dress, with her long blonde hair tied up. The tension within the square began to grow as Carmen joined Adam, standing by his side.

'I had wondered where *you* had gotten to,' Evelina said to Carmen. 'Still denying what must be done...' Her statement appeared to anger the blonde goddess.

Here we go... Brandt felt his palms begin to radiate. Even the air felt tense as they all stood rigidly, waiting for the other to act. Brandt could see the blue sparks begin to flicker within Carmen's honey-coloured eyes.

'Eve...' Adam attempted to dissuade her from what was inevitably about to happen; 'there is always another way...' But Evelina's mind was already made up, made clear to all as she once again unsheathed her blades.

'Weapons?... How mortal of you.' Carmen chortled and then smiled as she began to rub her fingers together, sparks of blue light flickering about her hands and scurrying up and down the golden skin of her arms.

Evelina hurled her khopesh blades, one towards Adam, the other at Carmen. Adam managed to dodge the blade; however, Evelina took the opportunity to land a blow to his chest, sending him falling backwards. Brandt threw himself at Carmen, landing a swift backhand across her face that sent her hurtling across the make-shift garden. Brandt and Evelina then switched targets, and Brandt focused his efforts on Adam. As he descended on Adam there was a thunderous noise from the heavens above, and a bolt of blue sparks exploded from one of Carmen's hands, narrowly missing Brandt, forcing him to alter his trajectory. He looked to Carmen with such fury in his eyes that they felt as if they had melted within their sockets, but it was Evelina that struck Carmen first, allowing Brandt to continue onwards to Adam.

'Brandt! You don't have to do this!' Adam moved away from Brandt as he advanced. But Brandt knew what had to be done, Adam would only get stronger with time. He grasped Adam by the forearms and unleashed his rage upon his flesh, burning hotter than ever before. Adam screamed in agony, but managed to pull himself away, enough to spring up and dropkick Brandt in the chest, flipping away from him. As Adam spiralled through the air he changed, landing on the ground as a huge ferocious lion with a glorious golden-brown mane. He roared, shaking the foundations of the city, and as the tremors forced Brandt to lose balance momentarily, Adam leapt upon him. He scratched and pounded Brandt with his huge paws and sank his gigantic teeth into his flesh; it took every ounce of Brandt's strength to hold him back. Brandt tried to burn him, singeing fur and melting flesh, trying anything to stop the beast. Yet, it was an arrow that distracted Adam long enough for Brandt to throw him off, an arrow that struck true into the lion's side.

Pentaur glided down from the roof tops, notching arrows and letting them fly towards Adam. The beast roared and lashed out as Brandt and Pentaur closed in and cornered it.

'We've got this,' Pentaur said to Brandt as he loosed another arrow and hit the lions hind leg. Brandt glanced at Evelina, seeing that Matthias and Serena had joined the fight, helping to contain Carmen.

'Enough!' Evelina commanded them all to stop. 'Adam! Enough!' At her command Adam began to transform back. He knelt in his human form, pulling arrows from his flesh, his wounds instantly closing and healing.

'Even if I knew where the tree was, I would never –!' Adam began to say, but he was interrupted by Evelina as she threw one of her blades at him in frustration. He caught it effortlessly.

'You... You drive us to this!' she exclaimed in anger. 'We take your memories, because with them, you'd destroy us all! The tree can end it all, it can end this torment!' She looked at Adam, pleading with him. Brandt looked at him, wondering if he would give in, but Adam simply stood there, confident that he was in control. His defiance forced Evelina to react. 'Serena, burn it down!' She said the words through gritted teeth and with such malice to her tone.

Serena began to set alight to the grass, the plants and trees. Matthias held Carmen back, preventing her from rushing to Adam.

'No!' Adam yelled as the fire began to spread, destroying his creation. 'WHY?!' There was such pain in his voice. Brandt could feel Adam's emotions ripple out across the courtyard. Adam moved towards Evelina, but Pentaur intervened and pushed him back. Trying again, Adam was forced back by Pentaur, this time losing his patience. His eyes glowed brighter as his anger built, his fury could be felt by all. Seemingly losing control, he spun the blade in his hand and thrust it forwards, plunging it into Pentaur's chest.

'ADAM! NO!' Evelina cried out. Matthias released Carmen from his grasp and moved to Evelina's side. Serena extinguished her flames and Carmen stood unmoving, a look of fear possessing her face. Brandt flew to the aid of his brother, catching Pentaur as he fell; he embraced him as his life left his body.

'What have you done?!' Brandt yelled at Adam as he knelt with Pentaur in his arms.

'AHHH!!!' Adam screamed in pain as he dropped to his knees, clutching at his head. Brandt, panicking, looked to Evelina; he knew what was happening.

'Quickly!' Evelina ordered, 'stop him!' She was

panicking, her words trembling as they left her lips. Serena lit her hands on fire and Carmen, stood beside her sister, prepared herself, her skin alive with the power of lightning. Brandt clambered away from Adam as he continued to scream in agony, dragging Pentaur's body with him. Matthias stepped forward and picked up the blade that Adam had used to slay his kin, attempting to cut Adam down where he knelt. However, Adam quickly raised a hand and caught the blade; he stood up and removed his other hand from his face to reveal his eyes, blood shot and glowing red instead of green.

'I remember...' Adam looked to Matthias and the blade he held turned to dust and fell to the ground. He then turned his attention to Brandt. 'Cain.' He said the name with such hatred before charging towards him. Matthias attempted to grab Adam, but he effortlessly sent Matthias flying, crashing against one of the stone walls. Brandt could not move as Adam continued towards him. The hate, the fury that Adam held, Brandt could feel it all. It paralysed him. But whilst Adam's emotions were concentrated on Brandt, Evelina had the opportunity to move to Adam and grasp him, placing a hand on either side of his head.

'Enough, my love,' she said softly. And then, as she snapped his neck, Brandt could see the emerald-green return to Adam's eyes, and the feeling of remorse pulsated from within them.

The journey from Kadesh to Abydos took them six days, twice having to halt and extinguish the light from Adam's eyes. Brandt had happily taken his life the second time, his anger towards Adam having consumed him for the entire journey. The ritual was almost complete. Hanging within one of the temples were twelve souls connected to the high priest, YuYu, a man chosen for his faith and his distaste for the weaker side of humanity; he saw mortality as a sickness and prayed to Osiris for strength. Instead, it was Matthias who had answered his prayers. To Brandt's surprise, Carmen played her part without dissension. She had taken Adam's side, and would no doubt do again, but she knew as they all did, that he must be controlled. There was but one way they knew how to do that. The high priest stood robed, with long purpley-grey hair that had made him stand out from all of the other priests and worshipers. He wanted this, a chance at immortality, and had helped sacrifice those closest to him without hesitation. As Adam woke, Evelina was at his side, the blade of bone and wood in her hand. 'Come my love, we have a job to do,' she whispered to him as she lifted him up to his feet. Adam was weakened due to his rebirth; he would be easily manipulated. Evelina placed the blade in his hand and ushered him over to the last sacrifice. The elderly woman hung, hands bound, unconscious due to the time she had resided there, waiting for Adam to wake. 'Finish the ritual my love.' Evelina spoke softly, almost a whisper.

'Please... Don't make me...' Adam pleaded as he stood before the helpless woman. His words, however, were pointless, and Evelina continued to encourage him until he was forced to comply and carry out the deed, spilling the woman's blood. As the life left her body, Adam too looked to have lost something from within him; he stumbled and turned to look around at the others. He looked at Brandt, possibly searching for help, or maybe it was forgiveness he sought after. It mattered not. Brandt walked up to him, he who could no doubt not recognise his own flesh and blood, looked him in the eye and allowed the rage he felt inside to set ablaze within his veins and cause his eyes to burn with hatred.

'Your task is complete...' Brandt looked down on Adam. A small part of him wanted to call him father, but the word stuck in his throat; for what father would want to kill his own son. '...Adam.' Brandt rested his palms on Adam's cheeks and pressed his red-hot thumbs into those green eyes as hard as he could.

It had been over three millennia since that day, yet the burden still weighed heavily on Brandt's heart. 'The Poem of Pentaur. Do you know what that is, Adam?' Brandt asked the question as he stood before their prisoner. Nahki had reluctantly arranged for Brandt to visit the site where Adam was being held captive. His cell, as it were, was located underground in a dark, dank hole that the C.I.A would use for interrogation purposes, but never admit to being associated with.

'Time is almost up, brother,' Nahki admitted. 'It would make no sense for you to be seen here, my cover would be blown.' Nahki could never comprehend the desire Brandt held in his heart, the pain he wished to inflict on Adam. Devoid of hatred, how could Nahki understand how he felt, even after all this time. 'I believe the poem to be an account of the battle of Kadesh, no?' Nahki stated, ruining the game.

'Pentaur was one of the Avunaye, one of us. And that is all history has to remember him by. You erased him from time, from the memories of the others, but I remember, Adam. I remember the look in your eyes when you took my brother's life. The look of hatred you had for me... You will remain down here until such a time we require you. You will suffer alone, and the world will forget you.' Brandt looked Adam in the eyes as he lay chained to the walls within his prison. 'We *will* find the garden, Adam. We *will* find the tree. I will leave my mark on this world...' He grasped Adam by the throat, lifting him to his feet. 'And I will take passion from its despair.'

7

Seamus McCarthy

Declan and Alannah had left the house to collect their evening meal. They had the place to themselves for at least half an hour, Seamus surmised. Since returning home, he was finally feeling good. He was finally feeling himself again. Work was less stressful and he had successfully resisted chasing possible leads regarding the Avunaye, not that there had been many; they had been unusually quiet. Lucy had thus far failed to find anything suspicious about his father's death and his relationship with his wife had been reinvigorated. It was rare for them to have time to spend together, and even rarer for them to be home alone.

He chased her up the stairs to the bedroom. Slamming the door behind him, he frantically pulled his shirt up over his head and undid his pants. Moira stood beside the bed doing the same, the pair of them giggling like adolescents, their excitement shining brightly. He paused for a moment as he watched her finish undressing, standing beautifully naked, brushing some of her curls behind her ear as she climbed under the covers and waited for him to join her. The corner of her mouth held a smile.

'Stop gawking and get in here!' she grinned. 'We haven't got all day.'

I don't think time will be an issue, Seamus almost chuckled to himself as he finished stripping and hopped into the bed beside her. Experiences of passion had been few and far between for as long as he could recall. Despite their clear love for one another, life had just gotten in the way. They lay on their sides, facing each other as they kissed. He ran his hand down from her shoulder, along the curve of her body, and down to her arse, caressing her soft skin. He grasped the cheek gently, pulling at her, closing the space between them so that she could feel his strength. She responded by lifting her leg and wrapping it over him. She ran her fingers through his hair as she kissed him, sliding her tongue against his. The desire between them was insatiable. Seamus began kissing her softly on her neck as he gently slid himself inside her moistened vagina. She moaned in ecstasy into his ear as his length filled her. She grasped at his hair and dug her fingers into the skin of his back as he proceeded to slide his penis three-quarters of the way out of her, before thrusting it back inside, clutching at her buttock and her leg as he did. Seamus rolled her gently onto her back and lay on top of her as he continued to make love to her, looking her in the eye as she lay perfectly beneath him. She smiled at him and then held him tightly, kissing him as he came inside her; she grabbed at the hair on the back of his head and brought her legs up, wrapping them around his waist. She hummed with satisfaction as they embraced, and then they lay still, forgetting the world around them.

'We leave you alone for five minutes!' Declan's voice sounded from down the stairs, followed by the bang of the front door. Seamus and Moira looked at each other sheepishly; they had been caught out.

'Oh my god,' Moira expressed in embarrassment before kissing Seamus once more. She quickly slid out from under him and wrapped herself in a sheet. 'Busted...' She giggled as she opened the bedroom door a crack and checked that the coast was clear before tip-toeing to the bathroom. Seamus not so gracefully, stumbled out of the bed and quickly put his clothes back on before composing himself and heading down the stairs to join the kids.

The smell of freshly made pizza filled the house. Combined scents of baked doughy crust, melted cheese, oregano and pepperoni had Seamus' stomach groaning in anticipation of having its fill. He entered the dining room to find Declan stood by the table, devouring a slice, as if afraid that he would not receive another. He wore a dark blue hooded top, skinny jeans and a pair of black and white Vans. He smiled at his father as he entered the room. Alannah appeared from the kitchen with a handful of plates.

'Hey! Save some for the rest of us!' she groaned, telling her brother off. She too smiled at the sight of Seamus as she placed the plates down upon the table and pushed some of her long hair from her face. She was wearing blue jeans, torn at the knees, a dark blue, long sleeved top and a red, blue and gold coloured, plaid, blanket scarf about her neck; she looked so grown-up that her appearance disheartened Seamus a little, as the realisation that his little girl was not so little anymore, struck him once again. 'We ended up getting three, so there should be plenty to go around.' She wasn't wrong, Seamus thought, a little surprised by her words. Three pizzas were one too many as far as he was concerned.

'Three?' Seamus was curious as to his children's reasoning.

'Yeah... We figured it would be enough for the five of us...' She smiled; her cheeks slightly flushed.

'Five?' Seamus was confused, he had not expected any guests. Yet, following his question, came a knock at the door. Alannah bounded past him as she rushed to answer it, with Seamus still slightly confused as to who was joining them for dinner.

'We ran into him on the way to the pizza place...' Declan sounded, with half of a second slice of pizza filling his mouth. 'Alannah invited him, so don't blame me.' Seamus turned on the spot to head towards the front door, but before he could move his daughter re-entered, followed by a friendly face.

'Edgar...' Seamus was caught off guard by his friend's attendance.

'Well, before you blame me, you should thank Edgar,' Alannah smiled again as she spoke, 'he paid for the pizza Dec is currently scoffing down like nobody's business.' Seamus was at a loss for words.

'I hope I'm not intruding.' Edgar spoke quite formally, breaking the silence that Seamus was creating with his lack of a response.

'Nonsense, Edgar,' Moira announced from behind their guest, 'please excuse my husband's lack of... well, everything. It seems he has lost his tongue.' She smirked at Seamus as she passed him and gave him a quick peck on the cheek. Edgar stood in a limbo of sorts, unsure of what to do as he awaited a response from the man of the house. He was dressed casually, wearing a blue denim shirt, dark coloured jeans and brown shoes; very different to his snappy suits.

'Edgar, sorry... come on in. Join us for dinner, and thanks...' Seamus blurted out the words, trying to cover all the bases at once. His reply, however, did seem to put his friend at ease.

'You can sit here,' Alannah piped up, suggesting that Edgar take a seat beside hers. Declan laughed at the suggestion, drawing a scowl from his sister and catching Seamus' attention, initiating a chorus of fatherly alarm bells within his head.

'That's okay, sweetie,' Seamus quickly blurted, 'Edgar can sit next to me, we can catch up.' His daughter was unimpressed by his decision, slumping into her seat, arms folded. Seamus looked at her, and then at Edgar. *He's a good guy, but she's my daughter...*

'Well, now that my family have made you feel oh so welcome, would you like a beer, Edgar?' Moira held a large bowl of prepared salad in one hand, and two bottles of cold beer in the other.

'Thank you, Mrs...' Edgar began to say.

'Edgar, please, it's Moira. Take a seat, relax and enjoy, and ignore everybody's weirdness,' she smiled at Seamus at she passed him a bottle and gave the other to Edgar. She and Declan then took a seat and began to dig into the food. Seamus took a large swig of his beer hoping to ease his nerves and lower his paternal defences.

'Yeah, sit and enjoy.' Seamus reiterated his wife's words whilst patting Edgar on the shoulder, before sitting down himself. Edgar dutifully waited for Seamus to take his seat before sitting himself.

'Thank you. This looks great, Moira.' Edgar was most courteous, despite the obvious fact that it was a simple takeout, that he himself had paid for. 'You have a lovely home,' he acknowledged, before helping himself to a slice of pizza. Seamus' family had only met Edgar the once before, bumping into him whilst out for dinner, but they had all hit it off. It was as if he was a long-standing friend, rather than someone that had just entered their lives by chance. Seamus was still dubious of the man. Yes, he owed Edgar a lot, but he still had many unanswered questions for the man that had saved his life, and while they remained so, he felt the need to be cautious; a feeling that was made harder by his families instant liking of him.

Perhaps he can give me some answers tonight... Seamus sat back in his chair and tore into a slice of warm, delicious pizza; the warm gooey cheese drooping down onto his chin.

The five of them ate and drank, laughing and chatting about anything and everything as a family would. Edgar asked the children how their studies were going, offering to help Alannah with her history dissertation. He spoke to Moira about the hospital and to Declan about attending an upcoming football game. In all, he was charming and attentive; he was the perfect guest. 'So, Edgar,

I told Moira and the kids all about how you saved my life,' Seamus interrupted the general chatter and sullied the mood with a more serious topic. He knew Moira could tell where the conversation was headed just by looking at her sudden glare. Edgar simply smiled. 'Obviously I am grateful for all that you did, but I have been wondering recently as to why you decided to take me to Brooklyn. Surely it wasn't the most logical hospital to take me to? There are closer emergency departments to where it happened...' His questioning of Edgar received looks of disappointment from his wife and daughter. Declan, however, showed some intrigue into the subject. 'I haven't had the chance to ask you about it. I mean, two months passed with me going undiscovered...'

'Seamus...' Moira's voice carried a tone that he recognised all too well.

'It's okay, Moira, I am happy to explain.' Edgar sat back into his seat and turned slightly towards Seamus. 'After finding you lying in the street, bleeding out, I contemplated taking you to the nearest hospital...'

'So, how come you didn't?' Seamus queried.

'Someone had attacked you... It's not something I am accustomed to dealing with, so I thought that I had better take you away from the danger, somewhere safe, where you could be seen to without the risk of whoever it was that had stabbed you finding you again. It was a risk, but one that paid off.' He was sincere, but something still nagged at Seamus.

'But, how come no one found me? How has my wound healed so quickly?'

'Well, I'm no doctor, so I'm afraid I can't advise you on your wound, that's beyond my credentials... but as for no one finding you, I made sure that no one knew where I had found you. As far as the hospital staff were aware, you were an unnamed man that had been attacked on the streets of Brooklyn. I knew you'd wake up at some point and that you'd sort yourself out when you did. My priority was simply to keep you safe and alive.' It was a good answer, and one that had Moira and Alannah swooning over his honour and Samaritan-like act of kindness.

'And we are all so very grateful for everything you did, aren't we, daddy...?' Alannah urged Seamus to change the topic of conversation.

'Yes, of course,' he replied unconvincingly.

'Tell you what, how about I help you get to the bottom of how you healed...' Edgar began to speak once again, yet this time Moira interrupted him.

'Enough shop talk for one evening. How about we concern ourselves with how my husband is still alive, another day... or not...' She raised her eyebrows and smiled at Seamus, letting him know that that was enough.

Edgar stayed late into the evening, answering everyone's questions about where he was from, what his parents were like and if he had any brothers or sisters. Seamus was interested to learn that this wealthy Wall Street businessman was an orphan. His parents had died when he was young and he had been taken in by an orphanage, so in that right, he felt as if he had many siblings, blood related or not. He was currently single, a fact that peaked Alannah's interest, forcing Seamus' fatherly senses to tingle once again. As he listened to Edgar's story, Seamus was reminded of just how lucky he was to have a family such as those around him. For all the money that Edgar had, it appeared that having no one to share it with was one of his regrets.

As the evening drew on, Edgar took his leave, thanking Moira and Seamus for their hospitality and bidding them goodnight, before the roar of his car's engine ferried him off into the night. Waving off his friend and locking up the house, Seamus took a moment for himself, processing Edgar's explanations. And as he slowly accepted the information that he had been given, his heart felt that much lighter. He took a deep breath in and smiled.

All is well.

The following morning Seamus arrived at work with minutes to spare. He had managed to fit in his morning run, and for the first time in a long time, he had completed his once *daily* routine with ease.

'I can't believe you're back already! You're nuts, McCarthy!' McCabe chuckled as he laid eyes on Seamus. 'If I were you, I'd be making the most of time away from this chaos.' He lifted a stack of paperwork up of off his desk as he spoke. The jolly looking sergeant appeared happy enough to be here, but Seamus knew that the chaos he referred to was most likely that which resided outside of the station's walls, the gruelling battle that each and every officer had to return to on the city's streets each day.

'Serg. You know I can't just sit still. I was asleep for two months!' Beside his desire to get his life to resemble something like what it had done before all of the craziness, Seamus had always loved his job; his duty to his city. It wasn't a hardship for him as it was for some of the others.

'Well, well, look who's back in uniform.' The words carried a hint of resentment and could only belong to one fellow officer.

'Malik...' Seamus said as politely as he could. He hadn't spoken to Malik Seif since bloodying his nose. *This is going to be fun...*

'McCarthy.' Malik stopped in front of him. He then did something uncharacteristic, and definitely not what Seamus would have expected; he held out his hand. Seamus looked at him for a moment before hesitatingly grasping his colleagues out stretched hand. Malik gave Seamus' hand a gentle squeeze before shaking it. 'Been a while, mate, just wanted you to know that there's no hard feelings.' Seamus could barely believe what he was hearing.

'Er, yeah... I mean, I'm sorry for the nose... you know.' Seamus rambled, dumbfounded by Malik's act of kindness. He was almost waiting for the other shoe to fall, for Malik to begin laughing or something equally cruel. The longer the gesture appeared to be genuine, the more disconcerting it became.

'Forget about it.' Malik accepted the apology, much to Seamus' and McCabe's, surprise, whom stood blank faced as he witnessed what was happening. 'End of the day, we're all family, right?' He seemed to be making the statement as well as fishing for confirmation that Seamus was indeed still one of them.

''Course,' Seamus responded. Despite their differences, they were both officers of the law.

'Good.' Malik then waved over someone from the opposite side of the room and Seamus realised that there it was; the other shoe. It was detective Jack Cannon. He had light brown hair that was just long enough for him to frequently have to run his hand through it, pushing it back away from his face. He kept a short, tidy beard and had a broad, strong face. He wore a walnut-coloured shirt and dark blue pants. Cannon was an experienced homicide detective, one that Seamus had had few dealings with in the past. The detective had a volatile nature. Like a blood hound, he had always tracked his prey with little care as to his methods, yet despite his lack of respect for protocol, he was highly revered for his success rate when it came to catching his man. 'Seamus, you know Jack, right?' Seamus nodded in response. 'Jack has been busy since new year's... Tell 'Carthy what you told me.' Malik held a look of concern that worried, yet also intrigued Seamus enough for him to want to know what was going on.

'String of murders, supposedly connected to your freaky super powered friends...' Jack looked at Seamus with disgust in his eyes. A look of judgement that was undeserved.

'Hey!' Seamus exclaimed before moving towards the room's periphery, encouraging Malik and Jack to follow. 'Hey...' he repeated, this time quietly. 'Those assholes are not my friends…' Seamus felt the need to defend himself. He had already been judged by some as a nark, spilling department secrets to the feds, but he would not be put into the same category as those whom had caused him so much pain over the last year.

'It's okay, McCarthy, Jack here is joking.' Malik glared at the detective at he spoke.

'Okay, not your friends.' Jack's words said less than his expression, and Seamus could tell that he didn't fully believe what he was saying. 'Anyway, these murders, so far there has been five, all women aged between twenty and twenty-five. We 'ent seen anything like it, each girl, woman, blood drained in the same way, look of terror on their faces… '

'What has any of this got to do with me?' Seamus really didn't want to get involved with anything Avunaye related right now.

'Glad you asked,' Malik grinned. His smile made Seamus' skin crawl.

'Look, we got no leads,' Jack admitted, 'more women are going to die and if what I believe is true, that your… that those super freaks are involved, then we are fucked.' The detective was frustrated, but sincere in his words.

'I still don't get what this has…' Seamus began to say.

'Look, I got a tip off for another victim,' Jack lowered his voice, almost to a whisper. 'Basically, I want you to be the first on the scene.'

'What the fuck?' Seamus attempted to control the level of his voice whilst backing away from the pair slightly.

'McCarthy, listen… There's a rumour that Axe was dirty, that he was working with Markovic and the freaks. There's no way that's true, and the only way we can clear his name is if we manage to catch one of the fuckers, make them talk…' Malik was serious. Insane, but serious. He actually wanted to take on the Avunaye.

'You're crazy…' Seamus voiced his thoughts.

'No, what's fucking crazy is that I investigate the murders of five women and at every turn I get blocked off by a bunch of suits, feds, C.I.A... And your colleague, *your* brother, Axel, he gets listed as a fucking traitor...' Jack was angry, a dangerous flare of fury flashed in his eyes. Seamus did not like what they were suggesting, but he also knew Axel; he knew him to be a good man.

'McCarthy, look. You turn up at the scene and instead of calling it in to the station straight away, you call your contact at the feds. They come and confirm whether it's the freaks or just another non-super powered sicko... You tell them that seeing as you've scratched their backs, maybe they can scratch yours... If we can get ahead of one of those fuckers... There's a lot of officers in this city that want payback, justice for all our fallen comrades...' The more Malik spoke, the more desperate he seemed. They made their intentions clear; it was revenge they wanted, plain and simple, however, some of what they said was right. The Avunaye had plagued his city for god knows how long, and thus far nothing had been done about it. Seamus' head pounded with his thoughts, unaided by the pressure that his colleagues were exerting on him, on his conscience. Somewhere out there was a woman that had been murdered. He couldn't help but picture her, only, when he pictured her face, he saw that of his daughter's. If he helped Malik and Jack, he would undoubtedly be starting something that could result in countless more deaths, but regardless of who was doing the killing, they needed to be stopped. Maybe he could use this to get close to the Avunaye himself, to get to Adam, to get the answers he had always wanted.

But what about Moira... the kids... I promised to walk away and never look back... Seamus' mind wandered as his colleagues waited patiently for his response. *But what if it is Alannah that becomes the next young woman to turn up dead...* He knew he had to do something, say something, but fear and uncertainty gripped his tongue.

'So, McCarthy? What will it be? Figured you'd want these freaks brought to justice.' Seamus wasn't sure whether he said it just to shut Jack up, or if he thought that he could actually make this work, but his passion to protect his city, his family, overwhelmed him, and he accepted the mission laid out before him.

The building was located on 11th Avenue, in Chelsea. Unfamiliar with the rather extravagant area of Manhattan, Seamus circled the block before deciding this was the place he was looking for.

How the other half live... He couldn't help but be impressed as he entered the lobby. He expected there to be someone waiting at the desk, a clerk or someone of the like, but the place was desolate. *Maybe I'll wait a moment, see if anyone shows up.* He made himself comfortable on one of the large comfy seats. Staring at the clock on the wall, Seamus waited patiently for fifteen minutes before getting to his feet to have a look around. 'I haven't got all day...' The truth was he didn't want to be here. He looked behind the desk and then down the hall where the entrances to the stairs and elevators were. There was not a soul to be found. 'Hello?!' he called out, but there was no response. 'Weird...' Deciding to head to the apartment where Jack had told him he'd find the victim, Seamus pushed the button for the elevator and rode it up to the seventeenth floor. He exited the elevator into the apartment; his palms were clammy and his heart raced as his doubts forced their way to the forefront of his mind. He paced back and forth in front of the open doors until they closed and made up his mind for him. The apartment, as far as Seamus was concerned, was ridiculously expansive. 'This place is bigger than my fucking house,' he laughed as he slowly began to move into the lodging to investigate.

The hall had bright white walls and a smooth, shiny laminate flooring. It led through to a huge lounge-diner-kitchen combination, with floor to ceiling windows on its far side; the view took Seamus' breath away for a moment. As he looked out across the city he could see a multitude of buildings, parks and the Empire State Building in the distance. The pristine kitchen lay to his right, a large oaken table with four chairs before him, and a sofa capable of seating an entire football team to his left. The place was immaculate. *Doesn't look like anyone lives here...* He wondered if Jack was wrong about this. He walked over to the kitchen and opened the refrigerator to find it baron. *Something isn't right here...* Seamus began to head back to the entrance; he didn't want to waste any more time here. The idea that perhaps it was another one of Malik's pranks crossed his mind, but as he walked towards the hallway past the base of the stair case, something urged him to check the upper floor before he left. He stood at the bottom of the steps looking up, trying to decide whether the urge to investigate further was a feeling of his own or of someone else, it felt so alien to him. 'Couldn't hurt,' he said as he started the climb. The condo had two bedrooms, the first one he checked was furnished elegantly, just as the lower floor had been, as if no one lived here and it was up for sale. 'Last room...' he muttered as he pushed open the door to the second bedroom expecting it to be as identically laid out to perfection as the first, but what he saw, forced him to remove his sidearm instinctively. *What the fuck!*

He stepped into the room with his finger primed on the trigger of his gun. The perfect white walls were splattered with red. Cream carpet was stained red and brown. The double bed was broken in two, collapsed in its centre. Seamus looked about the room, searching for the body, only to regret his eagerness upon seeing her. Pinned to the wall, she was naked, her legs separated and her arms outstretched. There was, what appeared to be ice picks, embedded into her palms and feet, holding her in place. She couldn't have been much older than Alannah, and for a split-second Seamus could have sworn he saw his daughter behind the long black hair that covered a portion of the girl's face. There didn't appear to be many marks on her body, but the front of her throat had been torn asunder, and blood had flowed freely down her, resulting in a pool of red on the carpet. He decided that she must have been dead for a day or two now, as the scene was just starting to smell. He stepped forward but stopped as the carpet below his foot squelched. He felt sick. Lowering his weapon, Seamus went to pull out his phone, to complete the objective Jack had given him and call Lucy, but at that moment there was a sound that emanated from the adjoining en-suite; someone was here. 'N.Y.P.D!' Seamus exclaimed, raising his weapon again.

'Bloody hell... I'm coming out, don't shoot. I'm unarmed.' Something about the voice seemed so familiar, but Seamus couldn't envisage a face to put to it. The man that stepped out into the bedroom did so confidently, he was not at all fazed by the fact that he had a loaded gun pointed at him, or that he had been caught at the scene of a crime. 'Seamus,' he smiled. He clearly knew Seamus, but Seamus had no idea who this stranger was, despite the nagging familiarity of his voice and his accent.

'Raise your hands slowly and place them on your head, then lower yourself to your knees...' He wore a burgundy V-neck t-shirt, dark pants and a long black overcoat. He had short brown hair and an unnerving pair of yellow eyes. He began to raise his hands but then proceeded to place his index finger on his lips as if to silence Seamus. 'I said –!'

'I know what you said, Seamus. Lower your weapon and holster it.' Despite his head urging him to continue aiming his gun at the man, he couldn't stop himself from complying, as if he no longer had control of his own body.

'What the hell...' Seamus panicked as he unwillingly holstered his fire arm.

'That's better. It is so nice to see you again.' He

smiled again, however, as far as Seamus knew, they had never met.

'Who...'

'Who am I?' The yellow-eyed man said, finishing Seamus' question. 'Apparently, I am the bloody clean-up crew, dealing with my dear brothers mess.' He was so calm.

'Your brother?' Seamus looked back towards the poor girl's body.

'Yes... he has a tendency to over-indulge. It's what has gotten him such a bad reputation over the years.' One person came to Seamus' mind.

'Brandt? The beast?' Seamus thought it must have been him.

'Brandt? No... However, if you don't mind, when you get in touch with your F.B.I friends, and when you report back to your colleagues, could you tell them that this *was* him? I mean, that would just work out... perfectly.'

'What?' Seamus was confused.

'Seamus... I know you're already doing me a huge favour for which I am, or at least I will be grateful for, but you will do your best to convince them that this was Brandt.' His words possessed Seamus and as he listened, he felt himself make the decision to do as he was asked. 'I know! Crazy right... but no, I'm not a jedi,' he laughed light-heartedly at Seamus as if they were mere friends. 'These aren't the bodies you are looking for,' he chuckled as he waved about his fingers in jest. 'However, on a more serious note, you will forget meeting me again once I leave, and before I forget...' he smiled gleefully, '...when you see Lucy, do pass on this message...'

'Seamus?!' she called from downstairs. Lucy had arrived and as Seamus reached the top of the stairs, he saw that she was not alone. Her partner, agent Ward, was with her.

'Up here, Luce!' Seamus called and then headed back into the bedroom.

'Oh my god...' She placed a hand over her mouth as she entered the room and laid eyes on the body. Mike entered behind her; he seemed less shocked at the scene and gave Seamus a look that conveyed a less than pleasant message.

'I thought I'd call you guys first, before I notify the station...' Seamus admitted, just as Jack had suggested.

'Why us? Seamus, what the hell happened?' Lucy looked worried.

'I saw him... The beast... I saw him exit the building so I came in to investigate,' Seamus found himself saying the words effortlessly, truthfully. 'The Avunaye are your business, they need to be stopped.'

'We're not on the Avunaye case anymore, mate,' Mike responded, 'everything goes through the C.I.A now.' He looked about the room before staring Seamus in the eye, 'what are you doing here again?' His tone insinuated all manner of wrong doing on Seamus' part, to which Seamus did not take kindly to.

'Hey, I said, I saw that Brandt guy...'

'It's okay, Seamus, thanks for calling us.' Lucy quickly interrupted, preventing the argument that was undoubtedly about to start. 'Mike, go call this in, we'll take it from here.' As Mike left the room Seamus could feel the tension ease considerably.

'Lucy, there's something I need to tell you...' Seamus spoke without thinking. He felt awkward for a moment, as if he was reading from a script, however, he felt compelled to finish what he was trying to say.

'What's up, Seamus?'

'Luce, have you heard of Velocity?' She looked at him confused.

'I have... you think there's a connection?'

'I... I heard that a dealer was killed...' Seamus paused.

'Well, one less scumbag...'

'No, it's not that... Rumour has it that this dealer was

supplying a fed... You mentioned Mike was acting weird since, well, since he came back.' Her eyes questioned more than Seamus' word.

'Seamus...' Lucy looked at him sternly.

'Look, I'm just letting you know what I've heard,' he held up his hands in surrender, he did not want to upset her.

'Okay, well, thanks, but you've nothing to worry about,' there was an ounce of doubt to her tone. Seamus felt relieved to tell her, like a weight had been lifted, although, he didn't even understand where any of that had come from. The pair of them continued to talk privately whilst Mike reported the crime scene. Lucy had still not managed to find anything relating his father's death to the Avunaye, news that eased Seamus a little. Maybe his life was his own after all, and the last year had just been a bump in the road. Lucy asked Seamus to keep what he had seen here to himself, a request he had half expected, but one that annoyed him almost as much as the chief's request for him to spy on the F.B.I. He questioned whether or not his allegiances would be forever torn.

Leaving Lucy and Mike, Seamus returned to the station. He carried with him a heart filled with anxiety. Jack and Malik would want to know what had been said. Lucy's request for secrecy was redundant, as Jack had already found the crime scene, but what his vengeance-seeking colleagues didn't know, was that it was the monster that they had already dubbed "The Beast", that was behind the murders; a fact that would only add fuel to their fire and force them to accelerate whatever plans they were concocting. The entire ordeal was confusing.

'So, McCarthy? What did the feds say?' Malik had pulled Seamus to one side. Seamus knew in his heart that he should diffuse the situation, keep the information to himself; pretend that it had never happened. But he had no choice.

'I saw him, with my own eyes. The beast...' Saying it

again felt strange, almost as if he didn't truly believe what he was saying, but it had to be the truth, he knew what he had seen. Didn't he? He remembered it, and if he couldn't trust his own memory, what could he trust? 'The feds want us to stay out, they said it's up to the C.I.A now –'

'Course they fucking did,' Jack announced his presence as he turned the corner in the locker room. 'Fucking keeping it quiet whilst innocent girls are slaughtered!' He was furious.

'We have to do something.' Seamus did not like Malik's suggestion. What could they possibly do?

'Leave it with me... I got a couple contacts... If push comes to shove, can we count on you McCarthy? Will you help us bring these freaks to justice?' Jack looked at him with such hate in his eyes, he would do anything to stop Brandt, to stop the Avunaye, and that scared Seamus to his core. Yet, what option did Seamus have other than to help his comrades. The force had suffered enough already at the hands of the Avunaye, he couldn't bear the thought of anymore funerals. Brandt, Serena, Adam, and any others that were out there... they all needed bringing to justice.

'I'm in.'

8

Claire Davenport

'Fortune favours the bold...'

He's going to counter attack, you should wait.

'It'll be fine... Taste my dragon fire!'

And there it is... Goodbye dragon...

'Damn it, not again...' Claire sighed exasperatedly as she watched her life points roll down to zero.

I did warn you... Carmen pointed out; Claire could feel herself attempting to smirk.

'Hey! Not fair! Making me pull faces at myself...' Claire chuckled at the obscenity of her own statement. She had spent a fair bit of time of late indulging in games whilst at work. She had been tasked to put as much time as possible into tracking down the origin of the data hack that had destroyed the results for the tests on Cardoza's men. The problem was, she already knew who had done it, so when she wasn't trying to mislead the investigation by making it appear that the attempt was made from outside the bureau, she had a lot of spare time. Time in which she often found herself worrying about where the missing printouts had found themselves, or who it was that knew of her secret. Carmen tried to encourage Claire not to worry, reminding her that she was there to protect her, but Claire couldn't help recalling the names of those Carmen had killed. Enrique Santiago, Luis da Silva and the unfortunate

Lillian McLeodry.

The free time, along with Carmen's ever progressing recovery, also meant that the two of them had had the opportunity to get to know each other better. Claire was not Carmen's first host body. She didn't like to talk about her previous hosts to too much detail, but she did let on that she had been jumping from host to host now for over three hundred years. Carmen's memories were erratic at best, with the body swapping clearly not having helped, as she often confused her own past with those of whom she had inhabited. She was also very reserved when it came to questions about the other Avunaye and their initiation ritual, claiming she could not remember everything. Claire couldn't help but believe her, yet, there was a deep uncertainty to Carmen's past, blank spaces, as if someone had removed parts of it. They had spent days and nights talking to one another, the connection warming Claire, especially when she was alone at home. Claire would also have the most amazing dreams as her subconscious picked up on snippets of Carmen's existence.

You know, instead of playing this... game... we could be making progress on the whereabouts of Adam... Carmen often urged Claire to continue the search, however, she did not have to try hard as the subject of Adam would always give Claire an alien sense of duty and admiration. The only issue was that everywhere she had looked had come up empty. Claire had more algorithms and facial recognition searches running continuously than she'd care to mention, but nothing was working. She had also hacked into a couple of satellites and configured them to track the movements of Zane Brown, seeing as he had to know something of Adam's whereabouts; only Zane too appeared to be quite the ghost to the technological world. *You know I don't trust that guy...* Carmen announced her distrust as Claire scanned the search results regarding Zane.

'He is stealthier than stealth...' She had never had

such erratic results on a search. 'I mean, the guy barely goes outside, and even when he does, he seems to pop up all over the place...'

He's avoiding us, there's something I dislike about him...

'Avoiding us?' Claire couldn't help but question Carmen's logic.

He contacts your colleagues for updates on the Avunaye, yet we have not seen him in person, or heard from him since the turn of the year... Carmen's mistrust of the man was evident, but Claire could never decide as to whether or not it was warranted.

'Well, he is a big deal within the C.I.A, heh!'

'Who is?' Malique had entered Claire's safe haven and he was looking about the room, searching for whom she might have been talking to. 'Everything... Okay?' He expressed a look of concern.

'Ha! Fine! Just keeping myself company.' Claire chuckled, before looking for somewhere to hide her face as Carmen sighed within.

'You were talking about Zane Brown? To yourself, that is...' Malique had a glimmer of confusion in his eyes.

'Yeah... heh. When you put it like that! He is a big deal though, in the C.I.A... I was thinking that, erm, with his resources, I might crack this hacker, I mean crack the code, solve the puzzle... You know, shine light on, get the... cheese... work out who this hacker is, was, is...' Claire's babbling only caused further confusion for her assistant and Carmen could not refrain from laughing aloud within her head.

'You... like him?' Malique looked at her awkwardly, trying to read between the lines of her ramblings. Claire almost fell off her seat.

'What? No... no... I mean, he does have a confidence, and nice suits...' She paused for a moment as she and Carmen disputed their impressions of the man, which seemed to make Malique more uncomfortable as he stood in silence. 'But no. Definitely not,' Claire finally finished. She then looked at Malique curiously, wondering as to the reason for his enquiry.

'You know, Michael Corleone also wore nice suits... Just saying.' He responded to her look, seemingly understanding what it meant. 'I was just curious, I guess...' Something about what he said gave Claire a strange, warm, fluttery feeling inside.

Oh my... you like the help? Carmen gasped, catching Claire off guard.

'What! No!' Claire exclaimed in response to Carmen, before quickly covering her mouth with her hands. Malique's confused expression returned.

'You sure you're okay, Claire?' Malique was seemingly cautious as to what she might do next.

'Heh...' was the only sound she could muster, which didn't quite satisfy his need for clarity on her current mental state. The pair of them stood, simply, and awkwardly, staring into space as Claire, and presumably Malique, each waited for the other to make the first move. Thankfully for Claire, their silence was interrupted by another. As Lucy entered the room Claire felt a sense of relief, however, she couldn't help but notice the disheartened look in Malique's eyes as he slowly turned and exited.

'Claire, need your help with something.' Lucy appeared oblivious to Malique as he left, as well as the tension that rode on the air. She looked at Claire impatiently, arms crossed and feet apart. She was wearing a black, strapped, sleeveless top, a pair of dark pants, a belt with a heavy buckle and black boots. 'You good?' Lucy asked in response to Claire's lack of one.

'Yeah, what, whatcha need?' The truth was, what she had seen within Malique had her distracted, more so than she'd care to admit, and Carmen was not helping. The voice inside incessantly teasing her regarding her emotions.

'There's this new drug making the rounds, wondered if you'd look into it for me. I've managed to score a sample.

Hopefully you can run some tests?' It was a simple request, and one Claire welcomed as a convenient distraction for now. 'Oh, and could you see what you can dig up about a dealer than turned up dead recently, shouldn't be hard, apparently his heart was ripped from his chest...' Claire was intrigued, although, she was finding it hard to concentrate.

'Erm, yeah, sure,' Claire shook her head, attempting to cut out Carmen's running commentary about what had just happened with Malique. Lucy held out a clear bag containing a small red coloured pill.

'I'll run a few tests, see what this baby is made of.' Claire smiled as she took the sample. 'What are they calling this one? Red death? Crimson... Chaos? Heh!'

'Not that inventive,' Lucy laughed, 'supposedly it gives you a rush like no other...'

'So, it's not called sex then,' quipped Claire.

'Ha! No, I doubt it's that inconsistent, else no one would go back for seconds,' Lucy winked. 'No, they call this one Velocity.'

'Where did you get this?' She blurted out. The words came from Claire's lips, but it was Carmen speaking them now.

Hey! Claire exclaimed inside. It wasn't the sudden loss of control of her own body that she contested; it was the fear that Lucy might see.

'Okay, little more enthusiasm that I had expected... I have a friend in the D.E.A, although, apparently this stuff was available all over the city. It seems supply is having some ups and downs at the minute.' Lucy looked at Claire curiously. 'Claire, you wearing coloured contacts?'

'No!' Claire panicked, closing her eyes and turning away. She knew what Lucy was referring to. Recently, whenever Carmen took the wheel, her eyes would change colour to a honey yellow. Lucy's question terrified her.

'Hey, what's going on with you?' Lucy touched her on her shoulder reassuringly, only her body reacted by giving

Lucy a small shock. 'Ow!' Lucy yelped, pulling her hand away. 'What the hell?!'

'Lucy! Claire!' Krysta's voice sounded from the doorway. 'There you are.' Claire held her eyes shut, unmoving, she was routed to the spot in fear of being discovered.

'Claire? What the hell was that?' Lucy questioned again. Claire's heart beat faster and faster, she was struggling to hold it all in.

Claire, it's okay, I'm sorry... Carmen repeated again and again.

'What's going on?' Krysta queried.

'Claire just... gave me an electric shock...'

'Static!' Krysta quickly exclaimed in response to Lucy's accusation. 'Did it to me too, well, not Claire, Hale did... must be a lot of static in the building today...'

'Claire, open your eyes,' Lucy ordered. Claire hesitantly obliged. Maybe it was Krysta's presence that helped her to begin to calm down. 'I could have sworn they looked yellow before...'

'Must be the lights, Luce,' Krysta again jumped to Claire's aid. Claire could feel her own eyes welling up with a sense of relief.

'Seriously, Claire, what's up?' Lucy now sounded concerned, which was much better than the combination of curiosity and fear she had held in her voice before. Claire knew she had to react quickly, something to change the subject at hand.

'Sorry, Lucy, I have been a little static-y today, my bad. Heh. I'm okay just a little drained. Let me have a look-see...' Claire began frantically typing on her keyboard whilst Lucy stood staring, a look of disbelief on her face.

'That's our Claire, hey, Luce, quirky as ever!' Krysta quipped.

'Bingo!' Claire had quickly found some information.

Claire, there is something you should know about that

drug... Carmen interrupted Claire's train of thought.

'Erm, yeah, erm. That dealer, died on the corner of... Oh, there's a back-alley club nearby... I could do with...' Lucy seemed to grow more and more impatient with Claire's scattered half-sentences.

'We should go!' Krysta announced suddenly, preventing Lucy from saying whatever it was that was on the tip of her tongue.

'What?' Lucy looked confused again.

Claire, calm down... Krysta has your back, I won't do it again...

'Good idea, Krys,' Claire smiled, 'Lucy, we can go to the club, unwind, and maybe see if anyone knew the dealer.' Lucy was speechless, Claire and Krysta's tag team effort seemed to have completely thrown her. 'One question, why are we looking into this?' The question hadn't occurred to her until now, but Carmen's growing feeling of concern towards the drug was making Claire more and more curious.

'Just following a lead for, for Zane, that's all,' Lucy brushed her hair behind her ear.

'Okay then, it's a date! Heh! Let's go get dolled up and hit this club.' Claire was actually excited, she more than needed to unwind, and it had been a while since the three of them had gone out together. Lucy, still looking dumbfounded over what had just transpired, nodded reluctantly in acceptance.

'Alright! Let's go!' Krysta said excitedly. 'Oh, I can get my neighbour T to join us!' Krysta threw her hands into the air before giving Claire a friendly smile. The look in her eye told Claire that everything was going to be okay. Claire's heart felt ten-stone lighter as her friends turned and exited the room in high spirits. She was about to follow when she remembered the sample; she should leave it on her desk to remind her to run the tests tomorrow.

Claire, that drug... please destroy it... Claire could feel Carmen's restraint, she wanted to do it herself, but she was willing to place her trust in Claire.

'What is it?' Claire was curious as to why Carmen was so anxious.

It's made from our blood, the blood of the Avunaye...

'Oh...' Claire held the pill in the palm of her hand and subconsciously gave Carmen the go-ahead. Small blue sparks ran up and down her forearm before flurrying to the centre of her hand, disintegrating the red pill. 'Heh, pretty cool!'

The three of them had each returned to their homes to get ready and then Krysta and Lucy headed to Claire's, before they all got a taxi together to take them to the club. Krysta's neighbour had turned down the offer, meaning it would just be the three of them this evening, which Claire actually preferred. Lucy wore her hair down, curled; she had donned a black, ruched-top mini-dress, which helped to show off her amazingly coloured, smooth, toned legs. Krysta had opted for a burgundy, satin wrap-dress, which flaunted her legs and breasts, and she had tied her golden hair up into a bun. Lucy wolf-whistled at the sight of her friends, making Claire feel slightly more comfortable with her own attire. She and Carmen had agreed to wear a cream-coloured, high-necked, sleeveless midi-dress with a pair of beige coloured heels. She wore her long brown hair down, with her blonde streak falling over her shoulder. Just as they were leaving Claire's, Krysta had persuaded her to wear a pair of thin gold bar dangle earrings to compliment her outfit.

They laughed and drank and danced the stresses of the day away. The club was unique, which Claire admired. She particularly liked the view from the bar, looking down on the dancefloor below. There was something majestic about how their bodies swayed in time with the music; each soul moving in its own unique way, though with a certain symmetry to them all. As she stared and peeled away the layers of reality, she could see for certain, they were all the same, all as one.

'Looking for anyone in particular?' sounded a strong, yet, subtle voice, one that instantly snared Carmen's attention; Claire could feel her internal guest pulling at her, urging to see who it was. Claire turned to find one of the bar staff standing next to the table beside her. She was holding a handful of empty glasses that she'd just collected. Her short silver and black hair shimmered in the light and her blue eyes were like fathomless sapphire-coloured pools. It was as if eternity was incapsulated within them.

'Erm, heh,' Claire scratched at her head as she tried to come up with a reply.

Words would be good here, Claire, whenever you're ready...

'I'm not looking for anyone... well I am, but he died... wait...' Claire's babbling caused the woman to laugh and then smile.

'It's a good job you're gorgeous,' she said without even blinking, catching Claire by surprise. If she was struggling to say something before, she had now lost all ability to communicate. Claire opened her mouth to reply, but no sound transpired. 'How about we start with something simple... I'm Alexa. Now you try.' She smiled again, exuding such confidence.

'Claire...'

Honestly, Claire, if you wish for me to handle this, just say the word... This is beginning to look painful, and I have a limited view...

'No,' Claire refused Carmen's assistance. She then realised that she had said it aloud. 'I mean, hi, I'm Claire.' She held out her hand.

'Hand shake... Okay, that's a good start.' Alexa placed the glasses back down on the table and walked around it. She raised a hand to meet Claire's, and as their skins touched, they both felt a spark.

'I'm sorry!' Claire gasped and pulled her hand away.

Whoops, Carmen said, however, Claire felt no sign of

actual remorse.

'Wow...' Alexa responded, still smiling, much to Claire's surprise. 'That is literally some spark between us there, or are you like that with everyone you meet?' She had a mischievous look about her; she was toying with Claire.

'No, not everyone...' Claire confirmed, she was beginning to relax again. She began to feel a heat stirring within her, but could not be sure if it was Carmen or not.

'That's good to hear...' Alexa took a step closer and holding out her hand once again. 'So, Claire, how about we try that again.' Claire looked into her blue eyes and took her hand, this time without interference from Carmen's abilities. 'Firm, yet soft too... they say you can tell a lot from someone's hand shake.'

'They do?' Claire was still slightly off balance due to Alexa's advances.

'Yeah, but what's fun about a hand shake.' She took Claire's hand in both of hers and ran her thumbs over the back of it. 'I can think of better ways to get to know someone...' the glimmer of mischief returned to her eyes. Claire could feel her own skin begin to tingle with a sudden warmth.

'Erm, Dennis!' Claire cried out in response to the flurry of electricity she felt ripple outwards from betwixt her thighs.

'Okay... Dennis?'

'Yeah...' Claire quickly tried to shift the mood to something less sexual. She couldn't tell if it was Carmen's doing, but her emotions were on overdrive. 'Dennis, a dealer, a guy, was killed a couple of blocks from here. Did you... was he a customer here?' She finally managed to finish the sentence.

First Malique, now this woman. We are on fire today... Claire could feel Carmen's grin.

'Erm, okay, curveball. Yeah, D, I think some people called him.' Alexa appeared disheartened by the change of topic. 'Crazy what happened to him. Rumour has it, it was a fed that killed him, deal gone sour or something...'

'A fed? Weird...' Claire tried to think, but Carmen's relentless craving for a source of physical pleasure was beyond distracting.

'Look, should you grow tired of sour deals... and fancy something sweet...' as she spoke, Alexa dove into Claire's clutch bag and removed her phone without hesitation. 'Here is my number... use it.' She smiled again as she placed the phone back into the bag, and then she was gone. Claire was so stumped that she didn't even register her leaving.

We have definitely got to work on your seduction technique, Carmen quipped. *Good job you have someone with an eternity of experience in your corner.*

Yeah... Claire was still slightly dazed. *Right cougar you are! Heh!* She giggled aloud.

The evening continued with Claire spending much of it on the dance floor, purposely avoiding the bar and the possibilities behind it. Her head was a mess, yet thankfully, as she moved to the music, she was able to quieten the din and switch off from the world. The three of them were enjoying the respite from reality so much that they all almost forgot their reason for coming to this particular club.

'Hey, did either of you find anything out?' Lucy enquired as they paused to have a drink and catch their breath. Her question brought reality crashing back down. Krysta shook her head as she continued to dance on the spot.

'Oh,' Claire remembered what Alexa had told her, 'something about a sour deal... and one of us involved.' As she spoke, she began to realise that she had probably reached her limit with her drinks. Perhaps one or two drinks ago. She steadied herself. 'I think, I drunk,' she giggled, causing Krysta to laugh along with her.

'Wait, what do you mean one of us?' Lucy was clearly

handling her alcohol a lot better than the rest of them.

'A fed. That's what she told me...'

'Who?' Lucy was growing impatient with Claire's drunkenness.

'The goddess behind the bar,' Claire giggled again, 'she said apparently there was a fed involved.' Claire sighed as she looked up at the balcony above.

If you wish to court her, let her know... Carmen said casually.

'Court her...' Claire snorted, 'so old fashioned, heh.'

'Claire, what are you talking about?' Lucy's attention had been snared by the mention of a fed being involved, she was in full bloodhound mode.

'It's Car...' but the word stuck in Claire's throat, Carmen was preventing her from making a mistake.

'Car?' Lucy wasn't letting it go this time.

'Charisma!' Krysta piped up. 'Claire here got hit on by the silver-haired bar keep.' She looked at Claire wide-eyed, and then smiled at Lucy.

'Yep, she has something sweet for me,' Claire babbled.

'Okay...' Lucy began to lighten up as she grinned at Claire's intoxicated bliss. 'Think it's time we got you home.' She looked to Krysta, who reluctantly agreed, still moving to the music herself. 'When you start talking like a half-asleep infant, you've def had enough.'

'Excuse me... I... can handle my liquor,' Claire slurred.

'Yeah. Sure...' Lucy raised an eyebrow and smiled.

'How... how many fingers... hmm?' Claire waved her hands about erratically, resembling a panicked child attempting to swat a bee. 'Now who can't... can't handle my drink.'

As the three of them sat in the cab, Claire rested her weary head on Krysta's shoulder whilst holding onto Lucy's hand. There was a distinct warmth between them, a friendship, a kin-ship, for Claire would do just about anything for them, and she felt as if they felt the same.

'What… what does I do?' she muttered, her eyes opening and closing as she fought the need to pass out.

'About what, hon?' Lucy's tone could almost be mistaken for one of interest.

'Malique and A-lex-ahh….' Claire smiled.

'Malique?'

'He likes me….'

'We all do, sweetie,' Krysta commented, stroking Claire's hair. She then kissed her on her head.

'No! I mean li-ke….'

'Big day for you, hit on by a boy *and* a girl,' Lucy laughed.

'At least… at least you have… Mike…' Claire couldn't hold back the yawn as she spoke. Lucy suddenly went silent as Claire's unfiltered thoughts came out. 'It's okay… We all know, it's our secr… et!' Claire couldn't hold on much longer. Suddenly her phone beeped and she perked up and smiled. 'Wonder who…'

'Unknown contact, hon,' Krysta noticed, picking up Claire's phone after Claire had dropped it, attempting to read the message. Claire was barely awake, but Carmen stirred within as Krysta's heart began to race.

Claire, something is amiss. I'm going to see what it is. Carmen took the reins on Claire's body and sat up abruptly.

'Oh, someone's found their second wind,' Lucy joked at Claire's knee-jerk reaction.

'Krysta,' Carmen spoke with an authoritative tone, she could tell Krysta understood what was happening as she looked her in the eyes. 'What is it?' Krysta said nothing, but she gave Carmen the phone to look at. It was a single message that read;

"Your secrets will soon be unveiled. A friend should always underestimate your virtues and an enemy overestimate your faults."

Claire was fast asleep inside; Carmen did not have the heart to disturb her. Instead, she decided to delete the message. She knew the quote, and she had a theory on its sender; she would deal with the problem herself, so as to not worry Claire. As she exited the vehicle and said goodnight to Lucy, Carmen turned to Krysta. 'I'll handle it, no need to worry Claire,' she whispered, and then headed inside Claire's house to rest her host's tired body. She changed into her pyjamas and brushed her hair, before lying down on the bed and curling up. *Goodnight, Claire. Sleep well.*

9

Luciana Rodriguez

She may have intentionally neglected to set an alarm, but she had forgotten to draw the curtains at her bedroom window when she collapsed into her pit the night before. As a consequence, the early mornings sun shone brightly through, piercing the veil of her window pane and illuminating her entire room. She resisted getting up, for what felt like hours. She balanced on the edge of being asleep and awakening, but eventually she conceded defeat to the new day.

'Argh...' she groaned as she opened her eyes fully and became aware of the time. Contemplating a retreat to the sanctity of the space beneath her covers, she suddenly thought of Mike and clambered out of bed in search of her phone. The absence of any missed calls and messages forced her to pause and fight against the urge to read too much into her lover's lack of contact. 'Why are you shutting me out?' *Did I do something...* 'Ah!' She shook herself from her trance like state. *Don't go down that road.* Taking off the underwear she had slept in, she decided to tie her hair up and throw on her running gear; pounding the pavement felt like the best way to vent her frustrations, since her only other idea was to go out and shoot at things, and that would never end well.

She took the subway to Central Park and began to

run. A popular destination, Lucy was expecting the place to beaming with life, though, she knew of a quiet path or two where she could avoid running into too many people. The park was in its spring bloom, with the trees displaying an array of majestic colours as the rays of sunlight beamed through the gaps between their crowns. Lucy's path was sheltered by soft pinks and full-bodied cherry colours, whilst fallen leaves created colourful carpets for her to follow. Encapsulating true beauty, the trees flaunted a variety of bright yellows and vibrant greens, and her route was lined with multitudes of spring flowers. She could hear the babbling of a nearby stream as she ran, her feet pounding against the stone of a bridge as she battled against her own insecurities. She just needed to break through the barrier where freedom of thought, and hopefully, peace of mind awaited her.

The morning was warming up and her lungs were beginning to tighten. She continued to run until she reached a drinking fountain, with the thought of quenching her thirst making her mouth water in anticipation. Leaning over, catching the spray in her mouth, she was sharply interrupted as a hand struck her across her ass cheeks; water splashed across her face as she jerked. 'What the fuck!' she garbled as she turned to confront them. 'Who –!'

'Couldn't resist.' He shrugged his shoulders like an adolescent child that had been caught red-handed.

'Son of a bitch...' she grumbled, scowling at him as she wiped the water from her face.

'C'mon, Luce, it was a joke.' Mike smiled, further irritating her.

'Oh, you remember me. Well that's nice.' She was of course referring to his lack of contact, but she wanted to see if he knew what he had done wrong. Or perhaps he would be oblivious as always.

'How could I forget,' he smiled again, so cutely that it annoyed her. He was in his running clothes as well, hot and sweaty.

'Well, you don't seem out of breath. Taking it easy?' she teased.

'Ten-K done already. You look fucked,' he retorted, sarcastically, yet he remained infuriatingly adorable.

'Just getting warmed up,' she lied, punching him on the arm playfully.

'Then you'll be up for racing me to the fountain by the terrace then.' He began to step away from her as he laid down the gauntlet. Lucy laughed, as if to shrug off the challenge, but then she quickly took off at speed with the intent of winning the competition.

She put all of her effort into keeping pace with Mike, but she could tell he was holding back. Something was driving him. She only hoped it wasn't what she suspected, that he wasn't taking those pills. They reached the fountain together and Lucy was glad to finally stop and catch her breath. She leant on the fountains foundation as she breathed heavily.

'Want me to throw you in, so you can cool off?' Mike chuckled. Lucy couldn't believe how un out of breath he was.

'Whatever you're taking... maybe I should get in on it,' she laughed, but she was curious as to how he'd respond.

'One-hundred-percent me I'm afraid, love.' He was confident, unflinching at the suggestion that he was on something.

Maybe Seamus was wrong.... Lucy allowed herself to consider. She looked up at the Angel of The Waters and smiled. 'Never really noticed how powerful that angel looks. Kind of cool.'

'The thing gives me a chill...' Mike admitted as he glanced at the statue and then looked back to Lucy. 'Tell you what, you try and keep up with me, and I'll show you something that'll make your day.' Mike smiled again as he began to jog on the spot.

Curious as to what he could possibly show her in a

place she'd seen time and time again, she accepted; if nothing else, it meant spending more time with him.

'Okay then, Uno, Dos...!' he laughed aloud as he counted.

'Such a dick!' she laughed with him before the pair of them headed off, back into the depths of the park. They ran together until they were roughly half way down a section of path, surrounded by flowers and trees. Mike stopped and turned to her, grinning, before signalling for her to follow him as he diverted off the stones and into the foliage. Lucy could feel the looks of passers-by as she stood calling to Mike for an explanation, but he continued onward, until he had left her sight. 'Mike, what the hell...?' she sighed as she looked about to see who was watching. *He's lost it...* Making the decision to follow him, she found herself trying as best she could not to disturb the arrangements of spring flowers, before trudging into the thicker brush and trees.

She continued into the woodland for about a minute without any indication of where he had gotten to. 'Mike!' she called out, as she halted in her tracks. She could no longer see the path she had left, and all that surrounded her was nature. 'Seriously! Mike!'

'Shh!' she heard him say as he snuck up behind her. He wrapped his arms around her waist and pressed himself up against her back.

'So, where's this shit that's gunna make my day?' Lucy was growing tired of games.

'So... impatient...' He began to kiss her neck. She laughed in response.

'You're kidding, right?' her tone was stern. She couldn't believe his audacity. 'I haven't heard from you in two days –'

'Shh...!' He continued to kiss her neck before biting her ear lobe.

'In the park? You've got to be kidding!' She was annoyed, and she shrugged him off of her. He seemed to ignore her display of anger and simply advanced towards her again.

'Let me ease that mind of yours,' his words were euphonious. 'No more chasing, you're the one I want...' Lucy wasn't sure if it was what he said, or if she had simply craved his attention for long enough, but she wanted him. She stepped into him, and as he leant in to kiss her, she kissed him back. She wrapped her arms around his neck and kissed him, tasting his lips, feeling his tongue against her own.

He placed a hand on the small of her back and grabbed her ass with the other, giving it a firm squeeze. He then leant forward, forcing her to lean backwards, allowing him to grasp her upper leg and lift her off the ground. As he did, she instinctively wrapped her legs around his waist. He carried her as they lost themselves in each other's lips, pressing her up against a nearby tree. Lowering her feet back down to earth, he kissed her on her neck once again as he grasped the bottom of her top and slowly pulled it up to reveal her breasts. He paused and looked her in the eye, before pulling her top up over her head. She frantically untied his shorts and pulled them down to release his firm penis. Grasping it, she rubbed it up and down its shaft, feeling it pulse within her palm. The thought of being caught entered her mind, but it only added to the passion of the moment and exhilarated her. He grasped her wrists tightly, stopping her as she speedily caressed his penis.

'Not so fast...' he whispered as he pulled at her arms, turning her around, facing her away from him.

Mike placed her hands on the bark covered trunk of the tree, and with one hand, he grasped the back of her neck. His other hand touched on her chest, and then ran down her body, gliding over her breast, exciting her nipple. His fingers stroked her abdomen and then they slipped into her shorts. She tried to turn to look at him, but he wouldn't let her, holding her neck, forcing her to look at the tree before her. His fingers stroked at her clitoris before entering her now moistened vagina. He advanced and then retreated slowly, time and time again, all the while preventing her from turning to interact with him. Lucy bit her lip and softly moaned as he pleasured her. She could feel him pushing up against her; she craved his strength, she was ready.

'Mike... baby...' she breathed heavily with excitement. Her words made him stop; for a moment she was curious as to what he was thinking, but it wasn't long before she knew. He pulled at her shorts and she wriggled her legs to aid in the undressing. Spreading her legs, she leant forwards, resting her forearms against the tree and then she gasped with a sense of ecstasy as he entered her. His throbbing penis slid inside effortlessly, sending a delightable chill throughout her body. She wanted to scream out in elation as he thrust himself into her again and again, but she knew they must remain quiet, hidden. Lucy moved her right arm; touching herself, she ran her hand down her body until she reached her groin. She placed her finger tips on her vagina, feeling his penis as it entered and withdrew, feeling it throb. She reached between her legs and grasped his sack, massaging his testicles as he continued to drive himself into her. She could feel herself ejaculate and her head was awash with pleasure as she moaned aloud. Grasping his buttock with her free hand, she encouraged him to fuck her harder, and he obliged, dutifully. Harder and deeper he threw himself inside her until she could feel his legs begin to buckle. He exploded inside of her, filling her with his seed.

Unable to do anything but smile, the pair coyfully put their missing garments back on and made their way back out into the park, Lucy cutting a caper as the pair playfully re-joined civilisation. With the intention of heading back to Lucy's apartment to get cleaned up, they were almost at the subway station when Mike did something she did not expect; he grasped her hand and interlinked his fingers with hers. The act took her by surprise and her heart raced. Was it joy she felt? They rode the subway to the nearest station to her home and walked back together, all the while holding hands. *I love him*, she let herself think as they arrived at her apartment. Playfully wrestling and kissing along the hallway, she needed to let him go so that she could clean up and have a shower, but the feeling she currently had, the alien feeling of love, of passion, she didn't want to let go. 'Argh,' she giggled gleefully as she wrestled from his hold. 'I am going to get a shower.' She kissed him and then pushed him away, enabling her to do something other than fall back into his arms as her heart so wished.

She felt blissful as the warm water pounded on her skin and flowed down her body. The morning had been perfect. She couldn't help herself from smiling as she recalled them holding hands; something so simple, meant so much. She finished washing and switched off the water before turning to climb out, but her exit was blocked. Mike stood in her way, naked. His sweat ridden body gleamed in the light and Lucy couldn't help but notice his arousal.

'We're not done yet...' He jumped into the shower with her and turned the water back on. His sudden action took her breath away. Water streamed over their bodies as Mike kissed her on her neck, making his way down to her breasts. His tongue circled her nipple before he bit down on it gently. Continuing to kiss her, he hurriedly moved down her body, kissing her belly, hips and then her groin, before running his tongue across her clitoris. Lucy ran her fingers through his dampened hair as he licked, kissed and lightly sucked the prepuce. His tongue then encircled her vagina before finding its way inside. Her heart pounded, as once again, her entire body shivered with excitement.

'Yes!' she cried as he grasped at her ass whilst nuzzling his face in between her legs, lapping up the moisture from inside with his tongue. She tugged at his hair to encourage him to stand up, she wanted him now. He stood up and lifted her onto his penis. She wrapped a leg around him, allowing him to enter her, filling her. 'I... love you...' she accidentally revealed what she had felt within for some time. Panic struck her as he slowed in his pursuit for passion, but then he smiled, filling her with a sense of relief, before he fucked her until they both came once more.

That afternoon, they entertained an idea that Lucy had had for some time. They spent it as a couple. Each and every moment that passed, she questioned whether it was reality or just a dream. Only each time she was assured by his smile that the happiness she felt was indeed true. They made a lunch from scraps of edible foods Lucy had in her cupboards and refrigerator, and they talked. Their conversation for once didn't just cover work, they spoke about everything. Lucy talked about her father, her upbringing, and Mike shared stories of his college days. With each word they exchanged, Lucy felt as if their souls were growing closer together. It was no longer just a casual fling, what they had was developing, evolving into what she had hoped for all along.

Mike held her in his arms into the evening. They shared a bottle of wine and watched a film; it was so normal, but to Lucy, it was perfect. Mike then stayed the night, again, holding her, sharing his warmth as they fell to sleep.

Lucy woke the following morning with a huge grin on her face and an ache in her cheeks, as if she'd been smiling all through the night. She stretched out her arms before opening her eyes, and almost to her surprise, she felt him lying next to her. 'Good morning,' she smiled, rolling to face him, and then she ran her fingers through his hair, checking to make sure he was real. He opened his eyes in response to her touch, only his weary blue eyes looked tired and distressed. *I guess he didn't sleep as well as I did,* Lucy presumed.

'Coffee,' he muttered, sounding groggy and hungover.

'Sure. You not sleep well? You look a bit under the weather.'

'Nice... Saying I look like shit?' Mike grumbled. In an

attempt to reignite the spark of happiness that had encapsulated the previous day, Lucy ran her hand across his chest. She then leaned in closer as she moved her hand south towards his waist, but his response shocked her. 'Luce! Seriously,' he snapped, brushing her hand away. Deciding to do her utmost to avoid an argument, Lucy retracted bit her tongue and gingerly slipped out of bed to make the coffee.

And he says I'm not a morning person... she chuckled to herself as she made the drinks. She could hear him groan as he climbed out of bed and made his way to the bathroom, coughing and spluttering as he went. 'Okay if we grab breakfast on the way in?' Lucy called out to him. She wished that today was not a work day, that they could put yesterday on repeat, but unfortunately it was not to be. 'Your coffee is next to the bed.' She headed back to the bedroom, yet, again she received no response. She waited for him as she sat and drank her own coffee, though, as time passed, she really needed to get herself ready for work. After donning a pair of black suit pants and a white blouse with black stripes, she affixed her holster and her badge and then slipped on her shoes and grabbed her jacket. 'Mike? You okay?' She knocked on the bathroom door, his lack of response beginning to unnerve her.

'Yeah, course I am,' he finally replied as he opened the door. Lucy was taken back by his appearance. The tired, withdrawn, shell of a man that had entered the bathroom had transformed. Mike now looked the pinnacle of perfect health; he was glowing in confidence, stood in his joggers, his chest laid bare. 'I'll be ready in five minutes, babe,' he kissed her on the cheek and hopped off towards the bedroom. She was curious as to what had transpired behind the closed door, but she was happy to have her Mike back before her. Perhaps she was reading too much into it, after all, she knew that he still suffered with night terrors; that he struggled to rest.

Mike drove them both to work, stopping off at the

café on the way. They entered the elevator and held each other's hand until the lift stopped. Lucy couldn't deny that her heart sank as he let go of her, but she knew that it was necessary. Mike's eye was caught by Hale and the pair of them headed off to the briefing room. He didn't even look back. It was as if yesterday was now a dream, and Lucy hated the feeling. She decided to check in with Claire and Krysta and made her way to Claire's lab. Claire had had a day to look into the Velocity pill, so perhaps she had some news.

'Gone? What do you mean, gone?' Lucy grew more and more frustrated as Claire explained to her that the pill she had obtained had disappeared.

'I'm sorry, Luce, it was on my desk when we left the other night, but the next day, poof! Gone! Disappeared!' It was the only sample she had and its disappearance annoyed Lucy somewhat, but something about Claire's demeanour was off. If Lucy didn't know any better, she would guess that Claire was nervous, perhaps she wasn't being completely honest with her. Lucy made up her mind to confront Claire, based on her gut feeling that she was concealing something, but before she could, Krysta entered the room and interrupted.

'Hey, Lucy, good day off? Krysta smiled. 'Sol is looking for you.' Her smile vanished as quickly as it had materialised.

Deciding to put her and Claire's conversation on hold, Lucy followed Krysta as she left the lab. Krysta's mannerisms confused Lucy somewhat, friend seemed cheerful, there was a definite spring to her step, but her expression made Lucy think that Solomon wasn't simply wanting to chat.

Maybe she got some too. She does sometimes get weird after... Lucy thought as she walked behind Krysta, the thought only stirred up her own feelings toward Mike; she was brimming with emotion. 'Krys, hon, can we talk?' She wanted to tell someone, spill the beans, share her joy. She had kept their relationship a secret from everyone for so long, bottling up her feelings in fear of the consequences, that she really wanted to vent. Now felt like the right time to put her trust in her best friend. She needed a release. Her passion, her love, her fear and doubt; her head hurt with each attempt to work out her next move. She needed help.

'We can, hon, but first you should see Sol, he's waiting for you...' As she said it, she turned and smiled, a smile that suggested she knew more than she was letting on. It was as if she knew what it was that Solomon wanted. Like a child, Krysta was giddy with the knowledge of what Lucy and Solomon were about to discuss.

'You know, don't you? You know what all this is about...' Lucy called her friend out on her current behaviour. 'C'mon, Krys, at least give me a heads up,' she pleaded, but Krysta held firm, simply beaming with a delightful smile.

'Nope. No spoilers. In you go.' Krysta ushered Lucy into Solomon's office.

Solomon sat behind his desk. He was wearing a navy-blue suit with matching coloured waist coat and tie, and his shirt was of a lighter shade of blue, but the soft colours of his attire did nothing to lessen the look of seriousness in his eyes.

'Lucy, take a seat.' He spoke in an authoritarian tone, unnerving her. Lucy was anxious and confused; she could not work out why Krysta had seemed so happy, when clearly, Solomon was anything but.

'What's all this about, Sol?' Lucy questioned timidly as she seated herself. She braced herself for a verbal backlash.

'I like to think I run a tight ship. That everyone on my team knows and understands the rules, and what's more, abides by them.' Solomon stood up from his seat. 'I like to think that I have the respect of everyone on my team, and that if they had an issue, they'd feel comfortable enough to come and talk to me.' Lucy fidgeted in her seat. The temperature in the room felt as if it had risen ten degrees and continued to rise as his eyes remained fixed upon her.

Surely, he doesn't know about me and Mike... However, she then recalled what Claire had blabbered on the ride home from their night out. *Claire...*

'It has come to my attention that two members of my team have been fraternising, which of course you know, I disapprove of...'

Claire, for fucks sake...

'I cannot have my agents distracted!' he exclaimed, raising his voice.

'Sol, look, I can explain...' Lucy attempted to defend herself.

'No need.' He then he smiled, confusing Lucy all the more. She was a loss for words. 'We have all known about your feelings for Agent Ward for some time. You weren't particularly subtle about it when he was abducted.' Lucy stared at Solomon in disbelief, curious as to where this bizarre conversation was headed. 'Keep work and your personal lives separate. *That*, is my only order regarding this matter.' He smiled again. Lucy could not believe what she was hearing, she never would have imagined that Solomon would allow them to continue seeing each other. 'Speechless... Wow, there's a first.' Lucy could feel a smile spreading across her face like an uncontrollable wild fire. She felt such relief, happiness and joy that she was almost on the brink of tearing up.

'Thank you, sir,' she said whilst trying to keep her emotions in check. Lucy then stood up, gave Solomon a quick nod and proceeded to leave his office.

As she closed the door behind her she almost exploded with excitement. She looked about the office until she saw him; she needed to tell him. Mike was heading off down the corridor towards the locker rooms. 'Perfect.' Lucy set off after him. She burst into the changing room with the intent of grabbing her man and kissing him passionately, only she walked in to find him standing at one of the wash basins, a bottle of pills in one hand, and a single red pill in the other, about to place it in his mouth. 'Mike? What... what are you doing?' He glanced at her with a blank expression, as if she was no-one of import. He proceeded to put the pill in his mouth and then leant forward to take a swig of water from the faucet. 'Hey!' she yelled, pushing him away from the basin and snatching the bottle of pills. 'You're on this velocity shit?!' She required an explanation. 'Are you fucking crazy?' Seamus had told her the truth, but until this very moment, she had wanted to believe otherwise.

'It's nothing, don't worry about it.' His reply infuriated her further.

'Don't fucking worry? For a start, you're doing this here? Are you fucking stupid?'

'Just another secret...' He appeared unfazed by her obvious anger.

'Well, I just spoke to Sol. He knows! He knows about us, and you know what, he's okay with it!' Suddenly Mike's nonchalant demeanour transformed into that of a cornered, wounded animal.

'You... you fucking told him?! Are you fucking joking?!' He raised both of his hands to his head in an act of frustration and anger. 'You put both our careers at risk... and for what?!' He took a deep breath in, gritted his teeth and clenched his fists furiously. Lucy could swear that he was about to punch something.

'For what?! For *us* you dick! And I didn't tell him, he already knew! What the hell is wrong with you?!' Lucy repeated the question again, this time louder and in Spanish, but it appeared to strike a nerve. Mike retaliated by marching toward her and squaring up to her, forcing her to back up slightly towards the door. He attempted to swiftly swipe the bottle from her clutches but she resisted letting go of the pills, hoping that the man she knew from their day in the sun would miraculously reappear. But instead, he grabbed her by the wrist and squeezed it until it hurt too much for her to continue to hold on. 'Mike?! What the fuck?!' Lucy yelled before punching him in the chest. Managing to obtain his drugs, he merely barged past her and left the room. Lucy swiftly followed him in pursuit. 'Hey!' she yelled across the office floor. No longer caring about where she was, she wanted answers and he was going to give them to her. 'Don't you dare walk away from me!' Her outburst drew the attention of everyone around. Solomon emerged from his office, Krysta and Claire appeared at the entrance to another corridor; all eyes were on Lucy. Mike stopped and turned, looking at all the onlookers.

'You want an audience? You wanted everyone to know about us, well, I guess you have your wish!' Mike stood tall with his arms outstretched, pointing to everyone around them. 'Solomon,' he glanced to his superior before staring Lucy in the eyes, 'you have nothing to worry about, absolutely nothing...' He held his glare as he tore out her heart. Lucy was seething, but inside she couldn't feel more alone; she was breaking in two.

'Mike...' Krysta jumped in, attempting to diffuse the situation.

'Krys! I guess you knew all about us. She tell you all the gory details?!'

'Mike... Why are you...?' Lucy tried to question his actions.

'I am broken!' he yelled as loud as he possibly could. 'They *broke* me! You will never know what it was like! These pills...' he held the bottle aloft for all to see, drawing looks of concern or intrigue from everyone in view. 'They make me better, they're the only reason I can stand –'

'Then tell me!' Lucy exclaimed. She stepped towards him, hoping that they could have this conversation somewhere else, somewhere more private.

'Tell you?! You wanna hear?!' His anger was obvious. He stepped toward Lucy and swiped a stack of paperwork off of a nearby desk, scattering it all over the floor.

'Mike, I think you should step inside my office,' Solomon suggested. Solomon held a stern expression as he pushed his office door fully open.

'No, Sol, I think Lucy needs to know. I think you all need to know just how badly you all failed. I was broken on a daily basis. That big mother fucker tortured me, every, single, day!' Mike slammed his fist down onto the desk beside him.

'We know, Mike. Please, step inside, we're here for you now...' Solomon attempted to calm the situation.

'She knew. She knew about you,' Mike stared at Lucy. An insane grin spread across his face and he chuckled despairingly. 'She tried to make me forget you. She tried to force me to let go of you.' It was clear that Mike was beginning to lose control. Tears began to fall from his rage filled eyes, and in response Lucy too began to weep.

'I'm here, Mike, see. It's okay now... let's go and talk... ' Lucy blubbered.

'But *she* is in here!' he tapped on his head frustratedly. 'She raped me! Again, and again... She *broke* me!' Mike looked at Lucy and then looked around the room as he dug his fingernails into his temples and gritted his so harshly that his neck muscles bulged. He had borne his darkest secret to everyone, a secret that made Lucy feel sick to her core. She couldn't respond, she could barely breathe. She looked at him through tear filled eyes. He was spent; turning away from her, from everyone, he walked to the elevator and stepped inside it. Lucy wanted to say something, to call out to him, but she had no idea what to do or what to say. What he said, what had happened to him, it was beyond anything she had considered. What could she possibly say to him to make it any better? The doors to the elevator slowly closed, and as she watched him disappear, she could no longer see her Mike; he was but a shadow of a man, his essence shrouded by flame.

10

Claire Davenport

'Miss Davenport? Are you with us?' That voice. It was familiar, old-familiar, as if from a past life. She could hear their heavy breathing, weighted by expectation and frustration. She opened her eyes just enough to let the light in so that she could see the person before her, but not too much that her eyes would still appear closed. It wasn't her office, no, this place was from before that time, before the bureau. She recognised the off-white coloured wooden window frames, the pastel-coloured walls, the unforgettable smells: a mixture of too much cologne, an overdose of perfume and a hint of body odour. They coughed to obtain her attention.

'Hmm?!' she murmured, sitting up quickly and brushing the hairs from her face.

'There you are. So glad you could join us.' He spoke in a more than familiar tone, one that reminded Claire of exactly where she was, or better, when she was. She was in class, Mr Cuthbert's algebra class. Senior year to be exact. She had been up all night working on her latest project, she had barely slept and Mr Cuthbert's class had seemed like the most logical time to take a nap; Claire could undoubtedly answer any question he had for her, fully awake or otherwise. 'So, let's see if Miss Davenport can solve the equation, seeing as we have her full, undivided attention.'

There was that tone again; to the untrained ear it would denote a feeling of exasperation, but to Claire, it was yet another teacher conveying the fact that she simply was not living up to the potential they all associated her with. Claire looked at the equation he spoke of and smiled. It was a complex equation, one that ninety-nine percent of the students here wouldn't be able to answer. That was the point.

'Fifty,' she yawned, causing the students around her to giggle. Mr Cuthbert was less impressed.

'I'm sorry, but that is incorrect. Maybe if you stayed awake in my class you just might learn something.' He spoke with an air of condescendence, something that seemed to hit a nerve with Claire.

I'm right you... However, the thought escaped her and transformed into words. '... ignoramus.' As she said it, she shocked herself and quickly covered her mouth.

'I beg your pardon.' He heard her; she had hoped that he hadn't, he was usually reliably oblivious, but not this time.

'Heh! What I mean is, sir, Mr Cuthbert, sir. I happen to be correct, maybe you'd like to check. I mean, I'm not saying you're wrong, just, in this case, and a few others come to think of it...'

'Miss Davenport, please refrain from talking anymore.' There was a combination of fear and anger in his expression. He did not wish to be corrected by a student and he could not allow Claire's outburst and display of disrespect go unpunished. He stood for a moment, holding his glasses against his chin, glaring at her, before he proceeded to start writing down the solution for the equation on the board. He frantically and angrily wrote it down, to the point that Claire wondered if the pen he was using was going to survive. Once he was finished, he turned and looked at Claire again. 'Now, if you're satisfied, Miss Davenport, please leave my classroom and head to the principal's office.' Claire looked about the room and scoffed.

'Am I the only one...'

'Miss Davenport!' he exclaimed, stopping her from continuing. Claire gathered up her belongings; she was infuriated. As she went to leave the room, she stopped.

How about I teach you a lesson... She took out a permanent marker from her bag. She walked up to the board, ignoring the dumbfounded look on his face, and struck a line through part of his working, correcting it, so that it would now result in the correct answer. She then dropped the pen like a mic-drop to the sound of cheers from her fellow students and hastily left the classroom.

The meeting with the principal and her teacher that followed disinterested her. Once again, she was told of what potential she had, and what a waste it would be if she continued to treat school so frivolously. Little did they know, Claire had her own priorities. When she exited the principal's office, she had one more lesson to attend, but as she checked the messages on her cell phone, she made up her mind to leave. She had snuck out of school so many times before that she had perfected her escape. Avoiding the obvious exits, Claire knew of and often used one of three potential routes. This time, she had made her way through the gym and climbed out of one of the locker room windows. A path behind the building led up past the janitor's lodgings and there, within the fencing, was a gap just big enough for her to squeeze through. Once she had made it around the outside of the grounds to the far end of car park, she climbed into her car and drove, heading for a place she had come to call her workshop.

From the outside it looked like just another run down derelict church. Positioned on the outskirts of town, the building's white-slatted walls had long since lost their bright colour and were now a moss coloured yellow. Its rectangular shaped windows were topped by traditional semi-circular arches, and above the main entrance, as well as on the spire-topped turret structure that stood beside it, rose windows had once sat. All of the windows, however, had since been boarded up and the doors were sign-posted with warning signs, leaving the building, with its fractured shell and broken roof, looking very undesirable. Yet, it held such character, which is why Claire had decided that it was the perfect hideaway. She may have left the outer walls of the building to the will of the elements, but Claire and her partner had worked hard to create a space inside that was fit for purpose. Inside, the wooden walls had been painted white and the floor was half laminated and half carpeted with a shaggy grey carpet that cushioned their feet. The church consisted of a single naïve, divided into two levels. The lower laminated level sat a couple feet below the carpeted upper level; Claire had fashioned wooden steps up to the higher level and either side of the steps, sat a number of bookcases, brimming with books and disc cases. It was a tech-haven, with the upper-level housing a number of desks littered with computers, monitors and various pieces of other hardware. Police scanners sounded from atop a shelf on the back wall and the computers chirped with results for numerous applications every now and then. The high ceiling had a few lights, but mostly, the room was aglow with the light that emanated from the equipment.

'Hey there, Bueller, how was school?' she said sarcastically as Claire ascended the steps.

'Apparently napping in class is frowned upon, and the principal says "I am wasting my potential".' Her friend's name was Iris, or at least that was what Claire had come to call her. She had dark brown hair that fell to just below the shoulder line; it was straightened, giving her an oval-shaped face that was complemented by her bright-blue eyes and red coloured lips. She was wearing a black top with a brown leather jacket and ripped blue jeans. Iris was, what she and Claire liked to call, a hacktivist. Using her superior array of computer-based skills, she shone a light on areas of corruption and wrongdoing within society that would ordinarily remain hidden via legal methods of investigation. She had found Claire through the web and somehow managed to track her down, despite Claire's attempts to keep her identity a secret. They had since become friends and formed a formidable alliance. Most of Claire's time outside of school was spent assisting Iris in her work.

'Really puts the "pal" in principal that one,' Iris retorted. 'I'm glad you're here though, made some real progress on ol' Grammer.' She was referring to their latest quest for freedom of information. Iris suspected, and it was looking more and more likely, that the good senator, Charles Grammer, was in cahoots with not only the Russian mob, but with a Serbian gangster named Vladimir Markovic. They had been attempting for some time to trace large amounts of money that the senator's campaign had received back to its source, but hacking countless international accounts was proving difficult and time consuming. 'Managed to find a back door into the Serbian National Bank and pinpoint the origin of some of this cash flow.' She smiled at Claire as she explained her findings.

Their progress pleased Iris so much that her eyes flashed an amber, or honey colour in the light as she spoke. It was a strange phenomenon, but one that Claire had grown accustomed to. Iris loved her work; it was her passion. From what Claire knew, her life was bereft of family, although, on occasion, she would talk to Claire as if a mother would a daughter, so Claire had wondered if she did have a child or two out there and just wanted to protect them from her dangerous career choice. She didn't speak much of her life outside of the work-shop, but there were implications and subtle suggestions that Iris had had a privileged upbringing: she was definitely learned, and she sometimes spoke as if she wasn't from this time, as if quoting Shakespeare or Aristotle. 'C'mon then, let's get cracking,' she said, smiling again before diving in. Her commitment to the cause was more than admirable, encouraging Claire to sit down opposite and get straight to work.

It was the early hours of the next day when Claire awoke. She must have passed out, but as she realised the time she panicked.

'My parents are going to kill me!' She was still in disbelief that she'd fallen asleep. 'Fuck.'

'Shit, shit, shit...' Iris was seemingly oblivious to Claire's current predicament. She looked stressed.

'What's up, Iris?' Claire arched her back, stretching out, 'losing at bingo again?' she chuckled.

'No....' Iris was clearly worried. 'Claire, you know that hiding place you always tease me about?' Claire nodded in response, although a little confused. 'I want you to grab your stuff and get in there now.' She looked at Claire with fear in her eyes.

'What? Why?' Claire couldn't help but think that her friend was being paranoid.

'Just do it!' Iris screamed, her eyes flashing that honey colour again. Her exclamation scared Claire. Iris proceeded to march around to her, grabbing her by the arm and picking up her bag. She dragged Claire down the stairs towards the main entrance and opened up the concealed space that lay hidden behind the rooms interior wall. It was just big enough for Claire to squeeze inside.

'Iris, I don't understand...' Claire pleaded as she pulled her knees up to her chest and wrapped her arms around her legs.

'Listen. It's so much bigger than we thought. Grammer is in bed with Markovic, the Bratva, Department of Defence, the C.I.A...' Claire could hardly believe what she was hearing, surely they had what they needed to expose him now. 'He's linked to a military operation, code named "PRINCES"...' Claire could tell that there was more she wanted to say but something stopped her. There was the sound of a car screeching to a halt, but the sound wasn't out of place as the streets that ran by the building were often used for street races. 'Be silent, don't come out until they're gone. Promise?' Claire's heart was pounding ferociously within, she was in full panic mode. What the hell was happening? Iris covered up Claire's hiding place and slid a plant pot in front of it. Claire sat, huddled up in the darkened, uncomfortable space, her breath, heart and mind racing. She couldn't see her own hand in front of her face, but she could hear everything that was happening within the church. Iris was frantically typing on the keyboards. Then suddenly the front door slammed, causing Claire's whole body to jolt in shock. She could then hear footsteps.

'There's nothing here for you, it's all gone, I destroyed it all,' Iris hastily said, her tone quavering. Iris' words only confirmed Claire's fears, that there were others out there with her. Who was it that Iris was afraid of?

'You haven't destroyed everything.' The voice was cold. He had a strong accent; European. Claire stayed as quiet as she could, silently trembling in fear, covering her mouth to prevent herself from making any noise.

'I know who you are...' Iris said in a calm and confident tone. Claire was confused. She knew it to be Iris, but at the flick of a switch, she sounded completely different.

'And I know who you are.' His words were followed by several incredibly loud bangs. Claire bit down on her tongue and held her mouth shut, exerting such pressure that it hurt. She could only imagine what the bangs were, having never heard a gun-shot up close before. She heard a thud and pictured her friend falling to the floor. She wanted to cry, to scream, but she was petrified.

'Stop. She... We... I have a daughter.' The sound of Iris' voice brought a small sense of relief to Claire's heart that was swiftly blown away by the sound of another half-dozen gunshots. The room went quiet after that; for what seemed like forever, there was no sound. She contemplated moving but she was afraid. Then she heard his voice again.

'You best hope I never find her.' There was such malice to his tone. Claire heard the footsteps move across the floor, dissipating as they left the building. She remained deathly still for so long that she wondered if she'd ever have the strength to leave.

Small flickers of light crept through the cracks of the walls of her hiding place. Claire held out a hand and touched the rays; the sun had risen, its warmth granting an ounce of solace. She slowly pushed open the entrance to her hiding place, nudging the plant pot and knocking it over, the sound of the crash reigniting her state of shock. Slowly gaining the courage to move once more, she steadily clambered out onto the floor; her eyes already full of tears. She knew what awaited her and as she struggled to find the strength to stand, she crawled on her hands and knees across the floor to the steps. Each movement took all of her might, and as she reached the summit, she saw her. The carpet had been stained red and Iris' lifeless body lay there, unmoving.

'Iris,' Claire choked on the word, crying as she inched closer. 'I-ris...' she said again, hoping for a response. She coughed and spluttered as she struggled to breathe. Tears ran down her cheeks and wet the carpet beneath her. As she inched closer, she placed her hand down on the blood-soaked carpet, the feeling of Iris' blood on her hand causing her to choke on her tears and then throw up. Claire's stomach hurt and her chest was tight. She tried to stop her hand from shaking, but her gaze could not be shifted from the blood stain across her palm. Reaching out for her friend in a spasm of distress, she brushed the sole of Iris's boot. Her fingers snapped back, her arm pounded, and it felt as if someone had punched her square in the chest. 'Ow!' she cried out, feeling as if she had received a nasty electric shock. 'Ow!' she exclaimed again, shaking her arm in an attempt to deal with the pain. There was a sudden sharp pain in her head. Holding her head in her hands, she sobbed in pain, in grief. That was when she heard a noise from behind. She quickly turned to see who it was, clambering backwards in fear. Her heart was racing, she needed to get away from the man before her, but as she saw Iris' face, she stopped dead. Iris' eyes were wide open, but there was no light, no spark.

'It's okay, I won't hurt you.' He held up his hands. He was wearing a jacket with a hood, and with the light being behind him, Claire couldn't make out his face. 'I just need to know...' As he spoke, Claire could see his eyes glow from within his hood, an emerald-like shine. He stepped towards her, and as he did Claire suddenly felt a wave pass over her. She felt a calmness within and her tears stopped. Her heart steadily reduced to a normal rhythm.

'What...' She was confused.

'Carmen. Look after this one...' His words felt as if they meant something to Claire, but she had no idea why. 'Tobias,' he said, and as he did, Claire then noticed the second man stood behind him. 'Wipe the knowledge, make sure she's safe.'

'All of it? Even the woman? She discovered something... Princes?' Tobias questioned. He looked at Claire as if she was transparent, his yellow eyes piercing through her.

'Wipe it,' the green-eyed man said without hesitation.

'HOLY CRAP!' Claire exclaimed as she sat up in bed. She had been asleep, it could have been a dream, but her gut told her it was more than that. 'CARMEN!' she shouted out in her empty bedroom. *Don't ignore me! That was you, us!* 'Holy... shit...' *He wiped my memory,* 'but not yours...' *Who the hell is Tobias?* 'Another sibling I take it...' Her thoughts were bounding off the walls of her mind as she tried to piece together what she'd dreamt, what she'd remembered.

Claire, calm down. Carmen finally responded.

Calm down? Yeah... sure, why not. You! You were Iris! The more Claire thought, the angrier she became. *You... Adam...*

You kept this from me?

Claire, they took the memory from both of us, or at least parts of it... Memories take time to heal... Think of our minds like a jigsaw with missing pieces...

'Oh, great analogy! Doesn't make me sound nuts at all!' Claire shouted.

You are the one shouting at yourself...

Ha! A b-zillion year-old comedian, brilliant! She leapt out of bed and paced up and down the length of her room for a minute before deciding she really needed a coffee.

Claire...

Nope! Don't talk to me, not until I have had a coffee! She stomped into the kitchen like a petulant child, grabbed a mug and turned on the coffee machine. 'No...!' The machine did nothing. She frantically flicked the switch on and off repeatedly, but the machine continued to do nothing. The light was on, the other appliances were fine, so it must be the fuse she assumed. She could literally feel Carmen's stare, but she tried her best to ignore it; to request help would involve speaking to her and admitting defeat. Claire continued to flick the switch in a state of denial, sulking, but hoping that sheer will would prevail. As she flicked it on once again, she felt a spark leave her fingertip and the machine came to life. 'Aha! Finally, it works!' She was overjoyed with the realisation that she would soon have her coffee.

A thankyou would suffice... Carmen pointed out.

What are you...? It just needed a little perseverance, that's all.

Of course, what was I thinking. Go you. The pair began to laugh at how ridiculous they were being. Claire finally had her morning coffee, the smell of which was enough to perk her up a little. She was now willing to listen.

Claire and Carmen melded minds for a while. The conversation consisted mostly of Carmen trying to convince Claire that she had no idea that her memories had been tampered with, to which Claire could feel her sincerity; she was being honest.

'So, you don't know who Iris' daughter was? Or anything about that operation Princes? If they do in fact have ties to Markovic, this could be a huge break for us.' Carmen denied having any knowledge of either, but she did advise caution. Not only was this information worth Markovic killing Iris for, but for some reason, Adam had made the decision to wipe it from both Claire's and Carmen's memories; that fact worried them both. 'Aw, c'mon, this is what I live for.' Claire exhibited such passion; she was eager to chase the lead.

I know, but how will you explain to the others how you found it out? You need to be careful. Carmen was right, Claire would need to act with discretion for now. The bureau had been in a fractured state of late: Mike had been suspended, Lucy was still distraught, and Claire still did not know what had happened to the missing printouts that linked her to the murders of Cardoza's men. *You're going to be late for work,* Carmen halted Claire's current, erratic, train of thought.

'Shit!'

She arrived at work late, however, she doubted that anyone would have noticed if she hadn't turned up at all. Solomon was pacing up and down his office whilst on the phone, his hand gestures suggesting that he was in a very heated conversation. Kyle was outside, looking in. Claire attempted to avoid him but inadvertently caught his eye.

'Davenport!' he called as she tried to escape.

'Yes, Kyle?' Claire dropped her shoulders and sighed as she spoke.

'Cheer up. I know why Rodriguez is sour-faced, but what's up with you?' he smirked, but as Claire turned to walk away from him, he quickly manoeuvred around to block her path. 'I'm just joking, geez!'

That outfit is a joke, Carmen muttered. She wasn't wrong; once again Kyle had outdone himself, wearing a black and white, wide set, striped suit with a pink shirt and a navy-blue ascot.

'What do you want, Kyle?' Claire said exasperatedly. Her patience for Kit's nonsense was limited at best.

'With all the recent blunders, and with Solomon no doubt getting it in the neck from the D.O.J, I just wanted to make sure that you knew that, as an important member of this team, you had my support, should there be any changes in the hierarchy around here.' He stood there, expectant, with a sanguine expression. Claire said nothing, despite Carmen suggesting a few choice words for her to use. Instead, she remained equanimous, biting her tongue and stretching out her fingers behind her back to stop her from forming fists. She then turned and steadily walked away, managing to keep her cool, until she reached her lab.

'Argh! What a creep!' she shuddered.

'Kyle?' Malique sounded from the corner of the room. 'Give you the "I'm here for you" speech?' Something was off. With the acknowledgement of Malique's presence, Claire suddenly felt a sense of aggression that she didn't quite understand.

Carmen? What's wrong? But Claire did not receive an answer. Claire tried to ignore the feelings that were clearly not her own.

'Claire?' Malique waited patiently as she stood staring down at her hands, attempting to shake off Carmen's contempt.

'Yeah. Kyle. Heh!' She shook her head. 'I wish, I wish I could develop a shrink ray, you know?' Malique expressed a confused smile. 'Shrink him, stick him in a little toy boat and threaten to flush him every time he pissed me off. Heh,' she rambled. 'Be like... Honey, I shrunk the prick, in cinemas July fourth.' She acted as if a crowd was cheering and took a bow, before realising how crazy she must look to Malique and started to blush. She went to apologise to him for her weirdness but something was holding her back, and by the time she managed to shrug off Carmen's hold, Malique had left the room. 'You've got to be joking!' she exclaimed, furious at her co-inhabitant.

'Kyle got to you as well?' Krysta entered Claire's lab; it would appear that Claire wasn't the only one seeking refuge. Krysta looked well, her cheeks were full of colour, her hair shone in the light and she held a smile that quietened the din of frustration within Claire. She wore her usual work attire, black suit, white blouse, but something was new. 'Sorry, were you having a conversation with... you know...' Krysta appeared awkward. 'Can't wait for him to catch Lucy.' She looked back out into the hallway, 'she'll knock him clean out,' she smiled. Claire, curious as to the reason for Krysta's apparent bliss, pushed her friend for information. Krysta avoided the subject at first, explaining that Lucy was keen for Claire to help her look into the drug that Mike was using, the topic snaring Carmen's full attention.

After beating around the proverbial bush for a while, Krysta finally admitted that it was hope that had her in such high spirits. She had woken this morning with a simple, yet, powerful feeling. Hope. A hope that she'd soon find Adam, that she could soon move on with her life, whatever path she ended up taking. Claire decided that the idea was a nice thought, certainly a nice distraction from the fear of being found out, or the guilt of the innocent woman Carmen had killed. The conversation of Adam opened the door to the subject of Claire's own personal life, or lack thereof. As she spoke to Krysta and listened to Carmen's inner chatter, Claire was slowly suaded to giving life outside of the bureau a chance. She waited for Krysta to leave the room and then took out her phone. A giddy excitement, as well as a nervous flutter possessed her simultaneously.

'Hi, Alexa. It's Claire,' she said down the phone as a smile spread across her face.

11
Evelina

She was irascible; infuriated by the weeks of travelling that had resulted in little progress. For one as old as time itself, she found herself consistently angered with man's incompetence to record history accurately. She and Seymour had set out in search of information regarding Carmen's ability to transfer her consciousness from one host to another; the Avunaye had managed many spectacular feats, however, they had always remained tied to their original human shells. After trawling through reams of documents, Evelina had come to the conclusion that Carmen must have had some assistance, perhaps a person or some kind of relic that had allowed her to complete the transition. She had managed to rule out Adam as an accomplice, as at the time, he would have been under lock and key, but whoever had helped Carmen or whatever relic she had used, Evelina was determined to uncover the truth and had set out in search of it. Her travels had been extensive thus far, resulting in a strain on her patience. Seymour had insisted that a good place to start was Egypt; the ancient Egyptians, of course, having many tales of possession. However, their time there only resulted in the deaths of several scholars and archaeologists. From Egypt, they had moved on to Africa, to the Umbanda and their legends of African possession. Then, on to Haiti, to unlock the secrets of Voudou practices. Following that, they went to the remote islands of Japan in pursuit of the mythical Misaki. Unfortunately, the more myths and legends they pursued, the worse Evelina became upon their failure to bear fruit, which only resulted in more and more bodies being left in their wake. Their search continued across Europe. Ancient Greek Nympholepsy shined some light on the subject, providing a different perspective, but Evelina was tired of trawling through ancient manuscripts and looking at artefacts that had, more often than not, been incorrectly associated with time periods to which they did not belong. Upon leaving Greece, she and Seymour headed to Italy to investigate Christian legends that concerned possession, and this had eventually led them here, to Florence.

Evelina had previously spent centuries in and around the Tuscan capital, indulging in its wealth of culture. It was due to her time spent here that she became annoyed with herself for overlooking the secrets that the city held. As she looked up at a particular stain glass window, she recalled the thurible that was depicted within it, held some importance.

'The thurible, within that window?' Evelina asked of the priest before her whilst pointing to a stain glass window. He replied confidently, informing her that the relic was no doubt one of many thuribles that were donated by Emperor Constantine in the fourth century. 'Constantine?' Evelina questioned, her tone fuelled with frustration. 'Then I am in the wrong city!' She stood for a moment, fighting the urge to exact her anger on the poor man. Instead, she said, 'Pater gratias ago tibi,' thanking him in Latin, to which he replied that she was most welcome. She stepped out of the cathedral into the twilight and smiled. Finally, it felt as if she was making some progress. 'Seymour?' she spoke to the shadows and her faithful child appeared, his tenebrous figure materialising from the black. 'We need to head to the eternal city, San Giovanni, in Laterno. Make the arrangements.'

They travelled through the night and arrived at the church just as the sun rose. Eager to finally lay her hands on the object she desired, she burst through the main entrance, bursting through the metal gates and breaking down the wooden doors. She sought the cloister of the attached monastery, where she believed she would find what she was after. As she ascended the Scala Sancta, or Holy Stairs, she paused and smirked, reminiscing a time long past. Once within the quadrilateral enclosure, she searched for the relic but found herself empty handed. She then returned to the church, tearing through it in an all-consuming rage. It appeared that the object she wanted had been moved. 'AHH!!' she screamed exasperatedly, the ground trembling at her feet. 'Liberius...' she muttered as she took a deep breath in. She had shaken the foundations of the building, causing the large stone statues of the apostles around her to shudder at her presence. Before she left, she turned and looked into one of the chapel recesses. Marble pillars rose up from the floor either side of a large oval painting. Atop the pillars stood several statues of cherubim and angelic figures. Evelina stared at them with distaste, teeth gritted; time and scripture had immortalised the beings she looked upon, beings with immense power and purpose, glorified and worshipped by millions. As she stared at the purity of the stonework, she thought of herself and her children, how they had been shunned and feared by man, how unfair their existence was in comparison. Her temper got the best of her. She clenched her fists; her emerald green eyes glowed, and the stone before her began to crumble, the angelic figures cracked and slithers of marble fell, leaving them faceless and without wings. Evelina sneered in response, as if justice had been served, before leaving the building behind her.

Her next, and hopefully final stop, was merely a short walk away. The basilica had lost a little of its charm since she had last set eyes on it, but it remained impressive. It was early morning and the doors were open; queues of tourists waited to enter the structure and armed enforcers stood by, ensuring peace. *We will have to play our part here. We cannot afford any further delays.* She considered their options. 'Seymour, civilian clothing will be required here.'

Her companion stepped out of a darkened doorway onto the pavement beside her. He had tied his purple-grey hair up, with just a few strands cascading down the pale flesh of his face. He wore shiny black shoes that pointed at the toe, a pair of dark-grey pants and a jet-black shirt.

'Will this suffice?' His breath adding a deathly chill to the air. Evelina nodded. She was elegantly dressed. Wearing a white jumpsuit that hugged her figure, the material ran up to just above her breasts and was finished in lace that rolled over her shoulders; the sleeves were of a sheer mesh, and about her waist, extra fabric hung like a central-parted dress, flowing behind her as she walked. She wore a pair of silver lace-up heels and a bracelet about her left wrist that harnessed more diamonds than that of an average jewellery store. Her long golden hair was softly curled and hung freely.

The pair joined the queue and, upon entering, paid for a tour guide to show them around. Evelina chuckled light-heartedly at the notion that anyone could inform her of something that she did not already know. Seymour, however, did not appear amused by her whimsiness. 'Is this really necessary?' he questioned as the tour guide introduced herself, bringing a look of uneasiness to the woman's face.

'Ignore him, dear, please begin.' Evelina's words instantly washed away any sense of doubt the woman had.

The interior of the building encapsulated beauty. At least a dozen stone columns stood resolutely either side of the central naïve. Above them, Roman arches nestled below rows of windows that allowed the suns light to pour into the church and emphasise the splendour of the golden ceiling that ran its length.

'The impressive ceiling was completed by Antonio Guilliano...' the tour guide instructed, pointing up at the exquisite artistry.

'Yes, yes...' Evelina interrupted. The experience of a tour through history was not as fun as she had first thought. 'You know, the gold of the ceiling, donated by Isabella and Ferdinand of Spain. Supposedly from the new world.' She laughed as she reminisced. 'I'd like to see works regarding Saint Liberius,' Evelina requested, puzzling the tour guide.

'No, no. Liberius was never –'

'Never made a saint, yes, so they say...' Evelina interrupted once again. 'Shunned... I believe that was our fault, well, Adam's mostly, he does love to try and encourage you, mortals.' The woman was utterly perplexed. 'Now, if I recall, there was a mosaic?' Evelina waited for a moment, but as the confused woman before her struggled to produce an answer, her impatience shone through. 'The mosaic! My dear.'

'Yes... Erm, yes... the, the legend. The legend of the snowfall.' The woman trembled on the spot until Evelina gestured that they move on. Spinning on her heels, she ushered them to follow.

Legend, Evelina smiled as she thought. *Because a snowfall in the midst of summer could never happen.* They were led upstairs and out onto a balcony. Two angel-like statues stood clothed in gold either side of an intricately designed piece of art that depicted the legend that the guide had spoken of. 'I do not see it. Seymour?' Seymour shook his head. 'Where is it?!' Evelina was disappointed to not see any sign of what she sought. The guide looked at her blankly, which only infuriated her further. 'The reliquary... where is it?!' Yet, the tour guide remained silent. 'The crib, the thurible?!' Evelina was about to snap.

'There... there is a crib reliquary, but - but no

thurible, ma'am...' She was shaking, her voice quivering.

'This is a very special thurible, my dear,' there was an undeniable anger to Evelina's tone. She went to strike the woman, but then, she suddenly blurted out what Evelina needed to hear.

'The exhibition! A thurible... Emanuelle II galleries!' she cried out in fear. Evelina could feel it, the emotion leeching on every inch of the woman as she failed to fight the feeling.

'Remain calm, my dear, it is such a beautiful day.' Evelina begrudgingly said, her words filling the woman with a feeling of peace and tranquillity, almost to the point of collapsing in a state of euphoria.

Maddened by the day's events and the obstacles she had had to traverse, the only thing that prevented Evelina from losing her temper was the idea of making an impression on the world by attending the exhibition. She could easily take to the galleries and seize that which she wanted, but this gave her an excuse to flaunt all that she was to the masses of people that would be in attendance. She spent the afternoon shopping, preparing for the evenings event. Her search may well be over tonight, so she had decided to enjoy herself. As the evening drew forth, Seymour slipped away into the dusks thin veil, ready to appear as and when she required. Evelina wore her hair down, styled, so that it fell gently over her right shoulder. She wore earrings that dangled, and a necklace, all of which housed the finest, flawlessly impressive emeralds and diamonds the world would ever see. She donned a plunging, strapless purple gown that was intricately detailed on the back and train; the dress showcased her spectacular figure and was so long that she had to carry a portion of it as she walked.

The striking, resolute, white building shone in the dark with the assistance of many spotlights and fire-pit pedestals that were aflame at the summit of the main staircase. There were many people in attendance. Tens of people flowed into the structure as singles, couples and groups; some dressed casually, but most people had made the effort to dress formally for the occasion. The men looked dashing in their suits and tuxedos, and the women displayed an array of different styled and coloured dresses, yet, they were all flawed. Evelina looked at them all, all unique, however, all destined to wither and wilt, to lose their colour and fade into nothing. She made her way through the crowd, along the front of the monument, to the large open stone doorway. Within the entrance there were more stairs, with a large statue at their summit. People stopped and admired the angel riding the quadriga, basking in the masonry, the beauty. She understood why they looked on in awe: the flawless, heavenly being, encapsulated in stone, undying, unchanging, immortal. As many people as were basking in the beauty of the pieces on display, there were just as many stood in awe of Evelina, for her beauty was absolute.

'Magnificent gown,' a woman said, acknowledging her attire.

'Why, thank you.' Evelina chose not to return the compliment as she looked the woman up and down. 'I am looking for a particular exhibit, a certain thurible relic.' She spoke as if talking to a servant, asking them to lead her to where she wanted to go. The woman and her partner, both stood unmoving, speechless at her audacity. 'Perfect,' she sighed, before looking around for someone else to ask.

'The thurible of Selaphiel?' a voice asked. It was feminine, but out of place, a distinct Irish accent. She turned to look upon the owner of the voice.

'Well, yes...' Evelina was surprised by what she laid her eyes upon. She was petite, toned and she had wavy, deep red coloured hair that shimmered in the light, as if on fire. She wore a one-shoulder, body-con red dress that hemmed just below the knee, with a slit that ran half way up her thigh. Evelina smiled at the woman's slight resemblance to Serena, yet there was something else about her that hooked

Evelina's intrigue.

'That particular exhibit is this way, please follow me,' she said courteously and then turned to lead the way, revealing a large tattoo of a rose on the uncovered portion of her back.

'You're Irish,' Evelina stated as they walked.

'Very astute.'

'I meant that it surprised me. You stand out amongst the rabble.'

'I will take that as a compliment,' she laughed. 'I love history, and I adore travelling. I obtained my degree at Cambridge and have since travelled and worked in eleven cities in eight countries. In case you were wondering.' Even though Evelina could not see the woman's face, she could tell that she was smiling. Evelina could feel the woman's confidence.

'Impressive. I do like to travel myself. Whether for better or worse, the world is forever changing, so there is always something new.' Evelina was excited to finally lay her hands on the thurible, however, she couldn't ignore the poise and passion that exuberated from her would-be host.

'I have to admit, I have fallen in love with Rome, the _'

'Eternal City,' they both said in unison.

'I'm impressed.' The woman turned and smiled, catching Evelina's attention, before continuing to walk on. She had pale pink lips and her eyes were of a soft grey-blue colour. Evelina couldn't help but notice her uniqueness. 'May I say, you look stunning this evening...'

'My name is Evelina,' she responded, smiling back.

'Evelina. That is a beautiful necklace.' She stroked her own neck as she spoke. 'My name is Janet. In case you were wondering.' She was so brazen; Evelina admired her aura.

'Janet, that is a curious tattoo you have,' Evelina stated, testing the water.

'It runs *all* the way down... there are several petals delicately drawn just above my waist line.' Janet ran a hand down her back and across her ass as she continued to lead the way.

'I will agree, Rome has its beauties. There is an irresistible gelataria on Via Agostino Depretis. Just in case you fancied something –'

'Sweet,' Janet interjected, before turning quickly to face Evelina. She looked her in the eye and licked her top lip seductively. For a moment, Evelina could admit that she was distracted, but it was short lived.

Behind the scarlet seductress, the thurible rested atop of a pedestal, cordoned off by rope. Crafted in a brilliant gold, it had a black and gold chain by which to be hung by. The lid was curious, however, as it featured a cross in its centre, but also a number of other religious symbols, not all relating to Christianity. Evelina brushed past the red-head and moved towards the relic, a smile of success slowly spreading across her face. She walked up to the ropes, detached them and proceeded to pick up the thurible with both hands.

'Hey, you're not supposed to touch that,' Janet said, slightly downhearted by Evelina's ignorance to her advance.

'I can feel exactly what you're feeling, my dear. Don't flatter yourself. I'm sure I could have given you the night of your insignificant life, but some things are more important.' Janet was confused, exhibiting a puzzled expression that did not compliment her. 'Seymour...' The lamps flickered and the shadows within the small room shifted and wavered. From the corner of the room Seymour slipped into existence, walking out of the dark as if it was a mere doorway.

'Bejesus! Holy fuck!' Janet exclaimed, Evelina could hear her heart begin to race, and she could feel her fear.

'Call for help, try to flee and I will slaughter every last person here.' Evelina's eyes glowed green as she threatened the woman, taking her breath away. She would need to test her theory, and for that she would need Janet. 'Seymour,' she repeated, holding out the relic. He dutifully took it and began to place some items into it, materials that they had gathered on their travels; Evelina was willing to try anything and everything to make it work. As the thurible began to smoke, Seymour passed it back to her. She took it and walked over to the nervous, fearful woman that no longer exhumed any degree of confidence. She reeked of fear. 'I need to test a theory, my dear. I have an annoying sibling... daughter... whatever she is, she has an uncanny ability for survival that I do not yet understand, but one that I *must* understand if I intend on ridding myself of her for good.' Janet remained still, shaking, tears creeping from her eyes. 'Honestly, this is nothing personal, you are just conveniently placed. Now calm yourself.' As Evelina gave the command, she used her ability to fill the woman with a sense of safety and warmth, leaving her docile and waiting for Evelina to carry out her test. Evelina then held the thurible up, urging Janet to take hold of it. As they stood there connected, they both breathed in the smoke.

Evelina remained relatively patient, giving it a minute or two to work, but unfortunately, nothing happened.

'I... I don't understand.' Janet's voice quivered once again as she started to become anxious once more.

'Nor do I,' Evelina admitted angrily. She snatched the thurible away and threw it across the room. 'It was supposed to be the answer!' she yelled. 'This thurible, it has a legend, yes?!' She demanded some form of explanation.

'Y-Yes,' Janet uttered, her speech becoming increasingly quick. 'It is said that Selaphiel could use it to transfer his consciousness from one vessel to another, but it is just a myth. Please, just let me go –'

'Wrong! And by the way Selaphiel was female for all intents and purposes. Well technically she transcended gender, but if you wish to put a label on it.' Evelina was furious.

'Please, let me leave,' Janet begged.

'Argh!' Evelina erupted, slapping her across the face, sending her crashing against the fashioned back drop and cutting her cheek. 'Silence! I am trying to think...' She breathed in and out slowly as she tried to calm herself. Her heart pounded harshly, urging her to take her anger out on all those around her. 'Maybe... maybe *she* is the problem. Seymour, grab someone else. We will try again.' She refused to accept failure.

As Seymour moved towards the room's exit, Janet coughed and began to laugh. Surprised by her actions, Seymour stopped, and he and Evelina both looked at her curiously. 'Something amuses you, my dear?' Janet continued to cough as she chuckled. Evelina took a step towards her; she could hear her singing to herself under her breath.

'... must be, missing an angel...' she sang softly in amongst the coughs and spits of blood. Evelina looked closer, watching as the cut on her face closed and healed.

'Who are you?' Evelina's curiosity was piqued by what was happening.

'For when *he* takes a life coldly, shall they be freed of their restraints. With the drawing of blood –'

'Will they be set free.' Evelina finished, interrupting her. 'The curse of Adam, what has that to do with you?'

'You can so easily misinterpret these things.' Janet climbed to her feet and brushed off her dress. 'He unleashed against them his hot anger, his wrath, indignation and hostility.' She smiled.

'A band of destroying... Janet? Who are you? *What* are you?' Evelina was still unsure as to what was happening to the woman before her that was moments ago cowering in fear.

'Not quite.' Janet closed her eyes and breathed in deeply; there was a light beginning to glow from behind her, as if her rose tattoo was starting to shine, devouring the shadows. Seymour retreated backwards, towards the exit, covering his eyes. Evelina could feel his pain. As the light grew brighter, so did Seymour's pain; he apologised and vanished from sight.

'Enough!' Evelina demanded, before moving towards Janet within a blink of an eye. She grabbed the woman by the throat, but instantly relinquished her grasp. It was as if she'd tried to pluck a star from the night's sky.

'With the drawing of blood, *we* will be set free. A band of destroying –' Evelina did not wait to listen to anymore of her words. She turned and fled as quickly as possible, putting as much distance between her and the red-head as she could. There were many things that time had rendered that had surprised her, but she had never expected this. She would need help. She would need Adam.

12
Krysta Rose-Anderson

'You sure you want to do this, hon?' Krysta was struggling to see the benefit that could possibly come from the plan that Lucy had put forth, but Lucy seemed so determined; determined and distraught. Krysta couldn't recall the last time she had seen her friend so... broken. Lucy paced back and forth. Her eyes provided much insight into her current state of mind, despite the obvious attempt to conceal how she was feeling with her relaxed and casual attire. She had tied her long dark hair up into a ponytail, leaving her fringe to waft across her brow each time the breeze caught it. She was wearing a white, sleeveless, open-backed pantsuit with white sandals; an ensemble that emphasised her caramel complexion. If her friend was intending to look subtly desirable, Krysta was convinced she had achieved her goal. Yet, her eyes, her deep brown eyes gave away the raw emotion that she carried within. Krysta could tell that Lucy had been crying, and that she had not been sleeping well. Her attempt to disguise the fact were not fooling her friend, her face held all of the unmistakable tells.

Since that fateful day in the office when Mike had divulged his darkest secret to the team, Lucy had not been herself. She was distracted. She was desperate. Mike had managed to break down Lucy's emotional walls, their secret relationship opening Lucy up, allowing her to love. Yet, it had made her vulnerable. And it was in the same moment that he had let her fully in, baring all to her, that he had crushed her; her vulnerability allowing her heart to be effortlessly broken. *In true Lucy fashion, this is either going to work... or it is going to completely blow up in her face. Can only hope it's not the latter.* Lucy's plan was to speak to Mike face to face. She intended on confronting him about what had happened and to attempt to repair some of the damage that had been caused, to try and save their relationship. The only problem thus far, was that Mike had refused to speak to her. He wouldn't answer any of her calls, reply to any of her messages, and he would not open his door to her.

'It'll work,' Lucy replied, half-convincingly. 'He thinks he's meeting you, right? He likes you.' She spoke with an unassured tone, as if trying to convince herself just as much as she was Krysta.

'He is going to know that this is most likely about you... He's not stupid.' Part of Krysta would be surprised if Mike showed up at all. *Why else would I ask him to meet me?*

'No, he'll know. But I'm hoping he'll come anyway, Krys. I need him to come anyway.' She continued to pace, rubbing her knuckles nervously.

'I've never seen you like this, you know. I've seen you during breakups. I mean, usually, if you haven't knocked the guy out, you're out drinking for a night and moved on by the next morning.' Krysta was sat on a bench watching Lucy, trying to support her, but there was one thing that repeatedly plagued her mind. *I still don't understand why you kept it from me. I get keeping it from the bureau... but me?*

'I've never loved anyone before, Krys. Argh!' Lucy turned to Krysta with her fists clenched. 'This is a million times harder than any breakup. I don't hate him. When I think of Mike, of what we had... it was, good. We had a few fights, but...' she sighed, 'all I am left with is good memories... and it is killing me. I hate that my mouth wants to smile every time I think of him. I just... I can't just leave it.' Lucy looked at Krysta, her eyes glossed with unburst tears, resisting letting too much emotion show. It was clear that Mike meant more to her than Krysta had ever realised, a fact that saddened Krysta somewhat. With the Avunaye, Markovic, Adam and everything else in between, at some point, some stage, she had dropped the ball on being there for her best friend. 'Don't do that –'

'What?' Krysta replied innocently.

'I know you. You're taking on my issues as your own.' Lucy frowned briefly, a finger-shaking expression to dissuade Krysta from feeling bad. 'I know that I didn't tell you... that you pieced it together yourself and that you must think –'

'I don't,' Krysta quickly interrupted. 'I know you would have told me sooner or later.'

'I just... I liked the secrecy, I will admit. But I also didn't want to tell you until I was sure he was in the same place that I was... you know?' Krysta nodded in reply, drawing a small smile from Lucy's lips. 'Anyway, what time did you say to meet?' Lucy asked, even though she already knew the answer as they had gone over it ten times already.

It was a secluded and somewhat idyllic spot that they had chosen to meet at. Within Central Park, tucked away just off of the 79th Street Transverse was the Shakespeare Garden. Winding flagstone paths weaved in and out of picture-esc landscaped fractions, each harnessing different greenery and coloured flowers resembling that of the English countryside. A myriad of red, orange, pink, purple and yellow tulips at the tail end of their season provided an enchanted glow amongst the green backdrop of trees and shrubs. Rustic wooden fences lined the boundaries of the mini-garden extracts and Krysta sat perched upon a wooden bench situated at a fork in the path. 'I should probably hide, right?' Lucy asked with a slight grimace.

'I dunno... an ambush might go sideways?' Krysta

replied, concerned that this meeting might end up being even more disastrous than she had initially anticipated.

'If he walks up that path and sees me, he'll just bolt in the opposite direction like a...' Lucy continued to ramble frustratedly for a moment in Spanish. 'I won't jump out of a bush or anything, I'll just wait around the corner.' She had made up her mind and proceeded to head up the path a little until she was out of sight, leaving Krysta sat waiting on her own. Pushing her golden hair back behind her ears, Krysta sat patiently enjoying the gentle contrast of the combined scenery around her, the warmth of the sun and the coolness of the breeze. She understood Lucy's requirement for making amends, or closure, if that was how this was to play out. She couldn't help but relate her own personal struggles to those of her friend's.

Krysta had begun to daydream of Adam when she heard Mike approaching. He looked well, dressed in ripped blue jeans, a black short-sleeved t-shirt and grey sneakers. He had tided his beard and had had a haircut since Krysta had last seen him, and his cheeks were full of colour. He just about managed a smile as his eyes locked on her, a fact that made Krysta even more nervous.

He looks good... that's annoying, she thought as she rose from her seat to greet him.

'I have to admit, Krys, I did not expect to find you here alone.' Mike wasted no time with pleasantries as he reached Krysta. 'So, what is this about?' He took a seat on the bench, leaning back into it and stretching out his legs. 'She waiting in the bushes or something? Ready to pounce? Cus, I could tell you about a time –' He smiled wickedly.

'No. No, no,' Krysta desperately interrupted him, not wanting to hear of his cringe-worthy sex-capades. 'Just wanted to check in with you. See how you're doing...' She slowly lowered herself onto the bench, taking a seat as far away from him as the bench allowed.

'Well, as you can see, I'm doing fine. Be even better

once I'm cleared to come back to work.'

'Mike... you were using, I don't think –' Krysta began to say, but he quickly stopped her.

'I would hardly call it using, Krys. I take them every now and then, they've helped me get back on my feet quicker than any prescribed meds could ever do.' He appeared happy and assured by what he was saying, much to Krysta's disbelief.

I can't believe you're still taking them... 'You're still on them?' she said aloud, her eyes questioning his judgement.

'I can't believe you're that stupid!' Lucy announced herself as she walked around the bend into view. Mike's face dropped and his initial reaction was to glare at Krysta for her participation. He then stood up. Krysta half expected him to turn and walk away from Lucy, to refuse to deal with the situation at hand, yet, he stayed put, standing his ground he merely crossed his arms in a manner that emphasised his large biceps.

'I did wonder when you'd show your face. Just checking up on me, ey Krys?' He looked at Krysta again briefly conveying his disappointment.

'What? You honestly thought she'd just want to meet you to see how you were? I would say even you're not that stupid, yet...' Lucy continued to say something in Spanish that Krysta interpreted as derogatory, based on Lucy's mannerisms.

'I didn't know, that's why I showed. Who knows, maybe Krys figured that now we're both single...' Mike chuckled as if the insinuation was both funny and well timed.

'Hey! Don't bring me into this. You two need to talk, that's why I agreed to this. To get you both together.' Krysta was angered by Mike's obvious lack of respect for the situation. He had always been a joker, but he was usually more careful and considerate with his jokes. 'Besides, I'm not...' Krysta began to say, but as the words left her lips, she realised that she was unsure on what she wanted to state. Was it that she didn't see him in that way? Because she didn't. Or was it that she wasn't truly single; she had Adam. Or at least she hoped that she did.

'Not what, Krys? Please tell me you're not still holding out hope for that freak that played you?' Mike didn't hold back, separating his arms he took up a more intimidating stance, provoking Lucy to come to Krysta's defence.

'Back off, Mike. I had hoped to talk to you, to work things out. But you're still fucking taking those drugs.' Lucy was no longer displaying any nerves. She now looked ready to fight, which worried Krysta.

'Like I said before, they help. What is your problem?!'

'You don't see it, do you? Those pills are bad news. It was your dealer that ended up dead, wasn't it? You have no idea what you're doing.' Lucy's tone fluctuated between that of aggression and concern.

'They've become harder to get hold of, yeah... If it weren't for Serena –' Mike began to say, but then Lucy's dumbfounded expression stopped him from continuing.

'What the fuck does she have to do with it?' It was clear that Lucy's temper was flaring.

'Look, Luce.' Mike opened his palms in a plea for patience or mercy. 'I was at the club and she just turned up. Shit went sideways and then D saw me. She questioned him about the pills, but then she told D that I was a fed and –'

'I don't... I don't wanna know anymore.' Lucy waved her hand in defeat as her face conveyed a combination of fury and sorrow. 'Everything that bitch touches ends up in flames... and here you are almost defending her, after what –' Lucy covered her mouth with her hand and closed her eyes as she fought against her own emotions. Krysta moved to her friend to comfort her, but as she touched Lucy's shoulder, Lucy shrugged her off.

'Luce –' Mike moved towards them as if to offer some

form of comfort. His action surprised Krysta, but she felt that it was ill-timed.

'Mike, I think you should just go,' Krysta said, stopping him in his tracks. He looked at Lucy momentarily and then his and Krysta's eyes met. The suggested compassion he held moments before had vanished and he was back to looking as if he hadn't a care in the world. Shrugging his shoulders, he then turned and walked away, disappearing into the green beyond the bend.

Lucy stood strong for half a minute or so once Mike had left their sight, but then her foundations buckled and she fell to her knees. A sudden wave of pain, regret and sorrow appeared to crash against her and Lucy's eyes began to stream with tears. Krysta took to her knees and wrapped her arms around her friend, allowing Lucy to rest her forehead on her shoulder and sob into her chest. Krysta could almost feel the emotional fractures within her friend widen and swell, and she couldn't help but feel a pit of passionless despair open up within herself. Feelings of sympathy and anger clouded Krysta's senses as she tried to comfort Lucy, yet, she felt a rageful urge to chase after Mike. The meeting had not gone to plan, but part of Krysta hoped that the clash would at least make Lucy's chances of moving on a little easier.

'I... can't do it anymore...' Lucy struggled to say.

'It's okay, hon, I'm here. Anything you need...' *Let him go, Luce.*

'It's not just Mike, Krys, I can't do it anymore.'

'What do you mean, hon? Do what?' Krysta was slightly confused.

'I don't want anything to do with the case anymore. Everything they touch... everything about the Avunaye... about Serena... they just simply destroy lives.' Lucy pulled away from Krysta and attempted to compose herself, wiping the tears from her eyes and cheeks.

'I know it's rough...' Krysta was conflicted. Part of her

wanted to tell Lucy that it was okay, that she can step away and it will be fine. However, Adam was one of the Avunaye. He was good, and part of Krysta wanted Lucy to see that he was worth their time. She needed her friend to see the good in him, if for nothing else than to prove to herself that she was not alone in thinking that he was worth all this pain. 'Give it time –'

'No, Krys! That's the problem. *They* have all the time, *they* never fucking die! And here we are wasting our fleeting lives on them.' Lucy took a deep breath before looking Krysta in the eye. 'I hate them,' she said through gritted teeth and a fury filled her eyes like nothing Krysta had ever seen. 'I'm done.'

Ensuring Lucy made it home safely, Krysta couldn't quite bring herself to head back to her own apartment just yet. Instead, she took to the street. Intending on wearing out the small heels of her shoes, she walked without a destination in mind. With no heading, she wandered the sidewalks with a single purpose; she was searching, scouring the faces of every single person she passed. She knew that the odds were stacked against her, in fact, in a borough that on a good day housed over one-and-a-half million people, she would require a miracle. Yet, as far as Krysta was concerned, a miracle was not such a strange concept, and the odds of one happening, with the experiences she had had over the past year in mind, were far higher than she would have previously expected. So, she scanned the crowds and glanced at passers-by. Surreptitiously peeping into parked or moving vehicles, she was intent that she would inspect every soul that crossed her path. With hope in her heart, it wasn't a fruitless task she had undertaken; for with each check that resulted in failure, she considered it one less person that he was not, and that eventually, it would simply *have* to be him.

13
Brandt

He had endured much within his lifetime, from the hatred of those that had birthed him, to the fear and distrust of his siblings. He had suffered unimaginable torment at the hands of mortals that could not comprehend his purpose, being hunted and tortured upon capture, more times than he'd care to admit. Yet, nothing had blemished his sense of self-worth as the last year had, having been treated no better than a dog in order to protect an inconsiderable being on his mother's orders. If the first seven or so months had been bad, planning an attack that was destined to fail, the most recent four had been intolerable: for having complete freedom, yet still being on a leash infuriated him. He found himself being consistently dragged back each and every time they required him to watch over the whelp. He was jaded, which is why it came as little surprise to him when he eventually slipped up. Truth be told, if not for the impending chastisement from Evelina, he would not even care to rectify his error. But, once again, like a dutiful dog chasing after its master, Brandt had begun the hunt.

Brandt had checked on Markovic, and the Serbian had been in his Chicago hotel room roughly four hours before Brandt had realised he had slipped away. With that window of time, plus the time it had taken Brandt to decide whether he could be bothered to chase him down, meant that Markovic had at least half a day on him. He would have avoided the airports and travelled by car, which by Brandt's calculations meant that he was most likely back in Manhattan by now; exactly where they did not want him to be.

Brandt had not long set off in pursuit when he received a curious phone call from Tobias. He had requested that Brandt meet him in Winchester, Virginia, to aid him with a problem. The detour would only add a few hours to Brandt's journey, and Tobias had promised to then assist in the tracking of Markovic, so Brandt begrudgingly agreed to help. It was a warm day and the rusted pickup truck that Brandt had stolen had more dysfunctional mod-cons than ones that actually worked. The engine screamed as he pushed it harder and harder along the open roads, managing to get him across a few states, but its unreliability climaxed a couple miles out from his destination. Cursing the vehicle, he took his frustration out on it, flipping it and sending it crashing against a tree on the roadside, before stomping off towards the city.

He entered Winchester along one of its main roads, passing its medical centre; ambulance sirens filled the surroundings. It was May, and the city was celebrating its Shenandoah Apple Blossom Festival, so the streets were brimming with people. Moving onward at a steady pace, he pushed his way through the masses, negotiating many red-brick pathways, passing the city's quaint civil-war-esc styled yellow and red-brick buildings. Everywhere he looked, the green, pink and white decorations lined the streets, covered walls, and hung from lamp posts, creating an intoxicating carnival-like atmosphere. It was typical of his brother to summon him here on such an occasion. The crowds of people meant that an air of discretion would have to be maintained, Brandt couldn't afford too much of a delay in his chase of Markovic. Tobias had said to meet at the parade, but every street appeared to be filled with people celebrating, dancing and drinking; each one appeared the same to Brandt. Losing patience, he reached out with his bear paw of a hand and grabbed the first person he touched.

'Where's the parade?' he asked as politely as his deep, intimidating voice would allow, but all he received in response was a look of terror.

'Brother, you can let him go.' Tobias joined him at the roadside. Brandt released the child from his clutches and they tore off, disappearing back into the masses. 'We must work on your social skills, brother. "Where's the parade?"' he mocked Brandt with an attempted impression. 'You sound like that masked caped crusader. I'm Brandt-man,' Tobias grinned as he teased. 'Save the big scary voice for Markovic and his friends...' He wore a grey, long sleeved, v-neck t-shirt and jeans, with a pair of muddy brown hikers boots. 'Well, this is embarrassing. We look like we co-ordinated our attire, brother.' He laughed as he pointed out the similarities in their clothing. 'Make sure you keep that brown jacket on, else we'll look like little and large, you great lump.'

Brandt could care less about what they looked like, he wanted to know what the hell he was doing here. 'Okay, brother, straight to it... You recall the fun we had interfering with the rival tribes in this region all those centuries ago?' Tobias asked, but in response Brandt simply crossed his arms in a display of impatience. 'What is the point in living forever if you never reminisce?' Tobias continued to make light of the situation. 'Fine, have it your way. Kenan is here, in Winchester. He's been tearing through the contestants for this year's Queen of the blossom parade. I assume you noticed all the ambulances rushing about on your way through? Our brothers handy work.' Kenan was, and always had been, almost as much of a blight on the Avunaye as Tobias; more so in some ways. If it wasn't for his amicable alter-ego, they would have been forced to end him before now. 'Animal attacks, that's the story that I've fed the locals.

I swear, if he wasn't family –'

'You waste too much time cleaning up after him,' Brandt grunted. They both knew that they had no time to waste so they began walking down the streets, scanning the crowds as the decorated floats pass by.

Kenan had been a nuisance throughout his entire existence. The darker half of one of their kin, he was, by all means, an accident. Older than Tobias by roughly half a century, Kenan was initiated by mistake. Unbeknown to the Avunaye, a woman that they had chosen to join them was pregnant at the time of the ritual. A pair of twins resided in her womb, one alive and one a would-be stillborn. The initiation resulted in the twins being gifted with immortality, however, the two foetuses merged in the process. The body grew until maturity, but was inhabited by both consciousnesses; one brimming with life, and the other, filled with darkness. Kenan was the darker half, and he had made his presence known throughout human history whenever he had clawed his way to the surface. The origin of many tales of mythical creatures, he was the first monstrum. The undead half of his twin, Kenan thirsted for life's essence, for blood, and he took immense passion from extinguishing the light from others.

'I love my brother. It's not his fault that he has a dark side that refuses to listen to reason. I do recall a time when you encouraged the monster to torment the western continent. They even make movies these days about his blood-lust.' Tobias, too, had on occasion, goaded Kenan into causing chaos and instilling fear, but this time was different. If for no other reason, now was not the time for stories of monsters to be spreading across the country.

'Let's get this over with!' Brandt exclaimed as they continued to search the crowd. He had endured enough of Tobias' ramblings and was growing incredibly impatient. 'Where the fuck is he?!'

'You know Kenan loves a game of hide and seek...'

Tobias joked. However, his humour was lost on Brandt, whom could feel his body becoming more and more restless and agitated. 'If I know our brother, he'll be eyeing up the Queen of the festival, so keep an eye out for the float with all the pretty young girls wearing tiaras.' Brandt stopped and watched the floats as they passed by; a series of colourful creations designed to look like orchards, apples, castles and fairy-tale lands. Soon the floats stopped passing and marching bands, followed by groups of people, began to walk the parade. Brandt overheard many onlookers questioning where the coronation float had gotten to this year.

For fucks sake... 'Tobias! Where do these floats hale from?' Brandt could imagine that his sadistic kin had probably headed straight for the source. Tobias looked at him, exhibiting a grimace as the prospect of overlooking the idea entered his mind. He then hurriedly headed in the opposite direction to the parade with Brandt in tow.

Tobias was smaller and quicker, and so he had arrived at the scene first; it was the high school. Entering the grounds from off the road, Brandt headed across the football pitch. There was already an ambulance here, with several people rushing about.

'It was an animal attack,' they kept saying. 'That guy from animal control just ran up into the school.' Brandt knew it had to have been Tobias. The school buildings resided on a hill. A huge set of stone steps led up from the football field to the entrance. The school's façade was designed like an ancient Roman temple, with huge white columns spread out across the front, and above the entrance, atop the columns that rose up before the doors, a pediment, housing a rose window. Brandt knew which direction to head in, he just had to follow the blood. Consistent splatters and smears painted the floors and walls of the hallways leading Brandt through the school.

As he reached the door to the indoor gymnasium, he

found there was a little resistance when he tried to open it due to the body of a young girl that was slumped against the other side. She, like the four others he could see from the entrance, were wearing white gowns, each stained red. Brandt looked down on them all as he passed them, their throats had been ripped open, their gowns torn. The scene looked as if a pack of rabid wolves had managed to find their way in. Tobias, who was currently in the centre of the poorly lit room, was talking to a girl. Her gown was different to the others. Brandt surmised that she must have been the elected queen. Kenan had clearly saved her for last, forcing her to watch as he devoured the others. Once Tobias had finished talking, the girl stood up and ran, sprinting past Brandt as if he wasn't even there.

'What a fucking mess...' Brandt was angry, he didn't have time to be cleaning up after his brother. 'Where is he?!' Brandt didn't need an answer from Tobias, however, as after he asked the question, there was a light-hearted chuckle sounding from one of the darkened corners of the gym. 'Fun's over, Kenan.' Brandt clenched his fists; heat emanated from his hands and his eyes adjusted, allowing him to see his troublesome sibling despite the cloak of darkness. Kenan sat squatting in the dark, his arms dangling by his sides, his claw-fingered hands resting on the floor. He was wearing a white shirt that was spotted with blood down the front and around the collar. His skin was as pale as snow, which only accentuated the blood red colour of his eyes. Deep red veins ran close to the surface of his skin, spreading out from his eyes, running down his cheeks and disappearing up under his hair. His bottom jaw hung low, as if detached, and his animalistic teeth protruded from his upper gum. Thick coagulated blood slowly dribbled from his chin. He was, as ever, a monster.

'Has our brother not told you, the fun is just beginning.' Kenan's voice was deep and gravelled; the tone resembling one of someone with a sore throat. Each syllable sounded as if it scratched at his vocal cords, causing him discomfort. Brandt looked to Tobias for an explanation, only for him to simply shrug in response.

'Time for you to rest once more, Kenan.' Tobias stepped towards him. He had always been the best at calming Kenan: his ability of compulsion meant that he could bring their siblings alter-ego forth, silencing the beast, at least temporarily.

'You can force me back into my cage, Tobias, but it won't stop the chaos that's to come.' Kenan lunged from his hiding place, bounding across the floor like a four-legged beast, throwing himself at Brandt, teeth bared. He lashed out, clawing and attempting to sink his fanged teeth into him. Brandt grasped his arm and throat, attempting to stave off the animalistic onslaught.

'Night, night, you ugly bastard!' Brandt mocked. Kenan collapsed, falling to the floor as Tobias reached him. Brandt gave the limp body a swift kick and smiled, as it meant that they could now move on and leave this place.

The journey to Manhattan did nothing to ease Brandt's frustration. They had stuffed Kenan into the trunk of Tobias' car and set off at speed. He needed to track down Markovic as soon as possible. They had had to stop once already, so that Tobias could check that Kenan was still dormant, but once was one time too many.

'Relax, Brandt, this city is filled with Markovic's thugs.' Tobias had promised to help, and was listening in on the thoughts of everyone they passed as they drove through Hell's Kitchen. 'Ha! This city truly is fucked up, once you peel back a layer or two –' Brandt gave him a look to convey the requirement for urgency. 'Plenty of chatter... In fact, I believe you'll find the bastard held up in East Harlem, some abandoned production studio... Building's on Lexington. Happy?' Tobias smiled. 'I'll drop you off, but I'm done being your bloody sat-nav. I need to take Kenan back to the house and ensure his better half is back in the driving seat.' Brandt didn't care what Tobias' intentions were, as long as the information was correct. Soon he'd have Markovic back under control and he could stop chasing after him like a mangy mutt.

Tobias dropped him off at the location, leaving Brandt to finish the hunt by himself. It was now twilight and Brandt was unimpressed by the fact that the day was almost spent. He continually thought to himself that Markovic best still be here as he marched into the building, fuelled with intent, breaking down the numerous locked doors that resided in his path. He headed down a corridor and into a large open space. The floor was carpeted in a cheap thin grey that provided no comfort. The walls were white and to Brandt's left and right, there were pillars that rose up from the floor to support the ceiling. The room held no windows to the outside world and so, if not for the lighting built into the panelled ceiling, it would have been in complete darkness. He looked around and smiled, for Markovic was calmly sat in the centre of the room, bold as brass.

'Markovic, you fucking pain in the ass.' Brandt stepped further into the area. Part of him was glad that the bastard wasn't hiding, but he had also wanted to drag him out of some nook, kicking and screaming. Yet, acknowledging Brandt's presence, Markovic simply stood up from his seat and smirked.

'You took your time.' Markovic was confident. He was wearing a fine, black, three-piece suit with a black shirt and purple tie. He proceeded to take off his jacket, placing it over the back of his chair, and then he rolled up his sleeves.

'It was a waste of my time...' Brandt growled with gritted teeth. He watched as Markovic revealed and put on a pair of knuckle dusters. Brandt stroked his chin and smiled. *Does he truly want to fight?* The idea amused yet excited him. He took off his own jacket and then his t-shirt, revealing his tattooed torso. He rolled his shoulders and cracked his knuckles. 'You have no idea how long I've been waiting to do this...' Brandt grimaced with anticipation, he only hoped that the fight wasn't too fleeting; he had built up so much tension of late and this would provide an adequate release. As he moved to approach Markovic there was movement to his left and right. Half a dozen men entered from doorways either side of him, each armed with batons, baseball bats or crowbars.

'The entire building is sound proofed, in case you wondered why you didn't hear them before.' Markovic stepped back and gestured for the men to proceed. Brandt's blood began to boil, his scars aglow, and he smiled at Markovic. He wasn't at all surprised by the onslaught, Markovic would have to have been crazy to take him on solo. The men attacked, ambushing Brandt from all directions. As he snapped the neck of one and sent another hurtling through the air, he was hit a dozen times by their weapons. He took the blows, enjoying the pain, allowing it to feed his anger as he dispatched of his attackers one by one. He laughed as the few cuts he sustained healed within moments.

'Anymore? Or perhaps you wish to get your own hands bloody?' Brandt mocked the mob boss. He cracked his neck and grinned.

After dealing with a second group that had made their advance, Brandt felt like he had properly loosened up, warming up nicely for the main event. Showing his content with the situation, he picked up some of the bodies and tossed them aside, moving them out of the way and clearing a path for Markovic to come and face him. 'Do I get to beat you senseless yet?' Brandt goaded Markovic, hoping that he was done playing games. However, his opponent merely smiled again.

A third, and then a fourth wave of attackers descended on Brandt. These groups provided more of a challenge than the previous two, each of them carrying bladed weapons, increasing their threat. One of the assailants carried a short sword, which amused Brandt. As the attacker attempted to thrust the sword into him, Brandt snapped his palms together and caught the fuller of the blade. He held it there for a few moments, watching and laughing at the man struggle in an attempt to overpower him. Brandt then pulled his hands back towards himself, angling the blade to his side, drawing in his attacker that refused to let go of the weapon. Allowing the edge of the steel to bite into his hand, Brandt grasped the blade with one hand and used his other to grab his sword-wielding enemy by his clothing. In one swift movement, Brandt disarmed the man, tossed the sword in the air and caught it by the grip, before thrusting it upwards through the base of the man's chin, through his head and up into the ceiling. He allowed the body to dangle there for a moment and peered around it, giving Markovic a disdainful glance, before wrenching the body by its legs and tossing it to one side like a mere dummy. *Are you done?* Brandt thought, growing bored of the appetisers.

'Twenty-six point seven *million* dollars.' Markovic looked at Brandt as if the figure would mean something to him. 'That is how much you've cost me, leading me to believe that in the end, I would become one of you.' There was an anger to his tone, despite his calm appearance. A woman entered from the left; she was wearing what looked like motorcycle gear. She had blonde hair, with a black streak, and a thin scar that ran across her cheek. 'Brandt, meet Sinead.' Markovic introduced her. 'She's here to collect my twenty-six million pounds of flesh.'

'Her?' Brandt laughed, intending to goad the woman. 'Didn't she fail to kill that police officer? Punching a little over your weight...' Brandt began to whistle ebulliently; he was really starting to enjoy himself. As he bent forward, grabbing hold of another body to throw it out of the way, there was a loud bang, and then a searing pain in his right arm. He was surprised to find the tip of a harpoon protruding from his huge upper arm.

'I've been told they use these to hunt whales,' Markovic scoffed, but Brandt noticed that the woman, Sinead, had vanished from sight. He tensed his arm, the heat in his veins building, intending to melt the harpoon that resided there, but as he did, there was another loud bang, and a second harpoon pierced his left side.

'ARGH!!' he shouted angrily; he was all of sudden tired of this bullshit. Several men rushed out from each direction carrying heavy looking iron chains. They attached them to several points on the ground and then moved towards Brandt. *I am not some animal you can just chain down!* He grimaced as he pulled the first harpoon from his arm and launched it at some of the men like a spear, skewering one of them. However, as he went to fight off a couple of them to his left, he was hit again on his right, and this time the harpoon sank deeply into his thigh causing him to drop to one knee. Again, he howled in agony as he fought them off, but that was when *she* struck. Sinead came from behind and stabbed him with a large blade between his shoulders. She then quickly stabbed him with a second, just above his hip. 'ARGH!!!' he bellowed. Brandt tried to remove the blade from his back, but as he did, it gave the others the opportunity to attach the chains to his arms and then Sinead lashed one around his neck. The chains were instantly pulled taut and he could barely move. He just managed to grab one of the men that had chained him as he attempted to retreat; Brandt grasped his throat at arms-length and gritted his teeth as he forced all the heat from his body into his palm, practically vaporising the man's neck. Brandt laughed maliciously as the man's face set on fire and his body fell to the ground.

As Brandt knelt, harpooned and chained like a beast, Markovic and Sinead simply stood there, staring at him, exhibiting a confidence unbecoming of them. Three more men then entered the room: one was uniformed, a police officer; the second wore plain clothes, but the badge on his belt was clearly visible. The third, Brandt recognised. 'Kryln!' he guffawed. 'Come to get a lick in while I'm chained like a dog?!' He taunted the man. The officer, a sly weasel of a man, Brandt could swear he'd seen before, but Kryln Cardoza, he was a man worth fighting. The huge bald man had a sickening smirk on his face that Brandt couldn't wait to rid him of. Cardoza shook Markovic's hand and then turned to face Brandt; he cracked his jaw, causing the cobra tattoo on his cheek to slither from side to side. 'HA!' Brandt began to laugh as he looked at the five of them. He continued to chuckle for a moment, before beginning to whistle his favourite tune.

'Can we just shut him the fuck up?!' the officer asked nervously, 'Cannon, just end him!'

'Yeah, Cannon, come here and end me...' Brandt continued to whistle, all the while the temperature at his core rose higher. The metal of the blades in his back and the harpoons began to liquify and they fell from his body, causing his audience to panic. His fire filled eyes shone brightly and his scars looked as if they were about to erupt. The chains began to buckle and weaken. He'd soon be free. 'We own you...' Brandt pointed at his audience, holding his aim on each of them just long enough to hear their heart skip a beat. 'We fucking own you!'

Cardoza walked towards him, his fists clenched, the veins in his forearms and on his neck pulsing. As Brandt broke free from the last of his restraints, Kryln clocked him across his jaw. It had taken a lot of his remaining strength to break free, which would make this fight almost fair. The two giants exchanged blows again and again. For a moment, Cardoza had the upper hand, hitting Brandt hard on his open wounds, but Brandt managed to swipe his legs from under him and then as Cardoza hit the floor, Brandt lifted him up and threw him against the ceiling. As Cardoza fell, crashing back down to earth, Brandt was ready to finish him, when the officer shot him. Two bullets in the chest halted Brandt momentarily, causing him to stagger, but then his anger was directed towards the uniformed officer.

'Seif, what the fuck are you doing?' the other badge asked, but as Brandt charged, he too drew his firearm. Brandt only made it a few feet before dropping to his knees, his fists crashing onto the ground as they emptied their clips into his flesh. He could feel his body attempting to heal, but his wounds were too many. Kryln now got to his feet and grabbed Brandt by the hair before striking him hard in the head with his knee. Scoffing, as if he pitied Brandt, he then moved to stand beside Markovic.

'Do not pity me, mortal!' Brandt grunted, spitting up blood.

'For all your power, you *are* still human.' Markovic held a subtle smile. He walked up to Brandt. With one hand he held Brandt's chin and lifted his head up, before striking him across his face with the other, the brass knuckles breaking Brandt's skin. Brandt could feel his own blood entering his lungs and he began to cough, spitting blood in Markovic's direction. As Brandt knelt, sitting back on his heels, he just about managed a smile as blood dribbled from the corners of his mouth, antagonising them all once again.

'Whatcha smiling at, FREAK! You're gonna pay! You're all gonna pay!' the one they called Cannon shouted. Despite his current condition, Brandt could still sense their fear. He smirked and coughed some more.

'I… know… what awaits you…' he struggled to say as the blood gurgled in his throat, hoping to instil more fear. His lungs felt heavy and his breathing was extremely laboured. The discomfort was something he had not felt for a long time and he could sense that his death was not far off. Yet, despite the inevitable end that faced him, he could feel it deep inside of him. An unrelenting passion; one final act.

'And, what might that –' Markovic began to ask in a cocksure tone, but he couldn't get the words out. Brandt looked at them all with such hatred, such distaste as he knelt, struggling to stay upright. He swayed slightly and began to fall forward, but managed to stave off hitting the floor, planting his fists onto the hard ground. His slowly lifted his head, his eyes burning with a malefic fire. Each of them winced as they received his mark. Clawing at their throats and exchanging glances as what looked like an underlined number seven, followed by an apostrophe, was seared, branded onto the skin of their necks.

'Vengeance... seven... fold...' Brandt mustered before Markovic drew his own weapon and shot him three times between his eyes, and his body slumped to the floor.

14
Tisa and Bomani

More.

She smiled as she dropped the body to the ground and wiped the blood from her lips. Her venom was potent, fast acting. None of them stood a chance which is why she liked to switch between her animalistic epithets between kills. She had killed the first guard at the door, tearing his arms asunder with the strength of a silverback, before sinking her teeth into the neck of the next victim like a king cobra. The building was full of Markovic's vermin and she and her brother had taken it upon themselves to exterminate each and every one of them. Considering their task, she had dressed plainly, wearing a white scoop vest top, light blue jeans that cut off half way down her shins, and a pair of white lace-up sneakers. She had also tied her hair up and donned a pair of large hoop earrings.

'Sister, don't play with the vermin.' Bomani snapped the neck of another guard and then dusted off his hands.

'Just remember, brother, we need one alive to question.' She exhibited a smile, but conveyed a look of seriousness with her eyes. She knew all too well that it would be hard for either of them to resist simply slaying every last one of them.

'No promises.' Bomani grinned in response and then grasped one of the buildings supports. Inch by inch, the metal appeared to slither over his skin, sliding up his arm and under his t-shirt. It continued under his clothing and crept up his neck until his entire body was coated, hardened and metallic. Once complete, he took Tisa's hand; his heavy, alloy-enveloped flesh was cold to the touch. He kissed the back of her hand and then rushed off down the hallway to their right.

Tisa looked across the foyer that lay before her to a large stairway at the far end. The building was an industrialised office block of sorts, comprised of five floors. Its many rooms were used for multiple purposes; Tisa had seen it's like before. Predominately a make-shift barracks for Vladimir's soldiers, it was also used for the storage of narcotics and weapons, and a number of offices had been converted into cells to assist with his human trafficking and kidnapping enterprises. She could hear the commotion on the floors above as the fear-filled mortals scurried about; their presence here was now known, but it would only make the fight that much more intense. She bounced up and down and shook herself as she buzzed with excitement before charging towards the stairs.

Two men, armed with handguns, were rushing down towards her. She proceeded to run up the wall in an attempt to avoid their gunfire, and then lunged over them, landing on the steps behind. She swiftly kicked one and sent him hurtling down the steps head first. The other quickly turned and tried to shoot her, but she quickly disarmed him. Tisa laughed at him, goading him to attack. He thrust forward, grabbing her by the wrists, but this only made her laugh all the harder.

'You know, some of the most venomous animals on this Earth's poison glands are located just below the skin, making them deadly to the touch.' She smiled as she watched the thought be processed by the man. He slowly let go of her, staring at the palms of his hands. She watched on intently as he gasped, his eyes growing wider with apprehension, and a mere prod to his chest sent him tumbling backwards to meet his comrade. Tisa then continued on to the first floor, mowing down two more attackers, exhibiting a true incarnation of the animal nicknamed "Black Death". The power she exerted splintered bones and ruptured organs, smashing their mortal sacks of meat against the walls, forcing them through the boundaries into adjacent rooms. She raged onward, taking pleasure in each life she took.

Bomani ascended the floors on the opposite side of the building. Less swift than his twin sister, he used the elements around him to his advantage, hardening his skin, enabling him to take their gunfire in his stead as he took them on one by one. His flesh, deflecting a bombardment of ammunition, allowed him to steadily march along a hallway. The repetitive, endless fusillade only ceased as he came face-to-face with those attempting to resist his assault. Clenching an iron-forged fist, he bludgeoned one enemy across their face whilst quickly grasping a second by their throat. A third continued to empty his weapons magazine, carelessly firing bullets that ricocheted off of Bomani's body as he slowly squeezed his hand around the man's neck, and like a vice, crushed his airway and compressed his neck until it gave way under the pressure and was pulped. The onlooker, seeing the decapitation of his ally, attempted to turn and flee. Bomani took to one knee and picked up a broken shard of glass, debris from his attackers attempts to slow him down. He grasped it between his thumb and index finger as his hand slowly transformed to reflect the sharp, smooth, vitreous material. He chased after the man, and as he caught up to him, he thrust his razor-sharp glass-formed hand into his back, pushing through to his chest, penetrating his core and lifting him up off the floor before slamming his body down forcefully.

The twin's foray continued until but a few remained alive. On the uppermost floor of the building, three of them had barricaded themselves in a room. Tisa and Bomani both reached the room simultaneously, each leaving death and destruction in their wake. 'Ah! I love a good bloodbath!' Tisa rejoiced in her triumph as she stood by her brother's side, covered in the blood of her enemies. Bomani simply smiled, expressing he felt the same. The passion she had exerted into each kill, the power she held over these mortals, it exhilarated her. She pushed her herself up against her brother and licked the blood from his cheek as she grasped at his crotch. She expressed a wicked smile as she dove into his torn pants, however, she found herself disappointed as she began to caress his manhood. 'Metallic...' She began to laugh. 'I suppose, there will be time for that once we're finished here.' She tilted her head back and ran her tongue across her teeth. As it glossed over her incisors, her tongue tore down it's centre and the teeth grew larger, forming venom filled fangs. Her nails grew longer, becoming talons. A true therianthrope, she was primed to tear through the last of them.

Bomani also prepared for the final battle by reaching into his pocket; he often carried a number of little tokens or trinkets with him, each one formed from a different material. On this occasion, he rummaged until he found a diamond ring. He twiddled the ring between his thumb and finger until his skin came into contact with its stone and then, inch by inch, he transformed. It was exhilarating. As his skin gradually took on the complex composition of the gemstone, the feeling of permanence excited every molecule of his being. It was time to finish this.

He threw his weight into the door, forcing its hinges to crumble and the lock to shatter in the splintered frame. His action was met by an eruption of defensive shotgun blasts that obliterated the falling wooden door before him. Much of the pellet-like shot struck his impenetrable flesh, ricocheting and scattering in all directions. Bomani stood resolute before the open doorway, chuckling at their foolishness as they wasted their ammunition shooting at him, all the while ducking and dodging the return of their own gunfire. He became further amused by the fact that they were unaware that Tisa had slithered into the room unnoticed. He kept their focus as Tisa moved like a shadow amongst the room's furnishings. They required one to survive, for now at least, but the others were expendable. They each wielded a twelve-gauge shotgun and were wearing military-style clothing and equipment: camo-pants, stab vests with extra ammunition lashed across their torso's. However, one of them stood out from their peers. Barely visible, just above the neck line of her top, the mark of Cain resided. Bomani silently conveyed his observation to his twin, signalling for her to pounce.

Leaping into the fray, Tisa took the nearest man by surprise. She sank her fangs into his neck just above his collar, injecting her poison before he had the chance to react, whilst simultaneously lashing out at the second man with her talons, shredding through his flesh, opening up his throat and spraying blood everywhere. The poisoned man buckled and as the venom coursed quickly through his veins, fell to his knees. Torn between continuing to shoot at Bomani and defending herself against Tisa's sudden onslaught, the woman tossed her bulky shotgun to one side and drew two pistols, foolishly hoping to take on both of them at the same time. Bomani kicked a chair towards her and, as she moved to avoid the projectile, Tisa lunged forwards and slashed at both of her arms. As her flesh opened up and her life began to pour out of her, the woman dropped her weapons and threw herself backwards against the wall. She curled up submissively whilst grabbing at her wounds, surrendering herself to the inevitable. However, the inevitable would have to wait, for the twins needed answers. Tisa halted in her attack, retracted her claws and fangs and wiped the blood from her lips.

'Two. Two of you,' the woman mumbled as she

cowered on the floor, shaking her head. Tisa moved to her side and squatted. 'There's only two of you. How? Such, bullshit.'

'It does not matter. Both victory and defeat were out of your control. Unfortunately, you did not put up the kind of fight that would make the earth shake.' Tisa poked at the wounded mortal, taunting her.

'Please... don't kill me. Help me...' she pleaded as her blood ran freely from her arms, slipping through her fingers.

'You were already dead, my dear. From the moment you participated in the fall of Brandt, from the moment you received his mark...' Tisa pushed the woman's head back to reveal the brand.

'I... I didn't know...'

'You mortals never do. You are but fleeting moments in time, and now your moment is about to end.' The woman began to cry, however, she was very weak, so it was more of a pathetic whimper. 'We know that Markovic and Cardoza were there, but we wish to know who else was. Who else bares the mark?' The woman struggled to remain conscious, her hands slowly slipping away from her cuts as she lost the strength to hold them up.

'A name!' Bomani commanded, breaking his patient silence and slamming his fist into the nearby wall.

'There was a cop... and a – a detective...' The woman's head dropped as her light began to fade. She was about to die, to slip off into the void, but out of nowhere she found the strength to chuckle to herself. Tisa, perplexed, looked at her brother, wondering if he had noticed something she hadn't.

'You laugh in the face of death. Why?' Tisa wished to know what this insignificant being could find amusing at such a time as this. The woman coughed and then smiled, seemingly at nothing.

'If nothing else... we at least showed the world that you bastards...' She was spent. The second hand on her life's clock had struck its last.

'That we what?!' Bomani grabbed the woman's body and frustratedly shook her before dumping her back onto the ground.

'That we can be killed, brother. *That* is what she was trying to say.' It wasn't fear that her twin's expression conveyed as he looked down upon the woman's body, but more of aggravation, as if he was struggling to calculate a solution to their problem. 'More fool them,' Tisa said, smiling. Despite the knowledge that the Avunaye could be killed, the mortals did not know the whole story. The witnesses, the ones that had received the mark, their fate was already set. As for any others that may try to come after the Avunaye, they would find the task of extinguishing Tisa and her family more difficult than they could possibly fathom. It was not the first time that they would have to stare death in the face. Working behind the scenes had become more and more difficult as humanity had made advancements, but there were many ways to distract, or if necessary, destroy any and all evidence of their existence. 'I pity the rest of these branded fools. Evelina will know what action to take against Markovic and his men, but perhaps we should find this... detective, ourselves.' Tisa yearned for more action. This fight had been interesting, but she remained restless.

It was a little after nine o'clock and the evening was relatively warm, despite being overcast. Bomani had sensed the impending rainfall just before they had entered the building. Their target was of little significance, but he would serve a purpose as bait, drawing in the person whom they truly desired to meet. Three floors from the roof, his office window overlooked the street. He sat, typing away on his keyboard, unaware of the dangers that surrounded him. Tisa was fuelled by adrenaline; she enjoyed the hunt, but more than that, she lusted for the chase. She had exchanged her human form for that of a chocolate, shaggy-haired beast. She had soft white paws and a strip of white fur that ran from the tip of her snout down under her body to the base of her tail. She skulked quietly through the adjoining offices, stalking their prey, unseen, waiting patiently for the right moment.

Purposely knocking over a swivel chair, she made sure that she was out of sight when he emerged from his office to investigate the sound.

'Hello? Is anybody there?' he questioned the darkened empty offices that surrounded him.

Tisa could smell him; a hint of deodorant, masked by the scent of sweat and body odour from sitting, stewing in his own juices all day in his stuffy office. Yet, there was now something else that rode on the air ever so slightly, something she could play on and encourage. He went to re-enter his office, eager to dismiss the noise that he had come to investigate, when, with a sharp whip of her tail, Tisa knocked a coffee mug from a desk, allowing it to fall and smash on the floor.

'Hello?' he called out again, making an immediate about turn, heading towards the disturbance. 'John? If that's you... I'm tired of these bloody pranks – Okay?' There was now a distinct flutter in his breathing as uncertainty crept in. Tisa's heart warmed to the thought of his fear. As he reached the broken mug, he cautiously looked about the room before stooping to touch the debris, as if he didn't quite believe, or didn't want to believe, what was right before him and what it suggested; that he was not alone. 'Hey! C'mon, this is pathetic'. He was growing impatient and began to exhibit signs of anger. He was angry at both the person messing with him, but also with himself, and as the pungent scent of fear escaped his pores, Tisa knew it was now time.

Tisa growled in the darkness, capturing his attention before allowing herself to be seen. Entering the light, she stared at him, lip raised, teeth bared as the rumbling of her growl continued from deep within. He stood motionless for a moment, a bead of sweat slipping down his brow as he contemplated his options. She barked, forcing him to make a snap judgement and he chose to take flight. He rushed towards the elevator, pushing chairs from his path as he fled, but she required him to head elsewhere. Springing forwards, Tisa bounded through the office, leaping over desks and bark-howling at the man as he ran. She needed to cut him off so she threw herself into a desk and sent it crashing into its neighbour, cutting off his escape. Panicking, he grabbed a number of items off the nearest desk and hurled them at Tisa. A stapler hit her on the head, so in response, she let him know her contempt by baring all her teeth and barking violently at him until his fear had completely possessed him. He headed back from whence he came in a panic, rushing past his own office towards the stairwell. She knew his first instinct would be to run down the stairs so she needed to keep up with him. She chased after him ensuring she was on his heels as he reached the entrance to the stairwell; he attempted to shut her out but Tisa crashed through the door, tumbling onto the stairs, blocking the way down. She snapped at him, filled with a sense of glee as his parasitic fear fed on him some more. Altering his course, he headed for the roof.

Sauntering after him, Tisa remained close enough to encourage him to keep pushing onwards without forcing him to stumble or fall; the sooner he made it to the roof the better. Her plan was almost scuppered as he reached the door to the roof and found it locked. Pushing off with her large hind legs, she scurried up the last few steps and ploughed into him, knocking him back into the door and forcing it open.

'Oh god! Help! Help me!' he screamed as he just about managed to remain on his feet and ran out onto the rooftop. Briefly glancing behind him to check that she was still there, he clumsily lost his footing and fell.

Tisa walked out onto the roof and let out an almighty howl at the moon. She then shook excitedly, shedding the fur coat that covered her body. She sat on her back legs and stretched out, reaching for the stars. Her front legs transformed into arms, fingers extending from her once paw-like hands. The white streak of hair fell away and her breast laid bare. Her golden-brown skin shimmered in the moonlight and she opened her big brown eyes to look upon the terrified mortal before her.

'How? What –' the man began to say.

'How did you do that? What are you? Why are you doing this?' Tisa mocked the man as she climbed to her feet. 'Why is it always the same drab questions. It is so boring!' Her raised voice startled the man.

'I don't understand...' he quivered as he loosened the collar of his shirt. Tisa smirked; of course he did not understand, how could he? He was insignificant. Tisa half-heartedly smiled as she walked towards him.

'You are a means to an end.' She breathed in the mild night air and then stared him down, biting her lip, relishing the look in his eyes. He clambered to his feet and hurriedly looked about at his surroundings, no doubt hoping for a means to escape. Tisa continued to inch towards him and in response he backed away from her, growing ever closer to the roofs edge. Becoming bored of thc slow dance that they appeared to be performing, she charged and shoved him, throwing him from the roof and sending him falling to the street below. She listened to the thud of his body hitting the ground and waited in anticipation for the screams of the first person to find him.

Sat patiently, perched upon the edge of an adjacent building's rooftop, Tisa watched and listened as the evening's events played out below. Soon a crowd had gathered and the police had cordoned off the area. She watched as her brother joined the scene, spotting him as he moved through the crowd wearing a pair of sleek black boots, dark denim pants and a burnt orange, three button, long-sleeved shirt. *Here we go*, Tisa thought excitedly as the officer in charge of the scene finally called Bomani forward as a witness.

'You saw what happened here?' Bomani simply nodded in response to the officer's question. 'Head over to the detective, give your statement. Then, come back and wait here, we might need to speak to you again, so we'll require your contact details.' Bomani said nothing to the officer, it was the detective that intrigued him and his sister. He proceeded to walk across the street towards the detective, who was currently taking the opportunity to have a smoke in peace, away from the bustle of the crime scene.

'Detective?' Bomani queried as he approached the tired looking man. Dressed in a dark grey suit, with a dark red shirt, he flicked his cigarette butt to the ground as he turned to look at Bomani. As his investigative stare attempted to sum Bomani up, Bomani too studied the man before him. His beard looked to have been left to grow uncontrollably and the discolouration under his eyes showed evidence of sleep deprivation and stress. He was well built and could no doubt handle himself, whilst tiny scars on the back of his hands suggested either a history of poor firearm handling, or, more likely, a trigger-happy temperament. Bomani surmised that he would no doubt be easy to bring to anger.

'You the one that saw the victim fall?' The detective placed his hands on his hips, parting his jacket to reveal his badge and holstered weapon.

'I saw him.' Bomani paused for a moment and then looked up at the roof from where Tisa had thrown their victim. The detective also looked up, providing Bomani the opportunity to inspect his neck. 'He was pushed. There was a woman,' Bomani revealed, obtaining the detective's undivided attention.

'Pushed? You sure?' He looked at Bomani curiously

and then looked up again, this time revealing a mark that had been mostly concealed by his shirt collar.

'I am sorry, detective, I did not catch your name.'

'Detective Jack Cannon.' His expression displayed a sense of mistrust. Perhaps he was curious as to why Bomani wanted his name, or maybe he was playing out the scene in his head and did not quite believe Bomani's account.

'He was definitely pushed by a woman,' Bomani said passively as the detective continued to stare up at the roof. The detective half-heartedly listened to Bomani's description of the woman before palming him off onto another uniformed officer, who would take the full eye-witness statement; he then slipped back into a contemplative state and lit another cigarette.

Having received a signal from Bomani, confirming that this Jack Cannon was indeed their target, Tisa made her way down to the street. She found a pair of hole-riddled jeans and a dirty hooded-jacket in a box in the alley at the base of the building that would clothe her for now. Walking out into the street, bare-footed, she walked up to the detective, brushing past him and continuing up the street away from the commotion.

'Fucking, excuse you!' he grumbled after being knocked and almost losing his cigarette. He tutted as Tisa continued walking, but then she did something that she knew would catch his attention. She began to whistle a tune that, if this was indeed the detective that had assisted in putting Brandt down, he would undoubtedly recognise. Tisa continued to walk away as she whistled, but she could hear his footsteps as he began to follow her. Her heart beat with such joy as she heard him turn down the alley, continuing his pursuit. His pace began to hasten as he attempted to inconspicuously catch up with her, but it was not quite time to spring the trap. There was a door down the next alley, to the left. It had a dirty green ribbon stuck across it, decorated with four-leafed clovers, stretching from the top-right corner to the bottom left of the door; a decoration from a past celebration. Beyond the door was an empty store room that belonged to a restaurant that looked out onto the next block over. Tisa had rigged this door so that it could only be opened from the outside.

As she picked up the pace, she heard her pursuer follow suit and then remove his fire-arm from its holster. Tisa paused for a moment, looking up and down the alleyway as she opened the door, ensuring that he saw her enter. He hadn't called the chase in yet, such was his confidence. She could hardly wait, the suspense making it all the more thrilling. The room behind the door was in total darkness. There was a light, however, to turn it on he would have to come further into the room and step away from the door. Tisa waited in the darkness as she listened to him cock back the hammer on his handgun and then turn the handle on the door. Rays of light flooded into the room revealing a few boxes and the light switch that hung from the ceiling, but Tisa remained concealed for now. Then, as the detective stepped inside, he reached for the switch, allowing the door to close behind him. A look of surprise sprung to his face and he turned and hurriedly tried the door handle, only to find that the door could not be opened from this side. The trap was sprung.

The detective moved about the room, searching for her, looking for a means of escape that she might have used, but there was none. 'Alright, come out, whoever you are.' He held his gun up, turning, aiming in every direction. She closed her eyes as she listened to his heartbeat gallop. His fear was palpable, it flooded her senses. She would take such passion in this kill that she wanted to savour it. 'Where the fuck are you...?!'

Tisa made him jump as she stepped out from her hiding place, but she was not what he was expecting. She had assumed the form of a black tabby cat, and walked slowly over to the detective, brushing up against his leg whilst purring, subtly disarming him. 'Ha! A fucking cat!' he sounded, relieved that the animal was the only thing to be found. Holstering his weapon, he bent down and stroked her behind her ears and under her chin.

She played with her prey for a moment, rolling onto her back and allowing him to stroke her belly. Then she struck. The tip of her soft, fur covered tail harnessed a stinger that held a particular venom that, upon envenomation, will paralyse her victim. Whipping her tail, she stung the detective on the wrist, causing him to fall backwards away from her. He shook his hand to deal with the pain, but Tisa could tell from the look in his eyes and his erratic breathing, that he knew that something was wrong. He grasped at his wrist with his other hand and tried to shuffle to the door, finding his legs unusually heavy. Panicking, he attempted to pull his phone from his pocket, but failing that, he then tried to crawl to the door, but as he reached it, it opened, and stood in the opening was Bomani with a pleasing smile spread across his face.

The detective did not fully lose consciousness, but he was powerless, unable to act as the twins transported him. It was the early hours of the morning and the city was mostly asleep. Yet soon it would awaken, and they wanted their message to be heard, loud and clear. They propped him up against the fountain in the park. His tongue was no longer numb, but he was yet to regain the use of his arms and legs. 'You're them... Avun...' he muttered as his voice faded in and out.

'Avunaye, yes. Like our brother, Brandt. Do you recall him?' Tisa held his chin and turned his head to take a look at the mark. His breath was heavy; the venom had affected his respiratory system more than Tisa would have liked. She wanted answers from him. 'Jack... How many of you *people* did it take to take down our brother?'

'A lot... The bigger they are...'

'The harder they fall! Ha! Good. There will be plenty

more of you then.' Tisa's words appeared to confuse him. 'Why did you do it?' The detective smiled in response to her question.

'He deserved it... He killed...'

'He has killed so many people throughout time. Why was this personal to you? I can see it in your eyes... This was a crime of passion.'

'The girls he killed... He was a monster...'

'Girls?' Tisa tutted as she looked to Bomani, whom in response, merely shrugged at the accusation. She began to laugh as she realised that the detective had been misled into thinking that Brandt was his man. 'Brandt didn't kill any girls... Brother, he is all yours. Detective Jack Cannon here received the mark of Cain for nothing.' She couldn't help but chuckle as she stepped away from the detective.

'Mark of Cain?' Cannon questioned.

'You helped take down the son of Adam.' Bomani squatted before the man and tore open his shirt. 'You should be grateful.' Bomani then revealed a blade from his belt.

'Grateful?!' His adrenaline had spiked, shaking him out of his daze. Terrified and confused the detective grimaced as he tried to move.

'Grateful that it is I exacting punishment. For the others, they will receive his vengeance seven-fold.' Bomani took hold of the detective's chin and turned his head to one side, pressing his face against the coarse stone of the fountain. Cannon tried to struggle, to wriggle free, but Bomani held him sternly as he began to cut away the flesh from the detective's neck that held the mark. Cannon's screams, due to his lack of breath, were more of a wounded pup's whelp, the sound amusing Tisa as she urged her brother to take it slow. Bomani cut until he was able to lift the mark from the detective, blood flowing freely from the open wound. Cannon's eyes welled up, tears running down his cheeks as he acknowledged the fact that he was about to die. Grasping the stone of the fountain, Bomani absorbed its properties, converting his own flesh into hardened rock. He clenched his stone formed fist and punched the detective in the chest, feeling his sternum crack. Bomani proceeded to hit him again, harder this time, breaking through his flesh and bone. He wrapped his cold hard fingers around the detective's heart and pulled fiercely, tearing it from his body. Then, opening the lifeless hands of the body before him, Bomani placed the marked flesh in the left hand and the un-beating, blood-soaked heart in the right. 'The best of people, are those that come after.'

15
Luciana Rodriguez

'Very nice work, Rodriguez.' Kyle had a smile from ear to ear. If he was to appear any more pleased with Lucy's work, his cheeks would likely tear under the stress. He lingered, perhaps hoping for a fist-bump, a high-five, or some other form of acknowledgement, however, Lucy was merely wanting to be left in peace to finish off the paperwork for the case and move on. 'I mean, we knew we had him for bribery and embezzlement, but somehow you...' he paused for a second, smiling again and shaking his head in disbelief. 'Somehow you get him to own up to forgery and money-laundering as well.' Kyle might have shown surprise in her abilities, but this was what Lucy had always been adept at. Before the Avunaye, before Markovic, she was an outstanding agent, and without the distractions that the Markovic case had brought she had been able to get back to her best.

Solomon had assigned Lucy to a couple of different cases for the time being. Lucy knew that he had done it out of pity for her but she didn't care. In fact, she appreciated the reprieve from all of the madness and it had helped her to focus on her work, which in turn helped to distract her from her personal issues. Kyle was still hovering by her desk like an irritating fly waiting for something, anything, that she could give him by way of recognition. It seemed he had no intention of leaving until he got it.

'Yeah, well, job done. Am I right?' She said the words as she slowly tore herself away from her computer screen, but as soon as the sentence was complete, she sprang back to paying him no mind. Thankfully, and oddly satisfyingly, Kyle then finally decided to leave her be. In truth, she was trying her best to avoid looking at his face. For when she looked at Kyle, she remembered how euphoric it had felt to punch him in it, but that only reminded her of Times Square, the Avunaye and the red-headed bitch that fuelled her temper of late. The thought of Serena balanced on Lucy's last nerve constantly as it always led to thoughts of Mike. She would think of how much it still pained her to not be with him, how she had been falling asleep each night with her phone resting on her chest in case he called or text, how she was here, waiting, and even though she still had doubts, she'd instinctively accept him back with open arms. She was broken at best, and in her worst moments, she found herself contemplating dark deeds. She was falling apart at the seams and there was but one person to blame. It was this fact, that she had someone to blame, a target to aim her anger and hatred towards, that helped her climb out of bed each morning and get done what she needed to. Serena. The Avunaye. She had found herself loathing them, for they had turned her world upside down.

Lucy sighed heavily and exasperatedly, throwing a hand down onto her desk in an act of discontent. She accidently knocked over the obscure looking desk-tidy that Claire had bought her, spilling her pens and other stationery over the corner of her desk and onto the floor. 'Argh!' she threw her head back and grunted at the realisation that she would need to clear the mess up.

'When they said that you were hard at work, this wasn't quite what I was expecting.' She knew the voice. He stood by the entrance, feet together; his shoes were polished so well that they caught the light and shined. He was wearing drab-coloured pants and an olive-drab coloured coat, holding his cap under his right arm and his left arm behind his back. Clean shaven, with short brown hair, he looked just as she remembered him, however, one thing was definitely different; the golden oak leaf that denoted his rank.

'Major, Jackson Torrent.' Lucy couldn't help but be impressed by her old friend. The last time she had seen him he had been a first lieutenant; major was a huge step up in such a short space of time.

'Hmm... Is that surprise, disbelief, or perhaps something else I'm reading on that face of yours, L?' He smiled.

'How does a gun toting, whiskey smuggling, backroom gambling den coordinator from Phili, make it from LT to Major in... two years?' Lucy teased him.

'It's been four years since you've seen this pretty face, and if you don't mind, can we keep the whiskey business on the d-l.'

'At ease, soldier,' Lucy quipped and they both chuckled light-heartedly.

'Have to behave myself around the general's daughter, you know that.'

Four years... Has it really been that long? Lucy had spent much of her childhood on the move, going from camp to camp, fort to fort, base to base. She and Jackson had met when she was twelve at Fort Lee. As the years passed, they had run into one another again and again, each time in a different location and a different stage in their lives. When Lucy was seventeen, her father had been stationed at Fort Leavenworth for a time and her and Jackson's friendship had been rekindled. If her father knew some of the things they had gotten up to over the year, it would be safe to say that Jackson would not be with the military anymore, possibly not even with the living. Their secrets bound them and had formed a formidable friendship. 'Not that I mind, but what are you doing here?' The army and the F.B.I had a long-standing respect for one another, with many ex-military personnel finding a new home within the bureau; Hale was one such example, however, majors didn't usually just turn up out of the blue.

'The general is currently in a meeting with deputy director Stanwell and... someone else from the D.O.J. You know me, I rarely listen to all the boring details.' He held his hands up in a sign of admittance. Lucy's heart jumped.

'The general is here? Now?' Her tone revealed her panicked state, to which Jackson could only laugh. 'Hey. Stop it!' Lucy ordered. His mockery was not helping. Lucy's father was a giant, and a perfectionist, and her life right now was far from perfect. It barely resembled that of someone with any level of control.

'C'mon, L. Lighten up. Honestly, I'm pretty sure he just wants to see where his daughter works.'

Bullshit. Lucy knew that her father's visit was more than a quick check on her. *Something is happening. All these years, he's never come to see me at work. He's got to be checking to see if the bureau is a useful tool or something like that...* 'Where're you based?' she quizzed frantically.

'Fort Hamilton.' She suspected he was lying. She had known him for far too long to not know his tells. 'Can't say it's the best, but anything beats Rock Island. You remember?' He laughed as he reminisced. Lucy half smiled in response, but she knew that something was off.

Proceeding to take Jackson to the canteen, the pair caught up over a coffee, sharing recent war stories. Jackson told her of his last tour in Afghanistan and Lucy mentioned their crusade against Markovic, leaving out all the more sensitive details. They laughed about past misdemeanours, including their famous skinny-dipping incident. Lucy found herself feeling relaxed; it was nice to reconnect with a friend that knew nothing of her current predicaments. 'Well fuck me, Paul Hale! In the flesh!' Jackson sounded as he noticed

Hale making himself a coffee. The announcement was probably a little louder than Jackson had intended, with a number of people turning their attention to him. He gingerly raised his hand to apologise and then they all went about their business. 'Tough crowd...' he jested as Lucy almost spat her drink out at him as she tried to hold back her laughter.

'Jackson,' Hale acknowledged as he walked over to them both. 'Long time.' Hale looked to Lucy for a split second, a big-brother glance, as he made sure she was okay.

'You two know each other?' Lucy was surprised. Even though they were both in the army at one stage or another, it had never really occurred to her that they might have met before.

'Enlisted at the same time, L. Me and Hale go *way* back.' Jackson smiled at Hale, but his hands told a different story as he played with his coffee cup.

'Well, that pretty much sums it up actually.' Hale shone no further light on the subject, which only made Lucy more curious. 'I had better get back to work. Good to see you, Luce.' Hale's exit drummed up more questions for Lucy.

'Okay... What the hell was that?' There was clearly some tension between the two of them, and knowing what both of them were like, Lucy was intrigued.

'Nothing, L. We're good.' Jackson's response was less than convincing.

'Aw, c'mon... Or I'll tell the general –' she teased him.

'No fair, L,' Jackson rubbed at his eyes. 'Look, all I'll say is, how much do you know about Hale?' His vagueness and slight concern interested Lucy.

'He's a great guy. Ex-army, good agent. Awesome tats.'

'So... nothing? Look, we enlisted together, but he... Hale advanced quicker than anyone would think possible. Special forces scooped him up and everything else is classified. I mean, we did one mission together about six years ago and to this day I am not sure what it was that we actually did.'

'Yeah right!' Lucy laughed momentarily, but she could tell that Jackson wasn't joking.

'Hale is, was, what the army would consider an appreciable asset. I, I still can't believe they let him go to be honest...' A look of worry crept into the corner of his eyes as he spoke. Lucy went to probe further, but she was interrupted by a deep resounding sound as her father cleared his throat, calling for attention. Lucy and Jackson both instinctively jumped up out of their seats to greet the general formally.

'Sir!' Jackson saluted and acknowledged his superior.

'General,' Lucy followed suit, almost saluting as she awaited her father's response.

'At ease.' Lucy felt a sense of relief wash over her as the general allowed her to relax. His presence, however, was still enough to keep her anxiety levels at a steadily high. He looked down at his daughter, but the warmth that a daughter would usually receive from her father's eyes was not present. It never had been. Their relationship had never been one of kisses and cuddles, instead, the general had spent most of their time together teaching Lucy war tactics and training her to take care of herself. Her childhood vacations had consisted of extreme survival exercises in foreign environments. Lucy had often felt an air of disappointment from him with regards to the fact that she hadn't ended up within the military herself.

Six-foot-tall, the man was well preserved for someone in his early sixties. He was well built, and healthy, emphasised by the colour in his cheeks and in his hair, which was not yet completely grey. He was a proud man, with darker skin than his daughter, a fact that he would often remind her of; "You'll always have to work a little harder" he'd say to her, "but it will be easier for you than it was for me at your age". He wore a similar outfit to Jackson, however, his was a dark shade of blue and clearly showed his station with an array of decorations. 'Was that Paul Hale I saw?' he asked, but Lucy knew it to be rhetorical. The general rarely missed anything. 'Hmm...'

'Jackson suggested that you'd be interested in a tour?' Lucy was eager to move on. The quicker the general moved on, the less likely he was to notice all the cracks in her life.

'A tour?' The general appeared to question Jackson with his tone, no doubt questioning as to why Jackson felt the need to talk about him behind his back. 'Perhaps you can introduce me to your colleague. Krysta, is it?' Lucy was surprised by the request. Of course, she had mentioned Krysta before, and the general had met her once, yet the fact that he had asked for her specifically had caught Lucy completely off guard.

'Follow me...' Lucy said slowly. She knew better than to dwell too much on what the general was thinking, and so she moved away from her seat and led Jackson and the general to Krysta's desk, however, she was not there. Deciding that Claire's lab was the next best bet, she quickly altered course, hoping that her father did not take note of the error.

'Hey Krys,' Lucy said as she laid eyes on her friend. Krysta was undoubtedly busy, working hard alongside Claire, but Lucy couldn't disappoint her father.

'Hey, hon,' Krysta barely lifted her gaze from her screen as she acknowledged Lucy. It was Claire who gave Krysta an awkward nudge as she laid eyes on Lucy's uniformed guests.

'General, you remember Special Agent Krysta Rose-Anderson, and this is Claire –'

'Oh, heh... Don't – don't let me get in the way,' Claire interrupted awkwardly, causing Lucy to frown.

Claire, now is not the time to be all... quirky... Claire fumbled momentarily, drawing looks of curiosity from everyone before she took her leave.

'General Rodriguez,' Krysta smiled, before giving Lucy a look of reassurance. She knew that Lucy would be nervous with her father being here, and now was especially bad timing, what with Lucy's current personal catastrophe. Uncharacteristically, the general stepped forward and offered Krysta his hand to shake.

'All is well, I hope,' he said mysteriously. Lucy was dumbfounded. The handshake he and Krysta exchanged exhibited more affection than he had shown his own daughter in some time.

'Chaos, actually.' Krysta admitted. 'I hate to be rude, but I have to get going...'

'Something wrong?' Lucy had been grateful for being left out of the main investigation, but she was now suddenly wondering what she might have missed.

'A detective was murdered. The scene is a mess and I have to confirm potential suspects before, well, before the C.I.A inevitably take over...' Krysta was trying to be discreet whilst giving Lucy a clue as to what was going on, but she was failing miserably.

'When did...' Lucy had wanted to steer clear of the Markovic case for the time being, but she had assumed that she would still be kept in the loop by her friends. It seemed clear to her that, had the general not have requested to see Krysta, she probably wouldn't have been informed of the new development.

'We're fully aware of the Markovic case. And of the Avunaye,' the general cut in. It was at that moment that everything seemed to become clear for Lucy. The reason as to why the general was really here. It created a sinking sensation within her. 'Please, don't let us keep you.' Krysta smiled once again and then headed out in the same direction Claire had previously, leaving Lucy alone with the general and Jackson once more. Lucy turned to the general to ask him what, or who, he would like to see next, her tone undoubtedly to carry a hint of sarcasm. However, he managed to put his thoughts into words quicker than her. 'Luciana, I'm afraid we will have to cut this short. I have some business to attend to.' Lucy wasn't sure if she was disappointed or relieved by his decision to leave. 'Call the base, if we have time whilst I am close by, perhaps we can have dinner.' The idea seemed like a consolation prize, but before Lucy could convey her feelings, the general was already making his way towards the exit.

'I know that look...' Jackson had been left behind to make whatever excuse he thought necessary for the general's lack of fatherly compassion.

'Jackson, don't worry about it.' Lucy's words cracked as they left her lips; she fought against the urge to sulk.

'Look, L, I probably shouldn't be saying this but –'

'Then don't say it, dumbass.' Lucy placed her hands on her head and expressed a dejected sigh.

'We've been assisting the C.I.A.' He looked at her, wide-eyed, waiting for a response.

'Hence you know about all the shit we've been going through...'

'Yeah. Yeah, I know. I know all about agent Ward as well. If he were my colleague, my partner... If he were one of my guys, I know what I would want to do.' Lucy chose not to respond. She was tired of revisiting the same subject again and again. On some level she knew Jackson could sense her disinterest, but despite it, he still patted her on her upper arm before saluting her. 'In case the Lucy Rodriguez I know wants what is due,' as he spoke, he handed her a piece of paper. Then, as everyone else had, he left, leaving her alone again. She was tempted to simply screw the paper up and throw it in the trash, but her curiosity nagged at her.

What the fuck? She asked herself as she read what was written. It was a time and an address. *Sorry Jackson, not interested. Not now...* She saw it at first as an invite for the two of them to meet up, but after staring at the address for a minute she realised that she recognised it from somewhere. She took out her phone and searched the address to find that it was for an Italian restaurant over in Tribeca. What was unusual was that as far as she could recall, Jackson hated Italian food. Deciding that if she was quick, she may still be able to catch him before he'd had the opportunity to leave, Lucy headed for the stairs and rushed down them to the ground floor. She reached security by the entrance, but there was no sign of Jackson; she must have just missed him. *Only one way to find out what this means...* she decided. She would have to head over to the address at the time stated and find out for herself what it meant.

'Oh! Agent... Rodriguez?!' A man called to her from the other side of the security check in area. He clearly did not have authorisation to enter as the security guards cut off his advance. 'Agent Rodriguez! One minute of your time? Please?!' Curious as to what this man wanted, Lucy passed security and walked over to the entrance. The man rushed over to meet her. He was scruffy, wearing a brown leather jacket and beige coloured pants. His tie was barely tied and hung loosely about his neck. 'Agent Rodriguez, thank you.'

'Who are you?' Lucy asked bluntly, crossing her arms and looking him up and down. He was carrying a phone in one hand and what looked like a notepad in the other.

'Alex Cross. I'm with the news, daily news...' He opened his notepad and tried to find a pen, awkwardly, whilst attempting to hold his phone.

Press... Fuck sake. 'Sorry Alex, I'm busy.' Lucy attempted to dismiss him.

'Agent! I'm writing an article on erm, the occurrence, no, appearance of certain people in the city...'

'You're babbling Mr. Cross, if you write as well as you speak, god help you.'

'People with super human abilities!' he blurted out as Lucy turned to walk away. She paused for a moment and turned to look at him before continuing back through security. As far as she was concerned, he was just another reporter wanting to stick his nose where it wasn't wanted.

Lucy arrived at the restaurant fifteen minutes before the time on Jackson's note. She was more than prepared for one of Jackson's infamous pranks, knowing that if this was a wind-up, she'd probably catch him in the act. As she sat in her car, patiently waiting on the opposite side of the street, she couldn't help but run through several different scenarios in her head. Could it be Jackson up to his old tricks? Perhaps her father did actually want to meet for dinner? The idea that this was, in some way, actually related to Mike crossed her mind and made her heart ache. The time on the note came and passed and Lucy had seen no activity. She was jaded, to the point of renouncing this stake out of pure curiosity when something occurred to her. *It's Wednesday night... The doors are open... Where the hell are all the people?* It was at this point that she also realised that since arriving she had not seen a soul; the beauty salon just down the street looked to be open with a couple of staff members inside, but no customers. The restaurant's lights were on and usually at this time of night the place would be packed, yet there was no-one. 'What the fuck is going on tonight?' Lucy asked the darkness as she turned in her seat to look up and down the street once more. *Fucking Jackson has sent me on a wild fucking goose chase...* As she decided to give up and leave, reaching for the key in the ignition, a set of headlights flashed across her mirror. A car had pulled into the street and parked up outside the restaurant. It was a white S.U.V that ominously had no plates. Lucy watched the car in her sideview mirror intently. The driver's door opened and a tall suited man stepped out; if his suit and body stance didn't make it obvious enough, his earpiece certainly gave the impression that he was private security. *Okay... now I'm intrigued...* Lucy didn't have to wait long, however, to have her curiosity satisfied. She ducked to avoid being seen as she realised whom it was that the driver opened the rear door for. Her heart pounded furiously and her mind raced as it tried to process what her eyes had captured. It was a woman. She had stepped out of the vehicle wearing a pair of caramel, open-toed heels and a burgundy, ruffled charmeuse mini wrap dress. Her golden skin and fiery hair both shimmered under the street lights as she made her way into the restaurant, leaving her driver with the car. Lucy grasped at the steering wheel, her nails digging into the leather as she tried to contain her rage. Serena was here, not fifty feet away. The only problem was, Lucy was alone. She pulled out her phone, calling the first person that came to mind. 'Pick up Mike... Pick up... C'mon, don't be a dick...' But there was no answer. Selecting a different contact, this time, her luck was in. 'I've got the red-headed bitch in my sights. Get over here. Now.'

If she had managed to get hold of one of her team, no doubt the C.I.A would have interfered and her opportunity for revenge would have been lost within a sea of bureaucracy. She had needed someone close to her, someone she could rely on that understood what this meant to her. She wanted Serena to feel her pain and Lucy knew that there was at least one other that would wish the same ill against the fire brandishing bitch. He approached her car cautiously. Out of uniform, he wore a pair of brown suede shoes, ripped blue jeans and a light brown jacket over a t-shirt.

'Where is she?' he asked as Lucy wound down her window. His expression was one of utmost seriousness, knowing that he was here for a single purpose.

'She's in the restaurant. Seamus, she's alone. You armed?' Lucy knew he would be carrying, but it was her way of offering her friend some form of pleasantry. They needed to remain focused, but she was glad that he looked okay. 'Serena is quick, don't underestimate her.' Seamus had had more experience with Serena than anyone, other than Mike, but Lucy felt the urge to remind him to be careful.

'So, what's the plan?' He was agitated, hardly able to remain still. No doubt he had an itchy trigger finger too. Lucy would deny it, but she just wanted to put Serena in the ground right now.

'I figure if we sneak round back, clear out the kitchen, then we should have her to ourselves. From what I've seen the driver is the only security she brought with her.' She gestured towards the S.U.V as she spoke. Seamus looked down the street briefly towards the restaurant and then nodded. He didn't need to over think it.

'Let's get this over with...' Seamus took out his gun and double checked that the magazine was full.

Moving down the adjacent alley to the restaurant with Seamus in-tow, Lucy's heart and mind raced together in anticipation. Conflicted by feelings of both wanting it all to be over and wanting it to last, to make Serena suffer for as long as possible, Lucy was swimming in a pool of emotions. She felt passionately about one thing though, she wanted to cause the bitch some harm. Finding the back door open, Lucy and Seamus headed straight inside and moved quickly down a short corridor towards the kitchen. Lucy held her weapon in one hand and her badge in the other, ready to usher any bystanders from the premises. The first person they came across was a chef, who dropped a pan of water and vegetables at the sight of Lucy and Seamus.

'It's okay. F.B.I,' Lucy said quietly, attempting to reassure the panic-stricken cook. 'Out the back, quickly and quietly.' The man nodded and hurriedly made his way past them. Entering the kitchen, Lucy held her badge aloft, and whilst Seamus made his way along the cook line, she continued to alert as many staff members as she could and encouraged them to leave.

'We had no choice,' one of the chef's said with a thick accent, his voice quivering in fear. Lucy simply nodded and gestured towards the exit.

'You ready?' Lucy asked Seamus. However, it was her

own doubt she was hoping to quash. It was the point of no return. Her conscience told her that she needed to bring Serena in, but her heart yearned for retribution, to simply end her with a hail of bullets.

'Let's get this over with.' Seamus' tone suggested that he didn't want to wait any longer. Pulling back the hammer on his firearm, he opened the door to the restaurant floor and headed out. Lucy followed him this time, as if her internal conflictions had manifested themselves in a shift of leadership.

The dining room was void of people. All of the tables were set up ready for service but all but one was not in use. In the centre of the room were a group of six booths that sat back-to-back. Serena sat in the middle booth on the far side to Lucy's position. She sat unfazed by their presence, simply enjoying a glass of red wine, with a slice of cake sat on the table before her. She looked at Lucy and then at Seamus. There wasn't an ounce of fear in her eyes, such was her confidence. Or perhaps she welcomed the end. Whichever it was, Lucy felt perturbed by Serena's lack of reaction.

'It's over Serena,' Lucy said angrily, but even she didn't quite believe the words leaving her lips. 'What you did... What you deserve...'

'Seamus, are you of the same opinion as Lucy?' Serena tilted her head to look Seamus in the eye, almost smiling at him as she did.

'We're doing the world a favour!' Seamus was angry. He pointed his weapon at Serena's head, caressing the trigger.

'Well. It seems you did not feel the same way about my brother Brandt. Or at least you did not participate. You do not carry the mark.' Lucy, annoyed by Serena's attempt to confuse them, pointed her gun, her hand squeezing hard on everything but the trigger. 'I see.' Serena appeared disappointed. 'Please, take a seat.' She pointed to the seats within the booth at which she sat. 'Before you pass judgement, let us talk.' She sliced through the cake in front of her with a fork and exhibited a pleasurable moan as she delicately placed it in her mouth. Lucy lunged forward and swiped the plate off the table, sending it flying and smashing on the floor.

'We have fuck all to say to you!' Seamus exclaimed.

'Lies!' Serena slammed her fork down onto the table. 'You, you are dying to know why, why you, why *your* daughter! Why your partner! And Lucy here wants to know why I did what I did to Michael!' The mention of Mike's name forced Lucy to lose it.

'Do not say his name!' Lucy's tempter got the better of her and she discharged her weapon. Serena moved unbelievably quickly, sliding across the seat a few inches and dodging the shot, with the bullet embedding into the leather.

'Velocity.' Serena adjusted her position and sat back comfortably, ignoring the fact that Lucy had just attempted to shoot her. She waited for Lucy to take the bait.

'What of it?' Lucy wanted nothing more than for Serena to shut up, but the nagging suggestion that Serena had answers to Mike's current condition tore at her.

'Lucy, who gives a shit.' Seamus shuffled his feet, growing more and more impatient. He was nervous, as an outstanding officer and a good man, this was a difficult position for him to be in.

'Seamus, just... hold on a sec...' Lucy stared Serena in the eye, asking her to continue.

'He's still using, isn't he?' Serena asked and Lucy nodded in response. 'It's made from our blood. I have yet to find out who is behind it.'

'Who the fuck cares! Seriously, Luce, don't let her –'

'Seamus! Please....' Lucy begged him to have patience.

'He will die.' Serena looked at Lucy, and for the first time, Lucy could see the fear in her expression that she had wanted – but she didn't understand why.

'How can I help him?' She wanted the answer, but Serena's sudden but evident concern for Mike infuriated her. 'Tell me!' Lucy screamed, pointing her gun at Serena once again.

'I am sorry for what I did to him.'

'You don't! You think that matters?!' Lucy felt her finger brush the trigger of her gun, hungry to bite down and feed her anger.

'Regardless of what anyone thinks, I will do my best to help young Michael.'

'Help? How could you possibly help?' Lucy shook her head, trying to force Serena's words from her mind and make sense of the situation she was in. She was seething inside, her rage unbridled. She hated Serena, she despised everything she stood for. Lucy's finger glazed across the trigger of her weapon, but as she went to breathe and squeeze, the front door to the restaurant swung open with a loud bang.

'N.Y.P.D! Drop your weapons!' Seamus shouted at the two men that had burst in, each brandishing a shotgun.

'Seriously, what the fuck!' Lucy tried to hold her aim on Serena whilst turning to look at their new guests and side-stepping towards Seamus. 'Serena, call off your dogs or I swear to god –'

'They're not with me, sweety.' Serena appeared unafraid, however. 'I imagine they are here for the same reason you two are, is that right boys? Here to take me out as well?' Both men said nothing as they cocked their weapons and began to raise them.

'Whoa, whoa!' Lucy diverted her aim from Serena to the two men. 'Drop your weapons!'

'We ain't here for you, cop, stay out of it!' The man yelled, causing Serena to laugh, which only pissed Lucy off even more.

'Serena, shut the fuck up!' Lucy now realised that she

had completely lost control of the situation. *What was I thinking?...*

'Markovic sent them,' Serena continued to chuckle. 'All four of you, here to kill me, yet, arguing over who gets to do it.' She sat back in her seat again and drank some more wine. 'Lucy, swear to hear me out, and I'm all yours.' Lucy wasn't sure if she could trust Serena, but the current situation couldn't really get much worse. The two men were sweating with the decision before them, but Lucy could tell by the looks in their eyes that this was not going to end well.

'I'm...' the words stuck in Lucy's throat; she sighed '... I'm all ears.'

'Luce!' Seamus contested, but Serena moved so quickly that neither he nor Lucy could have done anything. Serena rushed towards the men, dodging one shot and redirecting the other man's weapon, forcing his shot to hit the ceiling. She stripped away their shotguns and whipped each of them around their heads with the butts of the guns, the force knocking them both unconscious. Dropping the weapons, Serena turned back towards Lucy, curtsied, and then walked back to her seat.

'Please, sit,' Serena said calmly. 'I would offer you some cake, but –'

'You think taking out those two thugs proves anything?' Lucy reluctantly kicked over a lose chair and sat down.

'They're alive, are they not?' Serena looked at them as if she deserved some form of commendation. 'It shows growth... Or at least I feel it does.'

'Cut the crap. You're a cold-blooded killer. Now tell me how I can help Mike before I put a bullet through that thick skull of yours!' Lucy's leg was shaking as she sat facing her enemy, her sidearm resting on her thigh. 'Just say whatever it is you wanna say...'

'This is bullshit!' Seamus exclaimed, beginning to pace back and forth frustratedly.

'You see me, all of us, my siblings and I... You see us all as killers.'

'Because you are!' Seamus slammed his hand down onto the table between them.

'Why? Because that is how you perceive us? How history perceives us?' Serena finished her glass of wine and then poured herself another. 'Until Adam killed Cardoza's men that night, to save *your* colleague, Krysta, until *that* moment, we were cursed.'

'This bullshit again?!' Seamus interrupted. He grasped at his firearm and Lucy could tell that he was so close to using it, just as she was.

'When Adam closed the entrance to Eden, he cursed his bloodline, the Avunaye. We are brimming with power, but were unable to use it as we wished. Cursed to only be able to take a life in self-defence or during an initiation. This is until Adam set us free.' Lucy grinded her teeth whilst listening to Serena's words. She took them in, but all she wanted to know was how to help Mike. For even though he was free, he would remain under the thrall of this freak as long as he was using. 'For when he takes a life coldly, shall they be freed of their restraints. With the drawing of blood, will they be set free.'

'Very moving, but can you *please* get to the fucking point,' Lucy scoffed. A countdown had begun in Lucy's mind, ticking down to point where she could no longer listen.

'Often with power, comes vanity. We were fools to think that our actions had no consequence. Time distorts everything. Did you know that the Greek god and goddess, Apollo and Artemis, were based on Adam and Evelina. I know, I know, you would probably mistake Adam for someone more important, like Zeus –'

'Argh! Enough! I mean, what the fuck are you talking about?!' Seamus lifted his gun in frustration.

'There are worse things than us out there now, Seamus.' Something was recognisably different within

Serena. Lucy looked her in the eye and she could swear that there was fear there once more. 'The Greeks believed in Zeus, the Romans were smarter, they named it Jupiter. The so-called king of the gods, the ruler of the planets, leader of the guardians.' Serena stopped talking and drank the rest of her glass in one go. Lucy gave Serena a moment to continue, the fear expressed in her eyes granting her that courtesy, but Lucy's patience was thin.

'You're stalling.' Lucy contemplated that this whole conversation was a trick, a rouse.

'You always require proof... unfortunately, you're about to get it.' Serena stood up sharply, drawing Seamus' aim. 'You should leave.' There was an unbelievable concern to her tone.

'Sit down and shut up!' Lucy demanded, yet she was undoubtedly thrown by Serena's sudden demeanour. *Is this her plan? Is she trying to throw me off?*

'Attempting to help the mortals won't save you, Serena, for you *are* an abomination.' The voice seemed to sound from everywhere and yet nowhere, causing Lucy to spin on her heels, searching for its source. She had an Irish accent, and as she slipped out from behind one of dining room's divisional walls, Lucy chose to aim her gun at her.

She was petite. In fact, if this was whom Serena feared, Lucy would be surprised. She had red hair that was tied back in a pony-tail and she was wearing a tight, black, long-sleeved top and black camo pants. She reminded Lucy of herself a little; perhaps she was an army brat like her.

'F.B.I,' Lucy asserted her authority. 'How about you show me your hands and tell me who you are?' The woman slowly raised her hands with her fingers outstretched and took a step towards Lucy, moving away from the wall that had concealed her.

'With the drawing of blood, will *they* be set free.' Serena said, taking an obvious defensive stance after navigating her way out from the booth.

'And what does that have to do with any of this?' Seamus questioned. He was still anxious, clearly unsure of who he should be aiming at.

'Not us. Her.' The words quivered as they left Serena's lips.

'Okay, I'll ask once more. Who are you?' Lucy sighed once more.

'Zeus,' Serena began to chuckle nervously, drawing a smirk from the unnamed woman. 'Zeus, Jupiter... Evelina awoke *it* in Rome. We were vein to think that the curse was all about us. *She* is here to ensure that the Avunaye never return to the garden...' Serena almost sounded defeated.

'Someone, please, just tell me her fucking name! For fucks sake!' Lucy did not feel in control. She was not comfortable standing between Serena and whoever this woman was.

'The vessel is called Janet. My name, is Barachiel.' The spoke calmly and clearly, she seemed unnerved by the whole situation.

'Sorry, what? Which is it? Janet? Or... the other one... ?' Lucy was tired of mind games; Serena had already spun her head enough for one day.

'But my name is unimportant. For what is a name.' She did not avert her gaze from Serena as she spoke. 'Names can often be confused. Take Serena here. Hestia. Vesta. Rhea Silvia. Should I continue?'

'Please don't. How about you just get down on your knees and –' Seamus began to add.

'Enough. Serena, why involve mortals? It is beneath you.' Janet clenched her fists and lowered her arms, taking another step towards Lucy.

'Whoa! Back up there, lady, or I'll have to shoot...' Lucy aimed at her, finger ready on the trigger. Janet said nothing, she simply smirked again and suddenly there was a bright light being emitted from behind her. *What the fuck?!* Lucy began to panic.

'Time to fight fire with fire,' Serena said assuredly as the light grew brighter. Before Lucy could even think of what to do next, she found herself being dragged backwards and then she was hurled over the booth where Serena had been sat, landing on the floor, Seamus landing beside her. Serena joined them momentarily, squatting beside them. 'To help Mike, find me the source. Soon as you can, get the hell out of here.' Serena's eyes flashed a bright red and the veins beneath her skin began to glow. As Serena leapt over the booth there was an explosion of heat and light that shook the room. As flames flashed across the tops of the booths, Lucy dared not move, but she soon had no choice as the booth she was hidden behind began to lift from the floor and slide into her, pushing her and Seamus towards the room's periphery. There was a sudden blast of fire, as if someone had set off a bomb and the booth took off, flying up over their heads across the rest of room and crashing against the wall, leaving Lucy and Seamus unprotected.

Seamus quickly grabbed Lucy's arm, shaking her from her shock-induced daze. He ushered her to get up and follow him to a nearby exit that led out into the street. Lucy attempted to look back at Serena as she fled, but the light was far too intense. They moved as quickly as they could whilst tables and chairs flew through the air, smashing against the ceiling, the walls and other pieces of furniture. As she and Seamus made it to the exit, the doors frame began to crumble and the ceiling above them ruptured, forcing them both to dive out into the street. Laying on the ground, Lucy looked back at the restaurant; a beacon of fire and light, it shone brightly in the dark before its windows shattered and its foundations erupted, reducing the building to a pile of rubble.

16
Claire Davenport

Spring was drawing to a close and the days were beginning to grow much warmer. The heat and humidity within the city seemed to reflect the increasing pressure that Claire and her colleagues were feeling; the intensity of the threats against them continued to grow and incidents were becoming more common. Claire was especially starting to feel the pressure of the impending actions of the Avunaye, with the presence of Carmen magnifying said burdens. It had become clear to Claire that the looming threat of someone revealing her involvement in the deaths of Cardoza's men, and of course Lillian, the innocent bystander, was ever present, and that Carmen had taken it upon herself to rectify the issue. Carmen was smart, she had managed to destroy the evidence that connected Claire to the murders, and Claire had a gut feeling that she was doing her utmost to protect her from harm. But Claire had also come to find that she did not cover her tracks very well and that Carmen was, without a doubt, taking full control of her body as she slept. Whilst Claire appreciated the idea that Carmen was looking out for her, she did worry that it could only lead to further problems, one being more blood on her hands. It was this concern that had recently thrown their symbiotic relationship off balance. Claire had also not found it easy dealing with Carmen's feelings of guilt regarding Mike's condition and the destruction of the only sample they had had. Lucy, of course, endeavoured to help him, but she too was struggling emotionally, and knowing that they may have had a chance to make things right, but that the chance was squandered due to Carmen's fear, only added further stress.

Today Claire found herself out in the field, assisting Krysta. The heat had helped her decide her attire, opting for a pair of sneakers, black suit pants, a grey short-sleeved t-shirt and a bullet-proof vest. She may have gone with a pencil skirt and blouse, but certain inner flutters, undoubtedly persuasive feelings from Carmen, nudged her towards a more sensible option. It had only been a few days since their last outing, investigating the crime scene of detective Jack Cannon, the same day on which Lucy had found herself barely escaping a restaurant explosion. This time around they had been sent to oversee the investigation of an office block that was littered with the bodies which, they'd come to realise, were Markovic's associates. A stronghold of sorts, the building had been ravaged within approximately twenty-four hours of the detective being slain, leading to suspicion that the two events were connected.

Krysta was waiting at the front of the building when Claire arrived. She was accompanied by a police officer and a member of the forensic team, distinguishable by their white overalls.

'F.B.I are a welcome sight,' the C.S.I woman smiled. 'Office building turned massacre site, with a shit load of crazy thrown in, just to make it all the more interesting.' Krysta introduced Claire and then suggested that they all get moving. Her search for Adam still remained fruitless, so perhaps her urgency in this case indicated that she hoped that this site might result in a lead. 'Call me Dawson,' the C.S.I said. 'Let me show you what kind of shit we're dealing with.' Leading them through the blood-spattered and body laden corridors and stairwells of the building, Dawson reeled off their findings thus far, much of which made little sense to her, but to Claire and Krysta, it was clear that the Avunaye had been involved. It was a large crime scene and by the looks of things, no expense had been spared as far as staffing was concerned; there were investigators spread out all of the place, all dressed in white overalls. Although the bodies had barely began to decompose, the pungent stench of death saturated the air. Many of the corpses had had their lower abdomens slashed or blown open, revealing their intestines. From the smell of it, Claire could swear that a large number of them had most likely lost control of their bowels during death. She was managing to bare the effluvium, but Krysta appeared to be struggling, moving the C.S.I on quickly whenever she could.

'We have bullet casings everywhere from over a dozen different types of firearms. There's a shit ton to go through, but from our initial findings they all seem to belong to the victims. Looks like whoever they were shooting at didn't feel the need to shoot back. Crazy, right?' As they walked, stepping over what seemed like hundreds of evidence identity markers, Dawson pointed out each body they came across and provided their first assumptions for the cause of death, or at least her best interpretation of the evidence. 'So, we have stab wounds, broken spines, blunt force trauma... I have sent so much blood back to the lab to be worked already. We also, get this... we have a herpetologist on the team that swears that one guy was killed by a poisonous frog, and another by a snake bite. It's... it's a first for me...' she shrugged her shoulders and looked at Krysta in the hope of some form of explanation. '...well, whatever happened here, the animals seemed to have gotten away unscathed, despite the hundreds of rounds that were popped off, at first glance there appears to be no dead reptiles or amphibians.' As Claire studied the evidence around her, and with the information the C.S.I had already gathered, it was clear to her who had done this. She had continued to dream about Carmen's past, and that, combined with what Carmen was willing to share, had taught her much regarding Carmen's siblings.

This has got to be the twins... Tisa and Bomani. Claire continued to examine the devastation that surrounded them; she could feel Carmen pulling away from the subject but also felt a sense of disappointment, perhaps guilt. *Carmen? This wasn't you, you're not responsible for this...* Carmen did not reply, but Claire knew that she would have heard her thoughts. Letting out a loud, exasperated sigh, Claire drew the gaze of all of those around her that were trying to work, to which she expressed a sheepish, apologetic expression and covered her face with her hand.

'Whatcha thinking, Claire?' Krysta asked, breaking the awkward silence that had filled the room. She then tapped her finger on her temple, suggesting that Claire confer with her co-inhabitant. Claire had thus far kept her and Carmen's current issues to herself. She had also not disclosed her recent discoveries about the Avunaye either. Although she knew that Krysta had accepted the fact that Claire shared her body with Carmen, Claire still didn't feel completely comfortable sharing all the weird and wonderful details with her friend. Not yet anyway.

'I might have something...' Claire admitted whilst attempting to indicate to Krysta that they might want to speak about it elsewhere. 'Perhaps we can move on?' she asked of C.S.I Dawson.

The three of them continued through several other rooms on different floors until they reached the top. Dawson led them to the entrance of a room, but paused for a moment; she seemed especially excited about this one.

'I get the feeling you guys know something I don't...' She looked at Krysta, then Claire and then back to Krysta. 'Ah. One of *those* cases... Well, this room will hopefully make much more sense to you two than it does to us.' As she walked into the room, she described what the evidence told her. 'So, these three emptied twelve-gauge shotguns on whatever it was that stood here. Then they were attacked from the side, there, by something else.' She once again looked at the pair of them, silently pleading with them for answers.

'Crazy! Heh!' Claire blurted out under the pressure.

'Come on. You've gotta give me something. I mean, this shit is nuts.' Dawson stood there holding out her hands with the palms facing upwards, as if begging for an answer. She smiled slightly as neither Claire or Krysta provided any insight. 'Last chance...'

'We will take it from here,' Krysta said, destroying any hopes that Dawson had of finding out what they knew. Eventually, looking rather disappointed, Dawson rolled her eyes and agreed to leave them to it, explaining that she had so much more work to be doing elsewhere.

'So, Avunaye?' Krysta jumped at the opportunity to ask once Dawson was out of earshot.

'Yeah, looks like it –' Claire began to say, but Krysta quickly interrupted her excitably.

'Any sign?! Anything that could help?' She had hope in her eyes, a hope that Claire hated to see fade, but she couldn't lie about this. Claire simply shook her head and watched as Krysta's positivity diminished.

'There is something, however...' Claire pointed to a body of a woman curled up against the far wall of the room. Krysta turned to investigate and crouched down next to the body with Claire squatting beside her. 'It's exactly the same as the detectives.' She pointed at a scar, a mark that resided on the woman's lower neck.

'Any luck in finding out what it means?' Krysta frowned. It was a lead, but judging by Krysta's expression, not the one she had wanted.

'Well, I wasn't sure, but one mark... Could have been a birth mark or a scar? But two... exactly the same, same place. And on two different people?'

'So... this means that an N.Y.P.D detective and one of Markovic's thugs were connected.' Krysta stated the fact, but her tone suggested that she remained unsure of its relevance.

'Lucy said that Markovic had fallen out with the Avunaye. Seems the detective had joined forces with him to take out Brandt. This is his mark.' Claire hoped that Carmen would now chip in with a confirmation, but she still felt a sense of stubbornness from her and a silence which was, to tell the truth, deafening. 'For six months she doesn't shut up. Now she says nothing.'

'Claire? Is something up with you, two?' Krysta showed a blurred look of concern washed with confusion and scepticism as she spoke.

'I know it's weird, but I feel what she feels, so I know what's not being said, but I wish she'd say it... Does that make sense?' Claire sat back onto the blood-stained floor. She could feel Carmen sigh inside as she began to open up. *I swear... if you don't start talking to me, I'll... I'll give Gareth a call and I'll set up a session!*

Don't you dare. Carmen finally broke her silence.

'AHA!' Claire clapped her hands in celebration. 'Try me! Might make a day of it... Ten... Maybe twelve whole hours of D and D.' Krysta maintained a confused expression, but smiled at Claire conversing with the voice in her head. 'Maybe I'll even dress up... Wear the...'

You say it and I'll fry the first puppy we come across.

'Look, I get you were looking after me. Can we *please* move on?' Claire bore a huge grin as Carmen agreed to cooperate. 'Oh and, no dead puppies, that's not nice...' Missing half the conversation, Krysta's confused expression shifted quickly to one of deep concern, forcing Claire to quickly fill her in.

'Out of interest, what is it that you wear?' Krysta queried. Claire had never before revealed what she got up to outside of their shared social circle.

'For the sake of the puppy, I'd rather not say. Ha!' They both laughed.

With the inclusion of Carmen's input, Krysta and Claire began to discuss the evidence before them and the ramifications of such, if what they presumed was true.

'So, this mark. Carmen says that it is a sign that this woman was involved in killing Brandt? And that Brandt is actually Cain, which means he is, was, Adam's son?' Krysta slowly processed each and every piece of information that Claire and Carmen could provide, but she was clearly overwhelmed by it all. 'So, those who kill Cain receive his mark and, like in the good book, they will supposedly receive his vengeance seven-fold?' Krysta questioned, and Claire nodded in response. 'Is that Adam's vengeance?' Krysta suddenly appeared worried. Unfortunately, neither Claire or Carmen could ease her anxiety. As far as Carmen knew, no one had ever managed to kill Brandt before, so it was uncertain if it was Adam who would be carrying out the acts of vengeance on those who shared the mark of Cain or another of the Avunaye. Another concern was that they had no idea who else was involved. So far, it was one of Markovic's personal guard and a detective. They could assume that Markovic himself was likely involved, but how far did it go? Who else had the mark? For whoever they were, they would be a target now, and if Adam was to be the one to exact revenge, who, and how many, would he be killing? It was this question that clearly troubled Krysta.

Once Krysta and Claire had carried out their own investigation of the scene and discussed their concerns amongst themselves, Krysta contacted Solomon. She updated him with their findings and reluctantly confirmed the Avunaye's involvement, resulting in the crime scene now being declared under Zane's jurisdiction. Once Krysta was finished, the pair began to make their way back down through the building.

'So how come I have to find out from Hale that you

have another date lined up with Alexa?' Krysta asked, raising an eyebrow. Claire was caught off guard. In truth, she should have known that gossip spread through the office like wild fire. Yet, the problem wasn't that people knew, it was what their opinions of it were, because Claire wasn't even sure how she felt about it. She had always been attracted to men and only men. She had rarely dated and had never had a real relationship, but it had always been men that had interested her. However, it seemed that Carmen's interests were more exotic, with Claire often referring to Carmen's sexual preference as "anything goes". Claire had her own feelings but then she also had Carmen's, and sometimes it was difficult to tell them apart.

'I... Heh! Well, you see...' Claire was tongue tied.

If she's jealous, tell her there's always room for one more! Carmen suggested wickedly.

'One...? Ha!' Claire blushed. 'It's erm, date number two, no big deal...' Carmen scoffed at Claire's statement. Date number one was far from Carmen's liking. Claire had chosen the venue and so the pair had gone to an arcade.

Games... no fun... no sex... Carmen whined.

Hey! We did have fun! Claire was adamant that the date went better than Carmen had repeatedly suggested. However, tonight was Alexa's turn to choose what they'd be doing and so Carmen had high hopes that it would go a lot better.

'C'mon then, details.' Krysta probed.

'I have no idea. She said she'd surprise me. Heh!' The whole idea made Claire a little anxious. Krysta on the other hand seemed to love it.

'Excuse me!' a voice sounded from across the car park as the pair made their way to Claire's car. A man had somehow found his way past security and was jogging towards them waving his hands. He was wearing a shirt and pants that looked as if they had been slept in, and his hair was unkempt. He caught up to them just as they reached the car's doors. 'Hey! Thanks... for stopping,' he panted whilst gasping for breath.

'Sir, you can't be here,' Krysta informed the man as she looked around for the officers on guard. 'How did you get in here?'

'You are special agents Anderson and... Davenport, yes?' he wheezed.

'Who are you?' Claire questioned, wondering how he knew their names.

'My name's Alex, Alex Cross –' he began to say but Krysta interrupted him.

'Press? Okay, well, if you need anything, call the office –'

'So I can be palmed off to a drone, I don't think so.' He expressed a stern, adamant tone which appeared to irk Krysta. She seemed to have little to no patience for the man. Lucy had also mentioned that she had recently been ambushed, apparently, claiming that he had evidence of what was really happening within the city. The likelihood of him telling the truth was slim, but the team had been warned to not give away any information, assuming he was simply fishing for a story. Krysta gave the officers by the door a wave and as they began to walk over Alex conceded defeat and scarpered back from whence he came, with the officers now rushing after him.

Claire drove the two of them back to the office, pulling over at the main entrance to allow Krysta to get out, as she insisted on taking the stairs, leaving Claire to park the car alone. She was feeling good; it wasn't often that she got to go out into the field, but this trip had been a success as far as she was concerned. She drove down the slope and parked her little car in its designated space. The car park was only half-filled, a fact that brought a glimmer of pride to Claire's face. Many of the staff had started to cycle and use public transport for their commute and Claire felt as if she had had a hand in their decision. She had recently challenged her colleagues to be greener and had even started to design a renewable energy source to power her lab. It had been Carmen's memories that had spurred her decision to do something to do her bit for the planet; seeing how amazingly beautiful and clean the world once was had given her perspective on how far humanity had blemished the Earth. She climbed out of the car and started to make her way towards the elevator when the lights began to flicker eerily, placing the parking lot into split seconds of complete darkness.

Carmen? Is this you? Claire questioned, after all, electricity was her thing.

It's not my doing, Claire, be careful. Claire wouldn't have necessarily worried about it, but now that Carmen had suggested that there may be something to be concerned about, she couldn't help but wonder what it was. She stood still for a moment, watching the lights, waiting for them to flicker again. But they didn't. *Perhaps they're simply faulty.* Claire could tell there was an ounce of mockery to Carmen's words.

'Hmph,' Claire huffed, presuming that Carmen was toying with her. She continued to walk towards the elevator door, but as she moved, the lights between her and the elevator diminished once again. 'Seriously, Carmen! Cut it out!' Claire began to rush towards where she knew the elevator was, but from the dark someone rushed out just behind her, clipping her and spinning her round, almost causing her to fall as she hopped awkwardly to regain her balance. Whoever it was, they vanished back into the darkness before she had managed to see them.

It's not me! See! Carmen exclaimed. As she shouted, she simultaneously took control of Claire's body, throwing a bolt of blue electricity across the parking lot into the black. As the bolt struck a far wall, its tendril-like sparks flashed and reached out into the darkness, giving away the position of someone lurking there, just out of sight. They moved quickly, like a shadow, flickering amongst the pillars that supported the ceiling above. 'You're fast...' Carmen smiled as she turned slowly on the spot, estimating their location, preparing herself for another assault.

Claire did not resist Carmen's possession since she had come to learn that Carmen only took over in situations such as this, to protect her, to keep her safe. The knowledge warmed her heart.

Carmen turned to look back towards the elevator and that was when she saw them; a pair of red eyes glowing in the dark, encompassing two small flames flickering within their sclera. Carmen readied herself, electrifying her hands. The flames then grew and spread out revealing a face, and then flashed throughout their hair. Stepping forward, the lights above flickered and she was fully revealed. 'You've looked better, sister.' Serena stood reservedly. She wore a pair of small heeled shoes and black satin pants, however, where she'd usually wear something revealing, especially in this heat, she was notably wearing a camel-coloured, belted, wrap coat. Her face was noticeably bruised, which concerned Carmen; it was not often that the Avunaye suffered such injuries. Claire urged Carmen to ask her if she was okay, but the words lodged in her throat.

'You've looked better yourself, Carmen. Although this vessel you inhabit, it is not all bad.' Serena looked Claire up and down.

'You're hurt, sister.' It was the best Carmen could do, considering they would usually be fighting each other by now, having resided in the same place for more than a few moments. Serena frowned at her observation; she was clearly not accustomed to revealing such fragility.

'We were wrong,' Serena said bluntly before stepping towards Carmen.

'Wrong? About what?' Carmen questioned her sisters cryptic-ness. Was she playing at something? Was she attempting some kind of mind game?

'We assumed that when Adam broke the curse that it was us that were to be freed.'

Carmen? What is she on about? Claire wondered from within, allowing Carmen to remain in control for now. Carmen lowered her guard to signify that she was willing to listen.

'Evelina unintentionally woke one of *them.*' Serena grimaced as she spoke, as if she was still in pain.

'One of whom?'

'I'm sure that you've heard of Lucy's latest exploits, I was there. We were... interrupted... by Barachiel.' Carmen was in shock; Claire could feel her relinquishing control in retreat. She had never felt Carmen be truly fearful before and the emotion hit hard. 'As far as I am aware, she's the only one right now. But you've heard the stories... they're supposedly like fucking locusts, spreading like wild fire, leaving devastation in their wake as they hunt us.'

Oh my god, tell her about Brandt. Maybe this Barachiel – Claire thought.

'–It wasn't her, it –' Carmen spoke aloud.

'Ha!' Serena chuckled, 'It is interesting to witness you conversing with the mortal.'

'Brandt?' Carmen simply said in one short breath.

'Killed by mortal men. They all bear his mark, they'll pay soon enough. I believe Tisa and Bomani have been busy hunting some of them down.' Serena smiled at the fact. Claire couldn't sit back any longer and she forced herself to the foreground.

'They need to stop,' Claire insisted. 'There's too many bodies...'

'Oh, the mortal.' Serena looked at Claire curiously. 'You should know that they have taken Brandt. His body is missing, *our* brother is missing.' Serena was weak, but the fact that Brandt had been taken clearly infuriated her as the flames returned to her eyes for a moment.

'What I mean is – is... that they're drawing too much

attention. They killed a detective.' Claire was a little surprised by her own words. She was supposed to enforce the law, she should arrest Serena, yet here she was warning her. It was Carmen. Her relationship, her love for her sister, her unrelenting passion to protect her family despite all that they had done that was influencing her own choices now.

'The mortal shows more affection towards our kin than you. How curious...' Serena smirked. 'Our family is under threat and we hope to rely on Adam's support. Perhaps Carmen's also?' Claire could practically feel Carmen's blood, or technically her own blood, begin to boil as she raged at Serena's audacious request. 'The detective was not alone in the killing of our brother. Perhaps this is a line the F.B.I could pursue?' Serena looked Claire in the eyes, almost as if she was searching for something.

'It is... erm... may I ask, I mean... I will ask, however, what has happened between you, the Avunaye, and Markovic?' Claire could tell Serena was ready to leave and it was a question that had plagued her all day.

'A difference of opinion. We promised that which we could not deliver upon. Now it seems we are at war.' The lights began to flicker again. 'Family is all that matters now.' And with those final words Serena was gone, sinking back into the dark just before all the lights began to shine once again.

The final few hours of Claire's working day disappeared without her being able to keep an eye on the time. Her mind had raced with question upon question regarding their interaction with Serena. What had Markovic done with Brandt's body? Who was this Barachiel? And who exactly were "them", that Serena had spoken of. Carmen was once again shy with the details, claiming that "them" were something that had long been stripped from the Avunaye's memories. Yet, she did confirm one thing that caused a deep well of concern to open up within Claire; that this new threat was one only to the Avunaye.

Claire was also nervous about the impending evenings events, and whereas usually the time would pass by second by second, today the hands were galloping around the clock face. To make matters worse, she was currently arguing with the voice in her head like a maniac, debating on what she should wear. Carmen insisted that Claire needed to pull out all the stops to make up for her dismal first date impression, whereas Claire's anxiousness was swaying her towards the more reserved; she was opting for jeans and a hoodie, whereas Carmen encouraged leather pants and a plunging vest top.

'Argh!' Claire exclaimed as Carmen forced her to toss another outfit to one side. Her bedroom looked like a clothing stall at a yard sale. 'Seriously, we have like one hour before we need to leave and unless we're going in my underwear – We are not going in my underwear!' Claire couldn't help but chuckle. She was a complete mess of emotion. Anxious, tired, excited, horny; some of which she knew to be hers, some Carmen's, and the others, only god knew. One thing was certain though, she was almost out of clothes to choose from.

What's in that bag? Carmen attempted to divert Claire's attention to a garment bag at the very back of her wardrobe.

That? It's just a dress...

Then that's the one, grab it. Let's put it on.

I dunno... Claire was hesitant. She hadn't actually ever worn that particular item before, which is probably why Carmen was insistent that that was the perfect outfit for her date.

Perfect! Carmen smiled within at Claire's reflection in the mirror. She had donned the garment, which was a powder-pink, deep v-neck, mini wrap dress. The dress had a ruffled trim on its hem and a subtle flower pattern scattered across it. Finally, to complete the outfit, she chose a pair of black stiletto heels. Claire proceeded to apply a little makeup, but then she realised the time and panicked as she had still not touched her hair. *Calm down, Claire. Let your hair down and just watch.* Claire felt the warmth within her as she undid her hair. It stirred within her abdomen and she could see the occasional spark bounce off the surface of her skin. It spread from her gut, upwards throughout her body until it reached her head; she felt a little dizzy at first, but she trusted Carmen. Flickers of blue light bounced about her body and the charge caused the individual strands of hair to begin to lift and move.

'Heh! This is nuts. Not the talking to myself, well, you, but this...' Claire stretched out her arms and watched the electricity dance along them to her fingertips. It took a few minutes, but slowly, Claire's long brown hair began to look almost presentable, and by the time Carmen was finished, it was perfectly styled, tied back in a twisted crown. Claire's smile beamed for a moment, before it dawned on her that she needed to go and she practically sprinted out of the room, almost tripping over due to her choice of footwear.

Alexa had told Claire to meet her on the corner of seventy-ninth and fifth, leading Claire to believe that they were going to spend the evening in Central Park. Claire liked the idea; the park was a safe place. *Can't get up to too many crazy things in the park.*

You'd be surprised... Carmen chuckled, but Claire tried to ignore her as best she could. This date was going to be nerve-racking enough without the addition of Carmen's jibes, but everything changed when she saw Alexa walking down the path from inside the park. A mild breeze shifted her silver and black hair, causing it to shimmer in the sunlight. It was short and wavy with bangs, the style opening up her face. She ran her hand through her hair as she walked, lifting her gaze from the path she was following. As she spotted Claire she smiled, a smile that represented how Claire was feeling at that very moment; gleeful and happy beyond measure, if not a little nauseous. Alexa was wearing a pair of khaki green shorts and a black, long-sleeved shirt with the sleeves rolled up. Her outfit was completed by her beige, strapped, open-toe heels and complimented by a necklace and a small nose ring. Claire still had her doubts about how she felt, but either she felt nothing right now, or her and Carmen's emotions were in sync, as what she felt, felt undeniably true. She was so entranced that when Alexa mentioned how great she looked and asked how she was, she didn't answer at first, with it taking a full ten seconds for her brain to kick into gear and realise that it warranted a response.

'Ha! Sorry, erm, yes,' Claire babbled.

'Yes... yes, what?' Alexa smiled, almost giggling.

'Good. We're good,' Claire smiled dopily. 'I mean I! I'm good.' Luckily, Alexa seemed to find Claire's chaotic personality endearing. Smiling again, she reached forward and grabbed Claire's hand, gesturing with her other hand that they were to head into the park. The touch of her hand made Claire's heart skip and an excitable chill to flurry down her spine.

As they walked into the park, hand in hand, Claire began to feel conscious that other people would see them.

Claire, take a look around. Be thankful that you are accepted in today's society, as it wasn't always so. A sense of grief snuck in with Carmen's words, but then an easiness washed over Claire as she took Carmen's advice and glanced about to see that they were not being watched or judged.

'So, what's the plan?' Claire was curious and as she spoke, she found herself tightening her grip slightly on Alexa's hand, not wanting to let go. Alexa turned and continued to walk backwards, continuing to hold onto Claire's hand as she faced her, keeping constant eye contact. There was an air of mischief brewing within her sapphire-coloured eyes.

'Are you... hungry?'

Claire hadn't really considered eating until Alexa asked the question. Truth be told, her nervousness had eradicated her need for food for most of the day, but now that she was feeling more relaxed, she found that she was in fact starving.

'God yes!' Claire blurted out, causing Alexa to laugh.

'Good, just follow me.' She quickened her pace and dragged Claire along the path, leading her up to Belvedere Castle. The gothic, Romanesque structure stood resolutely amongst the green of the trees, watching over Turtle Pond.

'Not sure we can just waltz in here, can we?' Claire was growing a little dubious as to where they were actually headed.

'Trust me?' Alexa asked, taking Claire's other hand. The flutter in Claire's chest suggested that she did.

Alexa led Claire up into the castle and out onto the observation platform where there were a number of other people waiting. Four people sat on chairs with violins and other instruments by their sides. There was a table with two chairs in the centre of the area, and atop the table sat some covered trays. A waiter stood beside the table, eager to greet them both.

'Wow.' Claire stopped dead as she tried to take in what Alexa had arranged.

'It's nothing special, I just happen to know a lot of people in this city.' Alexa smiled and then waved at the musicians, who in turn began to play. Claire was in awe at how magical it all was; even Carmen was seemingly speechless. The waiter uncovered the trays to reveal a range of fast food, including taco's, which made Claire snort with laughter. Taking a seat opposite each other, Claire was stunned by the wonder of it all. The pair grinned childishly and gazed into each other's eyes before deciding to dig in to the food laid out before them. They ate and they drank, Claire consciously monitoring her alcohol intake, intending on remembering every second of the evening. The pair talked and laughed, and for the majority of the time, Claire felt relaxed and safe, so much so that she no longer felt the weight of the Avunaye, nor the worry of being found out. Alexa was practically dancing in her seat as the night drew on, with Claire emotionally swaying in time with her. Just as the stars began to become visible in the sky above, Alexa abruptly stood up. A man walked out across the stone platform before them and uncovered a piano that had been stashed against the wall of the castle's turret. He sat down and began to play a familiar tune. Alexa then slowly walked around the table and stood before Claire, holding out a hand, the look in her eyes conveying her hope that Claire would take it. Yet, Claire was hesitant. Perhaps it was happening too fast, or maybe she was still unsure of her feelings, or it was simply her dreaded insecurities resurfacing.

'Alexa, I...' Claire began to say, but then *she* started singing. A woman had snuck onto the platform without Claire noticing and she was now singing along to the piano. 'Oh my god...'

'Ella owed me one...' Alexa smiled. 'I want you to reach out...' she sang, along to the music. Something about the moment, the music, the stars above. It was possible that for a second, Carmen took over and forced Claire to her feet, but once she was there, the world melted away and she gave herself to the woman before her. Claire looked into her passion filled blue eyes and within them, she saw a light that helped her find her own truth.

Their hands and bodies touched as they danced to the song that Claire wished would never end. But eventually the song did come to a close and their dance ceased. Claire closed her eyes in an attempt to lock away the memory while it was fresh, and as she did, she felt Alexa's touch, her fingers against her cheek. Upon opening her eyes, Claire's stare was met by Alexa's, and as she moved into Claire, their lips touched, an unimaginable caress that bestilled Claire's heart.

Stars have formed and fallen without ever witnessing a moment such as this, Carmen said as their lips parted and the pair grinned gleefully at one another.

'Now for some fun.' Alexa raised her hands up above her head and clapped, the sound signalling the musicians to up the tempo. Then, from all corners of the castle, people emerged, rushing out onto what was now apparently a dance floor. 'What?' she said in response to Claire's wonder-filled expression. 'Told you, I know some people.' Alexa grabbed both of Claire's hands and they began dancing once again under the clear, star-filled nights sky.

17
Tobias

'C'mon then, let's have some fun!' He was restless. It was one thing mulling over his own thoughts, but to have to listen to the quandaries of six others, whom for at least the last four hours had all been thinking about the same issues. He needed a break, a release. 'Seriously, you are all literally giving me a headache with your obsessive worrying.' Most of them barely raised an eyebrow, and those that did were seemingly banking on another's reaction before saying or doing anything themselves. Tisa and Bomani were sat at the wooden table that was surrounded by floor to ceiling windows and glass sliding doors that led out onto the terraces. Sat in one of the large comfy chairs, Tisa, dressed in a pair of light-blue jeans and a white lace bodice, was perched upon her twin's lap as they competed against one another at a game of Bao. It was a favourite of theirs, a complex boardgame fuelled by strategy. Tobias noted that instead of playing with the traditional seeds, they had this time filled the board with gemstones, with Tisa choosing rubies, and Bomani, who wore only a pair of dark-blue sweat pants, had gone with diamonds. By the constant cursing within Bomani's thoughts it was clear that Tisa was winning.

Across the adjoining kitchen, Serena was sat at the end of the island with a glass of wine in hand. She scrolled through fashion articles on her tablet, attempting to distract herself. Despite the warmer temperature that had accompanied the official start to the summer season, Serena's attire purposely covered as much of her skin as possible. A terracotta coloured, ribbed, draped merino wool jumper and a pair of black, wide-legged linen pants helped her to hide her still-recovering bruises and burns that she had sustained in her clash with Barachiel. It was that fight that had everyone on edge, especially after Seymour's and Evelina's run in with her. Yet, even though Serena's body would heal fairly quickly, it was her mind, or state of, that concerned Tobias. Serena wasn't coping with having her emotions unlocked as well as he had hoped. Her relationship with the mortal F.B.I agent was still confusing her and causing her some pain. It had all taken some of the fight from her heart. *Time to cheer this one up...* Tobias grabbed a bottle of bourbon and made his way over to his wounded sibling. 'Please tell me that you are up for a bit of fun, sis?' Serena attempted to pay him no attention, but that only forced him to pester her thoughts.

'Tobias! Enough!' She put down her glass and gave him a firesome scowl.

'There's that fire. I was beginning to worry that you'd lost that eternal flame that we all love so much.' Tobias lifted the bottle in a silent request that she might join him for a drink. She was reluctant. 'How about a toast. To that red-hot fury that burns beneath your breast,' he smiled as he recalled a memory. 'You remember London... sixteen-hundreds... "the great fire" they called it.' Tobias span on his heels and grabbed two glasses, pouring Serena and himself a hefty sized drink each. The memory, or at least Tobias' attempt to prize a smile from her lips, forced Serena to sigh and close her eyes for a moment as she tried to expel her troubles.

'For twenty years I burned that country for treating me so ill...' Serena grimaced, before knocking back the drink that Tobias had given her.

'They got what they deserved,' he said, refilling her glass before downing the contents of his own.

'They got off lightly,' Evelina announced as she entered the room from the terrace, Seymour skulking behind her. She wore her long blonde hair down, draping it over one shoulder; she looked comfortable, wearing a dark-grey, sleeveless top and a pair of khaki coloured linen pants. It was certainly a different outfit from her usual, more formal attire. 'You're too young to recall the fire at the great library of Alexandria.' Evelina ran her hand over Tobias' shoulder and then softly caressed his cheek. 'If I remember correctly, she did it to spite Alexander...' Serena smiled and Evelina embraced her, placing an arm around her as they reminisced. 'Now, where is *my* drink, Tobias?' Tobias grabbed another glass and after pouring, went to pass it to Evelina when Seymour moved a hand towards it. A shadow of his arm and hand stretched out from him and snatched the drink from Tobias' grasp, sending a deathly chill up Tobias' arm.

'Easy, Casper...' Tobias smirked as Seymour handed the drink to Evelina. He forced his yellow eyes to glow as he stared into the grey-blue eyes, devoid of light, that belonged to his sibling.

Tobias... Behave. He could hear Evelina's thoughts and so, reluctantly, he obliged.

It was almost pleasant for the six of them to be together like this, sharing stories. Their common concerns gave them a platform from which to bond, however, as with all families, there was always one that was unable to simply join in with the fun and had to make matters more serious. In this case, it was Nahki. His inability to emotionally connect with the others made including him on such occasions impossible. It wasn't too long before he opened his mouth and disrupted the fun that Tobias had worked so hard to achieve.

'I would have to say that Serena's most recent escape

from the clutches of death was her most impressive feat.' Nahki had abandoned his meditation and decided to join in their discussion.

'There we go. The hollow one, as per usual, manages to paint the bloody elephant in the room in a fucking neon colour...' Tobias, having had access to all of his emotions for some time now, often found his brother to be intolerable. Nahki, the hollow one, as Tobias called him, was, as far as Tobias was concerned, empty inside due to his inability to feel as a normal human would.

'Careful, brother. Keep that temper in check.' Nahki was practically goading him, and Tobias was like a powder keg surrounded by flames at the best of times.

'Fine,' Tobias smiled, before knocking back another glass of bourbon. He then grabbed Nahki by the throat. In response, Nahki swatted away his hand and then drew a small blade from his own skin. Tobias' temper flared and his eyes glowed brightly. 'C'mon then!' he screamed before gesturing his anger towards Nahki with his hands. His fingers were outstretched, the tendons in his hands so visible they looked ready to burst from his skin. He used his ability to lift Nahki off the floor and throw him against the wall.

'Tobias. I said behave yourself.' Evelina's words were a warning, but Tobias knew he could push his luck a little further.

As Tobias pinned Nahki against the wall he began to extract some of the weapons from his flesh. Tobias revelled in the fact that the process caused Nahki immense pain as he tore open his skin and forcibly ripped the blades from his bone. Clearly growing tired of being ignored, Evelina soon began to flood Tobias with a tidal wave of self-pity and grief, forcing him to relinquish his control over his brother.

'Alright! Enough!' Tobias raised his hands in defeat and backed off. *Draw a blade on me again, brother...*

'Nahki has brought up a relevant point that we must

discuss,' Evelina stated, thus ending any sense of exuberance that Tobias had achieved. 'The emergence of Barachiel poses a threat to us all, but it could not have come at a worse time. With the death of Brandt, the disappearance of his body...' She paused for a moment. 'And with us now at war with the mortal thugs, I have made the decision to release Adam, in the hope that –'

'Whoa! Release Adam?!' Tisa interrupted, the conversation pulling her focus from her game. 'If what we know is true then Barachiel is just the first. You saw what she did to –'

'Exactly. And, *if* what we know is true, she will also not harm Adam. In turn, Adam will not allow any harm to come to his family. He is the key to keeping *them* off our backs long enough for us to locate the garden.' Evelina gave Tisa an authoritative glare. 'Nahki, you will work out a way for Adam to be released, or to escape, without destroying your cover. I believe that it is time for the C.I.A.'s investigation into our existence to come to an end. I would like you to ensure that the F.B.I take over once again and then *you* will find your brother's body.' Tobias watched as Nahki took his orders without so much as blinking. 'As for you two...' She looked toward the twins. 'Enough of the reckless killing for now. You draw too much attention.' Tisa's angered expression suggested that she utterly disagreed with what she was being ordered to do, but she would comply. Tobias scoffed at his sister's submission. 'Would you like to add something, Tobias?' Evelina's green eyes caught the light as she diverted her attention to him.

'Yes. Perhaps Toby has neglected to mention how he has been running all over the place cleaning up Kenan's mess's,' Bomani added, barely lifting his gaze from his game of Bao. 'The detective we killed believed it was Brandt who'd exsanguinated a number of female victims... but we know different... don't we, Toby?' Tobias could feel Evelina's disappointment.

'Argh!' Tobias sighed as he felt the pressure of his sibling's thoughts cascading upon him. He decided, however, to simply smile in response to their barrage of disapproval. 'Well, I see this party is over. I think I'll find some fun elsewhere. Coming, sister?' He looked to Serena, hoping that she would join him, not only for a night out, but to stand by him in defiance towards the others, but she was too deep in Evelina's shadow to disappoint and so she continued to scroll on her tablet. 'Fine! Shunned, as per usual! Enjoy your night of wallowing and contemplative fear!' Tobias was irritated and showed his frustration as he left the room by psychically flipping Tisa and Bomani's Bao board, ruining their game like a petulant child.

Tobias was frustrated by his sibling's actions, and despite the momentary distraction that their drinking and reminiscing had granted, he remained tense and went in search of some excitement and, perhaps, even a little chaos. *Their problems lie with their relentless attempts to control Adam... They will see, control is overrated.* He made his way into the city, pushing his yellow Ford GT to the boundaries of what the streets of Manhattan would allow. He knew exactly where he was headed, he had laid the groundwork a moon before and now it was time to see the start of his plans come to fruition. Pulling up and climbing out of the car, he walked under an archway and down the steps towards the bar's entrance. Deryk, the doorman, was currently busy refusing entry to a pair of men. Tobias could hear their drunken thoughts as he drew closer to them, the pair had ill intentions, looking to cause some mischief of their own, and Deryk knew it. Tobias smiled as he approached them. 'Deryk!' he held out his arms as he made his presence known. Deryk's face conveyed the fear that flooded his mind as he looked upon Tobias. 'Let them inside, Deryk, I'll ensure that they behave themselves. Isn't that right, guys?!' Tobias laughed as the men cheered in agreement, despite their intent. Reluctantly, Deryk opened the door for the three of them. 'Anyone of note tonight, Deryk?' Tobias smiled with his eyes, making the yellow of them glow eerily to unnerve the doorman.

'N – no-one out of the usual,' Deryk replied, however, his thoughts told a different tale.

'N.Y.P.D ey? Well, this will be fun.' Tobias ushered the pair of miscreants inside. 'Stay here, Deryk. If you make it through the night, you can go home at dawn.' Deryk, now panic stricken, unwillingly complied.

Within the bar, the sounds and smells of human dissipation caused a wry smile to rouse from the corner of Tobias' lips. The place was packed, with almost every table taken and every dancer occupied. Alcohol flowed freely from the bottles and taps and money left the palms of so many with such ease. The two men that had accompanied Tobias inside followed him as he made his way to the bar. He suggested to the first person he came to that they give up their stool at the bar for him and so they did, without hesitation.

'Fucking hell, man! You the fucking owner of summin?!' The intoxicated man chuckled. His companion was quick to remind him that this place belonged to Markovic.

'And don't you forget it!' she shouted across the bar. As her eyes met Tobias's he could sense her anxiety. Her fear was palpable.

'Gents, please... Go, drink, have fun, but don't leave.' Tobias turned on his seat to face Sinead. 'Pass me a bottle of bourbon, love. Make it the good stuff.' Rummaging amongst a number of other bottles, Sinead fished out an expensive brand that effectuated a sardonic laugh from Tobias. 'Angels Envy?' He stared at Sinead, searching her thoughts to see if it was merely coincidental. 'It'll do, I suppose.' He purposely made her wait, stewing in her own emotional hell as he slowly drank a glass full and then poured himself another whilst staring at her the whole time.

'I know who you are. Now, what are you doing here?' Her trembling words broke the silence between them.

'Look around, Sinead.' Tobias span on his stool and gestured to the people taking full advantage of her hospitality. 'Tell me what you see?'

'Same shit I see most nights...' Sinead pointed to the men and women clambering over the tables to slip dollar bills into the undergarments of the table-top dancers. She highlighted the ones sneaking off into the cordoned off area that housed booths for private dances and sexual encounters, and waved to a client at the end of the bar that was openly dealing drugs, before pointing out the police officer. Sat alone at a table, he nursed a short as he watched the ongoings of those around him without blinking. Tobias smiled again and then looked Sinead in the eye.

'Call the copper over, love. We *three* need a chat.'

Sinead did as she was asked and, reluctantly, the officer made his way over to the bar. He was wearing a pair of worn-out brown boots and discoloured light-blue jeans. His dark blue t-shirt had a dark stain on it, just above his waistline, and he wore a dark-green jacket.

'Who are you?' he asked bluntly, finishing his drink and then running his hand through his greasy slicked back hair. He was clearly fatigued.

'You look tired, Malik.' Tobias kept his eyes on Sinead as he spoke, watching her as she nervously dried a few glasses with a cloth.

'So? Seriously, Sinead? Who the fuck is this?' He was frustrated, and now his words carried an air of concern.

'He's one of them...' she simply replied, her words causing Malik's heart to almost jump out of his chest. Tobias sat quietly, holding up his glass, swirling around his drink as he listened to Malik run through a number of scenarios in his head.

'What do you want?' Malik questioned, reaching behind him and grasping the gun he had concealed under his jacket.

'Let go of the gun, Malik, and sit down.' Malik did as Tobias asked, exhibiting a dumbfounded expression.

'How...?'

'Quiet.' Tobias stopped him from voicing the question he despised above all others. 'This place reminds me of my Viking days.' Tobias banged his hands down onto the bar in a rampageous fashion. 'Pillaging and plundering! Ah, yes, there was Eric, and Harald... oh, and Ragnar! Ha!' He banged his hand down onto the bar again, drawing looks from those around him, but in raising his glass, he then received cheers of drunken admiration. 'But alas, mere mortals. They died and salted the Earth. Family is all that matters in the end.'

'Look –' Sinead began to say.

Tobias raised a finger to silence her. 'You both carry his mark.' He pointed to his neck, indicating the spot where they currently carried the mark of Cain. 'Yet, I am not going to harm you. Either of you.' He sat and slowly finished off another drink, allowing the uncertainty of his next action to eat away at them. He searched their minds for information regarding the location of Brandt's body, but alas, it seemed neither of them possessed such knowledge. 'Sinead, you are marked, and *he* will hunt you down once he is free. Go, now, you're dead already.' Sinead made no hesitation in grabbing some cash from the register and then her jacket, before leaving the bar. 'As for you, Malik, I will do you one favour before you die. Rattling around in that head of yours is the desire for revenge, for justice. Know this...' Tobias ushered Malik to come closer and then he whispered into his ear. 'F.B.I special agent in charge Solomon Grey is responsible for Axel's death.' Malik looked at Tobias, a vengeful glint in his beady eyes. He took Tobias' words as gospel and then, having sought permission, he took his leave. *Perfect... time to kick start this party...* Tobias threw his glass at the wall and leapt up onto the bar. 'Your attention, everyone, if you will!' His eyes shone their twisted yellow glow as he snatched the attention of everyone in sight. 'Time for a game! Drink! And have fun! Fulfil those nasty little human desires that bubble just beneath the surface of your putrid skins! However!' He grinned maliciously. 'If you should wish to leave at any point during the nights festivities... you will have to pay the piper! The toll being, three of your fingers. Now, crank up the music and let's party!' The compelled mass cheered, despite his words, and like mindless drones they continued on with their evening.

After an hour or so, having caused two bar fights, forcing two dancers to strangle a man to death and having satisfied himself in one of the private booths with a pair of intoxicated women, Tobias was losing interest.

'Hey, you!' shouted one of the men that had accompanied Tobias upon his arrival. 'You're to thank for all of this!' He was beyond drunk, and quite frankly very annoying. He smacked Tobias across the back in thanks, irking him greatly.

'Yes...' Tobias grabbed the man by the throat. 'Do me a favour, mate,' he said through gritted teeth. Tobias reached over the bar and grabbed a bottle at random. 'Hmm... Nope, I'll drink that...' He reached for another. 'Perfect.' Tobias proceeded to smash the bottle and with the broken top, he slashed the man's arm, causing blood to flick everywhere. 'Calm down now. Go to the entrance and tell our guest that we are ready for him.' The horror-stricken man precipitously made his way through the crowd, holding onto his bleeding arm. Moments later there was a shrill scream that brought a grin to Tobias' face.

He got up from his seat and made his way towards the entrance of the bar, where he found his brother waiting for him. He was dressed in blue suit pants, shiny black shoes and a white shirt that had been splattered with blood. Tobias placed a hand on both of his cold grey cheeks and looked into his blood-shot eyes, devoid of conscience. He took a napkin and wiped a globule of thick red blood from his detached mandible. 'As promised. A little treat, seeing as you've been behaving yourself.' Tobias folded the blood-soaked napkin and put it into one of Kenan's pant pockets. 'Remember the rules everyone!' Tobias called out to the crowd of customers as he and Kenan made their way inside. He held up three fingers and then made his way back to his seat. Tobias smiled at the chaos he had created. Free to leave as long as they sacrificed three digits, the room began to fill with a myriad of dreadful shrieks as Kenan proceeded to ferociously tear into his next victim.

18
Serena

She lay on the hard stone flooring, her arm outstretched, her finger playing with a single strand of straw. The coarse earthen rock on which she was forced to sleep was numbing, holding hiemal properties that were incongruous with the current month of August. It was torture. Beaten and fatigued, she was chained to the heavy stone structure, suffering their justice. She had known the trip to be a risk, the country was at war after all, but she had not foreseen this. She had scoffed at the named "Wars of the Three Kingdoms," insinuating that it was merely a quarrel between lovers. Having left the continent and sailed into London, she had made her way to the town of Manningtree in search of a rumour, a whisper on the lips of dead men. In hindsight, she should have heeded the glares of distrust and distaste she had received when inquiring about the tree, but her curiosity had gotten the better of her and she just sensed that she had found it at last.

Not far from where she had resided for a day, the village of Mistley was home to a famous tree that was said to be at least four centuries old. Mortals had never been too precise with their noting of history, thus, Serena had ample reason to believe that this was indeed the place where Adam had concealed the tree of knowledge. Unfortunately, she was incorrect, and upon discovering the old English oak tree was just a tree she had soon lost her temper. Within the woods, the old tree was wider than it was tall, yet it still stood at least three times her height. It was a strong, menacing, oaken sentry whose roots penetrated the earth, burrowing deep, yet, it offered her no respite from her family's endless search. She had cried out in anger and engulphed the tree in flames, unaware that she was being watched. Her actions were poorly timed in a place currently ripe with persecution, for upon her return back to town, she had instantly been accused of witchcraft. The mob had descended upon her in numbers, yet, uncharacteristically, she had decided not to react with a display of strength and power, for that was exactly what they would have wanted. It would have only encouraged them and made matters worse. However, her situation had only worsened since, due to *his* influence.

They had her stripped of all her fineries and now she resided in a torn up, grey, short-sleeved tunic over the top of a dirty beige coloured gown. They had wanted her to don a wimple, as her fiery hair offended them, but she refused, and so they had beaten her with clubs and forced it upon her. It was the morning after that *he* had begun her trial. Accused of performing witchcraft and of having intercourse with the devil himself, the witchfinder general set to ascertaining the truth of the matter. Hopkins was his name, and he had already sent over three hundred women to their deaths during his short career; the experience made him arrogant. As a form of torture, they had dragged Serena out into the centre of the village square and shackled her to a post. She had been forced to remain awake for the entirety of her trial thus far, which had now lasted over three whole days and, combined with the tests and the beatings, she was extremely drained. At the beginning she had protested her innocence, however, her supernatural abilities had made it so that Hopkins' witch-finding experiments worked against her.

'Many informants say jointly, that you, the accused,

four days past, did beckon with your hand and bring forth a raging flame that possessed a large oak tree! There, within the flames, you called forth Satan, whom, in the form of a man, did you copulate with freely!' As he read out the charges once again, Serena, as she had done before, could not refrain from smirking at the man's ignorance. 'Even now, Satan draws a smile from your lips! You have been tried and found guilty of witchcraft! Cut by a dull blade, your wound healed within minutes! Tested within the pond, you drowned and yet recovered!' The mortal could never understand who she was and therefore any attempt to dissuade him was pointless. Serena knew that the next step would be for her to be put to death, either by hanging or by fire, neither of which she feared. 'As one informant saith, you are ill afraid of fire and thus, at dawn tomorrow, you will be taken forth to Chelmsford and tried by the honourable Robert Rich, Earle of Warwick! It will be of mine own suggestion that you are to be hung...' Serena felt a sense of relief for a moment, but he continued. '... drawn, and quartered! So that to ensure your reign of terror ends!' He stood, dressed in a militaristic, buff, black coat and black rimmed hat, smiling gleefully as he watched Serena take in her punishment. For the first time in a long time, she felt a slight sense of fear, and the passionate rhythm of her heart changed to an anxious gallop.

'Until tomorrow then...' Serena muttered under her breath. She knew she had to do something, but she was weak and her steel restraints were too strong right now.

His smile sickened her and she wished for the strength to wipe it from his face. She gritted her teeth and pulled at her chains like an animal, taking some pleasure from the glimmer of fear that now resided in his eyes as he watched her. She grunted as she climbed to her feet and she could feel the blood in her veins rush thick and fast. Her heart beat strong and she looked up into the nights sky. The rage that burned within her, that she had always carried inside, filled every inch of her body and burst through to the surface of her skin. Hopkins and the others watching over her gasped and retreated in fear as her body became engulphed in flame. 'I will burn you, you insignificant wretch!' she cried. The flames licked up and down her skin and flowed, weaving between strands of her hair until it suddenly forced itself to a single point. Serena could feel the incredible ferocity of the fire, a yearning, a hunger, and looking up at the stars, the fire burst up from her into the darkness of the night, forming a bright hellish beacon for all to see for miles and miles around. And then, as quickly as it had manifested, it was extinguished, leaving Serena spent, lying exhausted on the cold hard ground.

As the summer sun pierced the horizon, the dawn had arrived and Serena's day of judgement was at hand. Hopkins stood before her, a bucket filled with water at his side, savouring every moment as the light snuffed out the darkness of the night.

'Your demonstration at the midnight hour only further damns your soul! For today, witch, you will be put to death!' His confidence only grew as more and more people entered the square to witness Serena being dragged away to Chelmsford to receive her punishment. Serena looked about their faces; both peasant and wealthy alike looked down on her in disgust, but they all exhibited a hint of something else in their expressions as well. Fear perhaps? Or intrigue? In amongst the crowd, one figure caught her gaze. Stood between a number of angry, hateful towns folk, was a man with long brown hair, dressed in a soft-lined, burgundy, short-waisted doublet, dark brown knee length breeches and soft leather boots. He was smiling, but it was his pale-yellow eyes that warmed her heart. She closed her eyes for a moment and took a deep breath in. Re-opening them, she noticed a larger figure that she recognised all too well towards the back of the mass of people. The fire in his eyes re-ignited her confidence and she began to laugh at her accusers; a vengeful laugh for the unfortunate mortals. 'She embraces the fact that she will be soon reunited with her master in hell!' Hopkins called out to the crowd, encouraging their wrath. Frightful jeers sounded out from amongst the rabble and some of the onlookers began to throw things: over-ripened fruit, mould-ridden vegetables and stones. One larger stone struck Serena on her cheek, cutting the skin. 'Satan's concubine bleeds! And yet, wait and see how her skin heals! Witch!' Hopkins reiteration of his assuredness that Serena was in fact a witch seemed to feed those around him, sending out shockwaves of fear-driven energy, fuelling their passion, their hateful desire for Serena to be punished. The only thing preventing this crowd from descending upon her and carrying out their own form of justice were the few law enforcers, the watchmen that helped ensure the countries laws were upheld.

Serena watched and waited as Hopkins continued to goad the public into not only believing the accusations he put forth, but also to begin shouting out their own imaginative and illusory indictments. A fair trial would have been impossible and Serena could only pity the many women that had already been put to death at the will of the witchfinder general. 'It is time for this witch to be judged! Chain her to the rear of my carriage!'

'Let her be dragged! If she survives, then it is once again proven that she is in league with the devil!' As the crowd grew bolder, more and more individuals took to the spotlight. Serena scanned the masses until she descried two more of her siblings, her family. Evelina wore her golden hair in a mass of tight curls and displayed a set of emerald earrings and an emerald stone filled necklace. She wore a long, tight white satin bodice with paned sleeves lined in pink and a matching petticoat. Nahki stood beside her. He was barefoot, but he had donned a pair of beige coloured breeches and a brown doublet.

What are you waiting for? Do you enjoy watching me at

the hands of these mortals? Serena couldn't help but wonder the reason for her sibling's inaction.

Fear not, sister. Tobias smirked as Serena looked at him. 'People of Manningtree! May I have your attention!' Tobias' voice sounded above the din of the crowd and caused the majority of them to silence and turn to look upon him. Jumping up onto a short dry-stone wall and hopping until he found some sure footing, he smiled as he gained control of the situation. Serena could tell that he had most of them enthralled, but there were a few that were obviously stronger of mind than the rest.

'Who are you, sir? Why do you beckon at this time?' Hopkins' body language suggested that he was perturbed by the interruption. He stood defiantly, staring Tobias down, but this was one battle of wills that he had no chance of winning.

'You wish to learn my name, witchfinder?' Tobias carefully took a few steps along the wall and stretched out his arms, raising his hands to interact with the crowd. 'My name is Nobody. Like the good people here, I am nobody!' As Tobias raised his voice, cheers sounded from within the towns people. 'But she...' He pointed at Serena. 'She is the hearth when all else is gone. Good people, would you have this man put out the fires in your homes that keep you warm?!' The crowd began to groan collectively. Tobias looked to Hopkins, his eyes grew wider and the yellow within them coruscated. Taken aback by the evil glow of Tobias' eyes, Hopkins stepped back away from him, backing up towards where Serena was currently chained.

'The devil resides in you, sir! Guards!' The confidence that had rode on Hopkins' tone during the entire trial had left him and now his voice was shrill and full of fear. Serena cackled at the weakened, misguided mortal. Three of the law enforcers responded to the witchfinder general's call for aid. The others simply stood still, as, like most of the town folk, they were no longer acting of their own free will.

'Fool,' Tobias smirked. 'Then come together again so that Satan cannot tempt you because of your lack of self-control!' He stretched out his arms, emphasising the fact that the people, Hopkins' people, still did nothing. 'Good people of Manningtree! Unfortunately, the witchfinder general, Matthew Hopkins, has taken ill! Leave and return to your homes, for tomorrow, you shall mourn his passing!' Hopkins moved to protest, yet the crowd began to disperse before him. He was perplexed by what was happening, witnessing the closest instance to witchcraft he had ever seen.

'Witch!' Hopkins cried out, but his cry fell on deaf ears as the town's folk left the square. All that now resided by his side were three of the guards. 'Seize him!'

Two guards rushed towards Tobias wielding pikes. The third stayed back; holding a musket, he aimed towards their target. Tobias remained still, smiling at his attackers as they advanced. Just before they reached him, he bowed sarcastically and then once they were within striking distance, Tobias proceeded to toy with the watchmen, dodging their swings and thrusts. The musket wielding guard fired, but before the lead ball reached its intended target, Nahki caught it, plucking it out of the air. He spun around and threw the bullet back at the guard, hitting him in the neck and opening his throat in front of Hopkins. Nahki then joined Tobias in playing with the two watchmen, goading them and then swatting away or dodging their attacks, whilst Evelina and Brandt moved to Serena's side.

'Thank –' Serena went to thank Evelina for coming to her aid, however, she stopped mid-sentence after receiving a look of disapproval from her.

'The tree?' Evelina asked in a dispassionate manner. Serena shook her head in response, invoking a deep green glow within a scornful look.

'W–W–Witches!' Hopkins trembled in fear, pointing his finger at Evelina and then at each of them. His passion for the hunt was lost as he faced the closest thing to the supernatural that he no doubt ever had.

'Enough!' Evelina commanded. Tobias and Nahki instantly stopped toying with the guards and, in self-defence, simultaneously snapped both of their necks. 'You!' Evelina expressed her anger towards Hopkins, forcing him to fall to his knees in an act of submission. 'You slaughter women in the name of your king, your god?! And yet you also preach, in your churches and in your streets, of their mercy! You...' Evelina took a step back from the man and turned to look upon Serena. The hint of pity in her eyes infuriated Serena. As far as she was concerned, this was Adam's fault. Once again, they had been crippled by his law, his curse.

I came here looking for your damn tree and you look upon me so... Serena glared back at Evelina and pulled on her restraints.

'You are all under arrest! Guilty of –' Hopkins attempted to regain some control of the situation, but Evelina put a stop to his yelling.

'You have shamed and belittled a goddess of the flame. My family may be cursed for now, but what you should know, Mr. Hopkins –' Evelina turned back to face the snivelling whelp, '– is that in order to test Serena, you *cut* her...' Evelina smiled wickedly and laughed before turning back to Serena and placing her hand on her bosom. As the emerald of her eyes shone, Serena could feel new life being blown through her. It was as if Evelina was throwing a mountain of kindling on the fire that burned within and now the flames raged throughout Serena, smashing against the confines of her skin, bombarding the ambit of her being. 'I consider Serena to be my daughter, witchfinder, and you have harmed her. In times long since passed she has been mistaken by some, revered by others. Whether they knew her as Hestia or Vesta, they all came to witness the passion that she carried within. The hearth from which her fiery rage emanates.'

'Satan resides within –!' Hopkins once again attempted to shout.

'Silence!' Evelina exclaimed furiously, before regaining her poise. She dusted off her hands and was done with the mortal. She then moved to stand beside Brandt, Tobias and Nahki, allowing Serena to act out her own punishment.

The heat Serena now felt within excited her. Her wounds healed and her full strength had returned. She effortlessly broke free of her restraints, and as she went to dust herself off, she began to laugh at the realisation of what she must look like.

'What the hell am I wearing... I don't know what's worse, this dress or the pathetic attempt at torture.' She could feel the fury spiralling within her head and heart; the fire was hungry for vengeance. Marching over to Hopkins, she grabbed him around the throat and lifted him to his feet. 'Do not ask for mercy, for I will never grant a man thus for as long as I carry the fire within.' With her free hand, Serena held out her index finger and created a flame that danced upon its tip. She waved it in front of his eyes and revelled in the fear and despair that saturated them. 'You believe in hell. Let us see if you'd survive in such a place.' She poked him with her finger, pressing and prodding at his navel. Concentrating her rage, the flame ate away his clothing and burnt away the small hairs on his abdomen. He winced in pain as the heat began to burn his skin, but due to Serena's grip, he was unable to scream, only able to sound out a muffled moan in response. She pushed her fingertip into the navel and stared into his eyes as the skin perished and her finger bore into his flesh. Rotating her finger, she enlarged the hole that she had now made and smiled at him with gritted teeth before thrusting her whole hand inside. Taking pleasure from his tears and moans as he attempted to cry out, she savoured each passing second until she was done with him. The flame on her finger enveloped her hand and she flooded his body with fire, burning away his intestines, his liver, bladder and stomach whilst he was still alive. Then, as his life ended, she released him, and his lifeless vessel fell to the ground with a thud.

She looked back on the days before Adam had unlocked her emotional capability with a simple fondness. Tobias had assured her that she would come to rejoice her newfound empathy for the human condition and that her power would only grow. It was a half-truth. She considered the fact that if it weren't for Adam and her new strength, Barachiel would have undoubtedly destroyed her. On the reverse side, if she were dead, she would not feel the way she currently did. It would be easy to hate Mike, to despise him as she had his gender for so long. It was gut-wrenching how she had allowed his existence to pain her so. She hated all the hurt that he had put her through and even more so, the fact that she blamed herself for letting him make her feel this way. It frustrated her that her emotions had latched onto a single being, and that no matter how many sexual partners she had had recently, not one had made an impact. Yet, despite contempt, she had come to his aid when he called. *I wish I could just let you die...* she thought as she looked at him. Mike was a shadow of his former self. He knelt, throwing up his last meal into his toilet as Serena sat, perched on the side of his bath tub. The only thing keeping him alive was the velocity, a concoction of one of her sibling's blood. However, the same drug was what was killing him, almost as fast as it was helping to heal him.

'I'm down to my last few v... it's... it's getting harder to get hold of...' he said between laboured breaths. Serena knew it would become harder to obtain. The Avunaye were not blood banks, there was only so much product available at any one time and as demand went up, it would prove harder and harder to keep Mike with ample supply. What she needed was the source, but each of her siblings had denied any involvement.

'Without knowing who is giving the blood... I don't know how to stop it from killing you...'

'Thanks for sugar-coating it...' Mike lifted his head long enough to smile.

'I did. Truth be told it will eventually liquify your internal organs...' She felt bad for baring the truth, which only annoyed her further. 'Argh!' she shouted as she stood up and stomped her foot, cracking the flooring. 'These infernal feelings! You do not care for me and yet I am willing to help you... save you... why?!' Serena pulled at her hair. 'You're an insignificant man! You'll age and rot in the ground. Why the fuck do I care?!'

'I'm not crazy about needing your help either...' his voice echoed slightly in the pan. 'Think I like this? After –'

'After what I did to you? Fuck you. If it were not for these relentless feelings of desire and a fear of loneliness, I would have drowned you in your own vomit the second I arrived!' The battle of snide remarks and sarcasm continued until Mike passed out on the bathroom floor. Serena had considered bringing up her recent interaction with Lucy, but had thought better of it. She also contemplated leaving him there – it would serve him right – but he was helpless and she struggled to simply turn her back. Serena lifted him up and carried him to his bed. As she lay him down, she proceeded to lay down next to him, brushing her fingers gently through his sweat-laden hair. Face to face, she considered taking advantage of his condition to satisfy her own needs. But despite her desire, as she stared at his face, a painful feeling lingered, pulling on her heart strings. It was his consent that was a desideratum.

19
Nahki

He stooped and lifted the chains up off the floor grasping them tightly, squeezing them as he contemplated his next move. Considering the condition of the restraints and scanning the room, noting the markings that had been left on the floor, Nahki surmised that there had not been a struggle. He deliberated on what he knew to be true, what he could trust. He had killed Adam roughly sixty hours ago so the likelihood that he was able to break himself out was minute. They had moved him to this particular site a week ago to the day; Evelina required Adam to be free, so Nahki had arranged for him to be moved to a black site on the outskirts of Tunkhannock, Pennsylvania. Situated in the once highly lumbered borough, the building was set back from any main roads and highways to ensure privacy. Fairly dated, the building housed a veranda that encircled around eighty-percent of it, with many bushes along its perimeter, a roof of mottled green colour and window shutters that were painted a darker shade of green. To the rear, a garden ran down to a stream and beyond that was dense woodland. This black site was closer to the city of New York, but still remained far enough away to avoid any unwanted attention.

Adam had been chained up in the basement of the house. No one was allowed in the room without Nahki's prior approval, so he doubted that the two agents that he had personally chosen to watch over Adam, could have been involved with his disappearance. Both of them single, without any family to speak of, logically, they were ideal candidates for secretive operations, as they would unlikely be tempted to give away their position, accidentally or otherwise. Nahki had been given free-reign to interrogate Adam to obtain whatever information he could to assist with concerns of national security, and to this end, he had only had to report to one person; the director. So, of the four people that knew of Adam's location, Nahki had surmised that the director was the most likely to have been compromised. Nahki sifted some of the dirt from the ground, rubbing it between his palms as he considered the possible motive for his superior to have taken Adam.

James insists that he did not see who it was that took Adam. Nahki knew his agents were flawed, they were mortal after all, so he had no reason to doubt their blunder; the question weighed on his mind, however. *The director denies any knowledge of Adam's disappearance, leaving only a handful of possibilities. Who else might have made a move for him?*

Nahki remained still, squatting in the dirt ridden basement they had used for a prison cell. He sniffed at the soil and woodchip that covered the ground, attempting to catch a scent of someone or something. Any clue. *One of the Avunaye, the department of justice, Markovic perhaps?* He ran through the most likely culprits in his head as he processed what his wolf-like sense of smell was picking up. Whoever it was, they had been within the city limits recently. There was an underlying scent that he caught ever so slightly, one that puzzled him for a moment. *Kerosene...* He stood up and dusted off his hands and then his pants. 'James?!' he called out to the agent that was posted just outside the room.

'Yeah, Zane?' he responded informally.

'Jet-fuel... Do me a favour and check out recent activity in the surrounding states, West Virginia, Ohio, New York... I'm looking for military personnel, Army, D.O.D, the works. Someone of import...'

'I'll get on it. You work this out from an empty room?' Nahki turned to James and exhibited a blatant look of impatience in response to his comment. Acknowledging the expression, the agent left to carry out his task. Whilst he waited, Nahki continued to examine the room.

Adam was most likely laying down, he deduced from the position of the restraints and impressions on the floor. *His abductors were careless, leaving two... no, three sets of footprints.* He continued to calculate what had happened, envisaging it all play out in his mind. *They carried him... he was yet to revive. They must have known of his ability to heal, else, why be so careful with a dead body?* He heard James' approach and turned to greet him at the entrance.

'Zane, nothing stands out within the last six months.' He was holding a tablet device for Zane to peruse. 'However, digging a little deeper, two weeks ago...' he pointed to the information on screen. It listed visitor details for the Jacob K. Javits federal building. Nahki pursed his lips and nodded in appreciation of the agents work. James nodded back and then backed out of the room, leaving Nahki stood, unmoving, contemplating his next move. Taking out his phone, he had made his decision.

'Solomon, it's Zane Brown,' he began the conversation. 'Something has come up in the Adam case...'

Nahki dressed casually for the meet, wearing light-brown, soft-leather laced shoes, a pair of dark-blue denim pants with the cuffs turned up, a white t-shirt and a light-grey, long-sleeved shirt that he left open at the front. He also wore his necklace, the rubies standing prominent against the white of his top. Ensuring that his meeting with Solomon was brief, Nahki took the opportunity to invite both Lucy and Krysta to chat at a local café. Agreeing to the meet, Nahki sensed an air of mistrust from the pair of F.B.I agents, however, he had their intrigue.

He knew the two women in depth, having studied

them and the rest of their team for some time now. He knew Lucy liked her morning coffee black, yet as the day went on, she'd add more and more cream. Krysta would also take hers in a paper takeaway cup, regardless of whether she was staying or not. Like a hunter stalking prey, Nahki wished to know every detail, every habit of those he considered integral pawns to Evelina's plans; it enabled him to anticipate their actions. For example, Krysta's bombardment of questions regarding Adam and his whereabouts came as no surprise.

'I'm afraid I can't help you with that...' Nahki told Krysta for the fourth time. They had barely exchanged pleasantries when her demands for information had begun.

'Bullshit, Zane!' Krysta said bluntly. 'Knowing the C.I.A, you probably know what I had for breakfast this morning. I want to know how he is, where he is.' Krysta frustratedly ran her hands through her hair, interlocking her fingers behind her head. Lucy on the other hand, seemed less interested in what Krysta had to say, she sat back, slumped in her chair, almost staring through him as if he weren't even there.

'It's a matter of national security. You know what an asset Adam is –'

'An asset? Fucking hell, Zane,' Krysta blurted out.

'Shouldn't even have said that. Just, trust me...' Nahki feigned a smile. He needed them both on his side.

'Just because he can't die, it doesn't give you the right to torture him for six fucking months,' Krysta said exasperatedly.

'I believe you recently had a run in with Serena?' Nahki tried to change the topic of conversation and rouse some form of response from Lucy, whom had so far seemed disinterested in the subject of Adam, uncharacteristically biting her tongue; perhaps the subject of Serena would loosen her lips. 'You give me this, and *maybe*...' He knew they would understand him and so he reclined in his seat and crossed his legs, opening himself up, awaiting their reply.

'Not so much of a "run in," more of an exchange of words,' Lucy finally responded, rolling her eyes. 'Of course, then some crazed bitch walked in and blew the place sky high.' She appeared unamused, but her mannerisms led Nahki to believe that there was something she wanted to ask him. She shuffled in her chair and then leant forward into the table. Nursing her coffee, she tapped her finger tips of the surface of the table and then sat back again. 'What do you want, Zane?'

'That all depends, what do *you* want to know?' he smiled.

'The crazy red-head, not Serena, the other one... She... Serena said that it was Adam that had made it possible for her... Ah fuck! I don't – I don't understand what the fuck is going on!' Lucy slammed her drink down, spilling some of it. 'As long as one bitch takes out the other, who cares...'

'Your father might.' Nahki said the words plainly, yet he knew that it would set off a proverbial bomb within the conversation.

'The general?' Krysta was quick to question Nahki's insinuation.

'What has the general got to do with any of this?' Lucy's grip of her cup tightened and she clenched her other fist.

'You are aware that he knows of the Avunaye. I need to know how much he knows.' Nahki waited for Lucy to say something, but it seemed her thoughts were working on overtime. 'Two questions. Is he still in town? And where is he based?' Nahki joined his fingers at their tips and looked Lucy in the eye, yet, she remained tight-lipped.

'Luce, honey...' Krysta gave her colleague a nudge before turning her attention back to Nahki. 'If she tells you –'

'Krys! what the hell?!' Lucy barked at Krysta's suggestion that they provide Nahki with anything.

'This information isn't free. You have to give us something.' Krysta's mood shifted as Lucy gave her a disappointing glare, however, she then focused her anger or annoyance onto Nahki. 'Zane. You will give us something on Adam, and you *will* keep us up to date regarding whatever business you have with the general,' Krysta said confidently. Nahki raised an eyebrow to the demands.

'We tested him. Adam. We killed him again and again.' Nahki smiled and then stood up from his seat.

'You son of a bitch! That's it?!' Krysta jumped up to confront him.

'I'll update you regarding the general's involvement, should it not jeopardise my own investigation. As for Adam, he lost every memory he had it seems, except those of his family. Well, that, and one other.' He smiled again and crossed his arms.

'What other?' Krysta quickly asked, yet Nahki was unwilling to say anymore until they answered his questions.

'Yes,' Lucy said frustratedly. 'The general is in town. Good luck finding him.' Lucy stood up as she provided the information, giving Krysta a sharp look before barging past Nahki, heading for the exit.

'Fort Hamilton, I think,' Krysta's anger subsided as her friend departed; she looked deflated.

'That other thing that Adam never forgot...' Zane pushed his chair in and began to walk away, having gotten the information he wanted. He had no need to continue the interaction, yet he looked back as he reached the door to see Krysta slump back down into her chair. Then, like throwing a treat to a pup, he gave her what she truly wanted to hear before he exited the café. '...It was you.'

Nahki had changed his attire before heading to the fort; he had visited the site a number of times before and could not afford to be recognised. Switching his civilian clothes for a simple pair of black shorts, he left most of his flesh uncovered, allowing him complete freedom of movement and the ability to shapeshift quickly. He reached the fort at nightfall and used his ability to phase through matter to stealthily make his way into the compound. As ludicrous as it might have seemed, Nahki surmised that Fort Hamilton was an ideal location. Surrounded by residential buildings, the fort was more of a tourist attraction than a military complex. If Adam was being held here, no one would suspect it. His mission was two-fold: firstly, he needed to search for any sign of Adam and secondly, he hadn't ruled out the possibility that the army had possession of Brandt's body. He made his way through several buildings and found nothing, but the next, the National Guard and Army Reserve Centre, was of particular interest, as there were a number of personnel performing patrols around the periphery, an unusually high level of security for such a building. He observed the building from the branches of a nearby tree, watching as the location appeared more and more promising. Nahki smiled, and then closed his eyes, mentally preparing himself for his assault.

He leaned backwards and tumbled from the tree, landing on the ground on all fours. Moving quickly, he sprinted towards the nearest wall, avoiding the patrols. Pausing briefly as he reached it, he then proceeded to walk through it, as if it were a mere doorway and found himself on the opposite side within a long hallway. Before him were signs for the cafeteria and information desk, but he was searching for the offices, or perhaps a medical or laboratory environment. He moved silently through the building, avoiding guards by adjusting his course where necessary or passing through walls into new rooms so as to not be detected. His search, however, was beginning to seem in vein. *Why the security if there is nothing here?* He contemplated the idea that this was perhaps the wrong location after all.

'The general is gonna bust your balls if he finds out you been drinking that shit.' Nahki heard someone speak from within one of the rooms further down the hallway; a mess of sorts.

'Fuck Rodriguez,' another voice sounded, 'this place used to be a piece of piss before he moved in.' Nahki was pleased to hear his time had not been completely wasted. From the sounds of things, the general was here on the base, yet, if Nahki was to learn as to whether the army was involved in the disappearances of Adam and Brandt's body, he would need to get the general alone. He could extract the information he required regarding the current location of the general from a guard, but he needed to ensure his presence here remained undetected, and so he continued his search quietly, moving back through areas he had previously searched to double check.

Nahki finally found the room he was looking for in an unlikely place. It appeared the general had commandeered the gymnasium for his own makeshift base of operations. The room had only one entrance, with two guards permanently positioned outside of it, not that this posed too much of a problem. Moving back along the hallway, Nahki managed to find an adjoining room and passed through a wall only to find the gym empty of people. However, he couldn't rely on it remaining that way for long, so he would need to work swiftly.

The gym equipment had been pushed to the outskirts of the room that was now full of tables topped with computers and a number of whiteboards detailing numerous military strategies. Making a calculated guess as to which desk belonged to the general, based on the fact that it was immaculately tidy in comparison to the mess that covered the others, Nahki managed to navigate his way onto the general's computer and discovered some interesting files that contained the blueprints for a panic-room of sorts.

Twelve-inch thick steel walls... keeping something in, or out? Nahki also found a series of lab-test results regarding blood work they had carried out on an unnamed subject. *Running tests on Adam?* Nahki assumed as he scanned through before deleting what he could. He searched for further intel, hoping to find a location for the proposed steel cage, yet, instead, he discovered something unexpected. *Operation PRINCES...* He clenched his fists as he began to read a preliminary report, but then the door opened.

She was stunning. Wearing a pair of mottled green camo pants, black boots and a beige short-sleeved top, her skin was a golden caramel colour, her long hair was mocha, and her eyes were a deep, smoky brown.

'...And *who* might you be?' as the words left her subtle pink lips, Nahki found himself having to shake himself from an induced daze.

'I could ask you the same question.' He held his ground, but subtly placed his hand on the opposite forearm.

'And I might answer, a dispenser of eternal and abundant mercy.' She closed the door behind her and then stood with a military-style stance, awaiting his next move, her hands behind her back.

'So, you are one of, *them*,' Nahki announced in a tone of distaste. Her presence more than complicated his mission.

'You use such a tone with me, yet, you are the filth that plagues this world. An abomination. If I had to guess, I would presume you to be Nahki, the twelfth.' Nahki attempted to calculate his odds of winning this fight, however, knowing that both Evelina and Serena had chosen to flee, he decided that his chances were unfavourable.

'Tell me, what is someone like *you* doing working with the military?' Nahki could feel the tip of the hilt of a blade on his arm, readying himself for whatever happened next.

'Common goals,' she simply replied. 'If you are searching for Adam, you have wasted your time, and forfeited yourself for nothing.' She slowly brought her right-hand round to her side, revealing that she was holding something; a rope of sorts, rolled in a loop.

'So, they do have him...' Nahki was working on borrowed time, but he needed further information.

'*Had* him. I insisted that Adam was to be held no longer. He is free.' Nahki chose to believe her as she had no reason to lie to him, and thus, this knowledge made staying in this position fruitless, so Nahki made the decision to leave. He would, however, require a head start.

He smiled at her and then swiftly removed the blade from his flesh. The blade hurtled towards her, but within a blink of an eye she deflected it using the rope, which as she unravelled it, Nahki could now clearly see was a whip. Cranking back her shoulder in a fast, fluid movement, she raised her hand and with a sharp flick of her wrist, lashed out at Nahki. The whip was three-thronged, with sharp metal tips at its ends. One cut Nahki across his cheek, a second across his shoulder. He managed to grab hold of the whip before she could recoil it and he quickly pulled another blade from his chest. The sheer velocity at which she reacted, however, shocked Nahki. She leapt forward and kicked one of the desks, sending it crashing against him and knocking him back against the wall. The room grew intensely bright as her skin began to emanate a breathtakingly white glow. The look in her eyes, for one who spoke of mercy, held none within them. For the first time in as long as he could recall, Nahki felt. He felt the distasteful feeling of fear as his mortality was in question. She pulled back on the whip, preparing to strike again and as she did, for an instant, the light that she emitted created a shadow across the room behind her. Perfect silhouettes spread out from her core, one either side of her, and in their penumbra was a profusion of divine feathers. Nahki closed his eyes and stepped backwards sharply, the molecules of his being phasing through the structure. Upon finding himself on the opposite side of the wall, he turned and fled, running in a direct path, passing through each wall until he found himself outside. He paused for a moment upon breathing in the nights air. Something within him was different; his heart was beating slightly faster and hands trembled for a split second. It was an alien sensation, but with the knowledge that she would no doubt not be too far behind him, and with a deep desire for survival, he leapt up into the nights sky, shedding his human form and taking flight.

20

Krysta Rose-Anderson

'C'mon, Sol, you've got to let me chase this. *Let us* chase this lead.' The connection between the Avunaye, or at least Brandt, and Markovic and the N.Y.P.D was clear in Krysta's eyes, but she was struggling to convince Solomon. She needed his approval to push it further, but he was hesitating. Relationships were in the balance.

'Krysta, relations between the F.B.I and the N.Y.P.D at present are delicate. We've kept them at arms-length this entire investigation and they've taken heavy losses. A detective was murdered and a sergeant has now gone AWOL.' Krysta was aware that another officer had disappeared, but it just made her case all the more important. 'Besides, you want to question these officers regarding their supposed involvement in taking down one of the Avunaye... This should be handed over to Zane.' Frustrated and baffled by Solomon's response Krysta struggled to hold back her passion to drive this investigation home.

'Zane? Seriously? I trust that guy about as much as you, or at least as much as you once did...' She needed help, another voice, some backup to help force Solomon's hand as he simply wasn't hearing her. *Where the hell is Lucy?* she wondered each time the conversation found a pause. Her colleague, friend and partner in crime was meant to be joining her in this meeting. Lucy had as much reason as anyone to want any connection to the Avunaye investigated. Krysta had banked on her stubborn determination to win the day, to persuade Solomon, but thus far she had stood her up. 'If it makes *you* feel any better, technically, we are investigating the connection between the N.Y.P.D and Markovic, they just happened to kill the same Avunaye... The idea that this should fall under C.I.A jurisdiction is circumstantial at best.' The fact of the matter was, Krysta was no closer to finding Adam now than she was four months ago, and it angered her. So, to avoid wallowing in self-pity at the realisation of her defeat, she was determined to finish what she had started; she was going to take down Markovic and all of his associates, and perhaps, when all of it was done, maybe she'd find herself closer to Adam.

Exhausting herself, Krysta continued to argue her case, despite Solomon's continued dismissal's. She could tell that she hadn't even begun to wear him down and was beginning to suspect that he was toying with her by not simply shutting her down and asking her to leave his office. But then he abruptly stood up from his seat and crossed his arms. The look in his eyes was all too familiar – he was tired and annoyed.

'Krysta, look...' It was the start of a closing sentence and Krysta could tell that her time was up. 'What you've got can be chalked up to mere coincidence and rumour. It's just not enough.' She ran her hands through her hair frustratedly. She had all the proof she needed, in Claire, in Carmen, but she could never, she *would* never use it. Krysta trusted Solomon, but Claire's secret wasn't hers to divulge and using it to win an argument would not only destroy her and Claire's relationship, it would place Claire in unnecessary danger. So, dejected, Krysta stood up and turned her back on her superior, ready to leave his office, when suddenly Lucy appeared on the other side of the glass door.

'I'm late, I know, but you won't give a fuck when you

see what I've got,' Lucy blurted out as she opened the door. 'Sol, you've got to let us push this N.Y.P.D angle. Interview room two.' She gestured to them both, urging them to follow her. 'C'mon then!' she ordered impatiently, sighing at Krysta's and Solomon's slowness to react.

Lucy had been more upbeat of late; a woman on a mission. She had clearly taken Zane's insinuation that her father was involved with the Avunaye to heart, and ever since, she had thrown herself back into her work. She had told Krysta that she was struggling to find Mike the help he needed, but she was never going to give up on him. It was probably both of these things combined that had spurned her on into jumping back into the Markovic investigation. No doubt of the same mind as Krysta, she figured that all roads will hopefully lead them to the same destination. Lucy marched ahead and held the door open to the observation room. As Krysta approached, Lucy gave her a reassuring wink, which helped to calm Krysta's nerves a little.

'Okay, Lucy, you've dragged us here. What do you have for us?' Solomon's tone was laced with scepticism which irked Krysta; she couldn't understand his reluctance in all of this. They all stood in the observation room, looking through the window into the empty interrogation room. Krysta was a little puzzled.

'Just wait here. Watch, and listen'. Lucy left the room, leaving Krysta and Solomon waiting in suspense. Krysta glanced at Solomon and tried to wonder what was wrong. Whereas usually he would hold such a rigid stance, attentive to all that was happening around him, today he fidgeted, and judging by Krysta's observations, he was disinterested in whatever it was Lucy had to show them.

Krysta and Solomon's awkward silence was thankfully broken when the door to the interrogation room opened and Lucy walked in with a woman beside her. Dressed in a grubby pair of beige combat pants and a black vest, her blonde hair with a thick black streak, combined with the scar across her right cheek, made it easy for Krysta to identify her. Lucy welcomed the woman inside and offered her a seat, which she reluctantly took. She was visibly nervous. Known to be linked to Markovic and his associates, they knew her as Raven, yet Krysta knew her name to be Sinead. Solomon's interest seemed to have finally been snared as he watched attentively through the glass. 'Your name is Sinead Hrafn, correct?' Lucy asked, to which Sinead rolled her eyes in response.

'Call me Raven.' She glanced at the glass, likely in the knowledge that there'd be someone watching her from behind its reflective surface.

'Raven. You manage the Twin Dice bar, right?' Lucy sat back, relaxed, no doubt hoping to help Sinead to relax as well.

'Not anymore...' She shuddered and looked about the room nervously. It was a hot day and yet Krysta noticed that she continually rubbed her arms as if she was cold. Clearly anxious, her mannerisms had Krysta distracted for a moment until she finally saw what was right in front of them. Sinead had a scar on her lower neck that matched detective Cannons and that of the woman from the stronghold. She was marked.

'Sol, look! She has the exact same scar as the others. Tell me now that it's just a "coincidence".' Krysta almost put her finger through the glass frantically pointing it out to him.

'You were picked up trying to board a flight to Europe, Raven. Does your employer, or ex-employer, know that you were attempting to leave the country?' Lucy remained calm, sticking to simple questions that would hopefully yield incriminating answers.

'Look, sweet. You know full well who I worked for, else you wouldn't have dragged me here. Let's not beat around the bush... Get to the point.' Sinead remained agitated as she provided the information. 'I worked for Vlad, not anymore. We took down that Brandt guy, did the fucking world a favour. But we got marked, now we're dropping like flies. Vlad and Kryln are gone, fucked off to South America, leaving the rest of us sorry bastards dealing with the shit they left behind.'

'What shit have you been left to deal with Raven?' Lucy asked. Krysta could feel how close they were to getting a lead that Solomon couldn't rebuke. She was also impressed by how collected Lucy was throughout.

'This!' Sinead shouted, pulling at her vest strap and pointing to the mark. 'Each of us got one, everyone involved in killing that big fucker! Vlad said we were taking the fight to them, but now... *He* came to my bar and told me to run. I went back a day later to grab some of my shit... but... the place was full of fucked up dead bodies.' Sinead pulled at her face and slammed her feet into the floor, pushing her chair back towards the corner of the room.

'Who helped you kill Brandt, Raven? And who told you to run?' Lucy's tone began to carry an air of urgency. Krysta almost smiled in anticipation of Sinead's response.

C'mon... say N.Y.P.D were involved... say Cannon...

'Mostly Vlad's and Kryln's guys. We thought nothing of the mark until one of our places got hit, and then that cop died...'

'So, N.Y.P.D officers were involved?' Lucy prodded.

'Only a couple.'

'And who told you to run, Raven?'

'The one with the yellow eyes... The sadistic fucker that can read your mind...' She retreated further into the corner. 'We are all fucked!' she laughed and then began to break down, lifting her feet up onto the chair and curling up into a submissive position, as her emotions climaxed and fear overcame her.

'Have Zane look into the bar, the guy with the yellow eyes, but we have proof – *She* gave us proof. N.Y.P.D involvement... C'mon, Sol, just give me the go,' Krysta begged.

Solomon stood still, taking up a stance that was more familiar to Krysta as he looked resolutely through the glass, processing everything.

'Work the Markovic – N.Y.P.D angle...' he said with some reluctance. 'You and Lucy, keep it formal, keep it delicate. We don't need a bigger rift between the agency and the police than we already have.' Krysta couldn't help but smile victoriously. Solomon then turned to look at her. 'I mean it, Krysta. Tactful. And nothing involving the Avunaye.'

Being asked to be "tactful" felt like an insult as she had always maintained a professional attitude towards work, but Krysta would let it slide. She understood that Solomon was nervous; he was once again under pressure to get results. He had to watch his step, which could explain his behaviour of late and, as he said, the bureau's relationship with local law enforcement was close to breaking point. Krysta arranged for her and Lucy to meet with Chief Pérez this afternoon, so, after grabbing some lunch, they made their way to the station. Krysta had thought it best to carry out the meeting on the police chief's turf, rather than call Pérez in. She had hoped that it would be seen as a good will gesture and work in their favour; they were looking to accuse some of her officers of being in cahoots with a crime boss and therefore they needed all the help they could get to stop this from blowing up in their faces.

'How long is she gonna keep us waiting, Krys?' Lucy asked as it reached the half-hour mark since they had been asked to wait in the departments interview room. 'I feel like we're the ones under the microscope. Sat in this dingy room...' Lucy impatiently tapped her foot on the table leg.

'Hon, calm down. You know the deal... She's just trying to disarm us. Make us stew for a bit.' Krysta remained patient, but if they were made to wait too much longer, she was afraid of what Lucy would end up doing. Thankfully, the door opened and the department captain, Captain Wu, apologised for the delay and invited them to follow him to the chief's office.

As they entered, Chief Pérez shook their hands. They had met briefly on several occasions, but Krysta couldn't help but replay the meeting at Times Square in her mind. She had shut Lucy down effortlessly during that meeting and pronounced Seamus dead, without even blinking. The captain, Daniel Wu, took up position beside the chief's desk. He had short black hair and a spotless uniform; he stood at the ready as if part of the military. His stance showed a clear respect for Pérez, Krysta surmised.

'Please, take a seat.' Pérez smiled and gestured to the chairs on the near side of her desk. She then proceeded to walk around it and sit down in her large comfy chair. She wore her long dark hair up in a bun and her honey-coloured skin was flawless; her beauty and soft, subtle features, were clearly designed by nature to mislead, for Krysta knew that she was known by her officers as "The Pitbull". 'So, agents, straight to the point if you will.' She was blunt and the look in her eye suggested she had little time to waste.

Krysta took the lead in the conversation, choosing her words carefully and adhering to Solomon's plea for subtlety and tact. She also knew that Lucy's and the chief's personalities would likely clash, so the less they interacted with one another, the better. Chief Pérez absorbed the information without contestation, no doubt waiting for Krysta to finish before she spoke her mind; the thought of which made Krysta anxious.

'These are the files and photos relating to the investigation.' Krysta slid a file across the desk, 'you can keep that, it's a copy.' Pérez opened the file and briefly flicked through it until she came across the crime scene photos for detective Cannon.

'Is this it? The mark you spoke of? The one that's branded onto the neck of everyone that was involved in the killing of this Brandt, which, apparently you have no evidence of, as there is no body to speak of.' Pérez stared at the pair of them, unconvinced and with a glimmer in her eyes that suggested she was about to explode. 'Do you know how many funerals I have attended in the last year and a half?' Krysta went to speak but was swiftly silenced as the chief gave her a sharp stern look. 'Each and every time I had to stand up in front colleagues, friends, families. Each time making poor excuses because all I am provided by the F.B.I are half-truths and bullshit excuses regarding national security. I currently have a sergeant missing and you come and ask *me* to help *you*?!' Like a volcano she had begun to erupt, however, it was clear she was just getting warmed up. 'Do you understand that, as a woman in my position, I am constantly under scrutiny. You come into *my* office and accuse *my* officers of being vigilantes! Of banding together with the scum of this city! Of being on the take! You have some nerve!'

'That's it!' Lucy leapt out of her seat and slammed her palms down onto the desk whilst blurting out something in Spanish. Her reaction prompted Pérez to also jump up in response. Krysta tried to grab Lucy, to reign her back in. 'No, Krys. She needs to hear this.' Lucy gave Krysta a recognisable glance and then stared back at the chief. 'This "bullshit" is real. You are not the only one operating with one hand tied behind your back, but do you hear us complaining about it? Markovic and Cardoza are our targets and they should be yours as well. Now, we have a witness that ties Markovic to your detective and at least one other unidentified officer.' Somehow Pérez was managing to bite her tongue and take Lucy's assault in her stride, but Krysta could tell from the look in her eyes that she was taking on board what Lucy was saying. 'We want justice for your guys, just as much as we do for our own, we have both lost good people, but wouldn't you want to know if one or more of them *are* on the take? We are giving you a quick and easy way to work out who you can and can't trust. Check their necks. It's as fucking simple as that.'

Tactics and subtly nil, Lucy, one. Krysta couldn't help but be a little impressed. The crazy thing was, was that it appeared Pérez admired Lucy's brazenness, and she agreed to look into the connection to her precinct personally. It seemed her pride came second to her badge.

After discussing chief Pérez's plan to weed out any corrupt members of her force, Krysta, Lucy and a group of officers headed to the Twin Dice bar to see if there was any truth to Sinead's story. The bar was in complete disarray: smashed glass, splintered tables, broken chairs and spilt liquor covered the floor. Light fixtures had been ripped from the walls and a door that led to the storage room behind the bar had been torn from its hinges. There was so much destruction, yet, not a single body to be found. Krysta arranged for C.S.I to examine the scene as there were numerous blood splatter patterns, but she had to admit that they, along with the devastation, could be chalked down to a simple bar brawl that had gotten way out of control. 'I dunno, Luce, it doesn't seem likely that the... you know... were involved here.' There were so many ears around that Krysta had to be careful with what she said. She couldn't help but doubt the idea that the Avunaye were involved, she had seen crime scenes in which they had been involved, and the level of destruction had been far greater.

'That's cus you're looking with your eyes, Krys,' Lucy replied. She then hurried over to the equipment that the C.S.I were currently carrying in. Pulling out a couple of strip U.V lights, she quickly moved over to where Krysta was stood and switched both of the lights on, holding them over a nearby booth and a table. 'Hey, you,' she called to one of the investigators. 'Spray that luminol stuff over here quickly.' The pair watched as the investigator sprayed the area. 'Holy shit.'

'Fuck,' was all Krysta could say in response as the U.V lights steadily started to reveal large stains that glowed a blue colour. She stood and shook her head slightly, regretting doubting what Sinead had said. 'You're gunna have to check over the whole place. Test all the stains to confirm the presence of blood, but it looks like something truly awful went down here.'

Having signed off the scene to the C.S.I team, Lucy drove the pair of them back to headquarters so that they could report everything back to Solomon. Upon their arrival, Solomon was quick to inform them that whilst they were out, he had had Hale interrogate Sinead, and after some convincing she had agreed to provide information on Markovic's and Cardoza's local enterprises in exchange for protection. *It's her only option,* Krysta thought. *But if Adam is the one to seek revenge, how the hell are we going to protect her...*

The afternoon raced by with Lucy uncharacteristically offering to write up their report, leaving Krysta with almost too much time on her hands. Claire was busy utilising the first pieces of information Sinead had provided, with her and Malique compiling a list of possible hide-outs and strongholds in and around the city. Hale continued to interrogate their willing informant; the quicker they were to obtain the intel and move on it, the better chance Sinead stood at surviving – or at least that was what they had told her. Krysta couldn't help but worry about what was yet to come. After making the rounds and finding all of her colleagues hard at work, Krysta then re-joined Lucy.

'Hey, Krys, do me a favour?' Lucy snapped, no doubt in response to Krysta's boredom fuelled lip-smacking and finger-tapping. 'I left one of my notepads in the car. Can you go grab it for me? Then I'll finish this up and we can go grab some food and a drink. Or two.' Lucy danced in her seat. Smiling, Krysta jumped at the chance to make herself useful and headed for the stairwell, skipping down the steps two at a time.

Reaching Lucy's car, Krysta unlocked and opened the rear door. She leant in across the back seat, reaching for Lucy's note books, but as her outstretched fingers touched them, she was forcibly dragged back out of the car by the back of her blouse. Before she could turn to see who it was that had pulled her back, she was then slammed up against the nearby pillar.

'Ah! What the hell!' she yelled and instinctively moved her hand to her waist, going for her sidearm.

'Ah, ah, ah...' he sounded, discouraging her. He had a gun of his own, which he currently pointed at her face.

'Whoa! Easy!' Krysta pleaded, still in slight shock of being jumped. As she raised her hands, she realised that she recognised her assailant. He was a police officer. 'Officer... Seif...' she read the name from below his badge. 'I'm agent –'

'I know who the fuck you are!' he exclaimed as he continued to aim his weapon at her head. He was twitchy, shifting his weight from one foot to the other, unable to remain still. 'But you... you had to read my name tag, didn't you? See, you don't care. We've met, what, two, three times? You feds... You fucking feds...' His glossy black hair was ruffled and his voice croaked with distress. There was a red to his eyes, a weariness, and his skin was a sickly pale shade of its former self.

'Look. Officer –'

'No! Not anymore... You don't even know, you don't even care!' He continued to wave his gun in her face, but with his other hand, he pulled at his hair sharply, ripping numerous strands from his scalp.

'I do. I do care...' Krysta tried to speak calmly despite her hearts attempt to burst from her chest. She tried not to panic, but everything about him screamed unpredictability.

'No, no, no!' he exclaimed, saliva flying from his mouth. 'First the cadet... then Axel... That agent – agent Grey... That black son of a bitch! He's the reason... And you! You stupid bitch! Why? Why did *you* come?! Now it's over. It's all over!'

'Seif... Malik... What's over? How can I, what do you need? I can help –'

'No. I devoted my life to this job, this city, the people. And now it's all gone! I... I've nothing! NOTHING!' As Seif screamed at Krysta she heard the gunshots. In a split second the situation had changed. She winced at the boom and closed her eyes, feeling the blinding pain in her upper left arm. She wondered in that moment if she was going to die; if this was it. As her body forced her to concentrate on the trauma, her mind opened up to the fact that she had distinctively heard two shots. She clutched at her wound, squeezing her arm as she slowly opened her eyes. Malik was stood before her, but he wasn't right, he held his gun down, his arm hanging by his side. He looked at her in fear, with such pain in his eyes, taking in short sharp gasps of air. But then like a flame on a candle being snuffed out, his eyes began to flutter and his body slumped to the ground. His legs had folded underneath him and he laid on his back looking up at her, his lips attempting to mouth something. He began to choke briefly and blood spurted from his mouth with each cough. Still in shock and dazed by the event, Krysta couldn't divert her gaze, staring into his eyes as his life slipped away before her.

'Krysta, you okay?' Solomon asked as he made his way around the pillar to her. He had his phone to his ear. 'Shots fired in the parking lot. I have an agent wounded and an officer down.' Krysta said nothing, unable to look away from the emptiness of Malik's eyes. Solomon gently moved her hand to check her injury, the sudden pain reigniting her level of awareness.

'Ah! Shit!' she yelled at the pain receptors in her body as they all seemed to switch on at once. Solomon looked at the wound and reassured her that she would be alright. 'Sol... ' She wanted to thank him. It was likely his presence that had thrown off Malik's aim, but he had also saved her.

'C'mon. Let's get you to the hospital, yeah?' He pointed out the blood on his hands, showing her that although she would survive, she was still bleeding.

'Sol, he said –' Krysta began to say, still looking back at the body.

'Don't worry about it. It's over. Looks like officer Seif here has one of those marks...' Krysta hadn't noticed, but she could see it now and as Solomon helped her to his car, she felt the guilt of Malik's death. He had no doubt been fearing for his life, having received the mark, and then to lose his job; she pitied him.

Driving her to the nearest hospital, Solomon constantly asked if she was okay. It was endearing, yet a little unnecessary and annoying. It was a gunshot wound, one that she'd walk away from, but she felt as if he was making it a bigger deal than it was. Being a federal agent had its perks; she was seen to immediately upon arrival at the hospital, the bullet was removed and her wound cleaned and stitched up promptly. As far as Krysta was concerned, within the hour she was good to go, however, the doctor insisted she stay a while, showing a little concern about the amount of blood loss she had suffered. She stood up in protest, attempting to prove that she was fit to leave, though she soon found herself feeling quite dizzy and was forced to concede.

'Alright, alright. I'll stay for an hour or two.' Krysta surrendered to the doctor's and Solomon's requests that she stay put for now, ensuring she was in no danger of any complications arising. Yet once Solomon had left, shc found herself at a loss for something to do. She took out her phone and flicked through her social media accounts before deciding to type up her witness statement. *I've got nothing better to do and it'll save time later*, she told herself. She clock-watched for a little while and after calling both Lucy and Claire to let them know she was fine, she decided that she had stayed long enough.

She sat up with her legs hanging off the side of the bed and grabbed her jacket and shoes. But her escape was halted by a woman, whom Krysta presumed was a nurse, drawing back the curtain.

'Leaving so soon?' she questioned as Krysta attempted to put her shoes on. Krysta paid her little mind; she didn't want to waste any more time here. 'Here, let me help you.' The woman knelt down and took one of Krysta's shoes, helping her to slip her foot into it.

'Thank you,' Krysta said, appreciative of the assistance. 'I think they'd love for me to stay for the night, but I have so much to be getting on with.' Krysta expressed a sigh of relief as the woman finished helping her with her footwear.

'You should slow down, take advantage of the rest,' the woman said softly as stood up, her words causing Krysta to chuckle slightly at the idea. 'I'm serious, you are going to need your strength.' It was at that point that Krysta took a good look at her and realised that she was neither a nurse nor a doctor, but someone completely unexpected and incredibly dangerous. 'No need to worry. If I meant you any harm... well, you can imagine... Let's not have this little catchup end in misery, shall we?' She looked Krysta straight in the eyes and smiled innocently, the green of her eyes harnessing the glow of the fluorescent lighting and shimmering like precious stones.

'What do you want?' Krysta's words quivered as they left her lips. She simply stared at Evelina as she continued to help put her shoes on. What else could she possibly do?

'There. All set,' Evelina smiled as she plucked a piece of lint from Krysta's shoulder. She was wearing a black, floral, long-sleeved, off the shoulder summer dress and a necklace with a large central emerald stone that complimented her gaze. 'My love, honestly, you are saturated in fear. I can literally feel it. It is disgusting. There is enough of *that* in this place without you feeling it as well. I am simply here to ask you a quick question and to give you some advice.' Krysta's head told her over and over that she couldn't trust her, yet, it seemed actions, or lack thereof, spoke louder than words; if she did mean Krysta harm, then why delay? Evelina could snatch the life from her without breaking a sweat and there was nothing anyone could do to stop her. 'My family and I have, let us say, larger concerns than the F.B.I. Now, I am sure that you will continue your little investigations, and with regards to Vladimir, I may be inclined to assist you in one way or another. But I would appreciate you distancing yourself from my affairs.'

'Why the hell would you help us?' Krysta announced her distrust.

'Adam is free. No doubt curled up somewhere clawing at his head, trying to remember what the hell is going on.' A sense of relief washed over Krysta as Evelina confirmed Adam's re-emergence.

'Do you...?'

'Do I know where Adam is?' Evelina laughed. 'No. However, I am certain that you will find out shortly. My only request is that you help him.' Krysta was stunned by Evelina's words, a look of bewilderment possessing her face. 'You need Adam. We need Adam. For now, I believe, with your help we can keep him in check without killing him and he in turn can help us, my family and I, with our little *issue*.'

'Your issue? And *you* need Adam?' Krysta probed inquisitively.

'My issue, is nothing for you to concern yourself with. And yes.' Evelina pursed her lips, grimacing as she admitted her need for Adam's assistance. She then gently brushed some of Krysta's hair back behind her ear with her fingertips. 'Now, for my question, and I would appreciate nothing but the truth. Is the F.B.I in possession of, or know the location of Brandt's body?' Krysta couldn't be sure, but she could swear that there was an air of motherly concern to Evelina's words. Krysta shook her head in reply. She recalled that Brandt was in fact Cain, and that made him Evelina's son. A wave of sympathy flurried through her. 'Thank you, for your honesty and your sympathy, though unrequired. Now, as I mentioned, I have other matters to attend to.'

'Is it to do with the tree? And the garden?' Krysta asked, pushing her luck.

'No. Those will come in good time. This issue is more immediate, but as I said, you concentrate on Adam.' Evelina turned to leave.

'What if we don't?' Krysta paused as Evelina halted. 'What if we come after *you*?'

Evelina didn't even turn to look at Krysta. 'Then you would be putting yourself in a parlous position. Solomon, Lucy, Mike, Claire, Hale. I have decimated armies, my dear. Test my good nature and I will have no problem laying waste to all those you hold dear.' She simply made her threat and then continued to leave. But just before she disappeared from view, she stopped and said, 'you had better answer that...' And then she was gone.

Unsure as to what she had meant, Krysta picked up her phone. It wasn't even ringing, which puzzled her, but then it began to ring, sending a chill down Krysta's spine.

What the hell? She looked at the phone in disbelief but then she heard Evelina's final words once again in her head. 'Hello?' she answered the call.

'Is this Krysta? Of the F.B.I?' a man's voice sounded.

'Who is this?' Krysta replied defensively.

'It's Timothy McCauley. I'm the dean at the Cathedral of St. John the Divine.'

'I'm sorry... how did you get this number? And why are you calling me?' Krysta didn't recognise his name, which confused her further.

'He's here, at the cathedral. He asked for you. I assumed –'

'Who asked for me?' she sharply demanded.

'It's Adam.' Krysta did not need any further information and quickly gathered up the rest of her belongings. Rushing out of the ward, she ran towards the exit, filled with hope, her heart beating with a passionate sense of possibility.

21
Tobias

'Ben, it's almost four o'clock in the bloody morning. What is taking you so bloody long?' Tobias was growing impatient, yet his intolerance for delay was nothing compared to Evelina's, whom looked as though she was ready to bring the entire apartment block down upon them. Ben was nervously sweating as he rummaged through cupboard after cupboard. He was short and stocky, wearing a pair of brown pants held up by black suspenders and a scruffy white work shirt. He was an informant of Tobias', one of many, but Ben had a knack for finding things that people had wished to conceal. It was February, and to fight off the nights bitter chill Tobias had opted to wear an off-white, mottled, tweed overcoat and matching pleated pants with a blue shirt. Evelina toyed with the current fashion and wore a pair of knee-high black boots with brown tights, she had donned a butterscotch, cashmere, cut-in-on-the-shoulder turtleneck and a matching coloured mini-skirt. A brown cardigan was draped over her shoulders and she also wore brown elbow-length gloves.

Ben had led them to this particular apartment as he believed that the owner had in his possession the very item that Tobias sought.

'It's here somewhere, I swear!' Ben shouted. His voice was filled with an unsettling panic. 'Can't yous do something? X-ray vision, or sommin?' Tobias chuckled as he looked to Evelina and she rolled her eyes in response.

'Ben, who do you think we are?' Tobias laughed. Ben paused in his search and turned to look at Tobias, mopping his brow as he did.

'I dunno... I call you three days ago, says I found the blade you're after... You says you were in the Philippines. Few hours later, bang! You're on my doorstep. Plus, you always seem to make people do what you want, like mind control. And your eyes glow...' Ben looked at them eerily, his thoughts racing.

'Aliens? Seriously?' Tobias howled. 'Ben, it's 1986. I took a flight on one those amazing winged machines,' he said sarcastically. Tobias couldn't help but chortle at the man as his thoughts continued to run in circles, attempting to comprehend what Tobias and Evelina were.

'Ben, sweetheart,' Evelina spoke softly. 'Knowledge *is* power. Now, you told us you knew where my blade was being kept. Is that still the case?' Evelina looked to Tobias for the answer, knowing that he would be listening to Ben's every thought. Tobias grimaced at Ben's failure to produce what they were after and Evelina made her thoughts known.

Tobias placed a hand on each of Ben's shoulders and looked him in the eyes.

'Ben, you're going to take your thirty-eight and you're going to hold this entire block up until you find what we want.' Ben nodded, yet tears began to slip away from the corners of his eyes. 'If the cops show up, you try and run, okay?' Ben took a number of deep breaths as he unwillingly complied. Pulling out his firearm, he left the apartment and moved through the block, banging on doors and shouting.

'Well, this was a dreadful waste of time,' Evelina sighed.

'Ah, ah... Just wait. The fun is just beginning,' Tobias smiled.

It wasn't long before someone in the block had

called the police and then upon their arrival, the shooting began. Tobias and Evelina watched from a safe distance as Ben resisted arrest, exchanging gunfire with officers, before fleeing to the roof. 'Ha! Can't believe he jumped!' Tobias applauded as Ben jumped from one rooftop to another in an attempt to escape. 'C'mon, let's get a better view...' He grabbed Evelina's hand and dragged her along the hallway and down a flight of stairs towards the ground floor. As they reached the bottom of the steps, they ran into a police officer, knocking him over.

'Hey! Stop!' the officer yelled as he floundered on the floor and then proceeded to pick himself up. Evelina stopped in her tracks, forcing Tobias to do the same. 'You can't go out there right now. You not heard what the hell's been going on?' The officer dusted himself off and walked up to them.

'That's exactly why we're headed out there. Now we're missing all the action,' Tobias smirked, drawing a frown from the officer. *You inquisitive little bastard...* Tobias listened to the officer's thoughts; he suspected them of something. 'Look, officer...' Tobias fished for a name as he couldn't quite see his badge, but the officers mind was more complex than he would have predicted. In response, the officer rested his left hand on his hip and his right on top of his sidearm. 'You really don't want to do that, mate. You have a son, right?' Tobias' attempt to dissuade him only made the officer more concerned and prone to rash action.

It happened in a flash. The officer unclipped his gun and began to draw it, but Evelina flew at him, snatching the weapon from his grasp and shooting him with it. He didn't die instantly; he dropped to the ground, holding his chest. He had a look of disbelief in his eyes and his thoughts revolved around regret. He thought of his family, of his son, and he wished that he wasn't present in this particular moment as the light faded from his eyes.

'You had to push it, didn't you?' Evelina shook her

head in frustration. 'I suggest that you get the matter cleared up'. Tobias agreed to cover their tracks; making people believe that the officer died during the shootout with Ben should be easy enough. 'I dislike this city. I've no idea why you choose to return here so frequently.' She glared at him with intent, ensuring that he pay full attention. 'If the blade is truly here, find it. I am tired of complications and setbacks. Centuries of fumbling around in the dark due to Adam's interference. I want for you all to finally have your freewill.'

'You know, this city might be a good place to lure Adam. Break the damn curse.'

'Why on this green earth would Adam want to come here? Let alone fight for its dank existence. Enough of your games, Tobias. Focus your attention on cleaning up this mess and finding the blade.' Tobias and Evelina went their separate ways, with Evelina choosing to find the nearest club to entertain herself, whilst Tobias dealt with ensuring that their participation in tonight's events went unnoticed.

Tobias wasn't looking to get his hands too dirty, so he left the body for someone else to find and deal with on his behalf. Instead, he had preferred to put his true talents to good use and headed out onto the streets, feeding his story to any of the police officers that he came across. Each and every one of them absorbed the idea that the downed officer was killed in the line of duty during the attempted robbery, and should any evidence come to light to suggest otherwise, it was to be dismissed. Tobias was smug with his quick progress, but he knew that he would need to compel the station's chief to guarantee no loose ends. However, it seemed that he would have to venture into the belly of the beast to complete his task.

'The chief? Last one out, first one back at the station. You won't find him round here.' The officer stood with a docile expression, primed for manipulation.

'That's inconvenient,' Tobias replied. He was

beginning to become irked to be still working whilst Evelina played. 'Alright then, mate. Lead me to the chief.'

'I'll take you to the chief,' the officer responded in a flat, drone-like tone. 'Awful shame, that kid is gonna be lost without his father.'

'Kid? Ah, yes. His son...' It was the first anyone had mentioned of the deceased officer's family.

'Yeah. Ten-years-old. His old man was his hero. It's gonna be rough.'

Tobias travelled to the station with the officer and sat down with the chief. He made certain that the story he had fabricated was the only truth of the matter as far as the N.Y.P.D were concerned. He partook in a drink of the chief's secret stash of bourbon and extracted a few handy pieces of information from his loose lips, all the while with the thought of this now fatherless boy in the back of his mind. He had taken fathers from their sons, sons from their fathers and every other possible equivalent time and time again during his time as an immortal, but this felt different. He mulled over the details of the entire incident, attempting to find an answer as to why this scenario made him feel so different to all those that had come before. However, he was left stumped.

'You will honour the officer that lost his life tonight,' Tobias found himself saying, unsure as to why he should be concerned as to what happened after he left. *Perhaps I am growing a conscience,* he thought with a smirk. 'Is the boy here? I would like to meet him.'

As it turned out, the child had already been picked up by an officer and brought to the station upon news of his father's death. It appeared that he was lucky enough to have two families: one being with his biological parents, and the other an adoptive family, bound by loyalty and trust. The N.Y.P.D would help to bring him up now. He sat looking at the small, macilent boy. *He'll need to grow up fast to survive in this city.* Tobias couldn't help but judge the boy by his appearance, thinking that if the wind blew too strongly, he'd probably snap in two. He took a seat next to the boy. His eyes were now red-raw and tearless, waiting for his mother to come and pick him up. Tobias sifted through the child's scattered thoughts; thoughts of anger, of rage towards evil men, towards the system, the force – blaming the police for taking his dad. Many officers had attempted to console him, offering their condolences, but none of it would bring back what he had lost. Tobias looked closely at the kid, attempting to envisage his future, his chances of survival, when the boy turned to him.

'I don't need any more pity, thanks.' His words croaked with pain. Each of them laced with the sound of heartbreak.

'I offer no sympathy, boy,' Tobias smiled sarcastically, much to the child's surprise. 'I offer you only this...' He looked into the boy's eyes and saw a hidden strength buried within them. It made him smirk. 'Honour your father, protect your city. Never give up on what you believe. Life is short for a mortal, yet immortality can be achieved by several means.' The child took the words on board, yet he was confused by their meaning. Tobias then stood up and patted the boy on his shoulder before walking away, leaving him with his grief, but hopefully, also, with a purpose.

22
Krysta Rose-Anderson

It was late. She had taken a cab up town and had it drop her off at the foot of the steps to the cathedral. The city around her was silent; only the occasional sounds of life and of far-off traffic could be heard from where she stood, meaning she could just about hear the sound of her own anxious heart, racing away within her chest. The sky was black and starless with a few scattered cloud formations drifting across the face of the moon, briefly disrupting the search-light glow that it extended onto the huge rose window that loomed above the cathedrals main entrance. The buildings enormity gave Krysta a feeling of insignificance as her eyes followed its gothic structure up into the darkness. She took a deep breath in and took the first step to begin her ascent. It had been eight months since that night at Times Square; eight months spent searching, wondering, not knowing. The time had built a pedestal on which the up and coming moment perched upon, but she questioned whether it would all coming crashing down around her. The expectation was immense and Krysta, despite her fear, couldn't help but wonder what the future held.

I should report this. I should call it in... But I need to know, I need to speak to him, to see him... The needle of her moral compass span uncontrollably as she continued up the steps towards the doors. Towards Adam.

The doors were ornate. The lack of light made it hard to see, but they harnessed delicate etchings, carved into the numerous panels within them. She placed both of her palms on the large bronze door that sat within the central portal of the building and gave it a push, yet it did not budge. Stepping backwards, she scanned the whole façade of the building, looking for an open door, desperately searching for a way inside. Sighing, she decided to simply bang on the door before her. Clenching her fist, she struck the door four times, banging as loudly as she could, but due to the doors solidity she doubted that the sound even made it through to the other side. *You called me here... Least you could do is leave the door open...* She turned and began to walk back down the steps with the intention of trying another door, perhaps down the side of the building.

'Agent Krysta? Is that you?' A door to the left of the central portal had opened and a voice called out into the dark. Krysta span on her heels to find a man stood in the entrance. He was dressed in a purple cleric's shirt with a white collar and black pants. His head was topped with a short, thinning mess of hair and his face, although weary, was rounded and welcoming.

'Bishop McCauley, is it?' Krysta questioned, hoping that it was in fact the man that had called her here.

'Come on inside, quickly now.' Krysta hurriedly did as he requested, slipping into the cathedral. Inside, she found herself mesmerized by the huge open nave before her, swearing that it appeared larger from inside.

'Bishop –' Krysta began to say, yet he quickly silenced her, holding a finger to her lips.

'Call me Tim, please.'

'Okay, Tim. Why did you call me here? How did you –'

'How did I know to call you? Long story short, I've known him for some time. He's mentioned you once or twice, and now, it seems, you're the only person he knows.' He smiled but then looked down, seemingly troubled.

'Why did he come here?' Krysta looked about the room before her, searching the shadows, hoping to catch a glimpse of Adam. It wasn't that she doubted the bishop, but she longed for physical proof.

'Sheer luck, I guess. Or perhaps God's will...' He smiled again. The mention of God made Krysta's face screw up slightly. She wondered if Tim even knew who or what Adam was. 'You're wondering if I know who he is, aren't you?' he chuckled light-heartedly in response to her expression.

'What he is... Doesn't it –'

'Confuse matters? Make me question my faith?' Krysta smiled at his uncanny ability to finish her sentences. 'I live and work in a city that swings back and forth between light and dark. I've seen an honest, hard-working family man lose his job and then kill three people attempting to rob a store. I've heard of some religious people abusing children and others blowing themselves up, supposedly in the name of their faith. My faith is questioned every minute of every day.' He took one of Krysta's hands in both of his and gave it a gentle reassuring squeeze. 'I guess that's what faith truly is.' He smiled again and released her hand before gesturing that she followed him.

They proceeded through the nave, crossing where it intersected the north and south transepts. Beyond the choir stalls stood an alter with a number of chapels dedicated to saints surrounding it. Tim walked to the end of the alter and then looked back at Krysta with a look of uncertainty, as if he were lost. Krysta hurried to his side and there, curled up on the floor behind the alter, was the body of a man. He looked so at peace as he lay on his side, as if he were sleeping. His short, brownish-blonde hair was ruffled and he was wearing nothing but a pair of grey sweat pants. Krysta stared at him, studying every inch of his body, but she found her expression shifting from one of joy to have finally found him, to one of confusion. She ran her gaze down his back, down the tattoo of the leafless oak tree that she knew to be Adam's, yet, she couldn't bring herself to believe that this man was truly him.

'Bishop?' Krysta whispered, grabbing Tim by the arm and pulling him away from the body a few paces. 'This... This isn't Adam.' Tim looked at her, his wide eyes questioning her statement. 'Adam... He has scars, loads of scars... and a handprint on his shoulder... He's been tortured for months now. How could this be him?' She had so wanted it to be Adam, yet, this wasn't the man she had come to know.

'Krysta, what do you see when you look at me?' Tim smiled. Krysta wondered the point of his question, but for lack of a better option she looked him up and down.

'Erm... A bishop. A nice, kind man. A pinnacle of –'

'Alright,' he chuckled. 'That's enough flattery. No, be honest. Would you trust me with your life? Could you tell me your deepest, darkest secrets?' He raised his eyebrows as he spoke. Krysta couldn't help but be intrigued as to where his questions were leading.

'No...' she simply responded, apologising by way of shifting her stance.

'And why not? If I am such a nice, kind man. A pinnacle of youth and good looks, as I'm sure you would have said...' He chuckled light-heartedly again.

'I... I don't know you. We've literally just met.' Krysta didn't know what else to say, but she felt awkward for being honest.

'And you can't see past that fact?' He smiled, and as he did, it suddenly dawned on her what he was saying.

'Oh my god. Oh, sorry,' she winced. 'Are you suggesting that I don't see his scars because –'

'Because you choose to see him for what – for who – he really is. Adam's ability is rooted in emotion, and as human beings, our eyes are often clouded by how we feel. You can see beyond his flaws now and thus you no longer see them.' Krysta shook her head in disbelief. It may have sounded crazy, but somehow, she knew it to be the truth.

'How... How do you know all this?' Krysta questioned. She was more than curious as to how this bishop knew so much about Adam.

'Once you get to know him, he doesn't shut up. He's stubborn, that one.' Timothy smiled and then sighed. Krysta returned a smile to the bishop before returning to the alter. Carefully moving around it's corner, she cautiously knelt down beside Adam; she didn't want to disturb him but she wanted – she needed – to be close to him.

Timothy left them; noting that Adam was in good hands, he retired for the night. Krysta sat quietly, patiently waiting at Adam's side for him to wake, only moving occasionally to adjust her position whenever her body began to stiffen. As she watched him sleep, she knew that she had made the right decision to not call it in, at least not yet anyway. A few hours passed and Krysta found herself beginning to doze off. She was trying to find a comfortable position to rest herself when Adam suddenly stirred; his movement snapping her from a light drowse.

'Adam?' she softly asked, trying not to startle him. He groaned and kicked out his legs, like an animal experiencing a nightmare. Krysta wasn't sure what to do, so she rested her hand on his shoulder, but her touch appeared one step too far as the moment their skins met, Adam's eyes shot open and he looked at her in confusion and terror. His arms shot up and he grabbed the corner of the alter; in one quick movement he had pulled himself away from Krysta, launching himself across the floor, and crashing against the wall. He winced as his back smashed against the stone and he clutched at his face, forcing his eyes to close. 'Adam? It's me. It's Krysta.' She tried to mask her anxiety with concern, her words quivering as they left her lips. He appeared to be in pain, or in shock; she couldn't quite tell which as he continued to shake and pull at his face. Krysta crawled across the floor on her knees, using her right arm for balance. She stopped a couple of feet away from him and reached out, hoping to try and calm him, but just before she could touch him, he lowered his hands and looked at her. His eyes, at first, appeared a dull diminished green, but as the light soaked them and as he seemed to register who it was before him, they began to coruscate, brightening like polished emeralds beginning to show lustre. As the light returned to his eyes, the troubled expression washed from his face and he looked at her with a devoted solicitude that warmed her heart and brought a joyful tear to her eye.

Quietly basking in each other's presence, it was a number of minutes before Krysta decided to speak. Yet, as she went to, Adam interrupted.

'Krysta. I'm sorry.' He held his stare, his gaze piercing her flesh. She could swear that he could look directly into her very soul. She was about to tell him that it was okay, but a look of concern returned to his face. 'You're hurt...' Within a blink of an eye he was by her side, investigating her wounded arm. She watched his every move with wide eyes of fascination. 'You've been shot?' his words carried equal amounts of distress as they did anger. 'Who did this?' She was so lost in his presence that she was barely taking in his words, but as he moved her arm the pain wrenched her from her daze.

'Ah,' she groaned. 'Adam, it's okay, it'll heal.' She attempted to dissuade his fussing and grasped his hand, her touch stopping him in his tracks. She slipped her thumb under his fingers and ran it down his palm. Softly smiling, she gently squeezed his hand and briefly closed her eyes, clinging to the moment. He didn't pull away, instead, he shuffled closer, placing his other hand on top of hers. He leant forward and instinctively, so too did Krysta until their foreheads met. She closed her eyes again and breathed him in. Curiosity, however, forced her to open her eyes and look at him as he took a deep breath in and then exhaled slowly.

She could feel a warmth emitting from his hands and a gentle stirring beneath her skin; the flesh of her arm was rapidly sealing itself and underneath the dressing, she could feel her skin begin to replenish. It was like nothing she had ever experienced; a moment in which she felt more connected with her own body than ever before.

Undoing her blouse, Krysta uncovered her once wounded upper arm and was taken back by the absence of any injury. She ran her fingers up and down it, 'there's not even a mark,' she said, wonderstruck. Adam took her hand in his own and covered her shoulder back up.

'I don't... I don't remember everything...' He paused, looking down shamefully before finding the courage to look her in the eye once more, 'but I know I hurt you, and I'm sorry.' Krysta took a deep breath in and exhaled shakily, trying to calm herself. She took his hand and placed his palm upon her chest so that he might feel her heart beat beneath her breast, that he might know how she truly felt and that despite his absence, she had managed to forgive him and move forward.

Krysta updated Adam as much as she could with what was happening regarding the other Avunaye. He seemed deeply troubled by the emergence of Barachiel, but when Krysta questioned who she was or what she wanted, Adam began to struggle and dismissed the subject. He would need time to recover and remember before he could help, Krysta presumed.

'Brandt!' Krysta suddenly recalled and then instantly felt a huge pit in her stomach and a weight on her heart. Despite not caring that Brandt had finally been stopped, if Carmen was right, then he was still Adam's son, and she couldn't help but share in his loss. 'Adam, I'm so sorry...' she struggled to come up with the right words. 'It's Brandt, he – he's dead.' She squeezed his hand in an attempt to comfort him. Adam looked at her slightly puzzled; Krysta assumed he was in shock. 'I know that he... that he was –'

'Your phone is ringing,' Adam interrupted in a nonchalant manner. Thrown off by his abruptness, Krysta fumbled about searching for her phone. It was Solomon. She looked at Adam, silently asking if he mind her answering it, but he remained indifferent. Reluctantly taking the call, Solomon requested that she come into the office early as an urgent meeting had been called. Acknowledging Solomon's request, Krysta withheld the fact that she was with Adam, deciding that, at least for now, no one need know. She felt dejected as she told Adam that she had to leave, and although she informed him that she would be back later, his unresponsiveness confused her. The way that she was feeling, if she had to guess, looking at his dispirited, contemplative expression, it was his feelings bombarding her senses. She quickly got up and hurriedly made her way back through the cathedral towards the exit, her heart gradually feeling lighter as she distanced herself from Adam, but just before she reached the door, she came across the bishop.

'I'd suggest you get some rest before returning. You look tired,' Timothy said as she approached. Krysta smiled and went to continue to leave but then she suddenly had the urge to ask one last question.

'Why do you do it?' she asked and received a curious look in response. 'Why do you keep his secret? Why help him?'

He smiled. 'Today I help a friend. Tomorrow, he saves ten innocent lives.'

Krysta took a cab to the office and got changed into a spare set of clothes she had left in her locker. She also put her arm into a sling so as to avoid any curious questions regarding her injury, as now was not the right time for her colleagues to be wondering how she managed to heal overnight. She was physically and mentally exhausted and this meeting couldn't have come at a worse time, she could only hope it did not last too long.

'Hey, Krys,' Lucy said as she entered the locker room. 'How's the arm?' Lucy looked almost as tired as Krysta felt; she clearly was still having trouble sleeping.

'Sore, but I'll be okay,' she lied. 'They call everyone in?' Krysta hoped to draw attention away from herself.

'Yeah. Can't believe Solomon didn't let you sit this one out. But the whole team is here, including Kyle, Stanwell... Even Hicks is here.' Lucy splashed some water on her face. 'Something is definitely going down.' Lucy seemed excited, despite her tiredness. She was no doubt happy to have a distraction from everything else she was dealing with.

Krysta finished tidying herself up, allowing Lucy to help sort her hair out and then the pair of them headed through to the meeting room together. She looked about the room as she entered, her eyes drawn to the balding head of Markus Hicks. He stood beside Deputy Director Stanwell, talking amongst themselves whilst Solomon and Kyle stood obediently to one side, awaiting their superior's attention. She then clocked Claire and Hale. Claire was standing hunched over the interactive table, her hair tied back, her eyes locked on the screen. She was concentrating so hard that the lines on her brow above the rim of her glasses made her look ten years older. Hale stood beside Claire, his sleeves rolled up and deep in thought also, watching the numerous images and documents that flashed by on the screen as Claire ploughed through them. Krysta was about to subtly ask the pair of them what was happening when she saw an image on the table that derailed her train of thought.

What the... she thought, confused by the images and file names in view, each of them relating to the Avunaye. 'Claire? What's going on?' Claire looked up and grimaced, a look that gave Krysta no comfort. Claire went to open her mouth, however, it seemed that Krysta's question was just what the room was waiting for to get started.

'Aha, agent Rose-Anderson, nice of you to join us. And you, Rodriguez. Perhaps now we can begin.'

Condescending as ever, Hicks began the meeting by effectively silencing the room. 'News of Markovic's and Cardoza's retreat, most likely to Cardoza's home country of Nicaragua, has prompted me to make changes to your current investigation.' Krysta couldn't help but feel perturbed, they had finally made some headway in the case, they had Sinead in custody.

What the hell.

'What has also come to light is the incompetence of the C.I.A. Somehow they have managed to lose what was potentially the most likely solution to our ongoing Avunaye terrorist problem.' Hicks looked about the room, however, his gaze lingered on Krysta for longer than she would have liked.

Fuck... Does he... How could he know?

'They lost Adam?' Lucy piped up, a look of concern materialising on her face. 'Well that's just fucking brilliant!' Her outburst brought a flustered look of anger to Hick's face.

'Enough!' he erupted. 'Solomon, get your *team* in order.' His words fell heavily on each of them; Krysta could see the look of disbelief in each of her colleague's eyes. Solomon too was unsure how to react; he merely looked about the group and conveyed the necessity for obedience with his cold stare. Once the room had settled, Hicks appeared to be more comfortable and continued with his briefing. 'Judging by deputy director Zane Brown's files, the C.I.A failed to ascertain any valuable intel from the subject, Adam. As you can see on the screen before you, his notes ask more questions than they answer.' Krysta looked at some of the documents as Claire cycled through them. She then looked to Lucy, who in turn looked at her as documents incriminating the military flashed up.

'Operation Princes?' Claire muttered, expressing a sheepish look once she noticed she had said it aloud.

'Pure conspiracy, C.I.A nonsense,' Hicks was quick to

add. 'Here's the facts.' He paused for a moment and placed his fists down on the table. 'Adam is in the wind. Markovic and Cardoza are out of reach. We do, however, have reason to believe the remainder of the Avunaye group are within the state of New York and therefore, fall under federal jurisdiction. Do whatever needs to be done to bring them all to justice, and do it quickly. I don't believe I need to remind you of what a shit show this has been so far.'

Hicks had said his piece and had no time, or no interest in a response, indicated by his abrupt departure. The team had been handed back the Avunaye case, a fact that made Krysta feel sick to her stomach.

'Need I remind you all that should we encounter *any* of the Avunaye, we are to report it,' Kyle chirped up. His comment wrought looks of dismay from Lucy and Hale who did not like what he was insinuating. 'They're terrorists and we will treat them as such.' He glared at Krysta.

'Knock it off, Johnston,' Solomon ordered. He had finally said something, however, Krysta could tell that he was not right. Solomon had a look of uncertainty about him, as if his time was running out. Krysta presumed that he had had a preliminary meeting with Hicks, and that judging by his behaviour it had not gone well.

'You'll have no concerns from me. I'll happily put some of these bastards down.' Lucy's comment shocked both Claire and Krysta; it was the honesty in her words, the evident malice to her tone. Solomon, however, chose to ignore her and continued to speak on. The team were issued their assignments. Krysta, with her connection to Adam, was to look into his whereabouts. Claire was to piece together a detailed list of all members of the Avunaye, which Krysta knew would put Claire in an incredibly difficult position. Lucy and Hale were ordered to continue concentrating on Markovic and Cardoza's operations within the state, but were also given the green light to go after Serena, should the opportunity present itself. Krysta knew that Lucy would be content with hunting down Serena, however, she would probably prefer to be looking for Adam, hoping that he might have a way to help Mike.

When I see him, I'll ask him... Krysta made a silent promise to her friend, however, she did feel guilty for not thinking of asking Adam about Mike's condition when she saw him earlier.

One by one everyone began to leave the room and get started on their newly appointed tasks. Krysta was eager to speak to Claire alone, so she waited, rejecting Lucy's offer of breakfast, until the room was theirs. 'Claire, there's something I need to talk to you about...'

'Hell yeah there is! Heh, sorry,' she apologised for being so loud. 'Hell yeah there is...' she whispered. 'Operation freaking princes?' Claire looked around to check that no one else was within ear shot.

'What? No, that wasn't...' Krysta began to say before changing her mind, 'what is it?' she asked, shaking her head. Perhaps her news could wait a few moments.

'You remember I mentioned that mine and Carmen's memory had been altered? Well, erased... but not... because two minds in one, seems it's not straight forward... something about Carmen repairing one memory whilst the other gets wiped...'

'Claire!' Krysta tried to snap her out of her babbling rant. 'Princes?'

'Oh yeah. Well, anyway, the memory that got taken was of Tobias and Adam, taking the memory.' Claire smiled.

'I'm so confused...' Krysta placed a hand on her brow.

'They erased the fact that I, well we, me and a friend, had found a trail that indicated that Charles Grammar was dealing with Markovic and the Ministry of Defence. "Operation Princes".' Claire smiled again, seemingly happy that she'd finally said what she wanted to say.

'Charles Grammar?' Krysta questioned, to which Claire nodded in reply. 'Soon to be appointed vice president, senator Charles Grammar?' It seemed that the magnitude of Claire's intel hadn't quite dawned on her until Krysta said it aloud. Claire's eyes widened as she experienced the trepidation of what it all meant.

'Holy crap...' Claire looked around, searching for something. She grabbed a seat and sat herself down. 'Shit...'

'Yeah, shit...' Krysta tried desperately to think of what they could do. The intel came from Carmen, it wasn't like they could just go and tell Solomon what they'd found out. Krysta also had another pressing question on her mind. 'Adam took the memory?' she said, her tone full of concern.

'Well, no. Tobias did. But Adam was there,' Claire shrugged.

'Claire, I was with Adam last night.' Krysta finally blurted out her secret, feeling an ounce of relief as she did.

'You what now?' Claire questioned with a look of disbelief. 'Did you ask him about Mike... About velocity or Carmen... Or of the mark of Cain?' Claire blurted out her questions, each one adding a layer of guilt to how Krysta was feeling.

'I asked about the Barachiel woman...' Krysta said sheepishly, drawing a look of disappointment from Claire. Krysta proceeded to divulge the events of the evening past, retelling her and Adams conversation and explaining to Claire how amazing it had felt to finally lay eyes on him again. Krysta felt bad that she couldn't speak to Lucy about Adam, but she and Claire currently shared so many secrets between them that it had become so natural for her to want to share her thoughts and feelings with her confidant and colleague. One thing always lingered in the back of her mind, however. How long would it be before either one of them had their secrets exposed and what would happen when they did?

23
Luciana Rodriguez

'I'm telling you, Hale, the bitch loves her flashy, expensive crap. She's gonna be held up somewhere nice and it's gonna be either within the city limits or just outside it.' Having being given the green light to pursue Serena, Lucy didn't waste any time. She was like a caged animal that had finally been released into the wild and she knew her prey. Before, she had been ordered to steer clear of the Avunaye case, but now she could throw herself into it, one-hundred-and-ten-percent. Lucy had of course been secretly trying to keep track of the illusive red-head for some time now and she had kept a close eye on large transactions taking place within Manhattan: house and apartment sales, fine jewellery, even over indulgent clothes hauls had been flagged for attention. Unfortunately, all Lucy's results thus far had told her was that there were too many people with expensive tastes and far too much money.

'How about... Edgar Young? Two apartment sales in under five months, last one for... wow! That's more than my entire block is worth,' Hale laughed. His words carried similar levels of disbelief as they did jealousy.

Lucy was glad to be working alongside him on this. She knew that he had a steel-like determination with regards to work and that would definitely aid them in their efforts. She was also aware that he was keeping in touch with Mike, although he did her the courtesy of not bringing it up too often; it gave her a little piece of mind, knowing that if there were any major developments in Mike's wellbeing that Hale would clue her in.

'Don't worry about him,' Lucy quickly added as she sifted through more listings for property sales and transfers. 'He's a friend of a friend. I've already ran a background check. Some kind of wall-street Robin Hood... Makes a shit load of cash and gives half of it away or something.' She scoffed a little at the notion, yet, she secretly would have to admit that she thought it admirable.

'How about this one...?' Hale picked up the tablet he was using and held it for Lucy to peruse, however, they were then interrupted as Claire and Krysta entered the room.

'A little too conspicuous, don't you reckon?' Claire blurted out, snatching the tablet to take a closer look. 'Floor to ceiling windows? Heh... Not hiding anything in that place if you know what I mean.' Claire gave Hale a nudge with her elbow as she jested, but Lucy couldn't help but wonder the point of her colleague's interruption.

'Claire, despite you practically spelling everything out for us, we always know what you mean.' Lucy's gaze was stuck on the information she was scrolling through that she did not notice her friends shocked expressions at first. 'What?' she responded to their questionable looks as she lifted her eyes away from the screen. 'She always... argh! Whatever.' She was irritated by the intrusion and didn't have time for trivial matters. 'Claire, Krys? What do you want?'

'We've found something, Luce, something big.' Krysta's worried eyes told Lucy that it was worth listening to, however, she had Serena's scent, and like a bloodhound she stubbornly wanted to continue her pursuit.

'What is it? I have finally got the green light to chase down the bitch that tortured Mike... so it best be huge!'

Krysta and Claire explained to Lucy and Hale about Senator Grammar's link to Markovic and the D.O.D, implying that the Avunaye may also be connected. The trouble was, Lucy already had her sights set on a target and Claire's hole-riddled story about the connections simply didn't impress her. 'Let me get this right.' Lucy was short and sharp. 'The D.O.D, Markovic, Grammar – soon to be V.P I might add – and possibly the Avunaye, are all involved in a military op codenamed "Princes" that dates back over half a decade.' She wasn't the least bit convinced. 'We have proof?'

'Well, we have a source. We were hoping you might speak to the general...' Claire's tone was timid which only aggravated Lucy further.

'Whoa... you want me to what? Accuse the general of being –'

'No, not accuse, just inquire.' Claire shrugged slightly, making Lucy feel even more as if her time was being wasted.

'Inquire? The general will have my ass. Who's the source?' Lucy glared at Claire, watching her squirm under the pressure. She could tell by Krysta's expression that she should probably ease up a little, yet, she didn't care.

'Luce, ease off. We have good reason to believe this is good intel. Trust me.' There it was, the other shoe. Krysta's use of the word trust led Lucy to believe that this was all just a hunch.

'Look, Krys, Claire, I can't go the general with a fictional –'

'Hey!' Claire slammed her hand down on the table taking everyone by surprise. 'We may have a source on the inside. We can't disclose who they are, truth is we're not even sure. This isn't the first time they've provided us with information...' Claire looked Lucy in the eye with a stern stare. 'The intel is sound. Will you help, or should we bust down the general's front door ourselves?' Lucy couldn't believe her ears as Claire stood up and showed a side of herself that she had never seen before.

'Y'know, Claire. Sometimes...' Lucy clenched her fists and gritted her teeth for a moment, but looking into the eyes of her colleagues, she managed to slowly calm herself and decided to give them the benefit of the doubt. *I could be wrong, but this "source" screams mystery texter...* 'Sometimes I swear you are two different people, Davenport. I'll tell you what. *You* do your part and find Adam and the rest of the Avunaye, I'll handle the general.' *If we can find Adam, maybe I can help Mike...*

Lucy managed, to her own surprise, to get a message to the general and then rather quickly receive a response. The general was still close by and willing to see her. Lucy had never known him to be so available and it forced her to question if Claire's insinuations had merit. She was more than anxious; having enticed the general to the headquarters under somewhat false pretences, making him believe that she wanted to finish the tour they had begun on his last visit, and then for them to grab the meal he had suggested. Her hands were clammy and her heart beat at half a beat quicker than usual. She would have rather been thrown into a trench, to have to fend off an army of enemy soldiers single handed, than be in the position she found herself right now; staring disappointment in the face. She waited at security, keeping one eye on the entrance and one on the time, watching the minutes tick by towards the inevitable bombardment of her father's heavily weighted expectations. As the hands struck the agreed time, the doors opened, and in stepped the general, along with Jackson. Seeing Jackson helped to quell Lucy's nervousness slightly. *At least he will be reasonable,* she hoped. The general was wearing his black uniform with a pristine white shirt and black tie. His medals were on show; a reminder of how much he had accomplished but also, to Lucy, of how little she had done in comparison. Jackson wore an identical uniform, the only differences being their medals and insignia; the general's silver stars to the major's golden oak leaf. 'General. Jackson,' Lucy said, acknowledging them both as they were cleared by security. 'I hope you are both well?' She tried to smile but her anxiety levels remained high and in truth she felt nauseous. The general glanced at her, puzzled.

'Luciana,' he said formerly, barely looking at her. Lucy couldn't believe how the meeting had turned sour already; it hadn't even started. 'Let's not pretend that this is an informal visit. Major Torrent and I are here. Now, please lead the way to whichever room it is that we are to be interviewed in.' Lucy should have expected as much. She should be used to the general's cold, hard nature. Yet, part of her had actually hoped that they might have had a chance at spending at least a few moments as simply father and daughter. She stood dejected as she tried to compose herself, playing out how the meeting might unfold in her mind. 'Luciana? We do not have all day. Can we please get this over with?'

'Sir! Yes, Sir!' she replied sarcastically before turning to lead them to the elevator.

'I have no time for immature games...' The general's tone was filled with an all too familiar annoyance.

'General, I'm sure Lucy didn't mean any disrespect. Let's just head on up, grab a coffee and get this done. Shall we?' Jackson tried well to be the voice of reason, the bridge between Lucy and the general. The sad thing was, there had always needed to be a bridge; someone or something to help traverse the chasm that lay between them. As Lucy looked back at them, the general rolled his eyes and gestured that they should continue.

Lucy's only reprieve from the general's projection of discontent came when Hale joined them in the interview room. She secretly enjoyed the brief victory as she looked upon the general's somewhat unnerved and surprised expression.

'Okay, General Rodriguez, as the Avunaye fall under federal jurisdiction and not military, I would appreciate your full cooperation with regards to our questions during this interview.' Lucy felt unusual. Not for the fact that it was her father that they were questioning, but for the fact that she didn't feel at all awkward; it was not unlike questioning any other perp. The whole idea saddened her a little and she couldn't help but wonder how their relationship had become so estranged.

'Agreed. Regarding the Avunaye, feel free to ask whatever you feel the need to. We have nothing to hide, however, I feel you are wasting your time, considering they are not especially the military's concern.' He didn't even look at Lucy as he spoke. He occasionally glanced towards Hale, but mostly it was as if he were sat in an empty room, looking into empty space whilst responding to a radio call; as if Lucy wasn't even present.

'Does the military have, or have they had, any connections or dealings with the Avunaye?' Lucy asked bluntly. If the general was going to be cold and calculated, then she decided that she would be also.

'None,' was all he said. He placed his hands onto the table and interlinked his fingers.

'Has it ever had?' she quickly fired.

'Had what?' he replied. He finally looked her in the eye, unblinkingly testing her resolve.

'You know what... Please just answer the question.' Lucy wasn't in the mood for tests or mind games, whatever he was playing at.

'Agent Rodriguez, please, if you want an answer, phrase your questions appropriately.' His expression did not shift as he spoke, forcing Lucy to feel like a child once again, being taught proper etiquette.

'Please comment on your current knowledge of "Operation Princes".' Hale swooped in, hitting the general with the big question and catching him off guard.

'Doesn't exist.'

'Is the military currently affiliated with Vladimir Markovic and, or, Senator Charles Grammar?' Lucy could sense that Hale's quick-fire questions were beginning to get under the general's skin.

'No.' He fidgeted slightly before making a quick glance to Jackson; Lucy saw it as a small chink in his armour.

'So, department of defence, Markovic, Grammar, "Operation Princes". You know nothing of any of these?'

'I have nothing to comment.'

'A four-star general knows nothing of the D.O.D?' Hale stood up and leaned on the table. 'I find that hard to believe. Unless, of course, those stars are just for show?'

'I am not surprised Luciana brought *you* in on this.' The general emanated a smug, powerful aura. 'Interrogation was always one of your more valuable skillsets.'

'What is "Operation Princes", and what does it have to do with Markovic and Grammar?' Hale looked to Lucy and blinked; the stone-faced expression he had held thus far was beginning to weather and he was starting to appear uncomfortable.

'Interrogation would be putting it loosely though, wouldn't it, agent Hale?' Lucy could see how the general was goading Hale and she didn't like. She had made him come here; Hale did not deserve to be treated as such.

'General. Please just answer the question,' Lucy requested.

'Some people might refer to it as torture.' His words shocked Lucy, but not as much as Hale's reaction to them did. Slamming his fists down onto the table, Hale leaned forward as if to try and swing for the general. Lucy managed to quickly grab his arm and pull him backwards, with Jackson jumping to his feet at the same time in defence of his superior.

'You cowardly son of a bitch!' Hale exclaimed as he heeded Lucy's hold and broke off his assault.

'I suggest you get your *team* in order and –'

'Dad! Enough!' Lucy yelled. The general glared at her with scornful eyes and stood up from his seat.

'This interview is over. I have to say, I am

disappointed.' The combination of his words and the distasteful look in his eyes tore open a hole within Lucy. She stood destroyed as he exited the room without as much as a goodbye, leaving her once again feeling like the lost little girl she once was, with a daddy that didn't love her. The feeling, the reminder of her past, angered her.

The general had left. However, for some reason Jackson remained. Lucy hoped that he might once again be willing to help her; considering the last piece of intel he gave her almost got her killed, she figured that he owed her something.

'Luce, I've got to go...' Hale muttered as they were just about to settle down and speak with Jackson. She instantly felt deflated again; she needed something, someone to offer her some form of permanence right now, yet, it seemed everyone was bailing on her.

'Great, Hale, and what am I supposed to do now? Why do you have to go? If it's what the general said, I don't care...' She was almost whining as she questioned his desire to leave.

'It's not that. You don't need me on this... I'm pretty sure I made things worse...' There was something he wasn't telling her. Lucy crossed her arms and frowned at him, judging him with a look. 'I've got to go and meet up with Mike.' Lucy closed her eyes and sighed, fighting off the urge to start crying. 'I'm just helping him out where I can, until we find a way to help him properly.' Hale gave her hands a reassuring squeeze and smiled with his eyes before leaving her.

Determined not to let her emotions get the best of her, Lucy attempted to wield the turmoil inside that the general's disappointment and abandonment had caused, and focus her frustrations onto Jackson. She began by confronting him about the last piece of intel he had given her, driving home the fact that he had put her in harm's way, and piling on the guilt before hinting that he might assist her again. Jackson agreed to try and help, explaining to Lucy that he would always have her back, but then their conversation was interrupted. Hale had evidently felt bad for leaving Lucy to continue on her own, as he had attempted to enlist Krysta to take his place. However, according to Claire, who had actually ended up beside Lucy in the interview room, Krysta had taken ill and left the office for the rest of the day. Lucy was hesitant in accepting Claire's assistance, but then she recalled Claire's earlier outburst.

Perhaps if she brings the fire she had earlier, she won't be so bad to have around. As it happened, Claire turned out to be quite the asset. Her ramblings somehow managed to get Jackson so tongue-tied that he inadvertently disclosed information on a potential Avunaye target.

'Look. I haven't got long before the general court marshals me,' Jackson said jokingly. 'It's probably worthless to you now, but we discovered chatter regarding a site in Brooklyn. We sent in a team to check it out and it appeared to be one of Markovic's drug dens. But like I said, it's probably worthless intel as it has been emptied.' Lucy knew how much pressure Jackson would be under and how much trouble he'd be in if anyone were to discover that he was sharing information, so she promised to keep his name out of any reports. Jackson chose not to linger too much longer and once he had taken his leave Lucy began to vent her thoughts onto Claire.

'If there is no "Operation Princes", then why the hell are the military looking into Avunaye activity? What's their intention? They looking to recruit? I mean... the army, with the Avunaye working for them... They'd have a huge advantage over their enemies...' Lucy ranted for a few minutes without stopping for any feedback from Claire; she just needed to get it all off her chest. But once she was finished, she had decided on her next course of action. 'So, Claire. You up for a field trip whilst there's still daylight?'

Lucy had had enough of being cooped up in the office and whether Jackson's intel was worthless or not, it was something she could look into.

'Field work... I dunno... Is there no one else who...' Claire had seemingly lost her grit and slipped back into her sheepish self – the version of her that Lucy had hoped to avoid.

'We'll be fine, Claire. Come on! One little abandoned drug den. Best case, we find evidence or samples of velocity or perhaps something else that can help cure Mike. Worst case, we find jack.' Lucy pleaded with Claire to join her. It wasn't that she needed a partner on this, although she knew she should know better than to take on anything Avunaye related solo, she just didn't want to be alone again.

Finally managing to persuade Claire to join her, the pair of them headed to what turned out to be an abandoned factory and store front. Located on fifth avenue, Brooklyn, Lucy was surprised by the condition of the building as they arrived. The place couldn't have been empty for long, and if it was in fact a front for Markovic or the Avunaye, they must have kept the store running to help disguise their other activities. It was the fact that it was in such great shape that actually forced a sense of scepticism unto Lucy, and she began to doubt whether it would provide anything of use.

'I swear this place once sold pretzels or something... ' Claire looked the building up and down, holding a hand up to help shield her eyes from the glaring sunlight. 'Heh! Yep! Pretty sure I had some good food here once... or twice... I think there was one time... no that was the place on main... ' Claire chuckled to herself, which in turn made Lucy smile. Part of Lucy wished that her heart could be as unladen and care-free as Claire's seemed to be right now.

'Right, well, let's go inside and take a look around.' Although quickly judging the building by its exterior and deciding that it would most likely bear no fruit, Lucy decided that since they were here, now, and they might as well at least take a look.

The storefront was laid out like a small café or deli, with a few tables and chairs scattered about the room's periphery. There were chiller cabinets against both side walls, and a large counter towards the back. Beyond the counter was a long worktop with obvious vacancies where equipment had most likely sat between cupboards and storage shelves.

'Despite this place being baron, just the thought of pretzels is making me hungry.' Claire slumped her shoulders and dragged her knuckles like an impatient, hunger-driven adolescent.

Lucy raised an eyebrow to Claire's actions. 'Claire, they were probably cooking meth, velocity and who knows what else here...'

'Working for the mob or not, they made goo-od pretzels,' she smiled playfully. Claire continued to rummage amongst the shelves behind the counter. 'We should take a look in the back. There's nothing here, not even a...' she stopped and looked at Lucy who shook her head at the thought.

'You'd actually eat one if we found –' Claire shrugged and then grinned as Lucy spoke. 'Of course, you would...'

Moving into the back of the building they found a much larger room. No doubt once intended to be used for the preparation and cooking of food, it now held six long stainless-steel tables in its centre with strip lights hanging down over each of them. Lucy could picture a number of people standing along each table, either counting money or packing the drugs that had been manufactured. The cooking equipment was still here; it had been moved to the edges of the room to make space for everything else. As she looked around at the dust-laden tables and equipment, Lucy couldn't help but return to a state of frustration and disappointment. 'Claire, this is a bust. Waste of fucking time!' she kicked out, slamming the sole of her foot against the leg of the nearest table, forcing it to groan horrendously as it scraped across the floor.

'Hey, Lucy, look,' Claire chirped. She was smiling which only annoyed Lucy further. Claire was stood holding out her hands, gesturing towards one of the benches near the far corner of the room. Reluctantly, Lucy walked over to her, yet, all Claire was pointing at was another empty dust-stencilled space. Lucy crossed her arms and looked Claire in the eye. She couldn't decide whether Claire was nuts, or just trying to cheer her up by giving her something, anything, to cling to.

'Claire. There's nothing here,' Lucy said through gritted teeth.

'Exactly!' Claire replied, which only confused Lucy and in turn forced her to raise her hands over her face in frustration. 'Well, I mean, look...' Claire leant over the bench and struggled to reach for something. 'They wired it into the wall...' Lucy still didn't understand what she was harping on about. 'They left the... wire!' Claire exclaimed, managing to grasp what she had been reaching for. 'So I can tell what sat here. It's the right dimensions... chances are good.'

'Claire!' Lucy snapped. 'What is it?'

'Well, I'm not one-hundred-percent sure, more like ninety, or ninety-five... but it's a good bet...'

'Claire...'

'Right! Heh! A haematology analyser! For blood and, well, probably for use in producing velocity, seeing as that includes blood...' Although the evidence suggested that there may have once sat a piece of equipment here that could have aided them, Lucy still did not understand Claire's enthusiasm. She was also curious as to how Claire knew of velocity's composition, considering she had misplaced their only sample.

'Claire? How do you know that velocity contains blood?' Lucy stared her partner down. Claire suspiciously shuffled her feet and looked about the room, as if looking for an exit from this conversation. 'Claire... Serena told me that it was made from Avunaye blood, but I forgot to include that in my report. In fact, I'd forgotten it altogether until now. So, how do you know? You lost the sample, didn't you?'

'I did. Well, I mean, it got lost... I didn't lose it...' Claire looked as if she was panicking. 'You must have mentioned it, or something has... So many reports, so hard to keep track...'

'Claire...? What aren't you telling me?' Lucy couldn't help but feel as if she was being lied to. It annoyed her.

'This place has a walk-in refrigerator, right? Gotta be through one of those doors...' Claire pointed to two doors at the rear of the building. 'If there's any evidence here, it'll be in there. And who knows, maybe it was missed.'

'Claire?! Seriously. Enough.'

'I don't know! Lucy, I swear, the sample you gave me was lost. It must have come up in conversation, or... Mike's blood test results. Maybe that was it.'

'You'd better be telling me everything, Claire. I swear, if you're...' Lucy gave Claire a stern look, not wanting to let the subject lie, but her innocent expression persuaded Lucy to take her at her word.

Deciding to indulge Claire and her refrigerator theory, Lucy agreed to check out the doors to see what they could find, but she wouldn't forget their conversation; they would simply pause it for now. Lucy opened the left door and Claire, looking through a small window in the right, proceeded to open that one. Lucy's door led to a small outdoor space that connected to a back alley, no doubt for accepting deliveries and such. She sighed as she realised there was nothing here.

'Claire, I hope you are having better luck than me,' Lucy said as she sauntered back into the room, but Claire gave no response and her door was shut. 'Claire?' Lucy called, but then she heard a banging coming from the other door. Walking over to it, Lucy peered through the small window to find Claire stood inside, arms crossed, smiling in disbelief. 'Claire? Don't tell me you locked yourself in,' Lucy chuckled.

'Luce! the door won't open!' Claire shouted, but due to the thickness of the door, Lucy could barely hear her. Lucy tapped on her ear, indicating that Claire use her comms to communicate. 'There's no bloody door release! Please let me out,' Claire said over the comms before starting to laugh. Lucy waited a moment, jokingly starting to turn away and leave.

'Seriously, Claire. Only you would get locked in a fridge...' Lucy quipped. 'Maybe now you'll answer my question about the blood?' Claire didn't reply, she simply stood, unamused within the refrigerator. As Lucy pulled on the doors handle, however, the door would not budge. She tried again, pulling harder, yet she could not get it to open. 'Claire... it's stuck.' Lucy tried to remain calm, with the intention of not panicking Claire, but it seemed it was too late. Claire banged on the door again, attempting to push it whilst Lucy pulled.

'Lucy, this isn't funny...' The tell-tale pitch in Claire's voice indicated that she was beginning to panic. She banged on the window a few times before shaking her hands frustratedly.

'There must be some kind of release on the insidc, to stop this from happening. Look around.' Lucy stood and watched through the window as Claire began to look around the refrigerator. There was reems of abandoned plastic packaging lying on shelving. As Claire began to throw it all from one side to the other, Lucy could swear she could see something. 'Claire? What is that?' she questioned as Claire began to uncover something.

'Lucy! It's a body...' Claire looked to the window with fear in her eyes. 'Yes, okay, I'll check him...' Claire began seemingly talking to herself.

'What?' Lucy questioned Claire's ramblings.

'He has a pulse, Luce... He's alive, but he's hurt.' Claire cleared away all of the rubbish so that the man was visible to Lucy. Lucy's mind began to race as she tried to think of a way to get them both out of there.

I'll call for help. Get them cut out of there or something... Yet, before Lucy had even managed to contact anyone else, there was a loud groaning noise emitting from the unit and then a whirring sound. 'Claire? What's going on?' Claire, it seemed, had found a panel on the far wall of the refrigerator and had removed it in her search for a means to a way out.

'Lucy... I think I may have fucked up... Yeah... Think so...' Claire sounded disheartened and troubled. Looking through the window, Claire looked to Lucy and held up her hands; as she did, water ran from them. Claire rushed over to the window and banged on the door again. 'Lucy, the bloody thing is leaking... The rooms filling up with water!' The panic in her eyes urged Lucy to try and yank open the door again, but to no avail. 'Get us out of here, Luce!'

Lucy moved away from the unit momentarily, hurriedly looking around for something to help pry open the door, but there was nothing. She returned to the window to find Claire trying to sit the man up, lifting him up off the floor. Lucy's heart began to race and she ran her hands through her hair frustratedly as she realised that the water was already above Claire's ankles.

'I'm gunna call for help!' Lucy shouted and proceeded to call the office. She needed something to get them out of there; she'd blow the fucking door off if necessary. Her requests for help were met by news that the nearest fire departments were occupied with another incident. 'C'mon! I have an agent trapped with an injured civilian!' she screamed down the line before hanging up in frustration. Her phone then began to ring as she contemplated her next move. It was Hale. 'Thank god, Hale, give me something!' Her tone was full of desperation.

'Luce, we have a team coming to you now. How's

Claire doing?' Lucy looked back through the window and her heart skipped a beat as she saw that the water was filling up quicker than expected. Claire was struggling to hold the man up on his feet as the water had now passed their waists and was still rising.

'Not good, Hale. Water is flooding in fast. I don't understand what the fuck is going on! We need help now!' Growing more and more desperate, Lucy told Claire to get as far away from the window as possible. She took out her firearm and fired off two shots at the window and a few more at the door itself, only to find that the door and window were both too resistant. She was running out of options and her heart began to beat uncontrollably as she watched Claire struggle within the unit. 'Hale!' she screamed down the phone.

'Lucy, we're going to try and shut the power off from this end. If there's any sign of a power shut off switch, fuse box, anything at your end, take it out.' Lucy followed Hale's advice, searching for the buildings fuse box. As she found it, the lights switched off and Lucy surmised that it must have been Hales doing. Deciding to be better safe than sorry, she frantically shut the mains power off, along with everything else, not caring what each switch was for and rushed back to Claire to see if it had helped. Only, she could still hear the drone of the refrigerator whirring away.

'Seriously?! For fucks sake!' she exclaimed. Looking through the window, Lucy now struggled to see anything with the place in darkness, but she could just about make out Claire's body. The water level had risen higher than the window and the realisation forced Lucy to bang frantically on the door. 'Claire!' she yelled down the comms, hoping that Claire could still hear her. 'We need to cut the power! Short circuit! Blow the generator!' Lucy really wished she had Claire on her side of the door right now; her skillset would be perfect for finding a solution. But the reality was that Claire was trapped and Lucy, who now felt useless, was all she had. *How the hell do we... Think Lucy, think!* She had all but lost hope, resorting to kicking out at the door when there was a loud bang from inside the wall beside the refrigerator. Lucy jumped back as sparks of electricity zipped across the door and then the walls. Smoke began to seep out from the split between the wall and the ceiling and the groaning and whirring of the fridge ceased. Lucy went to look back in through the window to check that Claire was okay, but then she heard the sound of the front entrance opening and Hale, with a team of people, rushed in.

Equipped with welding equipment, explosives, drills and god knows what else, Hale's team set to work. 'Come on! Come on!' Lucy shouted as they simultaneously drilled through the doors handle and hinges. 'Faster!' She exclaimed, but then she was hit by a huge wave of relief as the door fell to the ground and water flooded out into the room, followed by Claire and the civilian. Lucy rushed to her colleague, frantically moving Claire's hair from her face to see if she was alright. Lucy's momentary sense of relief almost transformed into one of despair, but then Claire coughed and spat out water. 'Thank god...' she said in between racing deep breaths, before looking over to the man that had been trapped with Claire. Hale was attempting to resuscitate him, carrying out chest compressions again and again, but the man did not regain consciousness.

Ensuring that Claire was safe and secure, Lucy watched her colleague be taken off to hospital to be checked out, and then she headed back to headquarters. Whatever had happened to the refrigeration system, to short it all out, had probably saved Claire's life by giving them valuable seconds of time. Lucy was grateful for the luck that they had received, but as she began to write up her incident report, she couldn't help question how or why it had all happened. She had requested to be kept up to date with all findings from the scene and from the hospital, and roughly an hour into writing her report, she received a message from the coroner's office. *Preliminary report suggests John Doe died of electrocution. Not drowning.* 'So, when the generator blew, it had somehow electrocuted him?' No matter how many times Lucy went through the information, she couldn't make sense of it. Something wasn't right. *Was the fridge a trap? Was it set up to fill with water? How did the generator blow?* Lucy needed answers, otherwise her head was going to implode. She made a call to an engineer and left the office, heading back to the scene.

'Right. I want to know exactly how this thing was rigged. I want to know how the integrated water-cooling system, or whatever you call it, shorted out. How it overloaded... Two people were submerged in there, yet one dies of electrocution and the other is perfectly fine. Explain.' Lucy stood at the mouth of the unit, looking in, searching for answers but not finding any by herself.

'Well, I can't tell you how one person survived and the other didn't. Luck I guess... but, I can make an estimate on the cause of the pump failure.' The engineer had removed a number of panels from the inner wall of the walk-in refrigerator, enabling him to inspect its inner workings. He climbed down off his steps and scratched at his brow.

'Well?' Lucy pushed him for an answer.

'What you have here is a walk-in, with a traditional water-cooled chiller system. See, someone broke the pipe and fed it into the unit itself, no doubt rigged the pump to activate when the door was shut, or when that panel over there was tampered with. Somehow, an electrical current was introduced at the broken pipe, which travelled back up through the system to the condenser then the evaporator and blew the lot.'

'That... that doesn't make any sense.' Lucy looked at the engineer confused, although it appeared he too shared the same opinion. He opened his mouth as if to speak again, but as he did, he was thrown against the wall. Lucy instinctively reached for her firearm, but then she heard a voice and felt the need to stop in her action.

'This is unexpected. *You* are not supposed to be here.' He smiled at her with closed lips. Lucy's stomach twisted as she fought against her body's inaction, unable to defend herself as he stepped in front of her, looking at her with his unnerving, piercing yellow eyes.

24

Edgar Young

'Yes, John, technically I am a stock broker...' He was attempting to gain another new client. Walking along the busy streets of the city with his Bluetooth receiver in his ear, constantly working on the move, Edgar preferred to work outside; it allowed him to stretch his legs and exercise his mind, instead of dozing off behind a desk. His best work was achieved out amongst the hustle and bustle of the city he currently resided in. 'Think of me more as a wealth manager, because that's what I'll be doing from now on, looking after the wealth that you are undoubtedly about to accrue from trusting me.' The client, John Novak, was a successful businessman, but not someone that a typical stock trader would target. Technically, John had no money; he owned many assets in the forms of properties and real-estate that were mainly used as half-way houses and rehabilitation centres. Mr. Novak was a good man, putting all of his time and money into providing safe and secure environments for people struggling with addictions, the homeless and war heroes that had returned to their home country only to find themselves abandoned. John Novak was one of many people that did all they could to help others, but in the process found themselves in dire-straits, struggling to continue their great work without help. That was why Edgar targeted them and not the usual one percent. 'John, I realise that it will be all you have left, but that is why you can trust me. Over three centuries ago, London opened an exchange in a coffee shop. Over two and a quarter centuries ago, the New York Stock Exchange was opened when twenty-four brokers stood trading under a tree.' Edgar could tell that he had the client's ear, but he would have to nail it in one swift stroke. 'John, I have never – not once – failed to make a client money. I charge a commission of fifty-percent, and do you know why, or how I continue to charge such a weighty figure? It's because I take the ten grand you are going to give me and I turn it into a quarter-mil within a month. So, when you think of what you can do with the money you have, just imagine what you will be able to accomplish once I help you.' John was silent for a good minute on the other end of the line, no doubt seriously contemplating the offer that Edgar had put forward.

'Do it. God help me...'

'It's okay, John, you've got me in your corner now. I'll forward you the details and I will assure you, these stocks are primed to help you continue doing what you do best.'

A true modern-day Robin Hood, Edgar was wealthy himself, but he had always made sure that his financial success came hand in hand with that of someone else who truly needed it. Smiling, he felt that the morning had been a huge success and he had high hopes that he could continue spreading good-will to those who needed it most. It was a beautifully sunny summers day and he complimented his outfit with an expensive pair of square aviator sunglasses. He was wearing a royal-blue suit with a bright white shirt that he left open at the top two buttons. He stopped in his march to buy a hotdog from a nearby vendor, paying the weary looking worker twice the asking amount and receiving many thanks for his generosity. He had walked the city streets for roughly eight miles when he decided that it was time to head back to his apartment, and so he hailed a cab.

Edgar liked to move around a lot, never remaining in the same place for longer than a few months. He had purchased his current residence a little over two weeks ago; the apartment still smelt faintly of fresh paint. He did not like to be tied down and despite the expense and hassle that constantly buying and selling properties brought, he did it mostly because with each new home came new surroundings, new neighbours and new people to interact with. This particular apartment resided in NoHo, on the well-known Bleecker Street. Situated on a high floor, it was a lavish combination of two apartments converted into one. The entire eastern wall, running along the far side of the combined living and dining room, master bedroom and spare bedroom, consisted of picture windows that allowed for amazing architectural views and for the sunlight to flood in throughout the day. The apartment also had its own expansive foyer, which opened out into the living room and the kitchen, and an elevator.

'Productive morning, Mr. Young?' the doorman asked as Edgar approached.

'Sven, please, you know my forename. Use it'. Edgar wasn't one for formalities, he preferred things to be as relaxed as possible at all times, as no doubt, he would be moving on within a month or two.

'Will do, Mr. Young. No car today? Such a shame to keep such a fine motor locked up, and on such a fine day.' Sven smiled and looked up at the cloudless blue sky above.

'That is to say, you're disappointed to not be required to park it up for me?' Edgar laughed and patted the doorman on the shoulder as he passed him to go inside.

He had done some good with the day so far and felt good about himself. He was in the mood to celebrate, to share his tiny victory, but the downside of always living alone was that even during the good times, he always returned to an empty home. Orphaned at birth, Edgar had always been alone, however, his so-called adopted siblings that he had grown up with were always just a phone call away. Depending on where Edgar found himself, he would sometimes crash at one of their homes for a night or two in between moving lodgings. Those brief occasions were the only times that he felt the embrace of family. Regardless, today was a day to celebrate and he considered who he might invite.

Wild, crazy party with a room full of strangers? Or... He smiled as the thought occurred to him. He threw his sunglasses onto one of the white, fabric covered arm chairs in the living room and slipped out of his jacket. He undid the cuffs on his shirt and then the buttons down the centre, revealing his slender torso. Heading towards his bedroom and its adjoining bathroom, he took out his phone and dialled. 'Hey, Seamus, it's Edgar. How'd you like to bring the family over to my place for dinner tonight? Kind of a... business celebration. Hard work paying off. My treat.' He smiled gleefully as he and Seamus discussed the evening ahead. 'Perfect. I'll text you the address.'

Edgar had some time to kill before his guests arrived, so he pottered about the apartment for a while, tidying up and organising. The spare second bedroom had been converted into a home gym, so he had a quick work out and then a shower before getting himself ready for his guests. He donned a pair of dark-blue denim pants, a short-sleeved white t-shirt and a light-grey waistcoat, completing his smart-casual appearance. He had planned to cook one of his specialities in an attempt to impress his good friend and his family; pan-roasted fillet steaks with gremolata, a recipe that never failed to dazzle his dinner guests. As he was cooking, the buzzer on the intercom sounded.

'Mr. Young, I have the McCarthy family here,' Sven announced.

'Ah.' Edgar skipped over to the panel to reply. 'Send them up please, Sven.'

Edgar had resumed his position by the stove as

Seamus entered the foyer from the elevator. He was followed closely by Moira, Declan and then Alannah. Edgar turned to his right and smiled.

'Fucking hell!' Declan said as he looked about the living and dining room, receiving a sharp nudge from Moira, supposedly attempting to remind her outspoken son of his manners.

'Not too shabby hey, Dec'? Edgar encouraged Declan's wonderment and gave Moira a reassuring wink. 'Dinner's almost ready. Please, make yourselves at home.' He gave Declan a pat on the shoulder and Moira a quick embrace followed by a peck on the cheek.

'Something smells good,' Seamus acknowledged. He stood awkwardly, still in the foyer, almost clinging to the elevator whilst his family continued to move into the hearth of the home.

'Pulling out all the stops for you, mate.' Edgar shook Seamus' hand and tried to encourage him to come in further, inviting him once again to make himself comfortable. 'Moira, beautiful as ever. And Alannah,' he smiled. Alannah blushed in response. Seamus had dressed well for the occasion, wearing a short-sleeved, dark-blue, buttoned shirt, black suit pants and a pair of black and white sneakers. Moira looked glamorous, wearing a black jumpsuit with a pink blazer and matching coloured heels. Alannah coyly brushed her hair behind her ears as she smiled at Edgar; she was wearing a black floral tea dress with a pair of black sandals.

'This place is amazing, Edgar,' Alannah stated as she walked into the living room, she then leaned over the breakfast bar to take a look at what was cooking. Edgar quickly returned to the stove to check on the meals progress.

'I took the liberty of cooking everyone's steak medium-rare, but please let me know if you'd prefer it cooked more.'

'Mmm, sounds perfect.' Alannah continued to watch

him cook.

'Drink, Alannah?' Edgar leant on the opposite side of the bar. He waited a moment for an answer, but all she did was smile. Edgar found it sweet, but it didn't help him with his question. '...Seamus? Beer?' he asked quickly, causing Alannah to realise that she hadn't answered him. She awkwardly looked away towards her father, flushed with embarrassment.

Having poured the drinks and dished up the food, Edgar joined the four of them at the table to eat. He sat down at the head of the table, with Seamus and Moira to his right and Declan and Alannah to his left.

'So, what are we celebrating again?' Declan interrupted the small talk as they all enjoyed the food and drink. 'You were already minted, weren't you?' Declan teased before shoving another piece of steak in his mouth.

'It's not about the money, truly. What I achieved today will help a lot of people who need it. A lot of folks that are down on their luck.'

'Dec, Edgar is... Aww, he's that guy. You know...' Alannah paused for a moment as she searched for the words that lingered on the tip of her tongue.

'Oh! *That* guy,' Declan laughed, insinuating something other than that which his sister was trying to get out. In response, Alannah gave him a sharp jab to his upper arm.

'Fisher!' she blurted out, sighing in relief that she'd finally remembered what she wanted to say. 'You're like, a modern-day Robin Hood,' she smiled.

'Well, I think what you do is very admirable, Edgar. Congratulations.' Moira raised a glass to toast him. Seamus, however, remained fairly quiet. Edgar knew him to be a just man, perhaps he didn't quite agree with Edgar's methods of making money, playing the market, despite the good he did along the way.

Perhaps he doesn't see it as a hard day's labour... Edgar

pondered, watching Seamus' body language as the conversation continued. Edgar had noticed, however, how much Declan had bulked up since the last time he had seen him; he had clearly been working out. 'I imagine the gym I have set up in the spare room would interest you, Dec'. You're looking big, fella.' Declan was wearing a tight fitted shirt and ripped jeans. He goofed around in response to Edgar's compliment, flexing his muscles and mimicking a short strip-tease, much to Moira and Alannah's dismay.

'Declan's considering joining the force. After he graduates of course,' Seamus added. There was a definitive sense of pride to his tone. Moira's expression was less enthusiastic, exhibiting a motherly concern for her son.

'Well, if you are anything like your dad, this city will be gaining a fine protector,' Edgar added. Declan smiled, however, Seamus seemed to then retreat into himself a little. 'Seamus, I'm... I was sorry to hear about your colleagues,' he added awkwardly. It was a subject he had hoped to avoid bringing up, but Seamus looked as if he had something he needed to get off his chest. Edgar simply wanted to show his friend some support.

'Thank you, Edgar.' Moira spoke for her husband, who remained withdrawn from the topic of conversation. 'It has been tough, but we are getting through it together.' Seamus put his head into his hands.

'Cannon, Axel... Sam. Those officers were murdered. That I understand. I have closure, a target... I know who's to blame.' Seamus shook his head wearily as he spoke. 'It's Malik I don't get. Pissing his life away like that. What the fuck possessed him to shoot at an F.B.I agent?' He was angry and confused, searching endlessly for answers to the questions that continued to plague him. Edgar felt pity for him.

'If there's anything I can...' Edgar began to say sincerely, to which Moira smiled and nodded in response.

The conversation of Seamus' fallen colleagues

certainly put a dampener on the rest of the evening, but Edgar made the best of the time spent with his friend and his family. Moira continued to thank Edgar for his hospitality at regular intervals; Alannah, clearly besotted with him, attempted to flirt, however, Declan constantly ran interference like a protective big brother. They all watched through the windows as the sun set over the city, casting an array of beautiful hues, before the McCarthy family said their farewells and bid Edgar a goodnight. Edgar's thoughts lingered around Seamus' sullen manner after they'd left; he wished there was something he could do to ease his friend's pain, but how could he possibly help? *Money can't fix this... What use am I right now?* Edgar reached a point where he angered himself, resenting his inability to aid Seamus with his struggles. He worked himself up so much so, that he decided to get changed and head out into the city for a run in the cold night air, praying that it might calm his inner turmoil, otherwise he would only dwell on these thoughts and spend the entire night mulling over his feelings. Headphones in, he quickly completed a five-kilometre run and found himself back at his apartment, feeling a little less burdened. He entered his home and took off his top, slinging it onto the floor, and headed for the kitchen to grab a bottle of water. It was as he opened the fridge, he realised that something was out of place. His bedroom door was ajar and the light inside it was on, dimly, but he distinctly recalled turning it off. *Huh...* he questioned his own memory for a moment and then contemplated the idea of an intruder. Edgar was fairly confident in his ability to protect himself, so he headed through, entering the unknown brazenly.

He opened the door sharply, mentally prepared for a tussle with whomever had broken into his home. Yet, he did not expect to find *her* sat on the end of his bed. 'What... What are you doing here?' he asked, concerned. Usually, upon finding a woman in his bedroom, which happened occasionally, Edgar would be delighted and a night of passion would ensue. However, this instance was complicated at best, and it filled his stomach with a sense of dread. He rolled his eyes as he attempted to figure out how to handle the situation. She looked him in the eye and then looked down at her hands as she awkwardly twiddled her thumbs. She had a look of expectation, but also one of hope; a hope that Edgar could not oblige. *What was she thinking, coming back here?* She brushed her dark hair behind her ears and stood up.

'I'm sorry... this was... stupid.' She screwed up her face and bit the inside of her lip as she stood up and walked towards him and the exit. She was clearly upset that the moment had not played out how she had envisaged.

'Alannah, wait.' Edgar desperately wanted out of this situation but he was also concerned; it was late and the city was no place for an upset young woman to be walking around alone. Tears began to trickle from her eyes as she fought against her embarrassment. He held out his hands in an offer of an embrace, to which she rushed to, hugging him tightly as she wept. 'You're a beautiful woman, Alannah, but this is...'

'Wrong place, wrong time...' she sniffed.

'Let me drive you home.'

The drive was awkwardly quiet; neither of them wanting to reflect on what had happened. Edgar stopped the car up the street from her house; he didn't want to cause further issues by risking them being seen. They both smiled at each other and Alannah reached for the door handle. Edgar looked away, looking into his side-mirror to check that no-one was around, yet, as he turned back, he was met by her lips. She had caught him off guard and kissed him. It was just one quick kiss, but he found himself perplexed by the moment. The softness of her lips, the flurry of chills that ran up and down his body, his irregular heartbeat. He had to shake himself from a daze as she closed the car door and scurried up the street to her home. The drive back to his apartment was instantly forgotten upon his arrival; the world, and even time itself, didn't seem to make any sense to him right now. He undressed and laid down on his bed, but he wasn't ready to sleep. His thoughts were a jumble, trying to work out what had just happened and what he was going to do about it. Sighing heavily, he closed his eyes, half hoping it had been a strangely wonderful dream.

There was a buzzing in his head that was caught between his dreams and reality. He was on the cusp of waking when his body was shocked into a state of alertness by the realisation that the buzzing was coming from his doorbell. Someone was clearly desperate to speak to him. 'Alright, I'm up...' he told himself as he looked at the face of his watch. It was early, too early for visitors; the sun hadn't even been up long. Throwing on a pair of shorts and a t-shirt, he walked through to the foyer and answered the intercom. 'Who is it?' he asked wearily, half asleep.

'It's Declan, let me up.' Suddenly Edgar was fully awake, as if his body had been given a jump start.

'C'mon up,' Edgar replied as he pushed the door release button. Whatever this was, Edgar was sure he could handle it. *Nothing happened, so... let's just see what he wants,* he told himself. Edgar was making himself a coffee when Declan walked out of the elevator, he offered Declan a drink, but his offer was rebuffed as Declan began to pace frustratedly.

'You took advantage of my sister...' he said angrily. 'You know what she's... what our family has been through...'

'Whoa, Dec', nothing happened...' Edgar met Declan in the living room, stopping his pacing.

'Yeah right!' He was angry, clenching his fists.

'Declan, mate. Before you go and do something you'll regret, listen.' Edgar held his hands up in surrender, hoping that Declan would see sense before acting on his emotions. 'Honestly, I got back from my run, she was here... I drove her home. End of.' The look in Declan's eyes showed signs that he understood, that he was listening. 'Let's just take a minute, yeah.' The buzzer then sounded again. 'Seriously, who... let me see who that is...' Edgar tried to keep Declan calm as he walked back over to the intercom. 'Hello?'

'Edgar, it's Alannah.' Her words forced Declan to snap. 'Please let me in. We need to talk about what happened last night...' Edgar couldn't believe the timing and looked at Declan confused, unsure of what to say. As Declan's expression turned to one of rage, Edgar pushed the button to let Alannah in, hoping that Declan would believe the pair of them when they told him that they were innocent of any wrong doing.

Declan waited for Edgar to step back into the living room before he clocked him, swiftly landing a blow across his jaw with a right hook. Edgar took the hit without any intention of retaliating. The kid needed to get it out of his system; Edgar just hoped he was done.

'Oh my god! Declan! What the hell?!' Alannah exclaimed as she entered to find her brother also there.

'I'm not going to let him take advantage of a girl with a crush!' Declan shouted back at her. Alannah's face filled with fury for her brother. She marched towards Declan with intent, but stopped when she laid eyes on Edgar.

'Oh my god! Did you hit him?!' she exclaimed, frustrated and angry. She raised a hand to Edgar's face. Predicting an adverse reaction from Declan, Edgar quickly stopped her, grasping her wrist. 'You're... Your lip is bleeding... ' she said solemnly, upset by his reaction. Edgar hadn't noticed, but he could now taste the blood as it seeped into his mouth. The taste curdled his stomach.

'Let me...' Edgar closed his eyes for a second as he bottled the urge to vomit. 'Let me go clean up, then we can all talk.'

Edgar left the siblings to argue whilst he headed to his bedroom and then into the ensuite, listening to their raised voices bicker at one another as he left the room. It was only a small cut, but he had never liked the taste of blood. *I'll get dressed... dressed for work, then I'll deal with them...* he decided. He preferred an uncomplicated life, so he would need to deal with this quickly and preferably without including Seamus. He opened his wardrobe and pulled out a white shirt, throwing it onto his bed. Delving back in, he pulled out a blue jacket and matching pants. He got undressed and slipped on the suit pants, fastening them and sorting out the pockets. There was something in his pocket that wasn't meant to be there. A cloth, no, a napkin; it had been folded. As he unfolded it his stomach knotted and he choked on his own breath. At the sight of the red smear that stretched across the napkin, Edgars head was filled with the sounds of distant screams. He rushed to the bathroom and splashed his face with water from the faucet. Looking into the mirror he watched as his eyes began to become bloodshot. 'What...? No... no... no...' he began to panic, looking at the skin on his hands and arms as it began to lose its bronze tint and turn pale. The pain within his stomach was unbearable, a hunger like he'd never felt before. 'Ala... Alannah! Declan! You need... You... Go! Now!' he shouted, struggling to get the words out as his breathing became laboured. He felt as if his lungs were twisting, slowly failing him, unable to take in any air and his heart began to beat slower and slower, despite his distress. He clambered out of the bathroom and out into the hall.

'Hey, Edgar? You alright?' Declan asked, spotting him from the living room. Alannah rushed to his side.

'You need to... GO!!' Edgar shouted in a cracked tone. He was struggling to stand.

'What's wrong?!' she cried in a panic.

'LEAVE!!!' he snapped, staring her in the eye. He could see his own reflection in her now petrified, fearful gaze. His deep, red, blood-shot eyes, greyed skin and low hanging jaw. The pain was intense and he screamed in agony as his jawbone snapped and his cheeks tore, revealing teeth that were now extending, worming their way out of his gums as they grew.

As Alannah shrieked, Declan rushed to his sister's side, grabbing her by the arm and forcibly dragging her away from Edgar, towards the foyer. She resisted, paralysed by fear, but Declan was strong. Edgar could feel the hunger inside him, a painful, relentless thirst. He was dead inside and craved what all living things took for granted. He lashed out, punching the wall before him. *Leave them alone!* He screamed inside at the monster he was becoming, but it wasn't listening.

'I want to feel...' the monster, Kenan voiced, getting to its feet. Like a wild animal, he rushed without hesitation, throwing himself into the living room and then scrambling on all fours through to the foyer. Alannah screamed again at the sight of him and Declan frantically tried to close the elevator door. Kenan bounded towards them and grabbed Alannah by the wrist, pulling her back into the apartment, throwing her into the living room. She lost her footing and fell to the floor. Declan moved to his sister's aid but Kenan intercepted, digging his fingernails into Declan's chest and launching him into the living room alongside his sister. 'AH!' Kenan roared like a feral beast. Saliva dripped from his mouth as his hunger and excitement grew. Declan scurried towards the bedrooms, dragging Alannah with him. Kenan charged at them, tackling Declan to the ground and knocking Alannah back against the windows. Declan swung a fist and hit Kenan in the face, but it only infuriated the monster further. He scurried about, looking for an opening and then bore his fangs and went to lunge at Declan, when Alannah, finding an ounce of courage, raised a foot and kicked out at him, knocking him back. As Kenan scuffled on the floor, righting himself, the siblings made a move for the main bedroom, Alannah managing to get inside. Kenan was too quick for Declan though, and he barged into him again, shoving him down the hall. Alannah screamed for her brother, but at the sight of Kenan's glare, she slammed the bedroom door, sealing herself away.

Declan managed to get to his feet and bundled himself into the spare bedroom. He tried to close the door but Kenan threw himself at it, knocking Declan back into the room. The hunger within was too great, he needed to eat, to sink his teeth into someone and bathe in their blood. It hurt so much that Kenan banged his hands against his head to try and quell the thirst and quieten his conscience, Edgar, that cried from within.

Leave them alone! Edgar repeatedly cried inside, attempting to tame the blood thirsty monstrum.

'AHH!!' Kenan howled again before leaping towards Declan, only to be met by a barbell, with Declan striking him across the head with a weight. Kenan was dazed momentarily and Declan made a break for the door. The hit, however, had seemed to only silence the voice within, providing the animal with the clarity he needed for the hunt. He grabbed Declan from behind and sank his teeth into his shoulder, biting down hard as he forced him to the ground. Declan writhed and wriggled as he tried to get the beast off of him, but Kenan held him down and drank deep. Kenan urged himself to sink his fangs deeper, increasing the pressure and then he tore away a large chunk of clothing and flesh, causing blood to gush out over the floor. Declan continued to struggle for every second that his body would allow, but the more blood he lost, the less he moved, until shortly, he ceased to move at all. Kenan lapped up the blood from Declan's flesh and from off of the floor, indulging himself in his warm meal when he heard her whimper.

Alannah was in the main bedroom; Kenan could hear her heartbeat race and her breath quiver. He crept towards the door, scraping his claws along the walls. Stopping at the door, he pressed his ear up against it to listen, to take pleasure in her fearful struggle. However, he could hear her speaking, quietly whispering.

'Please... help me...'

'No! No one to help!' Kenan yelled at her through the door.

'I've called the police!' she screamed back amongst her tears.

Leave her alone!! Edgar bellowed from within, his constant drone forcing Kenan to claw at his own temple in an attempt to bore out the voice.

'AH!!' Kenan howled and he threw himself against the door again and again in a wild frenzy. Alannah must have pushed something up against it as it did not budge. He banged on the door frantically before throwing himself at it again. Struggling to get to her infuriated him and he was beginning to tire as his constant need to feed became insatiable. Throwing himself into the door again, it cracked, and one final lunge allowed him to burst through it, tumbling over furniture and Alannah whom had been sitting up against it. He turned and scurried towards her, pinning her down, drooling blood-filled saliva over her face like a rabid dog as his jaw snapped at her, tormenting her before he bit down into her flesh.

'Edgar...' she whimpered, and for a split second, Kenan saw himself in her eyes. Perhaps it was the sound of his name, or the look in her eyes, the thought of killing her, of devouring her; something caused a piercing screech to sound within his head and forced him to retreat to the corner of the bedroom. He grasped at his head, beating it as he writhed in pain. His stomach ached and his head throbbed as his jaw broke and then realigned itself. He could feel the warmth returning to his body, the beat of his own heart.

'NO!' Kenan exclaimed as he scratched at his chest, desperately trying to remain in control. 'No cage! No life!'

The world around him began to look less red and the pains within him subsided. Yet, as reality returned for Edgar, he was able to see the devastation, and the fear on

Alannah's face, the tears in her eyes and the blood. There was so much blood. He rubbed his arms, his hands, his chest, trying to wipe away the blood, trying to claw it off himself.

'AH!' Edgar cried out, tears breaking free from his eyes, spit flying from his lips. 'AH!' he cried again as an unbearable wave of despair came crashing down over him.

'Show me your hands, now!' an officer yelled from the doorway. Edgar slowly raised his hands and placed them on his head, his chest jerking and his teeth grinding as he broke inside.

'Tobias!' Edgar repeated again and again. 'Tobias! Make it go away! Take it away!'

25

Seamus McCarthy

Seamus ran to his car as fast as his legs would allow and he sped off out of the cemetery. They had taken Declan to the Mount Sinai Hospital. That was where Moira will be waiting for him. Seamus' heart beat so quickly that it felt almost like one continuous thump as he raced along the roads as fast as his car would allow. Traffic was beginning to pick up as the city began a new working day, but Seamus had no time to waste waiting on people he didn't even know. 'Out of the fucking way!' he screamed as he sounded his horn and swerved onto the wrong side of the road to overtake the car in front. He knew exactly how far away he was, but he needed to be there now. Every second he wasted in his journey to reach his family tore at him like a rabid animal; time itself was currently eating away at him.

He had barely slept. The evening at Edgars had started off as a pleasant change from everyday life, however, the topic of conversation at dinner had wormed its way, deep into his mind, and Seamus had struggled to shut it out. He had tossed and turned, disturbing Moira at least once as he had attempted to sleep, though, the harder he tried, the more it seemed unlikely to happen. He had left Moira and the kids asleep in their beds and driven for an hour to Brooklyn, hoping that facing that which tormented him would help put his weary mind at rest. In hindsight, he shouldn't have travelled so far, but how was he to know what was coming in the hours ahead. It had been roughly 6am and the sun had just begun to rise as he had reached his destination. Majestic warm rays of light stretched out across the world and caressed the stone before him, washing over the words, highlighting their significance to Seamus as he read, "Here Lies Samuel Lorenzo. A Beautiful Son – Taken Too Soon. Fidelis Ad Mortem". His badge had been etched into the stone next to his name, cementing his position in the department for all time. As Seamus had stood upon the earth that harnessed his late friend and colleague, a tear had crept from the corner of his eye.

'Hey there... Sam.' Seamus had choked on the words as he battled against his emotions. He had stepped closer to the headstone and taken to one knee, placing his right hand upon the hard surface that bore his partners name, running his fingers along the etchings in the stone. 'I'm lost, kid. I tried to get justice for you, but all I seemed to do was make things worse. Even when...' He'd struggled as he'd recalled Sam's cocksure nature and envisaged the kid telling him to "man up". '...Even when I promised Moira that I wouldn't get involved. It just... It doesn't seem to end.' Reaching down, he'd spread his fingers amongst the blades of grass that covered the grave, hoping it would bring him closer, that he might make a connection. 'I *hate* all the time, Sam. Markovic. The Avunaye... Talk of dirty cops. I looked up the name of the crazy bitch that blew up the Italian... Barachiel. History, religion, they have her down as an archangel. It's nuts, and yet, I can't help but wonder... If the angels are down here with us, fighting for us... against us... then who the hell is up there? Who's looking after you?' Seamus had clenched his fist, tearing the grass from the soil. He'd been angry and upset; mainly with himself and his own thoughts. The world was changing around him and he was struggling to understand it; to keep up. He had occasionally questioned what life was all about, just as he assumed every mortal being had at least once in their life time. The only problem was that his eyes had been opened to so many things recently, things that contradicted history, that questioned his faith. What was he to do about it all? What could he do?

He had been sat by the grave for an hour, talking to his figmental colleague – venting, seeking advice from the beyond – all the while holding the grass tightly in his clenched fist – as if without it, he would only be conversing with himself. That was when his phone had begun to ring and he had awkwardly tried to retrieve it from his pocket with the opposite, empty hand, stubbornly refusing to unclench his fist. He had fiddled and eventually pried the phone from his pocket only for it to slip from his finger tips and fall to the ground. It had been Moira calling, yet, the call ended before he could swipe to answer. *She's probably wondering where I am,* he had presumed, little did he know that she needed him so. 'I guess it's time for me to head home, Sam.' He had smiled and then sighed as he called Moira back. 'Good morning, sweetheart,' he had said in a rather chipper tone as Moira picked up the call. However, the sound of her broken voice in reply had stopped time where he'd stood. As he had listened to her painful plea, his fingers had slowly opened. The torn, narrow leaves of grass had tumbled from his grip, getting caught on the breeze and slowly drifted on the air until they crashed back down to earth, lifeless.

Moira hadn't said much, she didn't need to, and no doubt she couldn't have mustered the words anyway. All Seamus knew was that Declan was in trouble and, judging by the level of distress in Moira's voice, it was life threatening. He floored the accelerator pedal and tried to will his car to go faster, over-taking as many cars as he could, swerving in and out of lanes as he crossed the bridge into Manhattan. The traffic was starting to build up rapidly and Seamus side-swiped two cars in his attempt to not miss his turning once he made it off the bridge. *Home straight...* he told himself as his engine screamed, and for a moment he caught himself wishing he was driving Edgar's beast of a motor.

'C'mon!' he exclaimed in anger as he was forced to stop just shy of the hospital's emergency department. Making a split-second decision, he ditched the car and began to run as fast as he could. Following the large red "emergency" signs, he barged through the doors, barely allowing them to open, and scrambled across the grey tiled floor, looking for someone to point him in the direction of his family. He found himself not needing any help, however, as upon seeing him, Moira exhibited a heart-wrenching howl.

'Sea'!!' she wailed from across the ward. Seamus instinctively charged towards her, but before he could reach her, she fell to her knees. She had blood on her hands, her blue top and smeared across her face around her hair line, but Seamus could see no cuts or wounds. The amount of blood on her made Seamus' gut clench, his throat close and his heart stop. He slid onto his knees and grabbed her, holding her tightly.

'Moira, where's Dec'?' he asked cautiously, not really wanting the truth. Moira could barely cry for lack of breath. Seamus pulled back and placed his hands on her cheeks, looking into her red-raw, tear drained eyes. 'Where's our boy?' He was trembling. His arms were shaking as he tried to resist the urge to implode. He was torn between comforting his wife and leaving her to find his son. 'Moira?' he repeated as she offered no response, 'Moira?!' He tried to snap her into giving him the information he needed. She fell to the floor and let out an almighty cry as she pointed down the hall towards the operating theatres. Abandoning his wife, Seamus got to his feet and jogged, throwing his weight into the doors and heading down the hall. As he saw the entrance to the theatre he slowed, his legs wobbling slightly as a surgeon exited, his overalls saturated in red. Seamus walked up to the door and looked through the window. Placing his hands either side of it, he went to enter, yet his body refused to push. Instead, as he laid eyes on the body of his son, his legs gave way and he found himself falling into the room, hitting the ground hard. 'My...' he cried, laying on the floor, arms outstretched. 'My poor boy...' He reached out, his fingers outstretched, his vision blurred by the flood of tears erupting from his eyes.

Seamus felt as if he was in a daze. His body felt sedated and his mind refused to process what was happening around him. He and Moira had been moved to a private consultation room, although he couldn't recall how he had gotten there. A doctor had confirmed Declan's death and Seamus' colleague, officer Rivera, had said something about Alannah being safe. Seamus couldn't focus, his head felt light and his body weighted, as if his feet had been cemented and he was drowning in a river of despair.

'Officer Seamus McCarthy?' He heard his name being requested, and once his brain had managed to connect the voice to a person, he suddenly awoke from his subdued state.

'Krysta!' he shouted as he stood up and walked towards the door. It had been her asking for him, and her presence here, as far as Seamus was concerned, could only mean one thing. As he opened the door fully, Krysta was stood on the other side. Seamus angrily grabbed her by the arm and pulled her into the room. 'Was it one of them?!' he demanded, slamming the door behind them. 'Was it?!' Moira jumped up in response to his exclamation. She looked dazed and confused, glancing at Seamus and then at Krysta.

'Seamus, easy,' Krysta pleaded, raising her hands.

'Easy?! My son is dead!' His sorrow was now lost beneath a sea of rage as his pulse quickened.

'I'm sorry about your son, Seamus, I truly am. Mrs McCarthy... I'm just here to inform you that the F.B.I have your daughter, Alannah. We're keeping her safe.' Seamus rage distorted the sincerity in Krysta's eyes, nor could he hear it in her voice as she spoke. All he saw was red.

'What happened?!' Seamus exclaimed.

'Your daughter is the only witness. We are trying to piece together what happened, but she is not responding.'

'Her fucking brother is dead! What the hell do you expect?!'

'Seamus, I know. I'm sorry... but what can you tell me about Edgar Young?' Seamus was confused. What did Edgar have to do with this?

'What... What does he have to –'

'N.Y.P.D have him in custody...' As Krysta spoke, something inside Seamus broke. The world was clearer again and he knew what he needed to do. He walked to the exit and opened the door. 'Seamus, where are you going? You can't get involved –' Krysta tried to stop him, but Seamus shoved her backwards and marched out of the room. 'Seamus! Lucy is missing.' He paused for a moment upon hearing the news, however, "missing" was not dead, and he needed to be elsewhere.

Edgar... he thought as he clenched his fists and began moving at a pace. He wasn't sure if he was worried for his friend or angry at him, he just needed to get to him, to learn the truth; he would work out his emotions once he had the facts.

As Seamus reached his car and climbed in, he lifted his head to see his wife rushing towards him. He went to get back out, but she hurriedly made her way to the passenger door and climbed in. 'Moira?' he questioned, wondering what she was doing here.

'He was *our* boy. Don't you dare think that you are doing this alone.' She had a look in her eye that Seamus knew too well, identical to the one she had given him the night he left her to meet Dante. He said nothing in reply and started the engine.

Seamus was emotionally torn on the drive to the station. Part of him needed the answers to all of his questions, but part of him wanted to remain in the dark, for the truth might be more than he could bare. They parked up in the car park and headed in, heading straight for the holding cells. Seamus surmised that the less interference he had from his colleagues the better. The station seemed unusually quiet, which Seamus questioned for a second, but it was not of import right now, he was just grateful to find his path to the cells clear. He checked the log to see where Edgar was being held, but as he did, officer Rivera walked in.

'McCarthy? What are you doing here?' She was an honest officer that kept mostly to herself. Often caught with her head in a book, she was smart, but she was also tough; she had proved on several occasions that she could easily look after herself. 'McCarthy, you can't bring your wife through here...' She looked at Moira and expressed a look of sympathy. 'You guys shouldn't be here...'

'Ava, please...' Seamus pleaded. 'I just need a minute to ask a couple of questions.' Seamus hoped she would understand and give him the chance, but he was desperate and so prepared himself to knock her out if need be. Thankfully she nodded in reply.

'Make it quick, there's some people in with the chief looking to move him out of here... Could be the feds, who knows...' Rivera voiced her condolences with a heartfelt look and an elongated blink, before taking her leave.

A part of him hoped to find Edgar sitting in a cell, smartly dressed in one of his snappy suits, simply waiting for someone to admit that there had been some form of mistake made. Unfortunately, what Seamus laid eyes on, broke his heart. Edgar was sat on the floor in the centre of the cell wearing nothing but a pair of blue pants. His pants were stained and his hands, arms, torso and face were all smothered in a dried, red-brown colour. Seamus looked at him and choked on his own breath as he saw Declan's, his sons blood splattered all over a man that he had called friend.

'You son of a bitch!!' Seamus screamed, saliva flying from his lips. He banged on the bars, slamming his hands against them, ignoring the pain it gave him. He reached through the bars, unable to reach him, but it didn't matter. Edgar reacted to Seamus' voice, clambering away from him, retreating to the far corner. Seamus glanced at Moira, she simply stood by, crying in disbelief. 'It was Declan you son of a...! He was my boy! Our son! Why?! AHH!' Seamus began pulling on the bars in a crazed rage. He looked down upon Edgar, fury filling his vision, but he could see his child's murderer muttering to himself. 'What's that?!' Seamus shouted, 'What are you saying?! Why did you do it?! Answer me!!'

'Not me. Need Toby. Take it away...' Edgar repeated over and over.

'Take it... You can't take away what you did!! You murdering son of a –!'

'Careful, Seamus.' A familiar voice sounded from the entrance to the custody room, but as the man entered, Seamus didn't recognise him. 'Technically... that *bitch*, is my mother too.' He smiled with a closed mouth and his amber-yellow eyes widened. He was wearing a pair of charcoal-coloured pants, fastened by a brown leather belt, a white, long-sleeved ribbed top and a black summer jacket.

'Who the hell are you?' Seamus asked, grabbing Moira by the wrist and pulling her to stand beside him. The yellow-eyed man revealed a rosy-red apple and held up a finger, requesting a pause in the conversation. He bit into the apple and smiled as he chewed. 'I asked –!'

'Who the hell am I? I believe the more appropriate question is, who the hell are you, Seamus, or more adequately put, who are you going to be?' Seamus couldn't shake the familiarity of his voice, but he simply did not know the man before him. 'Queue the eery music. This is my favourite part, where the *big bad* reveals himself...' Seamus' head hurt from trying to force himself to recall how he knew the voice, the accent. 'You look confused, Seamus. Constantly asking yourself who the hell I am? What am I doing here? How do I know what you're thinking? Can I really read your mind? The answer to that last question is yes... Oh come on! One-hundred-and-three... seventeen, forty-two. Are we quite finished with the games, mate? I *can* read your bloody mind!'

What the hell is going on...

Moira moved into Seamus, fearfully holding onto him. Seamus was speechless, unsure what to say or think. He tried to control his thoughts but he could tell that he was failing to do so as the yellow-eyed man smiled again.

'My name is Tobias. We have actually met several times before now, Seamus, though you won't remember. I will say, however, I have not had the pleasure of meeting your wife before. Moira, is it? You can stop being afraid now, love.' At his command, Moira's grip loosened on Seamus' arm and she ceased her shaking.

'How...?' Seamus began to ask as he looked at Moira. Her instant reaction to Tobias' command frightened him.

'Enough of the how's, the why's... Do you like history, Seamus? "To every man upon this earth, death cometh soon or late. And how can man die better, than facing fearful odds, for the ashes of his fathers, and the temples of his gods..."' Tobias walked over to the cell door and with one sudden movement, he ripped the door off its hinges. 'I have a passion for history, Seamus, for knowing what once was, you can often control what will be.' He stepped into the cell and crouched down beside Edgar. Tobias grabbed Edgars hands and whispered something to him, before the pair of them stood up. Edgar's expression changed from one of guilt and insanity, to a look of relief, as if he now had peace of mind. 'All sorted.' Tobias patted Edgar on the shoulder.

'Sorted... What... You can't take him! He must answer for what he did!' Seamus' anger got the best of him and he stepped into the cell's entrance, blocking their exit. Tobias raised a fist to his mouth and looked at Seamus curiously, no doubt debating his next move.

'Seamus, mate,' Tobias began, 'Edgar did not kill your boy. Kenan did.' Seamus, unsure of what he meant, stood defiantly in the doorway. 'Buried within my brother here is a monster that he has no control over. Your son's... Declan's death is not Edgar's fault.'

'Then who? Why?' Seamus refused to move without an explanation. Inside, he was trembling in fear, but he refused to let it show. Tobias sighed in response.

'ME!!! Blame me if you need someone to blame!' Tobias shouted, the colour in his eyes flaring. Seamus trembled as he looked into Tobias' eyes, but then he noticed movement behind him. He presumed it was his colleagues, however, as he turned to check, he found a man and a woman stood behind Moira. 'Seamus, meet my dear brother and sister, Bomani and Tisa. Don't worry about your colleagues, I have dealt with them.'

What did you do?! Seamus feared the worst.

'Come now, I didn't kill them. I merely persuaded them to take the rest of the day off.' Seamus felt trapped. Caught between two immeasurable hard places, he didn't know what to do; fight, or flee? But if he was to get the answers he desired, he needed to fight.

'You didn't kill my boy,' Seamus stated, glaring at Tobias. 'He did!' He then looked to Edgar.

'Well, no, not physically, but I had a hand in it.' Tobias took off his jacket and placed it down on the bed.

'But why?' Seamus asked once again.

'Because I have had enough! Enough bloody waiting! Enough of Adam refusing to give us what we need! What *you* really want to know is, why you? And the answer to that question is simply mere convenience I'm afraid, mate.'

Seamus' rage returned with the suggestion that the nightmare his life had become was "convenient". He applied pressure to his head as he tried to comprehend the reasoning of it all.

'Convenience,' Seamus whimpered, but then his anger took over completely. 'Convenience!!!' he screamed.

'Silence!!' Tobias bellowed in reply, squaring up to Seamus. 'Bomani, tend to Edgar,' he ordered and then began pacing the length of the cell. Bomani barged past Seamus as if he wasn't even there, entering the cell to carry out his order. Seamus couldn't help but notice, however, how this Bomani carefully checked Edgar's condition. There was something between them; compassion perhaps, or love? 'You seem surprised, Seamus. You thought us beasts? It's not blood that makes us family, it's the memories we all share.' Tobias was sincere in his words, looking Seamus in the eye as he spoke. 'It is amusing really.' He smiled, almost chuckling to himself. 'As it is Adam's memories that have brought us all here.'

Tobias continued to pace the cell, as if he was waiting for something, but what? Seamus repeatedly looked to Moira to check that she was okay. The other one, Tisa, remained behind Moira, preventing them from escaping. 'Ah, here she is...' Tobias rubbed his hands together jubilantly, as if his efforts were finally baring fruit.

'Seamus?!' she called out; she was just down the corridor. Seamus sighed and rested his head against the bars of the cell. He was distraught. How had it come to this?

'Krysta! We're in here, love,' Tobias called out to her. Krysta turned the corner with her firearm at the ready. Her expression quickly shifted from one of determination to a muddled look of surprise and confusion. 'Put the weapon away, love.' Tobias smiled, his eyes glimmering. Yet, Krysta appeared to ignore his request; something that seemed to irk him. 'Strong-willed, that's okay. Tisa, if you would...' At his command, Tisa grabbed Moira, using her as a human shield, blocking Krysta's aim. Seamus yelled in protest and attempting to aid his wife Tobias stopped him, pinning him against the wall.

'What the fuck... T? What... What are you...?' Krysta continued to aim her gun at Tisa.

'Wait... you know her?' Seamus queried whilst struggling against Tobias' hold. He was initially surprised, but then he recalled that the F.B.I had always known more than they had let on.

'Yes, yes... No need for introductions.' Tobias released Seamus and clapped his hands together. 'Let's get the show on the road, shall we?'

'Tobias? We have Edgar, we should leave.' Tisa seemed unsure as to why they were lingering. Seamus looked at her, silently pleading with her to not harm his wife, however, Tisa's expression was one of doubt and confusion.

'Moira... everything is going to be okay... Please, let her go,' Seamus pleaded.

'All in good time, little sister,' Tobias looked to Tisa, 'but first, Adam should be here any second now...'

'Adam? Tobias?! What have you done?!' Tisa rapidly became nervous and she tightened her grip on Moira, forcing Moira to cry out in pain and fear. Seamus began to panic; he looked around at the people that surrounded him. Throw Adam into the mix, who knows what might happen.

'Adam? Why would Adam come here?' Krysta asked, maintaining her aim at Tisa. Seamus wished she'd aim elsewhere. He was anxious; one missed shot could hit Moira.

'Isn't it obvious... Because you're here,' Tobias laughed. 'I'll need him here to ensure that everything has gone to plan. Need to see the results.'

'Enough of this bullshit, Tobias. We should leave, now.' Bomani had decided to join the argument, agreeing with Tisa's decision to leave. Bomani attempted to grab him, however, Tobias retaliated by swatting his hand, grabbing Bomani's arm, wrenching it behind his back and pinning

Bomani against the cell bars.

'You long for the answers to all of your questions, Seamus. Well, I have them.' The grin Tobias exhibited sickened Seamus. It was a game to him, he was playing with people's lives, their minds. 'Now, Seamus... You owe me a favour...'

Seamus' head felt as if it was ready to explode. His thoughts were in disarray; it felt as if his mind was physically trying to reorganise itself and there were memories, commands, that had been buried and were now being forced back into place. He clutched at his temple and groaned in agony.

'Stop it! Stop it please!' Moira shouted at Tobias. 'What are you doing to him?!' she screamed in horror. Seamus continued to writhe in pain for what felt like forever but couldn't have been more than a minute, and then the pain suddenly stopped. Without blinking, without thinking, he quickly moved to Krysta and snatched her firearm from her grip and aimed it at Bomani. Seamus knew what he was doing, it felt right, but he also had no control. He took a breath and then pulled the trigger.

As the bullet reached its target, Bomani's skin had already started to change; it shifted from its natural colour and took on that of the cell bars with a metallic sheen. The bullet ricocheted off Bomani's forehead. Having failed to hit his target, Seamus' body began to act unwillingly, throwing the weapon back across the floor to Krysta and rushing towards Tobias. He felt an unstoppable urge to complete his task, a task he didn't even understand. As he reached Tobias, he instinctively lifted Tobias' shirt to find a blade tucked into his belt. Tobias stepped away, releasing his grip on Bomani, and as Bomani turned to exact revenge, Seamus plunged the blade of wood and bone into Bomani's chest, slicing through his metallic exterior as if it was mere flesh.

There were two distinct cries as the blade pierced the tribesman's heart. Tisa shrieked, her cacophonic scream-roar combination a mixture of human and animal distress at the demise of her twin. The second protest was from Adam, who had found his way into the corridor at that very moment. Seamus' gaze moved to Adam as he fell to his knees. Tears fell from his emerald-coloured eyes as he pulled at his hair in despair. He looked broken and Krysta rushed to his side, yet, as Seamus looked at Adam's eyes, they appeared to flicker before changing colour to a deep ruby-red. Adam cried out in pain and anger, his scream shaking the buildings foundations.

'Ha!' Tobias cheered at the scene before him, holding his hands up to his mouth, seemingly covering a smile of accomplishment.

'How could you!!' Tisa wailed, but she wasn't looking at Tobias. She glared at Seamus with an unrelenting fury. Seamus could practically read her mind in that instant and he tried to react, to stop her, but she moved too quickly.

Within a blink of an eye Tisa placed a hand on each of Moira's cheeks and twisted her head, snapping her neck. Before Moira's body had even hit the ground, Tisa moved to her brother and lifted his lifeless corpse off the floor. She then fled. Seamus dropped to his knees and crawled to his wife, a sense of denial forefront to any other emotion. He lifted her up onto his lap and clutched at her so tightly that his hands ached.

'You'll be okay. You'll be okay,' Seamus repeated, brushing back hairs from Moira's face. His heart began to ache as grief and sorrow sank in and his eyes were ready to erupt with tears. 'Stay... Moira. Moira! Stay with me...' Seamus blubbered, shaking his wife gently. 'Come back, Moira, honey... Come back. Don't leave me.' He shook her a little more violently before turning his gaze onto Tobias. 'WHY???!!!' Seamus exclaimed; his whole being shook, enveloped in a state of fury.

'For that! That look in your eyes! The fury you feel! What an emotion!' Tobias began to laugh; he was pleased with what had transpired which only infuriated Seamus further.

'Adam? Can you do something? Please, help her.' Krysta shook Adam as she pleaded for his assistance, but Seamus could tell that something was wrong with him, he could feel it.

'That's right, Seamus, Adam can't help right now. One of the twelve memories we took from him is worming its way back into his mind... but don't worry, he'll be back to his dull self soon enough.' Tobias crouched down and looked at Seamus, his yellow eyes full of wonder. 'Adam, go and find your son. Find Cain.' The mention of Cain appeared to shake Adam from his trance and he was gone, leaving Krysta to almost fall over due to the speed at which he abandoned them.

'What did you do to him?!' Krysta yelled, fear and concern consuming her.

'It's his default setting,' Tobias shrugged. 'Whenever an Avunaye dies, he resorts to hunting down Cain for a while. I figure he wants vengeance for Abel, or something. My concern, however, is with Seamus.' Seamus looked at Tobias through his tears; Tobias was monitoring Seamus' every move, but why? 'Your initiation, of course.' Tobias exhibited a beaming smile which only grew as Seamus and Krysta proceeded to question what he meant.

'Initiation?' Seamus and Krysta queried simultaneously.

'There hasn't been a ritual... I thought –' Krysta was cut short as Tobias stood up.

'Officer Connor Brennan. Remember him? Accidentally killed by Adam at the hospital. Then there was that professor, your kids' professor, killed by Serena.' Tobias was revelling in the moment.

'What? But they were accidents...' Krysta stated.

'Please... let me finish.' Despite wanting to scream at him, Seamus couldn't help but bite his tongue. 'Who do you think set up the massacre at the warehouse and ensured that Brandt and Adam clashed? Who do you suppose arranged the bloody meeting between Serena and the professor?' He smiled again, a corner-of-his-mouth smile. 'I made sure Brandt got his hands on Smithy.'

You bastard... Seamus thought as he sat weeping. But Tobias was just getting going and as he continued, Seamus' grief grew.

'I ensured that Seamus and Sam ended up at Hunters Point and that Axel lasted just long enough for Seymour to kill him at Times Square. Hell, I even freed agent Ward from Markovic's dungeon to make sure you all made it in time to thwart the bloody bomb plot.' Tobias laughed as if it was all a game; Seamus' blood continued to boil beneath his skin, yet, he longed for more answers. 'Then there was setting Brandt up, now that took some work, but the cops in this city are so easily manipulated. Receiving the mark made sure that the detective died at the hands of either Bomani or Tisa. Unfortunately for Bomani, that meant that he was expendable. Then of course I made sure that Edgar here spent some time with your family. Did you really think that you met him by chance? That he just happened to save you? I knew that with some time your relationship would end in tragedy as Kenan just can't help himself when it comes to blood.' Tobias crouched beside Seamus again, inspecting him, no doubt looking for indications that this initiation had worked, however, all Seamus felt was rage towards him.

'Where was I... Ah yes, Carmen. Forcing her to kill McCabe was fun but challenging, and working in Malik's death was difficult but – and here comes the cherry on the cake... This entire thing was made possible because Evelina killed your father.' He paused and watched as Seamus processed the information and began to break inside. 'Tisa kills Moira and that, mate, makes eleven sacrifices and one vacancy, thanks to Bomani's death.'

'You... bastard...' Seamus found that he was able to speak again. 'Why do this to me?' He continued to cling tightly to Moira, not wanting to let her go.

'I will do anything to find Eden. I don't bloody care if I have to crack the earth, burn the trees, boil the waters!' He spoke passionately. 'And to do that I need Adam to remember, which ironically requires some of the Avunaye to die. Now, I finally engineered a way to break our curse, but I can't take them all on, and besides, we're family. So, I need a tool, a weapon. Someone as strong as us, but who despises us. That's you, Seamus, *you* are my weapon.'

'I will end you,' Seamus said through gritted teeth. He wanted nothing more than to get up, to grab Krysta's gun, or the blade once more and kill Tobias. However, despite his desire, something within him prevented him from acting.

'I have been compelling you since you were ten! You are bloody hardwired *not* to harm me, mate.' Tobias was smug.

'Eleven sacrifices aren't enough...' Krysta stated, her voice laced in fear.

'No,' Tobias responded. 'But don't worry, love. I can't kill you, you're too important.' He smiled but it did not appear to calm Krysta's fears. 'I had a backup plan for each and every sacrifice. Do you think I would slip up now? Alannah has unfortunately slipped from my grasp, but I have two more, just in case.' He took out his phone and dialled. As it rang, he looked at Krysta, and then at Seamus. 'A good friend of yours slipped up and made themselves available.' The call continued to dial whilst Krysta pleaded to know who it was that he was calling. Seamus wracked his brain for who it might be; he didn't want anyone else to suffer, but he could feel a strength within him beginning to swell. Perhaps he'd be strong enough to fight back, to get justice, to save everyone else. 'Hello, you...' Tobias spoke as the call connected, 'it's time to stop fighting and let go.'

'Tobias?!' Krysta yelled as he continued to ignore her, he was too busy watching Seamus as the change began. Whoever it was that he had called, the twelfth person connected to Seamus, they had died. Seamus could feel their death, sense the loss of life as his own body flurried with a newfound feeling of strength. His mind began to sharpen, to work differently, and he suddenly understood every second of his existence up to this point.

'An Avunaye who has felt every emotion during their initiation. Like the fabled phoenix, you will rise from the ashes of despair.' Tobias grinned and beckoned Edgar to his side. 'What chaos we will reap upon the world.' And then the pair of them were gone.

26
Claire Davenport

Why do you feel the need to grieve for someone you've never even met? It was the question that continued to rattle around inside her head whilst Carmen's emotions pulled sharply and repeatedly on her heart-strings. It was developing into a burden, one which Claire could no longer bare. She felt Carmen's loss, her anger, her pain, but she also carried her own feelings of fear, trauma, anger and confusion. The combination was too much. Claire had almost drowned. The sharp reminder that despite sharing her body with an immortal, she could still die, terrified her. Yet, she had had little time to deal with her own experience as now Lucy was missing. Her friend and colleague had been taken, and from Krysta's description of what had happened at the police station, she may well be dead. Seamus had also been initiated into the Avunaye at the expense of his poor family and co-workers. And then there was Bomani, who was family to Carmen and thus the emotional cycle continued. To make matters even worse, Adam had gone, but where? To the best of Krysta's recollection, he had regained one of his memories and ran off, his eyes filled with a dark rage. The idea scared Carmen more than she was willing to admit, but Claire was left to wonder what it all meant. All in all, she was ready to explode.

Claire was at work, doing what she did best: hunting,

searching and digitally scanning the city for signs or clues to Lucy's whereabouts. She also, simultaneously, had searches running for both Adam and Seamus, however, all three were coming up empty. Krysta and Hale were working alongside her, yet their ability to keep up with Claire's technological prowess was lacking somewhat and so they regularly left the lab in an attempt to make themselves more useful by calling contacts or issuing orders to other agents.

'This is hopeless,' Claire muttered to herself once she had the room.

You'll find them, Claire. If anyone can, you can. Carmen tried to reassure her, but Claire just felt the idea was naïve.

'Why?' Claire said, deflated. ''Cus I'm the best? What's the point in being the best if you constantly fail...? Just means that there's no hope for anyone else.' Subconsciously, Claire felt Carmen punch her on the arm in response.

You think that it's not okay to fail every once in a while? Do you realise, that is how you become the best? I have probably failed at more things than the entire population of this country has even tried.

'Hmph...' Claire sighed. 'That just means you've been around... for a very, very long time. Heh!'

Claire, birds don't just hop out of the nest and fly. They fall, again and again, until... they don't. Now suck it up and think.

'I am thinking. I haven't stopped thinking. That man died so that you could save me. Tobias set it up and I fell for it, hook line and refrigerator. I didn't see any of the big neon signs, but Lucy did. She suspected something, that's why she went back there... and now she's... and it's my fault.' Claire's body began to shake with guilt.

Tobias will answer for what he has done. We mustn't lose hope that Lucy was not the twelfth sacrifice. Hearing Carmen say Tobias' name stirred an anger within Claire that she hadn't even realised was there. Her heart beat a little stronger and she could feel her hands clench and tense. *Claire...* Carmen's concern drew Claire's attention to the fact that she was inadvertently manifesting a tide of sparks to travel up and down her arms. She managed to snap herself out of it just in time for someone to walk into the lab; a someone that she had least expected to see.

He had managed, by the looks of him, to just about dress himself. His white shirt was untucked and creased, his tie crooked, and he currently had one sleeve down and the other rolled up, making him look awfully uneven. He looked at Claire and smiled, yet his tired, blood-shot eyes and pale blotchy skin gave him the appearance of someone in serious withdrawal or suffering with the world's worst hangover; Claire had never seen him like this. Yet, she found herself confused by her initial feelings towards him. She would have expected to feel pity, or perhaps worry or sadness towards her colleague and friend. But she currently struggled to feel any of those, instead, she found her herself quavering with contempt and anger.

'Mike? What the hell are you doing here?' she questioned bluntly and very much out of character.

'Good to see you too, Claire,' he replied. Claire stood defiantly, looking down on him, despite him being significantly taller than her. 'Seriously, the welcome committee having an off day?' He walked slowly into the lab, squinting, as if the lighting was uncomfortable for his eyes, yet, Claire couldn't bring herself to care about his condition.

'Considering the manner in which you last walked out of here... What did you expect? A red carpet? You have some nerve –'

'Claire, I'm just here to help. We've got to find Lucy... ' He was sincere but as far as Claire was concerned it was too little too late.

'You left. You left her without... Without ever giving her a chance to try and help you. And then you ignore and avoid her for months? Now that's she's missing you grow a pair and decide to show up? It's too late!' Claire's outburst brought a look of shock and surprise to Mike's face, however,

Claire wasn't quite sure where all this aggression had suddenly come from; she had thought about saying many things before, but never believed she'd actually voice them. *Carmen? Are you putting words in my mouth?!* She queried, confused. Carmen remained guiltily silent.

'There you are,' Hale said as he entered the lab behind Mike. He walked over to his ill colleague and gave him his arm to lean on. 'Everything okay?' Hale asked dubiously. He could obviously sense the tension in the room.

'Fine and...' Mike coughed and spluttered, '...dandy.'

'Argh!' Claire groaned aloud accidentally, sinking a little into her shell as the pair of men looked at her curiously.

'You okay, Claire? How's the hunt?'

'Claire's not best pleased that I'm here, mate,' Mike interrupted.

'Can you blame us?' Claire blurted out, 'me? You disappeared when she needed you, when we could have helped you... If it wasn't for you, Lucy wouldn't have been searching for a source for the drugs. *You* abandoned Lucy.' Claire didn't know what to do with herself. She could feel the pent-up tension under her skin. But why? Why was she feeling like this?

I'm sorry, Claire. I'm trying to hold it all in... my grief, my anger... but...

'I... We need to get out of here... I need some air...' Claire's anxiety levels peaked and she felt confined, pressured, weighted down by the grief of losing a sibling; a sibling of over a millennia-and-a-half.

'Claire, hey, wait up,' Hale left Mike's side and attempted to convince Claire to stay and talk, but she couldn't. What could they talk about? She could hardly confess how she was feeling, and to make matters worse, she wanted to confide in her friend, to tell the truth, but she couldn't. Claire stormed out of the office, rushing down the stairwell to the ground floor. She burst out of the building and took in a huge gasp of air, filling her lungs; trying to not self-detonate.

Claire, you need to calm down and breathe... Carmen calmly suggested, but Claire's world felt as if it was spinning out of control. *Claire, breathe, or you are going to pass out...*

She figured that she must have passed out as she slowly began to open her eyes. Yet, it appeared that she was no longer outside of the office. She had expected to see the sky above her, but instead, as she came to, Claire realised that she was in fact inside a vehicle of some sort, a van. And it was moving fast.

What the hell is going on? Claire asked herself and Carmen, wondering if Carmen had once again taken over whilst she was unconscious.

Claire, where are we? Carmen's question instantly shook Claire from her half-awaken state and caused her to panic a little.

Heh... is this a game? Are you messing with me? "Where are we..." nice one, heh! Claire didn't want to believe that she might well have been put in this van against her will. She quickly patted herself down, searching for her phone, but it was not on her. The vehicle was moving quickly; wherever they were headed, the driver must be in a hurry to get there. *If this isn't you messing with me, then what the hell is happening... Carmen?* Claire tried to climb to her feet, but the vehicle traversed some rough terrain and the rocking threw off her balance, causing Claire to tumble over. 'Hey!' she yelled at her captor. Crawling to the front of the compartment, she banged on the wall. 'Hey! Who are you and what do you want?!'

She received no reply from the driver. Instead, it felt as if the speed of the vehicle increased. Claire was ready to allow Carmen to punch through the wall, or perhaps bust open the rear doors so that she could jump out, but then the vehicle suddenly came to a screeching halt. Claire flew forward, face-planting the wall of the van as it stopped and she could hear the driver's door open. 'Hey! Let us out!' she exclaimed, but then Carmen reminded her that they did not know who they were dealing with and that to air on the side of caution might be a good idea. Moments passed and there was no sound, no one was trying to get in, the driver had not returned.

Something is not right... Carmen stated before urging Claire to move towards the rear doors. They had both assumed to find themselves locked in, however, as Claire investigated the door release, she found that she could simply open the doors and let herself out. *Claire, be careful,* Carmen suggested.

'Can't just sit here now, can we,' Claire sarcastically replied. She opened the doors and cautiously climbed out of the van, finding herself stepping onto a stone-slabbed pathway that appeared to lead up to a large house.

The front gardens, either side of the path that led directly to the building's front door, were well kept. The luscious green lawns and tidily trimmed bushes resembled a perfectly picture-esc setting, much like those often found in magazines, and there was a large tree in the centre of the left-hand side lawn. The house was immaculate. Clean, pearly-white walls housed large floor-to-ceiling windows, and from the inside, a gentle warm glow seemed to emit from the interior lights. 'I feel like we've stumble into Pleasantville... Where the hell... I recognise this place...' Claire slowly made her way up the path until she reached the front door. *Whatcha reckon, Carmen? Friendlies or...?* Claire attempted to peer through the windows, looking for any sign of movement.

I suggest we proceed –

With caution? Yeah, I know...

Claire gingerly opened the door and found a familiar face inside. *Ah, crap,* she thought as she took a step backward; her body was suggesting she run as fast and as far as she could.

'Finally! You're here. You can head straight upstairs

and clean yourself up. Feel free to help yourself to my wardrobe. Perhaps something a little more suitable.' Serena stood at the base of a staircase dressed in a sleeveless, black one-piece pantsuit with a plunging v-neck; she eyed Claire up and down with a look of distaste or disappointment. Claire was confused, but she couldn't help but be curious. Carmen tried to convince her that she should leave this place. 'Honestly, Claire, Carmen, whatever it is you prefer. We will be starting soon. You need to be quick.' Serena's eyes widened with a glare of impatience. 'There will be no fighting on this day. You have nothing to fear from us.'

'Us?' Claire blurted out, curiosity getting the better of her.

'Your, Carmen's, family. We will all be in attendance.' Serena then pointed up the stairs, reiterating what she had suggested earlier.

'All of you...?' Claire asked, her voice cracking slightly. 'Tobias will be here?' She watched Serena with intent to see how she would react to hearing Tobias' name, yet she appeared unaffected.

'Of course, he will. He is family.' Serena expressed a look of confusion before heading through an archway into another room.

Claire didn't have to argue her decision to head inside for long. It seemed that Carmen was just as curious to see what this was all in aid of and Claire knew that Carmen harnessed a buried longing to see her siblings.

Do you think Adam will be here? Claire asked as she dried herself after showering.

From what Krysta said, Adam will no doubt be absent for a few days. I have seen him regain memories before, from the death of one of the Avunaye. It takes it's toll on him. Carmen was solemn, speaking with a heavy heart. Quickly pulling out a navy, long-sleeved pleated midi dress from amongst a vast selection of fashionable and extravagant clothing options, Claire swiftly got dressed. She tied her hair up and began to make her way back downstairs.

Did you notice Serena's reaction when I mentioned Tobias? Claire was curious to know whether or not it was normal for one of the Avunaye to ignore the fact that one sibling had killed another. *Do you think she knows?* She quizzed Carmen.

I... I imagine Tisa would have reported the incident. That is, if she still holds the memory of it. Carmen's suggestion sent a shiver down Claire's spine and she recalled the memory she had once lost at the hands of Tobias.

'Well, we will have to wait and –' Claire began to say, however, she was interrupted as she reached the bottom of the staircase.

'Hi,' sounded the voice of a man stood in the centre of the foyer. He had a silverish-brown coloured beard and short hair. His face was kind and familiar. Dressed in a black suit with a white shirt and black tie, he held out a hand for Claire to take. 'You must be Claire, or Carmen. Apologies. I am Edgar, Edgar Young.' Claire quickly withdrew her hand, recalling the gruesome images from Declan McCarthy's crime scene.

'You killed that boy...' Claire's mouth operated quicker than her brain. Her words carried an air of disgust and fear, a fact that appeared to sadden Edgar.

'Claire? Carmen?'

'It's Claire...' she glared at him.

'I apologise, it is... confusing. But if anyone could understand what it is like to share your body with someone else, it's you.' He looked glumly at the ground. 'Kenan killed the boy. I live with the guilt.' Claire suddenly felt awkward. She had felt guilty now for some time due to some of Carmen's actions. Perhaps she and Edgar were not so different. 'Anyway, we're expected in the garden,' he said before proceeding to walk through to the room that Serena had gone to before.

Following Edgar through the kitchen and out onto

a balcony, Claire looked out onto the swimming pool and gardens below. Meticulously maintained lawns stretched out from the residence, ending at the bank of a small lake in the distance. She could just about see a small gathering of people, supposedly Carmen's siblings, at the edge of the water.

All these people we've been searching for... all in one place. Claire found it hard to believe. All the time she had spent searching for them, hunting them with the bureau, here they all were. Yet, strangely, she found herself without the urge to attempt to communicate with her colleagues. She didn't feel the need to contact the authorities; an unexpected feeling of being home spoke to her.

Thank you, Claire, Carmen said in response to Claire's lack of action; her words creating a warmth within Claire's heart.

Once she had made her way down to the garden, Claire could see plainly what this was all about. Bomani's body lay a top a pyre of tree branches and kindling; it was a funeral for their fallen kin. She looked around at those in attendance. Evelina stood next to the body dressed in a somewhat staid, classic black dress. Claire recognised the purple-grey haired man next to Evelina as Seymour; he was dressed in a black robe of sorts, standing stoically by his mother's side. Edgar took up position next to Serena, and who Carmen pointed out to be Tisa and Nahki. Tisa wore a black and emerald coloured shweshwe dress and her hair was styled into an array of bantu knots. Nahki turned to glance at Claire as she approached, forcing Claire's jaw to drop.

Son of a bitch! Her mind screamed as she realised who Nahki was, or at least who he had pretended to be all this time. *Carmen... that's... that's...*

It seems Nahki has played his part well.

Claire couldn't believe that that was all Carmen had to say on the subject, but she didn't spend too long lingering on the fact, as someone else caught her eye. He was tall and muscular, dressed in a pair of grey pants and a white shirt with short sleeves. He had mid-length, silky black hair and his eyes, which drew Claire's attention, were a solid black, as if his pupils, iris' and sclera were as one. Despite the occasion, he wore a devilish smirk on his face. *That, is Matthias*, Carmen spoke with an obvious tremor to her tone; clearly, he was one for Claire to avoid. Tisa turned around to see Claire's approach, however, as she looked, her expression of grief turned to that of rage.

'How dare you come here!' she wailed and then began to march towards Claire. Claire could feel the sparks between her fingertips as Carmen prepared to defend her, however, as Tisa approached, Claire was quickly dragged off to the side.

'You know the rules, sister. No fighting now.' Claire turned to find Tobias standing suited beside her, his yellow eyes giving away his identity.

'This is your fault!' Tisa cried, her eyes swimming with tears of despair. Tobias stepped between Claire and Tisa, hands behind his back with an almost-smile on his face.

'We are all here simply to mourn our fallen brother. You know that Carmen had nothing to do with Bomani's death.' Tobias didn't move despite Tisa's advance; so sure, was he, that she would do nothing but abide by the rule of no violence. 'The sun is about to set, sister. We can work out our issues another time.'

Once Tisa had calmed herself, she returned to the funeral pyre. Claire and Tobias remained further back from the others; Claire did not want to cause any further problems. *Us black sheep best stick together. Don't you think?* Tobias glanced to Claire, smiling. She could hear his voice in her head, which she actually found relatively normal. The fact almost made her chuckle, but she managed to hold back her emotion; laughing at a funeral full of superpowered people was not a wise move.

Looking up at the sky, it dawned on Claire for the first time how much of the day she must have missed being unconscious. She watched as Tisa looked up at the sky and said a prayer for her twin as the sun set above them. Tisa spoke of her brother being truly eternal as the sky glowed with deep reds and amber hues. Claire could feel Carmen's sadness, but she too found herself feeling pity for the family around her that had lost one of their own, despite the awful things that they had each done. As the sun shone it's last, and darkness possessed the world, Serena knelt down beside the pyre and produced a flame within her hand which she then engulphed the wood with.

'And as the shadow of the day embraces the world, and the sun sets on his life, may his fire burn eternally.' Serena glanced at Claire as she spoke before returning to her position next to her siblings. Claire could have sworn that, within Serena's expression, there was an air of gratitude for Claire's presence. As the flames rose around Bomani's body, Evelina solemnly moved away from the pyre, taking up a more central position, the other Avunaye roughly encircling her. She ran her hands up into her hair, and in one fluid movement, ran them down the back of her head and neck and brought them round to sit on her chest, shielding her heart.

'When we lose someone we love...' Evelina said in a broken tone. 'Our grief can often overshadow those around us. We can forget to continue to love. For in one's own search for solace, we do not see the suffering of others.' She held a hand and urged Tisa to take it, and as she did, Evelina's eyes began to scintillate with a bright green light. Her breathing hastened and she looked upwards into the night sky. 'As a family, we share in each other's glories, and burdens. We grieve as one. We heal as one.' As Evelina finished speaking, Claire suddenly felt a wave of intense emotion hit her. Like a wave crashing against a rock, for but a moment she felt the combined heart-wrenching agony and sorrow that nine despairing souls carried with them all at once. It passed as quickly as it manifested, but as Claire wiped the tears from her eyes, she knew it was a feeling she'd never forget. A scar upon her heart.

As the night went on, drinks were poured and speeches were made in honour of Bomani, leaving Claire to feel more and more awkward amongst the Avunaye. She had not known Bomani, nor did she know much about the rest of them, other than that which she had either seen or Carmen had decided to share; she was also struggling with the idea of where her allegiance should currently lie.

Hello, Carmen. It's been a while. Claire could hear Tobias' voice within her head again.

I have nothing to say to you, brother, Carmen sharply replied, however, Tobias appeared to be irked by her words. He walked towards Claire with an unsettling look in his eyes. He grabbed her by the arm and marched her across the garden to the house. Channelling Carmen's strength, Claire shrugged off his grip and shoved him.

'Take your hands off me!' Claire attempted to be as intimidating as possible.

'What the hell is going on here?' Serena questioned as she moved to Claire's side. 'Tobias? You cannot and will not start a fight. Not here, not now.' Claire found Serena's defence of her to be strange, but she was grateful for the backup.

'Everything I do, I do for this family!' Tobias yelled in response, his eyes glowing in the darkness. 'You treat me as the villain because I am willing to do what needs to be done!'

'You killed your own brother, how is that –' Claire began to say.

'What?!' Serena exclaimed, shocked. 'What do you mean?' she questioned Claire's accusation. There was a firesome rage in her eyes as she spoke. Claire did not want to be in the middle of whatever was about to ensue, and she subtly attempted to take her leave.

'Carmen, Serena. Stop.' At Tobias' command Claire could feel her body wanting to stand still, she could feel Carmen holding her in place. 'Bloody listen to what I have to say, then, you can leave or do whatever you want to do.' Claire continued to struggle within herself, caught between her own ability to move and Carmen's inability. Serena, however, remained silent and still.

'Why should we listen to you?' Claire snidely questioned. 'And why the hell can I... Argh! What the hell... Seriously...' she grumbled as she continued to combat Tobias' influence. *Carmen? A little help here?*

'Argh! Quiet! I did what I had to do... What do you bloody want from me? Do you want a bloody rendition of the parting glass? Do you want me to beg for your trust, for your forgiveness? To reach Eden there needs to be sacrifices. I swear to have your back, *if* you agree to have mine.' Tobias held a cock-sure smile as he waited for their reply.

'And if we don't? If the others find out what you have done?' Serena asked defiantly, seemingly starting to break free of Tobias' hold.

'Then I will squeeze the life from you,' Tobias grasped Serena by the throat as she stood unmoving. 'Here's the deal. The only deal. In exchange for your silence regarding our fallen brother, and your support when I require it, I will *not only* provide you with a cure for agent Ward –'

'Wait, you have a cure for Mike?' Claire looked at him wide-eyed, hoping that it was the truth falling from his lips.

'Of course. It is, after all, my blood that was used to produce the drug.' His smile at the fact made Claire feel sick and she could see the fury within Serena continue to grow. 'I will also ensure that agent Rodriguez returns to work, safe and sound.' Claire could hardly believe what she was hearing. The sudden injection of hope in her heart almost forced her to weep with joy. 'So, sisters. Do we have an accord? Of course, if you refuse, Mike and Lucy will no doubt perish...'

'Tobias. You bastard,' Serena said as Tobias slowly released her. She was physically shaking as she looked to control herself. Claire could understand how she was feeling as she felt it too, or at least she could feel Carmen's sense of betrayal. 'It was you...' Serena growled through gritted teeth.

'If we agree...' Claire spoke slowly, carefully considering her options. 'Mike and Lucy, there'll be okay?' She looked at Serena and attempted to convey a level of mutual understanding in her expression.

'If you two play nice, I promise.' Tobias held up his hand, wiggling his little finger in jest. 'But should you fight against me,' his tone deepened and his eyes glowed unnervingly, 'I will erase your memories, as I did Tisa's, and you will mourn the deaths of your friends –' He shifted his gaze from Claire to Serena, '– your lover, without any understanding of how or why they perished.' Claire felt as if she was choosing between letting her friends die and making a pact with the devil, but what choice did she have?

Having accepted Tobias' deal, Claire had been allowed to leave the residence, but not before Tobias ensured that she would not be able to find her way back by compelling her to forget the location. She took one of the many available vehicles that they had at their disposal and drove home. Her heart and head were at war with each other throughout the drive; her heart gladdened by the prospect of Mike and Lucy being okay, but her head was deeply concerned by the impending demands that Tobias might have. Carmen constantly suggested that Tobias was not to be trusted but, reassuring Claire that she'd made the right decision, Carmen swore to protect her. It was the early hours of the morning when Claire finally made it home, and to her surprise, she found Alexa waiting for her on her doorstep.

'Thank god you're okay,' Alexa said, punching Claire on the arm. 'I text, I called... I even rang the office. They said that you'd felt unwell and then disappeared...' She looked at Claire with a concerned, yet, doting expression. 'I finished work and thought I'd head on over. I was worried, so here I am. So, are you okay?'

'My phone... it... it got lost, heh. I've had, well... It's been... nuts! Crazy! I am so sorry...' It was as if in Alexa's presence, Claire had suddenly lost the ability to construct complete sentences, yet her babbling brought a smile to Alexa's face. Alexa ran her hands up Claire's arms, caressing them, and then she softly caressed her cheek with her thumb before kissing her, reassuring her that all was well.

The couple made their way inside and Claire started to make them both a coffee.

'So, where have you been all night? What's with the dress? Don't get me wrong, it's nice, but a little... formal...' Alexa quizzed Claire about her evening as she wrapped her arms around Claire's waist and kissed her on the back of the neck. Claire struggled to finish making the drinks as she found herself lost in the moment. Her breathing deepened and her heart fluttered as she ran her own hands over Alexa's. Alexa's hands moved across her waistline and then down onto the tops of Claire's thighs; she slowly lifted up the hem of Claire's dress until her fingertips found Claire's skin. Alexa continued to kiss her on her lower neck, just below her ear as she ran her soft fingertips across the tops of Claire's thighs and found the boundary of her underwear. Claire could feel the passion inside her, the warmth beneath her chest and between her legs. Claire turned around to face Alexa and grabbed her, kissing her passionately, wetting her tongue on Alexa's. The pair wobbled as they became further engrossed in the heat of the moment.

'Whoa, almost swept me clean off my feet there,' Alexa said softly as Claire began to kiss her on her neck, slowly inching downwards. 'You... never... did say... where you'd gotten to...' Alexa said between breaths. But as Claire heard the words and contemplated replying, she received a sharp stabbing pain in her temple.

'Ow!' Claire yelped and clutched at her head.

'What? What is it? You okay?' Alexa asked in a higher pitched, concerned tone.

'Son of a –' Claire winced as the pain struck again. 'He... My memory... He took it, but, but she... Ow!!' Alexa tried to help, but there was nothing she could do. She began to panic as Claire felt more and more pain; the more Claire tried to work around Tobias' compulsion, the more pain she felt. 'AH!' Claire screamed and inadvertently, a spark emitted from her hand. 'Shit! Shit!' Claire panicked as Alexa gasped and took a step backwards away from her. Her face was a flush with fear and confusion.

'What was that? What is going on?' Alexa asked as Claire attempted to compose herself, yet, the pain persisted.

Claire! You need to stop trying to remember! Carmen frantically pleaded.

'I'm not trying!' Claire shouted aloud. 'Ow! I can't stop it...!' As another needle-like pain thrust itself through her hippocampus, she jolted and span around still clutching at her head. Alexa attempted to advance, to comfort her, but Claire accidentally caught her with her elbow as she spun, knocking Alexa back against the kitchen counter.

'Ah... shit...' Alexa muttered with equal amounts of shock and pain to her voice. Claire managed to pull her hands away from her head long enough to see that Alexa had bashed her arm against the counter and cut herself.

'Oh my god! I'm so sorry!' Claire reacted, rushing to Alexa's aid. Suddenly, with her attention taken away from her attempt to recall the memories she'd lost, the pain in Claire's head subsided. 'I'm so sorry,' Claire repeated, looking at the cut on Alexa's arm. As Claire went to touch it, Alexa flinched.

'Hey, hey, babe. It's okay. Just a scratch. It's you I'm

concerned about...' Alexa looked Claire in the eyes and smiled, yet Claire could sense that Alexa was still afraid.

'Are you sure?' Claire asked, guilt-ridden and anxious. Alexa simply nodded in reply and moved into her. She closed her eyes and kissed Claire gently, the touch of her lips melting away Claire's fear and doubts.

'Ow,' Alexa grimaced, mid kiss. She pulled away slightly. Claire looked her in the eye, questioning again if she was in fact okay. 'It... It burns... Fuck...! Ow!'

'What burns? Your cut?' Claire was now frantic again.

'No... Ow... My back...' Alexa hunched over slightly to reveal the top part of her tattoo that was mostly covered by her top. Claire had seen the tattoo before; it was of a golden thurible that was surrounded by a rose, red on its periphery, blue in its centre. Claire lifted Alexa's top slightly to reveal the gold colour of the thurible emitting a bright white light.

Claire! RUN! Carmen screamed at the sight of the light.

'Alexa? What the...' Claire was terrified and unsure of what to do, she didn't understand; she wanted to help Alexa, who was clearly in pain, writhing before her. But Carmen urged her to flee. *I can't leave her...* Claire told Carmen, however, Carmen wasn't prepared to give Claire the choice. As Alexa's scream grew louder and more harrowing, and as the light grew brighter, Carmen took control of Claire and forced her to run as fast as she could. She moved through the city at an unnatural speed, hurtling away from the threat whilst internally wrestling for control.

You left her! How could you! Claire exclaimed within her thoughts as Carmen reached the F.B.I headquarters. *How could you?!*

The woman you know will be no more if we don't find Adam, Carmen insisted. She had brought them to the office in the hope of finding Krysta, although, at first glance she could not see her friend anywhere. 'Kyle!' Carmen shouted as she stormed towards the unexpecting agent. Kyle looked as if he were on his way to attend a wedding; dressed in an extravagant three-piece suit that included an eight-button jacket with tails. Carmen did not hesitate, she simply shoved him against the wall and asked if he knew Krysta's current whereabouts.

'Hey! Davenport, what the hell do you think you're doing?!' Kyle was angered and embarrassed by the manner in which he was forcefully pinned. As a number of other agents watched on, he tried to shrug off Carmen's hold, but he couldn't, resulting in further embarrassment and his anger growing. 'Get off me!' he squealed.

'Where is Krysta?' Carmen demanded again.

'Claire, hey, I'm here. What is going on...?' Krysta announced herself as she walked into the room and witnessed what was happening. Releasing the frightened Kyle, Carmen turned to Krysta.

'Krysta, where is Adam?' Carmen asked bluntly, disregarding all the ears surrounding them.

'Whoa... Claire?' Krysta questioned as she looked at Claire's eyes a little closer. She then smiled nervously and her eyes widened as she appeared to realise that it was Carmen at the helm. 'Look, let me speak to... you know... Claire...' Krysta whispered as she ushered them to move away from Kyle and the other agents in the room. Carmen, reluctantly, relinquished control and advised Claire to explain the situation quickly and precisely.

'It's Alexa, Krysta... She's... Something happened and I need Adam to help her.' Claire was terrified of what was happening, even if she didn't fully understand it. It had been such a long time since she had cared for someone so deeply and she couldn't think straight.

'Claire, I don't know where Adam...' Krysta paused as her attention was drawn away from Claire and towards a group of people entering the office from the elevator. Claire looked at them also, curious as to who they were. One member of the group made a bee-line for Kyle, whilst the others spoke to the nearest agent they came to and then looked directly over towards Claire and Krysta.

'Krys? what's going on...?' Claire murmured. The group consisted of four men and one woman, all dressed in suits. The group of four continued to walk towards Claire, and now Kyle and the fifth member of the group were also heading their way.

'Claire Davenport?' a deep voice sounded; the man stood beside Kyle pointed at Claire. Two of the group ushered Krysta to move away, to which she protested. The others surrounded Claire.

'Who are you? What... What's going on?' Claire trembled as they closed in on her.

'Claire Davenport, I am agent Thomas with Internal Investigations.' Claire was confused for a moment and then afraid. The feeling of fear seeped into her from every angle.

'I don't understand...' Claire muttered. 'Where's Solomon? Krysta?'

'Sol isn't in yet... Claire don't worry, we'll get to the bottom of this...' Krysta attempted to reassure her.

'Claire Davenport, I am placing you under arrest for the murders of officer Joseph McCabe, civilians Lillian McLeodry, Enrique Santiago and Luis da Silva, the destruction of evidence pertaining to said murders, infiltrating government systems and affiliating with known terrorists.' As two of the group grabbed her arms to cuff her, Claire debated whether or not to allow Carmen to break her free of this place, however, the arresting agent swiftly revealed a syringe and stuck it into her arm.

'What... What are you doing...?' Claire questioned as the drug took an instant affect. As the world began to fade away around her, Claire looked at the man before her. She looked him in the eyes and before she closed her own, she saw his eye balls turn completely black and a devilish smirk spread across his face.

27
Adam

Adam had once again been forced to take a life to extend their makeshift family. He had raised his hand to the young girl, bombarding her in emotion until her heart stopped. Upon completing the ritual, Adam had watched as Nahki lost the final piece of himself; he had felt the last ounce of Nahki's emotional capability slip away, and with it another of his own memories. It had felt as if an ethereal hand had reached into his head and torn a slither of his mind asunder, taking his memory, stealing his past and destroying a part of what made him who and what he was.

The five decades following Nahki's initiation was lost to Adam. Evelina ensured that he could not amass any measure of strength that would pose a threat to her or the rest of the Avunaye. When they were not exacting Adam's execution themselves, they left the duty in the hands of mortals under their thrall. Adam often awoke from his sleep screaming as memories of slow and pain filled deaths flooded his dreams; mortal man was not always as adept as the Avunaye at ending his life, with their attempts often being drawn out over a number of hours or even days. Adam sometimes wondered if feelings of jealousy or inferiority had a part to play in their torture of him.

It had been Carmen and Tobias that had come to his aid on one cool summer's eve. They had resided in a town known as Scupi for two seasons now, yet, plans that Evelina had put into motion – an attempt to disrupt mankind's trajectory – came into effect at an opportune moment for Adam. Sixty-eight years since the Avunaye became twelve, the earth shook violently beneath the town's foundations and the buildings around them began to collapse. During the commotion, Carmen made her move to release Adam, with Tobias aiding in their escape, compelling the town's folk to suggest that the escapees had headed west.

Carmen had carried Adam to the outskirts of the town as the ground shook beneath their feet. In an attempt to blend in with the common people, she had dressed them both in tattered oaken-brown cloaks, fastened on one shoulder, worn over long-sleeved tunics. She had thrown Adam across the rear of her silver-white coloured mare and then galloped off, heading east as fast as the horse would allow. They travelled across country after country, through one empire to the next, all the while avoiding contact with the native tribes and peoples. For many years Adam and Carmen clung to the edges of the known maps, manoeuvring along the borders of the seas, keeping as much distance between them and the rest of the Avunaye as possible. Occasionally they would hear stirrings, rumours of unnatural events and beings with immeasurable powers and they would swiftly leave their current dwelling behind and move on. As Adam's memory and strength recovered, they found that they felt safe enough to move further in-land, however, having resided within the Tang Empire for perhaps too long, whispers of their existence spread. After over a century without word of their siblings, rumours began to reach them once more of deities returning to earth and moving east across the continents.

'We have no choice. We *must* leave and find somewhere new.' Adam insisted that staying put, that fighting, was not worth the risk to the people. *We could head west once again. Avoiding the others as they head east in search of us.* Carmen stood looking down on Adam as he made the decision to leave and head west. A red pine towered above her; its grey-brown fissured bark climbing towards the heavens, rays of scattered sunlight breaching its pronounced, branched display of needle-like leaves. Like many of the local women, Carmen had her hair styled into a tall golden tower upon her head. She did, however, don a set of lamellar armour, drawing looks of curiosity and often disgust from onlooking men and women alike. Adam gave Carmen a look to suggest that it was time to go and then he rose from his seat on the ground. He knelt and planted his knuckles onto the soil. Closing his eyes, he concentrated, willing the changes within himself. Reopening his eyes, he felt the colour of them shift from green to yellow and he could see the specs of dust on the dirt before him. His brow stretched, the bones growing and evolving as his eyes expanded and his mouth and nose joined together and extended to form a hooked beak. His skin tingled and stretched, causing painful tears to form up and down the extent of his body. Through these tears, sharp barbs began to protrude, and from them, feathered plumes extended. Adam's plumage expanded to cover his whole body, with his head and his tail being covered in a magnificent bright, clean white colour, an array of strong dark brown feathers spread down his arms, consuming his hands and fingers and a tuft of mottled brown burst from his chest. The bones in his legs broke and snapped forward; the breaks slowly healed and reformed to allow them to bend in the opposite direction and the skin of his legs hardened and changed colour to form yellow scales. Lastly, his feet and toes split and merged simultaneously to form three talons and Adam shook his entire body to expel the pain and rigidity of the transformation and prepare himself to take flight. His new form was large enough for Carmen to climb upon and lay herself down along his back; grasping a handful of feathers, she rested upon him with ease, confident of Adam's ability to keep her safe. Adam then began to walk forwards, unfurling his wings and flapping with all his might to lift them both off the ground and take to the sky.

After over another century of running from and avoiding their family, Adam and Carmen found themselves within the Byzantine Empire at the turn of the ninth century. They had run into Nahki, Tisa and Bomani twelve summers before and barely escaped, with Adam falling at their hands and Carmen only just managing to escape. She had taken Adam's body and sought refuge, buying favour from the current emperor, Nikephoros I. In return for their assistance when required, the emperor kept them hidden and safe. Adam saw something within the emperor that gave him hope for humanity; an inner desire for peace and a passion for sharing hope and compassion, even with his enemies. Unfortunately, peace was further from reality than both Adam and Nikephoros would have hoped for and the land was thrown into turmoil with an Abbasid army invading the territory. Choosing to leave Adam and Carmen behind, Nikephoros rode out to meet his enemy, confident of his chances of victory, only to end up surprised at the battle of Krasos, surely to be heavily defeated.

Adam wasn't sure if it was the blood thirst, or the greed of the victors, whom in return for an agreed peace and the emperor's release, decided to take the fortunes of Nikephoros as tribute. Humankind had such flaws, and Adam could not help but see these weaknesses projected ten-fold in that of his kin. The Avunaye would stop at nothing to obtain what they sought after and it was now time for Adam to ensure mankind's future by crippling them. The Avunaye were already cursed to an existence in which their freewill was limited. Yet, there was always the threat, the fear that one day Adam would slip, falter in his duty and take a life in cold blood. When this inevitably happened, what could Adam do to protect humanity? How could he alone prevent the others from reaching Eden and the tree of knowledge? How could he stop them from claiming unimaginable power?

'Adam? Are you certain that *this* is what you want? There will be no going back.' Carmen was afraid. The two of them found themselves within the impregnable city of Constantinople, hidden away in one of its magnificent towers, yet, as what had always come to pass, word of their presence here had reached the other Avunaye; Evelina and the others were all headed towards them and Adam had little time and little choice.

'It is the only way. I cannot guarantee that I will not take a life. With their freewill, the others will find the garden, the tree. I must protect it.' The decision weighed heavily on his heart as he knew what it meant for all of his family. It was in mankind's best interest, but it would be an unforgiveable betrayal to the Avunaye.

'Then we must hurry,' Carmen urged him to proceed. Adam could sense the level of trust she had in him. 'We have each taken from you. A piece of you lives within each of us. If you must take something in return, then so be it.' She spoke callously, not fully comprehending what it was that Adam was about to do.

'For when the first man takes a life coldly, shall they, the Avunaye, be freed of their restraints. Yet, with the drawing of blood, the guardians will be set free.' Adam closed his eyes and held out his hands as he spoke. He could feel his connection to everything and everyone around him become stronger. Carmen stood anxiously at his side, waiting to see what would transpire, but even she was taken aback by what appeared along the far wall of the room in which they resided.

'Who? Who are they?' Carmen's voice quaked with a sense of uncertainty. Adam opened his eyes and looked upon the eight bodies that lay before him, each resting upon a bed of stone. He smiled and sighed in relief; the act had taken much from him. 'Adam? What... What are you doing? What good can come from more sacrifices?'

'No. Not sacrifices,' Adam replied whilst holding out his hand for Carmen to take. 'They will be vessels. They will become the guardians. A light, a source of hope. When awoken, they, and their descendants will protect the garden and fight to ensure that mankind is protected.' Although pleased, as Carmen took his hand Adam's heart ached. His hand was being forced into doing something he did not truly wish to do. 'Mankind will know of them. They will be feared and revered. A beacon of light, they will...' Adam paused for a moment as he sensed an impending interruption. A feeling of unease combined with ambition was being emitted by someone close by. 'Tobias.'

'Adam,' Tobias said quickly, slightly out of breath. 'You haven't long until the others arrive. You must leave.' Adam smiled at Tobias, silently thanking him for his warning, yet Tobias' gaze was drawn to the eight bodies and a look of fear filled his yellow eyes. 'Adam? What are you doing? What... What is she doing here?' Tobias moved past Adam, heading straight towards one of the eight; a young woman.

'You know this woman?' Carmen questioned, moving towards Tobias. Adam could feel her mistrust towards her brother.

'She... I... Her name is Iris. What have you done to her?' Tobias was filled with feelings of fear and anxiety, yet, to Adam's surprise, he was also full of a sense of admiration and love for the mortal woman.

'Tobias. I... I did not know... I am afraid it is too late.' Adam's words pained him twice-fold. He hated to hurt Tobias, and he could also feel the pain of his kin.

'Too late? What do you mean "too late"? Too late for what?' Tobias turned and glared at Carmen and Adam, his eyes filled with despair and glowing a twisted shade of yellow.

'For when the first man takes a life coldly, shall –'

'Adam?! Don't you dare... Don't you...! Don't you make her one of us!' Tobias marched towards Adam but Carmen intercepted, holding him back. Adam was bombarded by Tobias' fear and sorrow. As Adam continued to recite and repeat the curse tears began to slip from the corners of his eyes.

'With the drawing of blood, will they be set free to unleash his hot anger, his wrath, indignation and hostility... ' Adam grimaced as he attempted to finish what he had started. He was applying every ounce of himself to the task, but he was also taking in every ounce of everyone around him; absorbing their emotions, taking on their pain. '...They will carry the key to the garden, forever sealing the gates...'

'ADAM! No! Please!' Tobias screamed at Adam, begging him to stop.

'...A band of destroying angels!' Adam fell to his knees, exhausted. Carmen released Tobias and flew to Adam's side. Tobias, now released and unsure of what had just transpired, rushed to the woman. He looked at her with such passion, a passion that Adam had never seen or felt within Tobias before. 'Tobias, I am sorry.'

'Sorry?' Tobias looked at Adam with pain filled curiosity. 'For what? Whatever you did, it... didn't work, right?' He attempted to awaken the woman, but she did not stir. Looking back to Adam, the curiosity evaporated from Tobias' eyes as anger sank in and a vicious amber coloured rage swirled within his gaze. 'What did you do, Adam?! What – WHAT DID YOU DO?!'

Tobias waited for the woman he cared for to wake up, but with every passing moment he grew more and more furious. Adam was incredibly weak and was certain that the other Avunaye would be upon them shortly. Carmen tried to encourage him to leave this place but it was of no use, they would not be able to move quickly enough to escape. Tobias eventually grew too impatient and rushed towards Adam, grabbing him by the arms fiercely. 'Why is she not waking up?! What did you do, Adam?' His voice trembled.

'They will wake,' Adam replied, causing Tobias' yellow eyes to well up instantly. 'But when they do, you will forget.' As Adam confessed, he too found tears beginning to trickle down his cheeks once more. He could see the pain he was causing his kin, he could feel it, as if he was inflicting it all upon himself.

'Forget what?' Tobias panicked. 'Forget her...?' His love for the mortal was evident and it made the whole ordeal unfathomably worse. 'No! No, no, no –'

'You will all forget. Forget the ritual. Forget the path. Each of *them* will hold your memories and protect mankind and the garden. Once they wake –'

'How could you! WHY?!' Tobias was distraught, shaking Adam furiously.

'You would do that, to us? To me? My love.' Evelina had found them and she stood in one of the open windows. Her green eyes glistened with an anger and hatred at Adam's betrayal. Moving swiftly towards Adam, she hurled Carmen across the room as she attempted to intervene. Evelina grabbed him by the throat and lifted him to his feet. She looked into Adam's eyes and gritted her teeth as she wormed her way through his emotions, confirming what he had said to be true.

'Tobias,' Adam choked, knowing what was about to happen as Evelina dug her fingernails into his chest in frustration. 'Raphael.' He smiled, hoping that Tobias would understand. And then, as Evelina burrowed her fingers under Adam's flesh and worked her way to his heart, Adam watched on as the eight began to wake up. And as Evelina crushed his heart, and his life ceased to be, Adam felt the pain of the Avunaye as their memories were stripped from their minds.

28
Adam

He didn't have to search very hard to find the place to which they had taken him to. He was drawn to it, like a moth to a flame, driven by a sense of uncontrollable hatred; his eyes continued to burn and the world was ablur with a deep shade of red. The impression Adam got from the outside of the complex, was that it was indeed the military that had possession of Brandt's body. A high wall surrounded the periphery of the land and peering through the gates, Adam could see a few buildings set back from the entrance; one large building that was no doubt where they had the body, and a couple of smaller buildings that looked to be used for security purposes. He scanned the environment before him, but he was rooted to the spot. A typhoon of internal, emotional turmoil left him torn between two decisions; whether to use force and storm the place, or to use stealth in an attempt to cause no harm to those within.

Adam remained still for some time; his eyes closed. He was yet to be detected but he remained close to the main gate.

They killed him. It was not their place. They had no right. His thoughts were fixated on his desire to find Brandt, a desire he could not control and could not quell. Yet he was unsure if his desire was simply to find his son to mourn him, or that he just wanted to see the body for himself to find some closure. His senses were alive, listening and attempting to feel his way through the compound, searching for what he was here for. There was an air of despair that rode throughout the complex, an emotion that confused Adam a little. *Are they aware that I am here? Why don't they act?* He scouted the area once more, now noticing that there was no one visible; no guards, no sentries. *Where are they all?*

Adam took a deep breath in and then ran towards the wall. He pushed off from the ground and leapt the boundary, landing safely on his feet on the other side. After briefly checking to see if he could see anyone once more, he headed cautiously towards the nearer of the two smaller buildings. The building had two entrances, one on each side, and windows on each wall, allowing those inside to see out across the complex in all directions. There appeared to be some furniture inside, a table and chairs, a bunk and then a number of desks littered with surveillance equipment including screens for numerous cameras. There was, however, no sign of life. Wanting to not waste any more time, Adam moved on towards the main structure.

Built from a mottled coloured stone, the building became more and more impressive the closer Adam got to it. Castle like, it had a large open patio area in front of the main entrance, its borders trimmed with a stone wall, topped with a black picket fence. Small, tidy shrubs littered the outside of the wall, but within it, closer to the building, there were small lowered areas, trench-like, that had not been visible from outside the grounds. The large oaken door sat within a stone archway, with impressively large window formations on either side of it. Adam walked up to the door, noting the multitude of cameras that should have caught his image, and touched the wood, feeling for a presence on the inside, trying to sense where everybody was. *There's nothing. But where is this feeling of despair, of fear, coming from?*

He pushed the door, finding it to be unlocked. *Something is amiss,* he pondered; there was still no one to be seen, yet, looking through into an adjoining room Adam could tell that something had happened here recently. A dining room of sorts, there were a number of tables with benches either side of them. Each of the benches had been pulled out, unparallel to the table, as if whoever had sat there had gotten up in a hurry. Food and drink littered each table, most of it half-eaten. There was a glass on the nearest table to him that rested on its side, its contents had spilled out onto the table and was trickling onto the floor. Adam's heart beat harshly, each beat a heavy, angry pound. He clutched at his head as he tried to concentrate, to listen and feel. *Where is everyone!* His mind screamed with impatience and he stamped his foot down in frustration, causing the ground to tremble beneath his feet.

'Hey! Don't move!' a voice sounded from behind him. Adam turned to find a young soldier aiming a combat assault rifle at him, his aim shaking slightly. Adam could feel his nervousness.

'Tell me where he is. Where is the body? Then... You should leave...' Adam closed his eyes as he combatted his rage, his thirst for vengeance. He felt the soldier's reluctance, his fear was preventing him from making the logical decision. 'One last time. Brandt's body, where is it?' Adam's words carried a threat that the young soldier understood.

'There's a bunker, below us.' He had made the decision to save himself as he provided the information and lowered his weapon. The soldier then backed away slowly before rushing out of the building. Adam was appreciative of the man's exit; he was struggling to hold in the fury that currently possessed him and a part of him feared what he might do to anyone that tried to stop him.

Why do I feel so... Angry? Adam wondered as he began to search the rooms on the ground floor, looking in each and every doorway. Even though he knew where he needed to go, finding an entrance to the bunker proved irritating. He ran-sacked cupboards and turned over bookcases, just in case the entrance was concealed somehow. Yet, the longer it took the more his mind ached and the pain drove his rage.

'Where are you?!' he exclaimed as he planted his fist into one of the walls and pulled away a large piece of stone. Gritting his teeth, he pulled a slither of rock from between his knuckles that had embedded itself upon impact. The sight of blood running down his fingers only elevated his fury and he began wildly smashing the walls and floors, punching them, breaking stone, searching for an entrance. He punched the flagstone flooring and tore up broken slabs, frantically moving across the foyer, throwing each piece of stone across the room, obliterating them against the walls.

After minutes of uncontrollable frustration, Adam looked around at the destruction he had caused. His anger had devastated the rooms around him, yet, he had still not found the illusive entrance. 'AHHH!!' he wailed as he stamped his foot and once again caused the building to shudder in his presence. The power inside him was becoming too heavy a burden to carry and with another almighty cry, he expelled some of his fury and sent a shockwave bounding out from within him, shaking the earth beneath his feet and causing the foundations of the building to fracture. Stone fell from the walls, light fixtures exploded and as the dust began to settle, Adam saw a glow from the bend in the hallway. He moved towards it, but as he did, a shadow shot across the space before him and darted straight past him. Adam span around to question what it was and to see where it had gone but there was nothing there. 'Who are you?' he asked, questioning the empty corridor. He could feel something. Someone. It was somehow familiar, and yet, unknown to him. 'Who –' Adam began to ask once more, but as he did the shadow instantly materialised before him and engulphed him. He tussled with the apparition grasping at thin air, swiping at nothing, all the while hearing an unnervingly familiar laugh within his head. 'Who are you?!' he exclaimed, furiously lashing out. 'Who... Who are you?!

Who am I?!' he roared, and as he did, he dropped to his knees, the shadow dissipating from around him and for a split second, stood before him, an eidolon of himself with eyes of damnable red.

Adam's heart pounded ferociously and his mind questioned everything around him. The pain ate at him and as he bore his fingertips into his temple, desperate to calm the storm raging within his skull, he remembered where he was headed before the shadow had appeared. Turning the corner of the hallway, he had finally found an opening; a doorway that led to an elevator. He stumbled into the elevator and pushed the only button available to him, and with it, the door closed and Adam began to descend into the unknown.

Upon reopening, it took Adam a moment for his eyes to adjust to the lack of light within the depths of the installation. He exited the elevator, almost falling to the floor as his legs struggled to hold his weight, into a short corridor with a single door at the opposite end. He could feel life, emotion, as he walked along the corridor. The feeling granted him a minutes respite from the torture that stirred within his head. He paused for a moment as he tried to distinguish how many people were on the other side of the door, but the volume, and the level of fear, pain and despair overwhelmed him for a moment. *How could... Why are they so afraid?* Adam tried to block it all out so that he could continue, but each step was like wading through quicksand. The emotion from within bombarded him like ocean waves in a maelstrom. He finally reached the door and forced it open with every ounce of strength he could muster, only to find darkness waiting for him within.

Adam's eyes continued to burn and the rage he had felt had not dissipated at all, despite his numerous releases of anger. He could barely see, but what he could hear did not comfort him. There was gunfire coming from the darkness ahead of him and a myriad of screams, each carrying a portion of the despair and pain he had felt before. The further he moved into the dark the less those intense emotions became, as if the souls that were expressing them were being extinguished. Adam had felt like this before. In times of war, as people died, it was as if he could feel their lights go out one by one as they ceased to feel anything. It soon became evident that there was another room before him as Adam moved through the black; a room of steel, a cage, a prison. Adam banged on the metal of the wall and listened, only for the sound to disappear, the sheer breadth of the wall absorbing it. He moved along the wall, feeling it as he went until he found a set of doors. They were sealed, with no handle sign of a handle or control, intending to be unopenable from this side. Adam pushed with all his might, but they did not move.

Managing to find the split between the doors, Adam dug his fingers in, attempting to gain a grip on each of them to pry them open. Brandt's body was on the other side of the doors, Adam was sure of it, he could feel it. But who else was in there? 'AHHH!' He cried out as he grasped the edge of each door and could feel every inch of him having to share in the struggle to prise them apart. Yet, as he did, and he created a gap between the doors just wide enough for him to squeeze through, a red light began to flash throughout the room and he was hit by someone as they attempted to barge him from their path, knocking him backwards. He fell to ground and looked towards the opening before him, watching as a pair of armed soldiers attempted to hurry through the breach. One of them managed to climb out, but his partner behind him only managed to make it half way, before he was dragged backwards into the dark and a cacophonous scream followed his disappearance.

Adam climbed to his feet, the intermittent red light illuminating the soldier before him momentarily. The man was terrified, but Adam could sense a level of passion or duty that marginally overshadowed his fear.

'Help us. Please...' the soldier begged before turning and firing a burst of bullets through the gap in the doors. The pain in Adam's head increased and he clutched at his temple, wailing in agony as his eyes burned furiously and his mind felt ready to implode. His actions caused the solider further distress and he manoeuvred himself around Adam, holding his aim on the doors before them. 'They... They're all gone...' he muttered, his tone laced with a combination of despair and disbelief. Adam continued to writhe, battling against the pain within until suddenly, and unexpectedly, it ceased. Adam pulled his hands down from his head, and sighed slightly with relief as the burning behind his eyes stopped and he could feel them revert back to their pure emerald colour.

'What is this place?' Adam asked the soldier as he gazed through the gap in the doors. Between the flashes of red light, Adam could just make out an uncountable number of bodies littered across the floor. Blood began to ebb out across the floor between the doors and Adam had an unquestionable tightness form in his gut.

'We built it, to hold you... but then we were ordered to hold *his* body here...' As the solider explained, Adam moved an inch closer to the doors, keeping his gaze fixated on what lay beyond them. 'Oh god...' the soldier began to panic as a large set of fingers curled themselves around the edge of one of the doors. Adam stepped backwards as the door began to open wider and the deep, red, sadistic glow belonging to a set of eyes shone in the dark.

Brandt stood naked in the doorway, his muscular body pulsating with adrenaline and rage. His hair was drenched in blood, it ran down his face, his torso and legs as if he had bathed in it. He said nothing, merely staring down into Adam's eyes as his huge chest rose and fell with each breath. The soldier behind Adam shook uncontrollably in terror, and then fired a shot. Adam instinctively caught the bullet, and spun on his heels to face the soldier, disarming him within an instant. The soldier stumbled backwards, his expression questioning Adam's actions. Adam wasn't sure why he had done it, but something within him warmed to the realisation of protecting Brandt.

'Wh – why...? He's a b – beast...' the soldier stuttered as he began to back away slowly.

'He's my son,' Adam responded, and following his words, Brandt stepped through the doorway and walked over to the soldier, brushing past Adam as he did. He lifted him off of the floor and held him aloft by his throat. The soldier struggled against him fruitlessly; despair and desperation possessing him. Part of Adam wanted to stop Brandt from continuing, but in the back of his mind he could hear the voice of the shadow, an unbidden persuasion that vengeance was just. As Adam dropped to his knees in submission, Brandt proceeded to shove three of his large fingers into the man's throat and ripped away his lower jaw causing blood to spill out over his uniform, cascading over his name badge that read "Torrent". Adam watched on, his heart filling with a sense of sorrow, but also of relief as his son, Cain, tore away the soldier's head, along with a portion of his spinal column as he did. As he dropped the body to the ground, Brandt looked down at Adam, his fire-filled eyes brimming with expectation. Adam took a deep breath in. He could feel the red colour return to his eyes once more and he said, 'he does not eat. He does not drink. He does not sleep. For this is death. And he will wander the earth for an eternity.'

'Sevenfold vengeance awaits those that bare the mark,' Brandt grumbled, his hands aglow.

'And the world will know your despair.'

Acknowledgements

Writing is a passion of mine, if you'll excuse the pun. I was lucky enough to share the start of the Adam story, and now the story continues.

I have always been surrounded by people that love and support me and so there are many people to thank. Most importantly, I thank my family, my wife and children, my parents and all of my siblings.

I would also like to give special thanks to Justin, for continuing to assist me in bringing my dreams to print.

Ingram Content Group UK Ltd.
Milton Keynes UK
UKHW022018090723
424810UK00004B/15

9 781916 321687